Undara

Annie Seaton

This is a work of fiction. Characters, institutions and organisations mentioned in this novel are either the product of the author's imagination or, if real, used fictitiously without any intent to describe actual conduct.

Second edition
Copyright © Annie Seaton 2024
ISBN: 9781923048683

Annie Seaton lives near the beach on the mid-north coast of New South Wales. Her career and studies spanned the education sector, including working as an academic research librarian, a high-school principal and a university tutor until she took early retirement and fulfilled her lifelong dream of a full-time writing career.

Larapinta, the fifth book in the Porter Sisters series, won the Romance Writers' Association of Australia Ruby Award for long contemporary novel in 2023.

Kakadu Dawn, the sixth and final book in the Porter Sisters series, was a finalist in the Australian Romance Readers Awards for 2023.

Whitsunday Dawn, her first book with Harper Collins Australia, was a finalist in the 2018 ARRA Awards and was voted Book of the Year in the AUSROM Readers' Choice awards.

Kakadu Sunset, Annie's first traditionally published book with Pan Macmillan Australia was shortlisted by the Romance Writers' Association of Australia Ruby Award, in the long book category in 2015.

Each winter, Annie and her husband leave the beach to roam the remote areas of Australia for story ideas and research. She is passionate about preserving the beauty of the Australian landscape and respecting the traditional ownership of the land. For those readers who cannot experience this journey personally, Annie seeks to portray the natural beauty of the Australian environment—its spiritual locations, stunning landscapes and unique wildlife.

Readers can contact Annie through her website, annieseaton.net, or find her on Facebook and Instagram.

Also by Annie Seaton

Standalone Books
Whitsunday Dawn
Undara
Osprey Reef
East of Alice
Daughters of the Darling
From Across the Sea
Across the River
By the Billabong
Beneath Still Waters (Nov 2025)
Under Darling Skies (April 2026)

Pentecost Island Series
Pippa
Eliza
Nell
Tamsin
Evie
Cherry
Odessa
Sienna
Tess
Isla

Anthologies
Pentecost Island Books 1-3
Pentecost Island 4-6
Pentecost Island Books 7-10

Duckinwilla Days
Coming Home
Secrets and Surprises
Wishes and Whispers
Chasing Dreams
New Beginnings
Together Again
The House on the Hill
Beach House
Beach Music
Beach Walk
Beach Dreams
The House on the Hill Books 1-4
Sunshine Coast Series
Waiting for Ana
The Trouble with Joel
Healing His Heart
Sunshine Coast Books 1-3
Second Chance Bay Series
Her Outback Playboy
Her Outback Protector
Her Outback Haven
Her Outback Paradise
The McDougalls of Second Chance Bay-1-4

Richards Brothers Series
The Trouble with Paradise
Marry in Haste
Outback Sunrise
Richards Brothers Anthology
Richards Brothers Books 1-3

Love Across Time Series
Come Back to Me
Follow Me
Finding Home
The Threads that Bind
Love Across Time Anthology
Love Across Time 1-4

Bindarra Creek Stories
Worth the Wait
Full Circle
Secrets of River Cottage
Bindarra Creek Duo
A Place to Belong

Others
Four Seasons Short and Sweet
Deadly Secrets
Adventures in Time
Silver Valley Witch
The Emerald Necklace
An Aussie Christmas Duo

The Augathella Books
Outback Roads
Outback Sky
Outback Escape
Outback Wind
Outback Dawn
Outback Moonlight
Outback Dust
Outback Hope

Augathella Girls Anthologies
Augathella Girls 1-4
Augathella Girls 5-8

Augathella Short and Sweet
An Augathella Surprise
An Augathella Baby
An Augathella Spring
An Augathella Christmas
An Augathella Wedding
An Augathella Easter
An Augathella Masquerade Ball

Augathella Short and Sweet Anthologies
Augathella Short and Sweet 1-3
Augathella Short and Sweet 4-7

As always, to Ian, my ever-patient and loving husband.
You are always there for me.

7

The cruellest lies are often told in silence.
Robert Louis Stevenson

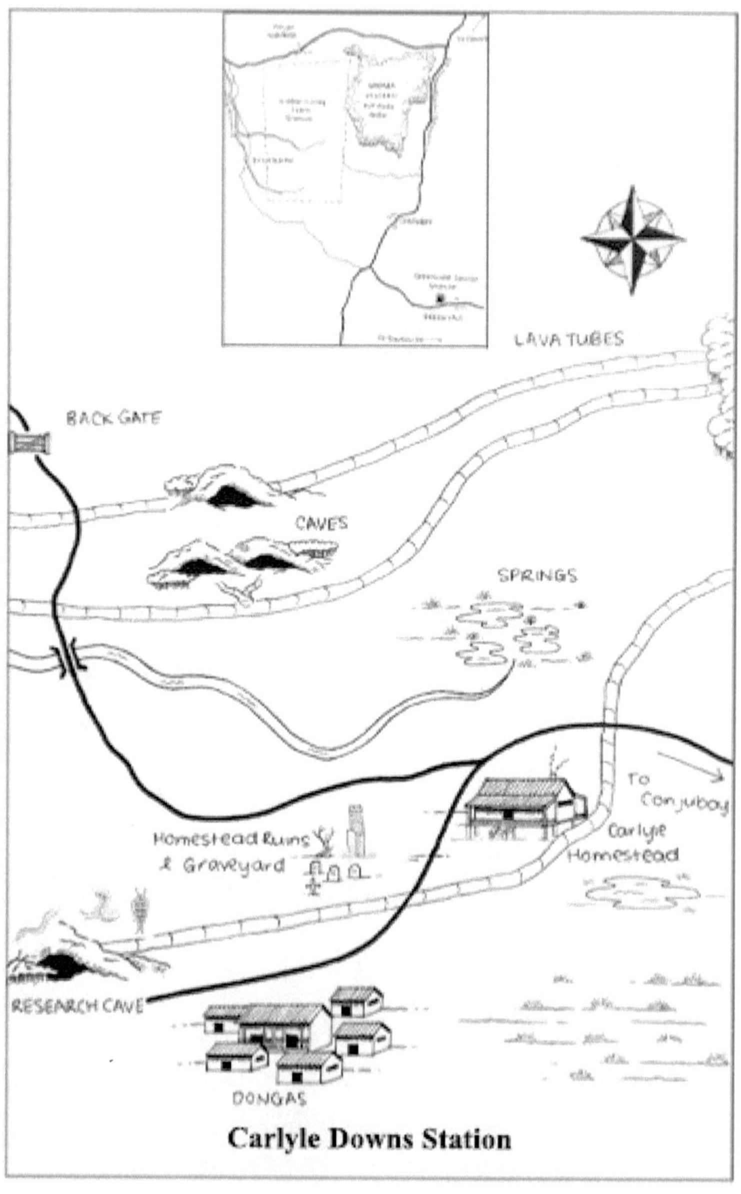

Carlyle Downs Station

Prologue

Emlyn tried to look out over the bright-white sand to the water, but her head was aching, and her eyelids were too heavy to open. Her arms burned as the tropical sun seared her skin. 'Pass my hat … please.'

She reached out to the beach mat to see if he was still there beside her.

Shimmering blinding light.

Damn eyes, why can't I open them? She raised her hand to her face and tried to force her eyelids open. She drew in a shaking breath, but her hands were still by her side.

'Am I asleep?' she asked. 'David?'

No answer. Of course, he wouldn't answer. She hadn't spoken to him since they'd left home. They'd hardly spoken at all since the fight about the wedding.

The first fight they'd ever had.

Why can't I hear the water anymore? Where is everybody?

Only low voices surrounded her. Maybe they've gone back to the bungalow for a nap.

Panic bubbled in her chest, and she willed her eyes to open. Fear took her voice, and her lips wouldn't shape the words.

'David. Where are you?'

No words. There was only a vibration in her chest where they formed.

'She's coming around.' The unfamiliar voice was calm.

She fisted her fingers into the sand to lift herself, but firm hands gently pushed her shoulders back.

'It's all right, Mrs Barber.'

No. There is no Mrs Barber. No more.

Pain rolled over Emlyn Rees in waves as conscious thought slammed back, and she turned into the pillow.

My heart can't bear it.

As quiet surrounded her, she opened her lips to catch the hot saltiness of the tears that trickled down her cheeks.

It's not real.

It's a dream. Only a dream.

Chapter 1

Carlyle Downs, **New Year's Eve.**

Emlyn Rees frowned and tapped her fingers on the steering wheel of the Troop Carrier she'd picked up in Townsville. The directions on the map that had been emailed to her outlining the route to the *Carlyle Downs* cattle station were detailed. Exactly thirty kilometres past Conjuboy, she'd turned left off the Kennedy Developmental Road onto an unsealed road, but there'd been no sign of any property name at the intersection. She'd been driving along the road for almost half an hour and was beginning to think she'd turned off too soon. The dirt road narrowed, and she had to grip the manual shift and change down a gear. As the road became little more than a goat track, dense thickets of black tea trees edged the road, and the front tyres of the four-wheel drive dropped into a deep rut that was obviously cut by torrential rain.

Biting her lip, she glanced over at the printed email that now lay on the passenger seat beside her. A stand of fig trees formed a canopy over the track ahead, and with an impatient huff, she accelerated out of the rut and steered the vehicle to the side before she switched off the engine.

Reaching for her water bottle, she took a deep swig before rolling the cool glass over her forehead; despite the air conditioning, she was still perspiring. The humid air pressed in close and heavy as a bank of dark cloud edged the sky ahead. Frustration filled Emlyn, and she frowned, ignoring the uncertainty that settled heavily in her chest. Flipping up her sunglasses, she reached for the piece of paper. Peering down at the printed map in the fading light, she traced her shaking finger over the route from Greenvale, the last town she'd travelled through, and then along to the small square that was marked 'Carlyle Downs'. This was the right road, although it was hard to believe that this narrow track could lead to one of the largest working cattle stations in the Einasleigh River area. After another kilometre along this track, she should go around a sweeping curve past the river where the homestead would be on her left.

With a shake of her head, Emlyn pulled her sunglasses back down and then flicked them up again before she put the map onto the dashboard. Despite only being mid-afternoon, it was quite dark. For the first time since she'd picked up the hire car, her unease grew, moving up her spine and making a home at the base of her neck.

The tension spread to her temples, a headache threatened, and her arm ached as it always did when she was tired … or stressed. For a fleeting moment, she considered digging out a paracetamol capsule but shook her head. She'd had enough painkillers—and anti-depressants—over the past months to last a lifetime; a simple headache wasn't going to kill her. As soon as she was settled in, she'd relax, and a good night's sleep would put paid to any tension.

With a determined set to her lips, she started the car and drove carefully down the track. Travis Carlyle, the property owner, had assured her that there would be someone at the homestead to meet her and take her across to the accommodation. His email assurance had been at odds with the disinterested tone of his voice in the three brief telephone conversations they'd had during the three months of planning. Making his preference to organise details by email very clear, it had seemed that Carlyle had done his best to delay the start of the research, which had originally been scheduled for late October. Carlyle had always had a reason each time he'd postponed the start date.

It was the first time Emlyn had been involved in negotiation with property owners, which the university usually coordinated; it hadn't been an easy experience. The delays now meant that their arrival coincided with that of the 'green' season when the rainfall could potentially be high, and they would have to work quickly as the threat of flooding in the tubes would hamper their efforts. The initial agreement was for a three-month minimum stay, and the six team members would be living in the dongas in the old resource centre.

The road ahead curved as she'd expected, and as soon as she left the river, relief eased the ache a little as a homestead appeared on the left, perched high on the hill just past the fork in the track. The sun broke through the heavy cloud for a few seconds and she caught a glimpse of water past the house. Gripping the wheel, Emlyn took the right-hand turn that led up to the building and pulled the car up outside the gate of the small house yard. Although there was no obvious need for a gate, the dilapidated fence did little to separate the front yard from the road. The building was surrounded by acres of dry brown grass, broken only by dead tree stumps and the rusting bodies of old cars. A water tank at the side of the house leaned drunkenly on uneven posts.

She shook her head. This was supposed to be the main house of one of the largest pastoral stations in North Queensland. Maybe this was a worker's house, and the main homestead was further ahead. She glanced at the map on the seat and wondered what to do.

Grey and box-like with flat fibro walls, the place looked to be uninhabited. David would have smiled and called it a "doer-upper". She closed down that line of thought before it could take root in her tired brain. A couple of small windows sat either side of a front door that was located at the top of a flight of stairs. As Emlyn looked up, the late-afternoon light left dirty blood-red shadows on the rusting roof and one of the curtains twitched. She blinked and then stared; maybe she'd imagined it?

Another shiver ran down her spine and she fought off the fingers of panic that threatened to take hold. Despite the heat, goosebumps prickled her neck at the base of her skull, and she forced herself to breathe deeply as the bands of tension tightened around her temples.

A flash of movement caught her eye, and as she turned a red kelpie shot down the stairs towards her vehicle. Emlyn sat back waiting for someone to follow the dog through the half-open door, but there was no sign of life apart from the dog now yipping and jumping at the wheels. Someone must have opened the door to let the dog out. Eventually, the kelpie lost interest and slunk off to the shadows at the side of the house. Emlyn laid her head back on the head rest and waited until someone appeared.

And waited.

A couple of times, she'd swear she saw the same curtain move, but no one came outside. Normally, being alone didn't bother her—in fact, it had been her preferred option over the past year—but the stillness of the landscape and the eerie light through the strange brownish-hued clouds were unsettling her. Not a sound and not a breath of wind.

The dead grass stretched to the top of the hill, broken only by the decaying bodies of the old cars. She brought her gaze back to the house and the dog's eyes glinted in the half-light as he watched her.

Glancing at her watch, Emlyn considered her options. There was no way she was going to get out of the car while the dog was around; she'd been terrified of them ever since she'd been bitten as a child. The red kelpie kept lifting its head and watching her. Maybe she'd keep driving and try to find the resource centre herself, but she needed a key to get in so that wasn't an option. Sleeping in the car wasn't terribly appealing, although if it came to that, she'd do it.

Damn, she'd just have to go up to the house and knock on the door. She knew there was someone inside, and she'd pound on the door until she got a response. Emlyn turned around and picked up the large umbrella off the back seat. If she needed a weapon to keep the dog away, that would have to suffice. Digging deep for courage, she smoothed her damp hands on her jeans and reached for the doorhandle. The dog lay in the shadows at the base of the water tank, but it was still very close to the bottom of the stairs.

As she opened the car door, a puff of dust indicated an approaching vehicle. The dog took off down the hill, and Emlyn climbed out of the vehicle and waited. It was a motorbike, and when the rider saw the Troop Carrier parked by the gate, he roared up the road towards her, closely followed by the yipping dog.

Emlyn swallowed. Surely it wouldn't bite now that its owner was there?

'Bits!' the man called to the dog as he stopped the bike close to her bull bar. He pointed to the dirt and the dog sank in the fine red dust beside the motorbike. He then swung his leg over the bike and walked over to Emlyn.

She leaned the umbrella against the car door and held out her hand. 'Travis Carlyle?'

He ignored her outstretched hand, shaking his head. 'Sorry, I'm filthy. You must be Emlyn Rees.'

'Yes.' She shoved her hands into her jeans pockets and waited for him to continue, but he just stood there watching her without speaking. Looking up at the dark clouds above them, she forced her voice to stay firm. 'Can you take me over to the accommodation, please?'

With a shrug, Carlyle whistled for the dog before he turned back to Emlyn. His words were curt. 'Follow the bike. It's another five kilometres west.'

What a charmer.

Shaggy fair hair in need of a cut surrounded a rugged face that held no welcome. He was younger than she'd expected—probably in his late thirties—but even less personable than he'd come across in the terse emails and phone conversations. With a sigh, she put the umbrella back into the car and climbed into the front.

* * *

The last thing Travis Carlyle wanted was a bunch of damn scientists poking around his property. Times were hard enough, and if it hadn't been for the payment already made by the university, he would have given this woman short shrift. He threw an irritated look towards the house as he kickstarted the bike. Gavin was inside, and he could have at least come out and taken her down to the dongas. He'd be on that damn computer.

In the months since the boys had gone back to Alison's at

the end of the last school holidays, Gavin had barely left the study. Dreaming about bloody cryptocurrency and how he was going to make their fortune when he should have been out helping Travis in the paddocks. At least the boys helped him with the cattle when they were home. That was the only way they were going to make a living, although any chance of a fortune had long gone with the fluctuations in the cattle industry. Hard work and skill weren't enough anymore. And only having the boys home in the school holidays made it so hard. All the other custody arrangements they'd tried hadn't worked, and in the end, Travis had agreed to school-holiday access. He had no other option when his wife—as they were still married—lived four hundred kilometres away.

There were cattle to be moved from the middle paddocks before the rain hit; Travis looked up at the sky and frowned. That was the last thing he needed, having the herd washed away in a flash flood. And rain it would, he had no doubt about that. As well as the dark clouds building since late morning, his right knee had been giving him gip since he'd got out of bed before dawn. With any luck, the tubes would flood, and these bloody scientists could go back to their laboratories and leave him in peace.

He glanced behind him and slowed the bike as they passed the vine thicket where the first lava tube crossed his land. The tubes functioned like giant stormwater drains as they collected and carried much of the summer rains. He had a feeling that Ms Rees—or professor or doctor or whatever she was—had disappointment ahead. He'd tried to tell her it was the wrong time of year to be poking about the caves, but like a typical woman, she'd dismissed his objections when he'd tried to put them off till autumn.

He muttered as he recalled the German blokes who'd first come looking at their place a couple of years ago. The Undara tubes fifty kilometres to the east had been discovered back in the sixties before Travis and Gavin had been born, and his grandfather and father had watched as the government had resumed part of that property as a national park. As kids, he and Gavin had played in the caves on their station—back in the days when Gavin had been a half-decent human being—and they'd taken for granted the strange beauty of their surroundings. Five generations of the Carlyle family had worked this land since one of their forebears had secured the pastoral lease over one hundred and fifty years ago. Now with the scientific interest and the ongoing negotiations of native title claims, the chances of holding onto the family land were becoming less certain every year. So when the university had offered a substantial payment for their research visit, he'd had no option but to accept. He shrugged; the three months would pass quickly, and they could get back to normal.

While ever there was breath in his lungs, he would not let the property go; he'd do anything to save it for the boys. There was too much history, too much family, to walk off the place. Travis gripped the handlebars as he went down the last hill and waited for the Troop Carrier to catch up.

He hid the smile that tugged at his lips as the woman parked the large vehicle. She stared at the neglected dongas for a moment before she crossed to where he waited on the bike. The buildings had sat empty for over five years; no one had been here since National Parks had built them when they'd charted the area around his caves. There'd been little feedback after they'd moved on, and the only communication had been a short email referring to the area as an undeveloped national park. He'd not followed up; if they forgot about it, that suited him well.

Large dark eyes smudged with shadows in a delicate face held his as the woman stood beside his bike. For a brief moment, he felt sorry for what she had ahead of her in the filthy dongas, but then he shrugged it away. It wasn't his problem. One of those university types, her hair—cut close to her head at the back with longer strands covering her forehead and reaching her chin at the front—screamed trendy at him. He looked down at the sturdy work boots and the brand-new, full-length khaki cargo pants. As he watched, she raised a shaking hand to her head and smoothed her hair flat against her cheek.

'Come on, I'll show you around.' Travis led her to the side of the first building and reached beneath the steps to locate the magnetised tin that held the keys. 'This is the main building. You'll find the refrigerators and the stoves in the back room, and there's office space in the front. I think you'll also find a land line in there, if you need it. As far as I know, it's still connected.'

'And the others?' She gestured to the five smaller dongas.

'The sleeping quarters.' He gave a short laugh as she took the keys from him. 'Don't know why they bothered locking them when they left. No one ever comes out this way. I suppose it keeps the kangaroos, snakes and bats out.'

'Thank you. I'm sure it will be fine.'

'Are the others far behind you?' He looked back at the road; there was no sign of dust from any other vehicles. 'You'll need a bit of a working bee to get it clean enough to stay in.'

'They'll be here soon.' Her voice was cold.

Travis narrowed his eyes and held his hand out for the keys. 'You can't stay here by yourself.'

'Oh, and why would that be?' She put the keys in her pocket and folded her arms.

As she lifted her head and stared at him with eyebrows raised, he noticed the fine tracing of silver scars on the left side of her forehead. When she became aware of him looking, she lowered her head until her hair fell forward again.

'Because it's not safe,' he said.

'The bats and the kangaroos? Believe me, Mr Carlyle, I've worked in much more dangerous environments than this.'

'I don't mean here. I mean in the caves.'

She lifted her head and held his gaze. 'I won't be going into the caves until the rest of the team arrive. I'll be getting the set-up here ready and taking delivery of provisions from Mt Surprise. And I believe we've signed an agreement that absolves you of responsibility for any accidents that may occur on your station, so you have no need to worry about me.'

'I'm not worried. I don't want you here, and I'm not responsible for you, but if anything happens, I'm the one who's going to be called out to help. And I don't have the time with the wet about to hit.'

Nature supported him as the first drops splashed the tin roof above.

'Don't worry. Your help won't be required.'

Travis stared at her. 'So how many days exactly until they get here?'

'When I find out, I'll make sure I let you know. They're leaving Brisbane tomorrow.' The raised eyebrows pushed him into not giving in, even though he didn't give two hoots about what was happening here.

She lifted her head and held eye contact with him. 'I believe there is mobile phone service, and you've agreed to let us log into your satellite internet connection until we get ours in place.'

'That's right.'

'Then thank you, Mr Carlyle. I'm sure you want to get back before the rain gets heavier.'

She was dismissive, and Travis fought the need to have the last word. With a terse nod, he walked across to his motorbike and rode off without a backward glance.

There was no doubt about it. Doctor Emlyn Rees was as cold as ice. But she and the rest of the university bods were the least of his worries, and the money that the university had deposited would stave off foreclosure for at least the next three months.

Chapter 2

Emlyn threw her backpack onto the single bed. She'd claimed the donga with the tiny bathroom that was furthest from the main building. She travelled light, and it didn't take long to unpack the essentials and put her toiletries on the single shelf in the tiny bathroom. As she went to zip up her pack, her fingers brushed the small box that held her jewellery. Unable to help herself, she flicked up the lid and stared at her wedding ring. The nurse had taken it off her finger in the hospital before the first operation, and Emlyn had seen that as a sign. Even when she was recovering, she'd not put it back on again. She stared down at the narrow gold band for a moment before shaking her head and snapping the box shut.

Emlyn stared through the window at the land surrounding the cabins. The glass was filthy—like the cabins—yet it softened the view of the harsh landscape surrounding the small buildings. Flat savannah grasslands burned off by the dry heat of the summer sun stretched as far as she could see. The rain had delivered only a few drops, and the sky had lightened. The dark, oppressive clouds became a sheet of steel grey stretching to the horizon, trapping the relentless heat above the land.

A few stumpy trees were scattered along the road that wound between the buildings, shading the camp site, and she made a note to check that the air conditioners in each of the cabins were working. It was going to get unbearably hot here over the rest of the summer. Even though the buildings were neglected and filthy, everything she'd tried so far had worked; lights were working, the refrigerators were humming as they cooled down, and the two chest freezers had come on as soon as she'd plugged them into the wall.

And there was nothing that a good scrub wouldn't fix. Emlyn had bought some basic cleaning products after she'd picked up the Troop Carrier. The thought of losing herself in preparing the rooms for the arrival of the rest of the team her spirits; cleaning during the day and reading through the academic papers about the Undara caves at night would give her a focus for a couple of days.

Apparently, the rain and the following green season were late arriving this year, and despite being early summer, the landscape still held the grim bleakness of the dry of winter. Emlyn embraced it; invisibility was one benefit of submerging herself in a new world. No one knew her, and no one knew her past. Even though she had only been here an hour, the isolation was a balm to her soul, and already she felt safe.

It had been a while since she had been out in the field, and this was the first time they'd had buildings to stay in. The nature of their research usually meant they camped in swags, with a large tent for their cooking and socialising at the end of the day. She hadn't been out in the field for almost two years, since—

Clenching her hands together, Emlyn swallowed and forced her mind back to the campsite in her immediate vision. She looked at the main building where the team would spend most of the time when they weren't in the caves; a high window had been left open, and it was in the worst condition, but scrubbing the bat guano off the benchtops could wait until tomorrow.

Her headache was coming back; she'd forgotten about it

as she'd dealt with the sullen property owner. It didn't bode well for the physical work she would be doing when the team arrived; this was the first time she would work in caves, and she wasn't sure how she was going to cope underground. Returning to the vehicle, she carried the two eskies she'd purchased and filled with food in Townsville to the mess area. The water from the melted ice sloshed as she set them down on the floor. She'd bought enough to keep her going until the grocery delivery arrived.

Her phone vibrated in her jeans pocket, and Emlyn jumped. It would be David; he'd keep trying until she finally picked up. Apart from her team of work colleagues, he was the only one who had this number. Her colleagues would be relaxing in Brisbane before they headed north. None of the team knew that she'd come up to the site today, and she didn't have a social relationship with any of them, so no one would be calling to wish her a happy new year. Emlyn hadn't forgotten the family traditions of a hot summer holiday, but she blocked the memories as the phone kept vibrating. Still, images of cricket in the backyard after a baked dinner cooked in the dripping heat of a Brisbane summer and plum pudding with Gran's saved sixpences doused in hot custard flickered through her mind like the jerky frames of a slow-motion movie. She'd spent Christmas Day packing for the trip and trying to forget about anything family-related, so why did she have to think about it now?

Because of David.

David who always did the right thing. Right now, he saw saving their marriage as the right thing to do, but for the first time in the ten years they'd been together, he hadn't been able to persuade her to come around to his way of thinking. It wasn't that he was a bad person or that he didn't love her. It was New

Year's Eve, and in her ex-husband's mind, by calling her, he would be doing the right thing.

She pulled out the phone and stared at the screen, trying to swallow the lump that had lodged in her throat, blinking as her eyes stung with the prickling of unshed tears.

Lots of laughter. Lots of love. But those days were long gone; happiness didn't last, and life was fragile.

There was no point trying to recreate everything she'd lost. Her family was all gone now, so there was nothing to celebrate. Emlyn was prepared to take full responsibility for the destruction of their lives; it was all her fault. It was easier than resurrecting a marriage that had no chance of surviving. She took a deep breath and pressed the "answer" button before she lifted the phone to her ear.

'Hello … David.'

'Hello.' His voice was wary. 'How … how are you, Em?'

'I'm very well, thank you.' The following silence was ripe with his unspoken frustration as he trod the minefield of what was left of their relationship. She knew him so well; he'd be worried she'd end the call if he said too much.

For the first time in her almost thirty years, Emlyn was unable to cope with what life had thrown at her, and as she'd learned to shut down, she'd become a different person. It didn't matter what anyone else wanted, or what they said, or what was the right thing to do—she no longer cared. Over the past few months, if anything overwhelmed her, she would remove herself from the situation.

Including a phone call from her husband—soon to be ex-husband—if need be.

'I'd like to come and see you this afternoon,' David said.

Oh God, how she hated the bleakness in his voice. Once

upon a time, back in the fairytale land of being in love, David's voice had been light and carefree. Always full of happiness. His handsome face had been unlined, free of worry, and the only expression that had been in his eyes was his love for her. Those hazel-green eyes once had the ability to melt her with a simple wink. The grief began to build in her stomach and made its way up into her throat until Emlyn fought the need to gag.

She bent and held her stomach with her free hand as she struggled against the clenching of her digestive muscles, dragging in a silent, deep breath.

'Are you still there, Em?'

'Why did you call me, David?' Her voice was cold, but at least she'd managed to get the words out. 'And no, you can't visit.'

'It's the first time we haven't been together to bring in the new year since we met.'

Silence.

'Can I come over after dinner? Please? I won't stay long. I promise.'

'It's impossible, David.' If she let him back into her life, it would only hurt him even more. Listening to her once-strong husband begging her for a morsel of attention was hard enough to deal with. It had been eight weeks since he'd last come to visit her and she hadn't been able to stand the pity in his expression as he'd looked at her.

'Impossible?' His wariness was replaced with a tinge of anger, and her finger hovered over the disconnect button. Anger was better than begging. Anger she could deal with. She straightened, and her voice built in confidence as she looked through the dirty window. 'Yes. Impossible. I'm away.' Three kangaroos hopped across the dry savannah grass, and the raw emotion that had her by the throat receded enough that she could finally swallow. She moistened her lips with her tongue, but the metallic taste filled her mouth.

'Away? Where? You didn't say you were taking a holiday.'

'I have a new contract, and I've left Brisbane. I suppose you still have the right to know that.' Emlyn closed her eyes and waited. The air that she managed to drag in filled her lungs, and she focused on breathing in and out.

'Of course I have a bloody right to know that. I'm still your husband, no matter how much you try to push me away.'

David would be running his hand through his black curls. 'David, we've separated, and we're getting a divorce. You have *no* rights to me anymore.' The words came straight from a cold, dead heart. 'I know it hurts you, but it's better for both of us this way. It's time for you to move on, too.' She squared her shoulders and rubbed her finger on the grime on the inside of the window and jumped when it gave a sharp squeak.

'No, it's not. Remember, you gave me a year, Emlyn. It's not up yet. And I'm not giving up. Where are you?'

'I'm in North Queensland. A research trip.'

'You're at work? Is there anyone else there with you? It's fucking *New Year's Eve*.'

'David…'

'Bloody hell. How long before you come home?'

I'm never coming home, David. Not to you, anyway.

She lifted her forefinger and stared at it, her attention on the red dust that had transferred from the glass to her skin. She could be cruel to herself, but David didn't deserve any more than she'd already burdened him with.

'Who's with you?' After the accident, she was sure the

hospital had told him to put her on a self-harm watch. She'd moved further away from him as he'd watched her closely. Ringing her constantly and calling in to her university office on the silliest pretexts—she'd seen through him; she'd soon learned not to ignore the calls because David would turn up on her doorstep—the same fearful look on his face—until she told him enough was enough.

'I'm by myself.' Emlyn held her left hand up to the light and stared at the white mark where her wedding ring had created a slight indent on her ring finger. Detachment didn't hurt. It would take time, but in the end, he would eventually accept what was best.

'Emlyn.' The anger was still in his tone despite the concerned words. 'Are you still seeing the counsellor?'

'Happy New Year, David.' Emlyn disconnected the call and turned off the phone.

How long would it be before David realised she was doing him a favour? How long before he would accept that and leave her alone? Leave her alone to try to resurrect some sort of life. A life for himself, accepting the way things were, and then she could get on with hers. How much longer did she have to push him away before he realised the only way they could continue to live was apart?

It didn't matter if she loved him. It was the future she couldn't give him.

* * *

Emlyn picked up a bottle of bleach and poured it on the stainless-steel workbench. The new skin at the top of her arm pulled as she stretched across with the scouring pad. The second lot of surgery had lessened the pulling of her skin, and if she wore a long-sleeved shirt with a collar, she kidded herself that the scars were barely noticeable. They didn't bother her; it was others who seemed to be ill at ease. Not Travis Carlyle. He'd looked curiously at her face, but he hadn't looked away when she'd stared back at him. Not like most people usually did.

Being alone didn't bother her. If she could have it her way, she would have preferred to carry out the research alone. Once she'd wiped down the benches, Emlyn pulled out her phone and reluctantly turned it back on. Surprisingly, there was a missed call and a text from John Kearns, the professor who was bringing the team from Brisbane tomorrow morning. They were travelling together in a van with a trailer.

We'll drive in shifts, Emlyn, and should be there within forty-eight hours. We've got all the equipment. Larry will be driving another van from Townsville and we'll meet him there and come up the range. When do you arrive?

Her fingers flew over the letters on the phone. *See you soon. Travel safe.*

With a determined grimace, Emlyn put the phone away and opened the refrigerators. They'd cooled down since she'd plugged them into the power points, but both were lined with mould. The eskies were no longer cold, so she unpacked the food onto the black-stained shelves in the small refrigerator. First job tomorrow would be to scrub them out, and then contact the grocery store at Mt Surprise after the public holiday.

A couple of hours later, Emlyn walked outside. She'd given in and taken a couple of paracetamol tablets instead of eating dinner and her headache had eased. Once the sun had gone down behind the Newcastle Ranges, the intense heat of the day had gone, and the humidity was bearable.

Emlyn looked up at the sky; the stars out here were incredible, and she held her breath as she gazed at the glowing pinpricks of life that formed a solid band of light from east to west. It soothed her and put everything in perspective. As a speck of microcosmic dust, her life was insignificant, her existence miniscule, so there was no point giving in to her emotions. She swallowed as she thought of the next three months. The night was still and quiet apart from the occasional baying of a beast in the distance and the occasional croak of a frog.

Would she make a resolution for the new year? It had been a tradition ever since she had married David. At midnight each year after they had shared a kiss, they would link their little fingers, look at the sky and silently make their resolutions. The deal was to keep them private until the first person broke theirs. It was always David because he made pledges that were impossible to keep. Emlyn had never broken hers because they were structured and planned.

No wonder our marriage failed.

Maybe she could vow to be happy next year?

She shook her head. Too soon. It wasn't in her yet. Maybe it never would be. A huge aching chasm opened up in her, and for a second, she wished she could be gone. Up in the heavens, where her grief couldn't define every living moment.

Emlyn lifted her face to the sky and let the cool wind brush her cheeks. The moon was rising, and the fat yellow orb hovered over the hill to the east, bathing it in an eerie light. She yawned and went back inside. It was almost midnight.

Tomorrow was a new day and she would look ahead. There was no place in her life for the past.

Chapter 3

Emlyn looked up as the thrum of a motorbike broke the silence. She tipped her head to the side and listened as she pulled off the rubber gloves she'd put on to scrub the hot plates on the stove.

Motorbikes.

The smell of bleach still filled the room, even though the windows were all open wide. Her eyes were gritty, but it wasn't just the smell of the bleach that had made them sore. When she'd woken at dawn, her cheeks had been wet. She'd stood under the shower and let the lukewarm water run over her hair and face until she'd shivered. Then she'd boiled the kettle and had a cup of strong black instant coffee.

By ten o'clock, the sky was bright, and sunlight streamed through the now clean windows. She'd called the store at Mt Surprise and finalised the order that was being delivered in a couple of days. The mess area was probably cleaner than it had ever been, and she was satisfied with the results of her morning's work. Once she attacked the large gas cooker that ran along from the sink to the door, she'd be done in here. Her stomach rumbled as she crossed to the door. She hadn't eaten anything since she'd left Townsville at lunchtime yesterday.

Hard footsteps sounded on the floor leading up to the mess. She reached for her long-sleeved shirt and slipped it over her singlet top before the screen door—with all the red dust now washed off—opened.

For a moment, she thought the man was Travis Carlyle, but then Emlyn realised this man was shorter and broader. Same blondish hair beneath his Akubra, a friendly grin and a pair of intense blue eyes met hers before the door squeaked again and her landlord came in behind him.

'We just came across to see how you were getting on,' Travis Carlyle said as he tipped back his hat.

Was that guilt in his voice?

'I'm surprised that you offered the accommodation with the condition it was in.' Emlyn spread her hands and gestured to the benchtops. 'But as you can see, I'm getting along just fine. I'll have this place shipshape soon.'

'For your information, the place wasn't offered.' Carlyle nodded to the man beside him. 'Dr …?' He quirked an eyebrow, and she nodded. 'Dr Rees, this is my brother, Gavin. If I'm not around, he should be able to help you with anything you might need.'

'Lovely to meet you, Dr Rees. You sure have done a . . . good job cleaning up . . . here.' The brother held his hand out to her but didn't quite meet her eyes.

Emlyn took it, and he shook her hand in a loose grip. He shuffled his feet and cleared his throat. When he looked up, colour stained his cheeks. 'I hope you have a good time at our farm. Um . . . what are you going to do here?'

Travis glanced down at his watch and Emlyn wished they'd let her get back to her cleaning.

Gavin looked at her expectantly, and it would have been too rude to ignore his question.

'We're here to explore the caves recently discovered on your property. I'm sure you're aware of the exciting discoveries made over the past few years in the main Undara tubes.'

'Yes, sort of,' he said slowly. 'But what are you looking for exactly? And where are you going to look?'

Emlyn's tone was measured. 'We are entomologists, Mr Carlyle.'

'I'm Gavin,' he said. 'Mr Carlyle was my dad.' He pointed to his brother. 'And Travis's dad too. What's an en. . .?' He removed his hat, and she stared when he put it on her clean benchtop, leaving a fine layer of red dust.

'Entomologist,' Emlyn replied. 'I study insects.'

'Insects? Like bugs?' His giggle was almost childlike. 'What's that got to do with our caves?'

'We're looking for new species. In the one hundred and ninety thousand years since they were formed, the lava tubes have provided a habitat for an array of insect life. As I'm sure you know, many of the caves have collapsed over at Undara, and the plants that have invaded through the holes in the tube ceiling have created whole new ecosystems.'

'All we've ever seen here are snakes and bats and silverfish. Not very interesting, and you're going to look at them? Crazy, hey, Trav?'

Emlyn flicked her gaze onto Travis, and the look he returned was cool and assessing. 'Yes, it all seems a bit of a waste of effort to me.'

'It's certainly not a waste of time. The preliminary findings from a couple of years ago are quite encouraging.' What might be interesting to her would probably mean nothing to a couple of cattle farmers whose land was being taken over. 'In the Undara system, many bizarre life forms have all adapted to the long and often hidden lava tunnels. White cockroaches and scutigerids are just two of the species discovered over there in recent years. Unique blind insects and colourless beetles have evolved because of the darkness in the caves.'

'And what do you think you're going to find in our little caves? They're nothing like Undara,' Gavin asked. 'We're much smaller over here. There's not a lot to see.'

'Time will tell. That's why we're here.' She moved across the room and opened the screen door, conscious of Gavin's eyes on her back. 'Now unless there was something else you wanted, I have work to do.'

* * *

'She talks like she's a bit up herself.' Gavin laughed as he started his bike. 'But she's pretty.'

Disgust curled in Travis's gut. 'I didn't notice.'

'No.' His brother looked across at him, and his lip dropped as he stopped laughing. 'I'm going back to the house.'

'I need you over in the dam paddock with me.'

'I can't,' Gavin called out as he shot past him. 'I have to go back. I'm waiting for an email.'

'I can't do it by myself again.' But Travis's words were lost in the roar of the bike as Gavin took off and accelerated until he was out of sight.

'Shit.'

Honestly, Gavin had the attention span of one of that woman's bugs. Sometimes, Travis wished that his brother would move to Townsville like he was always harping on about; life would be more bearable, although he'd have to hire more help on the station.

And he'd probably have to make sure there was someone to keep an eye on Gavin if he moved away. Over the past two years, Gavin had lost any interest he'd ever had in the cattle, and Travis had hired Jeff Collins, one of the sons from the Mt Surprise store, to help him and Bluey with the cattle work in the last six months.

Blue had the shits because he reckoned he didn't need a hand, and the sullen Collins boy was already on his third warning. Blue said he'd caught him smoking a joint when he was supposed to be repairing a fence at the yards. The kid had denied it, but Blue had sworn that he'd smelled dope. And Blue reckoned the days Jeff didn't show, he was in the pub at Mt Surprise chatting up backpackers who were here to see the lava tubes. It was a toss-up who to believe. Travis had no other option; he had to turn a blind eye because there was no one else available.

He glanced back over at the donga. The sun had disappeared behind the clouds, and the prefabricated buildings looked even more dilapidated in the shadowed light. For a moment, he felt guilty that he hadn't been more welcoming; maybe he should have invited her up to the house for a cuppa or a drink or something.

Then common sense prevailed; he didn't want her here and her comfort, and making her feel welcome, were not his concern. Nor was it his role to entertain her. And anyway, their house was in a worse condition than the dongas. Dad had always been going to build a new flash house for Mum after the original homestead had burned down when Travis had been at boarding school. But the years had passed—and the money was never there—and almost thirty years later, he and Gavin were still living in the old fibro house that Mum had once tried to turn into a home. Compared to the old original homestead she had moved to when she'd married Dad, the manager's residence had been a house without character.

Bloody hell, Mum would roll in her grave if she could see the pigsty he and Gavin lived in now. Since Alison had left, it had deteriorated into a mess. The thought of the university workers calling in to the house filled Travis with shame, and he vowed to have a clean-up soon.

When I have some time.

Between the cattle work, trying to maintain the fences and deal with the accounts, not to mention everyone who seemed to want a slice of his time—and his property—there was barely time left to sleep.

He hadn't had time for anything—or anyone—since the cattle industry had gone to shit. It was easy to understand why Alison had left and taken the boys. It wasn't just the state of the house or the lack of money to give her a new kitchen or fix up the bathroom. He hadn't provided the life she'd wanted. The property work had been gruelling, and some weeks he spent four and five nights out on the far boundaries camping with Blue as they'd moved cattle in closer to the springs. As much as he'd hated Gavin living with them, at least it was a male in the house at night, and he'd worried less about leaving Alison and the kids when he and Blue were out mustering.

They'd planned for the future before they'd got married, and hell, she should have known what it was like. Alison had grown up on a huge spread out at Boulia. They'd met at agricultural college at Gatton, and they'd connected the first time they met. Maybe they'd been too young to know what they wanted.

Travis stared out at the paddocks as he walked across to the bike. The first few years they'd worked together, things had been great. Even without money, they'd been happy, and Alison had helped on the property as well as tried to make a home for them. Until the drought took hold of the land. Until Carroglen started sniffing around the property. Travis was adamant that the family property was not going to be given over to a gold-mining company. Alison had suddenly taken Gavin's side and agitated for Travis to take their offer. And that was the one thing Travis wouldn't agree to. He'd held firm, never guessing it would lead to the end of their marriage.

But last summer, she'd changed. Almost overnight. It had happened so quickly. He and Alison had been working together, sharing their dreams and hopes, enjoying family life.

Then, only a few weeks later, he'd come in from the cattle one afternoon to find she'd packed up. She'd told him she was going and taking the children with her. He'd promised to do anything to get her to stay, but Alison had been determined. Even thinking about it now made him want to vomit.

'You care for nothing as much as you care for this land. I'm sick of taking second place,' Alison had said when they'd argued. Travis had tried to get her to understand that he had to work hard if they were to have enough money to give the kids everything they needed. The change in her viewpoint and the unfairness of her accusation had cut deep; he worked hard to provide for his family, not because he put the land over them.

She had done her best to make him angry; some of the things she'd said to him had been unforgivable, and it had hit Travis hard. The day Alison had walked out with the kids had been the worst day of his life.

He sighed and ran his hand through his hair. He needed a bloody haircut and he didn't even have time to go to town. He climbed onto the bike, but before he started it his innate sense of decency kicked in. Just because he was in a bad mood, there was no need to be the bastard that Alison had told him he was last year. With a grunt of disgust, he got off the bike, strode back to the donga and up the two steps and pushed open the door.

Emlyn was lifting the large cast-iron grill off the gas stove and turned with a gasp as the door slammed behind him. She dropped it and the heavy grill clanged when it hit the stove top. Her cheeks flushed pink as she pulled her long-sleeved work shirt back on, but she wasn't quick enough. The skin on the top of her left arm from her elbow to her shoulder, and up to the base of her neck, was white and puckered, and Travis drew a breath as she turned away.

'Here, give it to me. Where do you want it?'

'Over in the sink, please.'

He pulled a face as he picked up the heavy grill. Bits of dried, cooked meat and onion rings were stuck to it and the smell of bad meat pervaded the room. It almost slipped from his hands as he placed it carefully in the hot, soapy water in the sink. 'So the electricity's working okay, then? Water's nice and hot,' he commented in a friendly tone.

'Yes.' She nodded and avoided his eyes. 'But I forgot to ask you about the water situation. Should we take care with how much we use?' She gestured to the rainwater tank just visible through the window.

He shook his head as he rolled up his sleeves. 'Yes, with the tank water, which is piped to the kitchen and showers. There's plenty of bore water otherwise, but don't use it for drinking or cooking.'

'Okay. I guess I'll have to order in some more bottled water, then.'

'Have you got some here now?'

She nodded again.

'Put the jug on, and we'll sit down and go through some things. I could do with a cuppa, and it looks like you need a break, too.'

Without a word, she did as he asked, and he picked up the piece of steel wool on the countertop and scrubbed the grill until it was clean. He picked up the tea towel that was on the bench. By the time he had the cast-iron grill back on the stove, she was pouring hot water into two cups.

'I assume you want tea?' she asked. Her tone was still distant and formal.

'Yes, please.'

'How do you take it?'

'Black and strong, please.' He pulled out one of the old wooden chairs and sat at the laminated table. 'Look, I'm sorry I took off so quickly yesterday. I had cattle to move.'

'I don't expect or need your help.' She passed him an enamel camping mug.

By God, she was a cold fish.

He looked at her carefully. 'No?'

'No.'

'You probably need to know more about the set-up here. You wouldn't see that as too much help?'

She looked at him over the rim of her small teacup and finally her lips lifted slightly.

Maybe it was the beginning of a smile. Maybe it was just that the tea was hot.

'No. I guess that would be useful. And thanks for the help with the grill. It was pretty gross.'

He shrugged. 'No problem. If there's anything else that needs lifting, let me know and I'll move it before I go.'

'It's all good, the grill was the worst. But thank you for offering.' A glimmer of warmth filtered through the cold atmosphere and Travis relaxed into his chair, curiosity in his mind. She didn't look old enough to be leading an expedition into the caves.

Or strong enough.

There was an air of fragility about her, despite her insistence that she was independent. He wondered what had caused the scars on her arms; they looked like burn scars. But it was none of his business.

'The water pressure's not very strong. Is there a plumber anywhere around here?'

Travis shook his head. 'No, but we have Blue. I'll send him over.'

'Blue?' She screwed up her nose, and for the first time, her features relaxed.

'My stockman. He can fix pretty much anything.' Travis wrapped his fingers around the mug. 'Don't take too much notice of him, though. Bluey loves to spin a yarn or two. And he'll be in his element with someone new here to listen to him.'

'Thank you, I'll take that on board.'

'So, what else do we need to discuss?' He blew on the hot tea and then looked up with a grin as he caught her staring. 'Sorry, bad bushie habit.'

'I haven't set up my laptop yet, but I just needed to check that the passwords are the same as you put in the agreement for us to use your satellite connection.'

Travis frowned. 'As far as I know they are, but Gavin's the one who looks after that side of things. I'll check it out with him and get back to you if it's different. I can't remember what I sent to the university. Do you have it handy?'

* * *

Emlyn stood and walked over to the bag that she'd brought into the mess with her. She opened the zippered side of the laptop case and pulled out the backup printed file.

She always had a backup. Since the accident, she kept every facet of her life so structured, her counsellor had gently suggested that it was a mental health issue, but Emlyn disagreed. It was her way of coping. And she'd coped with the counsellor in her own way, too; she hadn't gone back again after that appointment.

There was nothing wrong with planning and having structure. She'd always been a bit on the obsessive side, always needing to know what was going to happen, and planning her day accordingly. David had smiled each night as they went to bed when she'd made her list of what she was doing the next day. 'Do we really need shopping lists *and* a calendar on the fridge?' he'd said as he kissed her in the kitchen one night. 'Fridges are for food and beer.'

'Emlyn?'

She jumped and stared at the man standing beside her. Her thoughts were foggy, and she looked down at the paper in her hand.

'Are you okay?'

As she'd stood there thinking, she'd folded the paper and refolded it, and now somehow, the sheets had become screwed up in her hand. She racked her brain, trying to retrieve what he'd asked her, but her short-term memory had shut down. That familiar sick feeling rose in her throat and she closed her eyes as she took a deep breath.

Trying to look normal, she moved back to the table, put the papers on the scratched tabletop and smoothed them out slowly and deliberately.

The password for the internet connection. That's what they'd been talking about.

'Yes, yes. I'm fine. I was just thinking.' Embarrassment

flooded through her as she wondered how long she'd stood there going off into one of her staring moments. Long enough for him to get up and walk over to her, obviously. She waved her hand. 'Capital CD underscore forty-two,' she read off the paper, trying to keep her voice even.

'Carlyle Downs, underscore and the year Dad was born. Okay. I'll remember that. I'll call back in later if it's changed.'

She held up a hand and looked past him. 'No. It's okay. Don't make a special trip back. I don't need it yet. I've got plenty to keep me busy here. Or you can text me. I'll give you my number.' As soon as she offered that she kicked herself. There was no need to have any sort of relationship with this man, no matter how kind he seemed to be this afternoon.

'You won't get lonely out here by yourself? Or scared?'

Her laugh was bitter, and she turned it into a cough. 'No. I like my own company. Thank you for calling in.'

'So what's your number? I'd need it anyway in case I need let you know anything.'

'Like what?' she resisted.

'Flooded roads. Any message that might come in for you.'

She recited it, and he put it into his phone.

Heat rushed into her cheeks as Travis sat down again and picked up his mug. Here she was trying to give him the hint to leave, and he hadn't even finished his cup of tea.

'So, tell me about your plans here,' he said.

Emlyn wondered why he was persisting. She glanced down at the papers in front of her and pulled out the last sheet with the map of the property. She traced her finger along the green belt by the river. 'We've decided to begin in the large cave where the roof is still intact. Once the others arrive we'll go underground and then set our research area. I imagine it will be very different from what the maps show us. The entry point is about three kilometres from the river, over some flat land.

'I know exactly where you're talking about. Some good grazing paddocks our there. That's where the property name *Carlyle Downs* comes from,' Travis offered, and she looked up in surprise.

'How do you know that?' she asked.

'Because it was my great-great-whatever-grandfather who called it that in 1862. The first homestead wasn't far from the bottom of that hill.'

'The first homestead?'

'Yes, it's actually not that far from here as the crow flies,' he said.

'So, this is a family-owned property from way back?' she asked, beginning to understand his reluctance to let them come on site.

'Yes, the first pastoral licence was issued for a block fifteen miles from north to south, and seven miles from east to west. *Carlyle Downs* was the centre point and my ancestors built the first homestead on the western side of the valley not far from the Einasleigh River. Over the years, it was amalgamated with many other runs to form the property we have today. The original settlement was a small wattle-and-daub shack with a woven grass roof. You can still see the brick chimney. It's the only thing left apart from the old cemetery. The next homestead built in the early 1900s was the beautiful old home that I grew up in. It was destroyed in a fire.'

'On the same spot?'

'Not far from here. It was at the top of a small hill near the river. The irony is, if anyone had been home when it burned down, the house was close enough to the water to be saved. It was a beautiful old homestead and was about to be heritage listed when it was destroyed. We moved to the manager's residence back then. And we're still there.'

'That must have been hard. To lose your home, I mean.'

'Yeah, it was. I came back from school that Christmas and everything was gone. All the family history, the diaries, the record books. All lost. There's still a cemetery there.'

'How big is your property now?'

'We're a hundred kilometres on our western boundary and fifty on the south.' He reached over and traced the boundaries on the map and she tensed when his shoulder brushed hers.

'That is big.'

'It is.' He stared past her towards the door, seemingly lost in his thoughts as she had been. 'We think how hard it was for the pioneers—my forbears came through not long after Leichardt discovered the area—but despite all our advances, I really do think we do it tougher these days.' He looked up and met her gaze. 'Sorry, I tend to get a bit carried away when I get started. I would give anything to see those family diaries again. I used to love reading them when I was a kid.'

'No. I know what you mean. I find it interesting, too. John—one of our researchers—will be keen to know more about the place. His wife is a lecturer in Australian history at the university and I know she's been involved in the study of Leichardt's disappearance. She was really keen to come up here with us when we first discussed the caves.' Emlyn paused, and as she looked at Travis Carlyle, she saw a much more fascinating man than the one who'd reluctantly given her the keys. 'But what do you mean by harder these days? Surely not?'

'The downturn in the beef industry, the change in live exports to Indonesia, the difficulty of getting workers to come out here, and to top it all off, a partner who would be happy if we sold the place tomorrow.'

'A partner?'

'Gavin. He's itching to sell up and move to Townsville.' His laugh was bitter. 'Thankfully, no one wants to buy it. There's a shortage of surface water on our property. We've only got a couple of perennial springs where we graze the cattle. The problem is they're all around the caves where you want to work.'

'So now you've got us here to compound your problems.'

'You want me to be honest?' His stare was intent.

'Yes.'

'It is a pain because I'm scared if you find something, we'll be resumed and turned into a national park.'

'Like Undara?'

'Yes. Although, to be fair, it was the Collins family who developed their own land and handed it over to the government. They run the tourist side of things there on the land they retained.'

'I guess you're hoping we don't find anything of significance.'

'Yes. This is our family property. My sons both love it up here.' His voice lowered as he stared past her. 'I want to be able to hand the property over to them one day. As a successful working concern.'

'You have a family?' For some reason, she had tagged Travis as a crusty old bachelor. *Okay, maybe not so old.*

'Yes, they're down with their mother in Townsville— we're separated. Once upon a time, I had plans to build a new home up here, but I didn't get around to it in time.'

In time for what, Emlyn wondered?

'They'll be home soon,' Travis said.

'How old are they?'

She was surprised when he answered.

'Twins. Boys just sixteen, and a small daughter. School finished at the beginning of the month, and they stayed down there for Christmas. I don't get to see my daughter very often.' His voice was bitter. 'Her mother doesn't trust me to look after her.'

'How old is she?'

'Four.'

Emlyn stood to go to the sink, and the room shifted. Her stomach churned, and her ears buzzed as she grabbed the edge of the table. She swallowed the saliva that filled her mouth and reached for the chair behind her, and sat down again.

'Are you all right?' Travis's voice came from a distance, but she was aware of him getting up from the table and heard the fridge door squeak. When she opened her eyes, he was crouched in front of her, a bottle of water in one hand. He lifted his other hand and put it on the back of her neck, the gentle pressure forcing her head down.

'Go with me. Put your head lower. You're as white as a sheet.'

Emlyn shook her head as the room came back into focus. Since she'd been discharged from hospital, her blood pressure had been okay. It had been so low after the last lot of skin grafts, the specialist had insisted she'd stayed in until it had stabilised.

'I'm fine. Don't worry about me. Please.' She focused on keeping her voice clear, all the while cursing herself for the physical reaction. She could keep her thoughts at bay, but sometimes her body let her down. 'I'm all right. It's just that …

I haven't eaten today. Low blood pressure.'

'Well, you'd better get something into you.' His voice was soft and kind.

Unwanted tears filled Emlyn's eyes as she stared back at him. Light amber-brown eyes full of concern held hers.

She sat up straight and reached for the water bottle. 'I overdid the cleaning in the heat. Thank you … for looking after me.' She blinked but couldn't help the stray tear that rolled down her cheek. Embarrassment filled her, and she looked away before she mumbled, 'I do appreciate it.'

'That's good.' He stood and pushed his chair in and then gestured to the table. 'Here's a muesli bar and an apple I found in the fridge.'

'Thank you.'

'Let me see you eat.' The kindness in his voice almost brought her undone. 'Then I'll go and leave you in peace. Although,' he frowned as she unwrapped the muesli bar, 'is it really safe for you to be here by yourself?'

Emlyn held the wrapper, and it crackled as her hand shook. 'Yes, I'm fine. Like I said, I overdid it. I'll slow down. The others will be here soon.'

'This heat creeps up on you. Make sure you stay well hydrated, too.'

'I will.' She lifted her head and held his gaze as she took a bite of the nut bar, forcing herself to eat. 'Thank you. And I'm sorry if I worried you.'

'All good. Why don't you go and have a rest? I'll call back and check on you later.'

'There's no need.'

He walked across to the door and threw a penetrating look her way. 'If you're sure.'

'I'm sure.'

'I'll ring later, then. Okay?' He cleared his throat and his voice was gruff again. 'Sorry. I probably bored you senseless anyway with all my yakking. You didn't need to know all that about the property.'

Emlyn stood and followed him across to the door. Her head was clear now, but her legs were still a bit shaky. After one conversation she knew more about Travis Carlyle than she did about any of her colleagues. The desire to end the conversation and retreat into her normal solitude was tempting, but the kind way he'd treated her prompted her next question. 'And your boys want to keep the farm?'

'Yes, they want to keep the *station*.' He pushed open the door. 'Would you like to come out for a bit of a tour with us later tomorrow? The boys will be here, and Jase and Joel will love showing off the place. The entry point you've chosen is a great place to watch the sunset.'

'Um.' She searched for an excuse, not wanting to be in company, but it was too good an opportunity to pass up. If they were with her, she could see the caves and decide whether she'd be able to go in and have a look by herself before the rest of the team arrived. Being guided in by locals with intimate knowledge of the landscape could save her a lot of time consulting her maps and notes. 'Yes. Thank you. That would be really useful.' Her voice was crisp and businesslike.

'Sunset is the best time to see the place in the green season. If it ever gets here this year. We'll come and get you. But I'll still call you later to check on you.'

He turned and was out the door before she could change her mind. Emlyn stood there hanging onto the door post as the motorbike disappeared over the hill.

* * *

Emlyn filled the kettle with bottled water and waited for it to boil. She'd eaten the food that Travis had laid out, and then lain down for a couple of hours and cleared her mind, although she was still kicking herself for reacting to his words. She probably should eat something more substantial, but the thought of cooking on the stove didn't appeal. In the end, she picked up another muesli bar and chewed on it.

Her teacup looked out of place on the chipped laminate of the kitchen bench in the donga. David had always smiled at her insistence that you should only drink tea out of fine china. She picked up the cup and twirled it around. It had come from a Royal Albert tea set that Nana had left to her, and she carried it everywhere she went. The gold rim was chipped, and the once bright flowers had faded, but holding it always soothed her.

She poured the boiling water onto the Earl Grey teabag, inhaling the refreshing sweet smell as she carried the cup across to the long bench along the wall where she'd set up her laptop. The password had worked. She sat down and logged onto the satellite connection. After glancing at the academic papers she hadn't completed reading yet, she flicked her eyes back to the screen. She'd deal with her emails first and then read until bedtime. Maybe she'd read some of the articles later.

A dozen or so unread emails filled her inbox, including one from John Kearns, which repeated the text message he'd sent her yesterday. There'd been some heavy rain around Gladstone and they were keeping an eye on the flood warnings as they planned their route.

Emlyn clicked on the last email before she realised it was

from David. She looked at the date; he's sent it to her soon after he'd called yesterday. There was no greeting.

Remember our first date?

You chose the movie and I went along with you.

Stardust? *Fantasy? Nuh, not for me. I pretended I was keen, but really, all I wanted to do was spend time with you. Watching you in the cinema that night is one of my best memories ever. Almost up there with our wedding day.*

I can't describe my feelings as I watched you stare at the screen, your mouth open with wonder, and your eyes glistening with tears when the witch locked the actress in the castle. I can't remember her name.

I never followed what was going on. But even though I didn't watch much of the movie, I still remember what made you feel sad. I fell in love with you even more that night. I knew we were destined to spend the rest of our lives together.

At least it gave me a reason to take your hand and you let me hold it.

It only seems like last week, but we had so much more happiness after that. We did, Em. Remember the happy times.

Everything makes our life. Happy times, sad times. That is life. *I want you to think about that.*

David had been so easy to live with. Whatever made her happy, whatever she wanted to do, whatever decisions she made. He was always happy to go along with her in his own cheery way. So when he'd first said no to going to the wedding, she'd been surprised.

Another *if only.*

She lifted her hand to her face, surprised to feel the tears on her cheeks.

It's New Year's Eve. Look at the stars and think of me

tonight. David.

Hurrying down the steps, she stood in the middle of the drive and looked up at the stars. The sky was silver, and the sparkling, shining stars blinked furiously as she stared at the ribbon that was the Milky Way.

The night sky always brought her calm. It hid her flaws and the scars burned into her flesh; it made the memories bearable for a short time. Tears pricked at her eyes, but tonight her grief was different.

How perceptive of David to know that of all things that helped her, it was the final scene from that movie that got her through when it all became too hard. He knew her so well, and she wished that their lives had turned out differently. She stared up at the stars and whispered the names of those she'd loved and lost as the pale starlight washed over the landscape in front of her.

Stardust.

* * *

The house was quiet and in darkness, and Travis sat on the back steps.

Alone.

The sky was clear and pricked with millions of stars, the moon high in the sky, bathing the bush in shimmering ethereal light.

When he and Gavin were small boys, their mother had sat out here with them when the moon was full. He could still remember her lilting voice reciting the poem about the moon and her "silver shoon" as her arms held them close. It was the only memory he had of his mother ever holding him.

Slowly, silently, now the moon. Walks the night in her

silver shoon. This way, and that, she peers, and sees.

What would Mum see now, Travis wondered? A shattered family. A property going to rack and ruin. Her request that he look out for his older brother, and her forethought in tying up the estate when Dad had predeceased her had been wise. She had made Travis the majority shareholder in the property because of Gavin's instability; Gavin was entitled to a monthly cheque under the terms of the will.

They would have gone under a long time ago if Gavin had his hands on the finances. If he'd had an equal say in how the property was managed, there would be a gold mine in operation by now. Gavin had seen it as the quick answer to their problems when Carroglen had first approached them two years ago. Travis had sat his older brother down and explained what it would mean if they took the offer. He'd had to work hard to get Gavin to see sense. When Travis had explained that their access to much of their land would go, Gavin had come on side.

The payment from the research team would have to suffice for the time being. At least the university people weren't making a visible difference to the land.

He raised the beer he'd been nursing for the past hour. 'Happy New Year,' he said to no one in particular.

Chapter 4

Travis's mobile rang late that evening and for a brief moment he felt guilty that he hadn't called Emlyn back as he'd said he would, but by the time they'd cooked, eaten and done the dishes it had been past nine o'clock. Anyway, he'd got a clear impression that she hadn't wanted him to call. Then Gavin had pulled out the ancient vacuum cleaner and started a mad flurry of clearing the living room and the entry foyer of all the junk that was lying around.

He obviously wanted something—and it would be money—and Travis was waiting for him to ask as they cleaned through the house.

'Do you want clean sheets on the boys' beds?' Gavin asked.

Travis had sighed. 'For God's sake, Gavin, just tell me how much you want, and cut this cleaning crap.'

'Why do you think it's about money?' Gavin's scowl had stretched to his eyes.

'Because it always is,' Travis replied tiredly. 'It'd be much easier if you'd just give me a bit of a hand with the cattle.'

Gavin unplugged the vacuum, threw it in the hall cupboard and disappeared into his room. 'I'm going to bed.'

Travis glanced at the screen before he answered; it was Alison's number. He ran his hand through his hair; he wasn't in the mood to argue with anyone else tonight. And then the guilt came chiming in; any arguments he and his wife had, he was always the instigator as his frustration kicked in. Frustration that he had to fight to see his kids, frustration that any spare money had to be sent south and just bloody frustration with the unexpected end to their marriage.

'Hi, Al, you're calling late.' He injected a pleasant tone into his words.

'It's me, Dad. Jase. I need to talk to you before Mum does.' His son's words were whispered and rushed.

Travis crossed to the window and looked out. The moon was slipping in and out as the clouds raced up high. The rain had threatened for two days, but there'd only been a few drops. 'What's up, mate?'

'I want to come home, Dad.'

'You are. I'm waiting to hear when to pick you up at the train station.'

'No. I want to come *home*. For good. To stay. I hate it down here on the coast. I hate the school too.'

Travis gripped the windowsill with his free hand. This was a discussion that came up at the end of every school year. He'd love to have his sons home with him all the time.

'Oh, I see. What does your mother have to say about that?'

The reply was sullen. 'What do you think?'

Travis took time to consider his words before he replied. If Jase came home, it would help him no end, but he knew how firm Alison was on the twins finishing high school. 'You've only got a year to go, mate. Actually, less than a year, and then you'll be here and working. And you'll be on the books.'

What he'd save on the private school fees would go straight to Jase and Joel as wages.

'I don't care about that. I just want to be there now. I hate school, and I hate not being up there. I know you need the help, Dad.' He was almost begging. 'What's the point of staying here at school, and learning stuff I'll never use?'

'If you want to go to college like I did, you have to finish high school.'

'I don't want to do that. You can teach me everything I need to know. Please, Dad, talk to Mum.' There was a muffled conversation in the background and Jase came back on. 'Here she is now. Love you, Dad.'

Travis closed his eyes. Ever since they'd left, his boys had ended each phone conversation with those words. He had Alison to thank for that and for a lot more. She'd come from a demonstrative family, the opposite of Travis and Gavin's upbringing. The first Christmas out at Boulia with her family, he'd been taken aback to see her brothers greeting their father with a hug and a kiss.

Now, he was comfortable hugging his own sons.

'Travis?'

'Hi, Al. How are you?'

'I'm fine. You?'

'Just the usual.'

Christ, he hated this stilted conversation every time they spoke. Their once intimate relationship had disappeared in one afternoon, and still, he was no closer to understanding why. What had happened to those loving and whispered conversations of the early years of their marriage?

The plans? The sharing? The joy in watching their boys growing, the joy of welcoming Cassie to their family.

Always together.

'We'll be up Thursday,' she said.

'Jase said they'd be on the train tomorrow.'

'Yes, they will. I mean Cassie and I. We'll get the train up the next day and stay over at Aunty Maureen's. Cass can have the days with you and I'll come and pick her up in the afternoons.'

The frustration started to niggle, but he held it back. 'That's a lot of driving back and forth for you.'

'I don't mind.'

'Are you getting the train, too or driving?'

'I've got a double shift tomorrow, so we'll get the train up on Thursday like I just told you.'

The frustration was replaced by anger. 'Shit, Alison. Who's with the kids when you do all these hours?'

'You know very well I make sure that I only work when the boys are home for Cassie or my regular sitter is available. And if I work at night, the sitter comes in, so the boys can do their homework. She's organised for tomorrow. I wanted the boys to come up tomorrow to give them as much time as I could. Don't worry, it's not coming out of the money you send.' Her words were calm and measured. He'd only ever seen Alison lose her temper once in all the years they'd been together.

The fourteenth of February, last year. How ironic was it that their marriage had died on Valentine's Day? He'd fought to get her to stay—begged, pleaded, even cried—but she was immovable. When she'd finally lost her temper, he knew it was real. Alison was going, and she was taking the children with her.

'I'm sorry. I know you do.' He calmed himself. 'So what's the go with Jase all of a sudden? What's got into him?'

'I don't know. There's been some incident. I overheard them talking about it one night, but they won't tell me what's behind it.'

'Do you think he's in trouble at school?'

'Honestly, Trav. I don't know.' Her sigh broke his heart. 'I've tried to talk to him, but he's been in a foul mood ever since school ended. Today he told me he wasn't going back next year.'

'Seeing you'll be up here, too, we'll both sit down and have a talk with him. Look, why don't you and Cass stay here in the house? Driving to and from your aunt's place is silly. You know there's room. The boys can sleep on the back verandah, and you and Cass can have their room.'

'What about Gavin? Is he home?'

'He is now, but he's going to Townsville first thing tomorrow. He spends more time there than he does here.'

'Be nice to have some time for yourself.'

I'd rather have you and the kids home. He didn't put his thoughts into words; it wasn't worth it. Travis flicked off the kitchen light and headed down to his room. Some nights, Alison was happy to talk for ages, and it looked like tonight was going to be one of them.

He tucked the phone between his shoulder and his chin as he used both hands to open his window. 'It is, but it gets mighty lonely, sometimes.'

The breeze coming through the window was moist and cool, and he sat on the windowsill as he settled in for a chat.

* * *

The forecast wind change was beginning to rustle the leaves of the tall eucalypts at the edge of the dry paddock. It was too dark to see the dust blowing across the bare dirt, but he knew it would be. The cattle would head to the lick trough against the windbreak for shelter and sustenance soon; they would drink there once the rain filled the trough. He stood with his head tipped to the side.

Listening.

Waiting.

Watching.

Not that there was anyone nearby to see him. The only ones who would be interested—and pissed off by what he was about to do—were asleep in the farmhouse three kilometres away. Or they soon would be.

Served them all bloody well right. He'd waited on the hill across the gully until the lights in the house went out. It had meant driving across the paddocks without the headlights, but the moon was bright enough to guide him; he couldn't risk being seen. The lights would have dipped down the hill across from the house if he'd taken the shortest route, so he'd turned them off and taken the vehicle cross-country instead, past an old chimney and some headstones.

There was rain in the wind, and the cattle smelled it at the same time he did. They showed their agitation: snorting, shaking their heads, and swishing their tails as the wind picked up. The clouds were moving fast across the moon, darkening the landscape. He waited until the moon appeared again and let his vision adjust before he moved over to the trough that ran along the fence line. Crouching down, he removed the plastic packet from his pocket and unwrapped it carefully, and then sprinkled the granules on the top of the hay in the trough. Moving his hand through the hay, he mixed the granules in. His fingers found the drainage pipe at the end, and he grunted with satisfaction. It didn't take long to unscrew the pipe and shove the plastic into the narrow opening. Once it was blocking the narrow neck, he screwed the pipe back onto the trough.

Now all he needed was the rain to fall.

Chapter 5

Emlyn had followed the three motorbikes in the Troop Carrier after Travis and his twins had swung by the camp. Although the boys were polite and personable, she still sensed a wariness similar to their father's. She was obviously unwelcome here. She didn't let it bother her; these days it was easy to separate the things worth worrying about from those of little consequence. One night before she'd left the family home behind her, David had told her that speaking to her was like talking to someone behind a glass wall.

'No matter what I say or do, I can't get an honest response from you, Em.' She'd closed her eyes and waited for the gentle tirade to end. It didn't matter, she was leaving anyway. If only he'd known that seeing him unhappy twisted the knife of grief even more, but it was the way things had to be.

'I can't get anything from you. Any response would be better than this polite person that I'm living with.'

'I have nothing to say.' She'd smiled and continued tapping away at her computer. Poor David had the patience of a saint, but she took comfort from knowing that would be the one thing that helped him make a new life without her. A few nights later when she'd made the arrangements for a small serviced room near the university, she'd told him she was leaving. His beautiful blue eyes had been awash with tears. That had hurt, but she'd covered up the pain and remained cool.

'It's the way it has to be, David. I can't go on like this.

We can't go on like this. I have my life now, and you need to make a new one. We need to move on, and you have to accept we can't do it together.'

Emlyn dragged her thoughts back to the present when Travis and his sons stopped at the base of a small hill, and she parked near the motorbikes. As she reached for her knapsack and torch, she frowned at the unexpected tear that plopped onto her hand.

Travis opened the door for her and she brushed the back of her fingers across her face.

'The temperature will cool considerably as soon as the sun sets,' he said. 'And it'll be quite cool in the cave. Did you bring a jacket?'

She nodded, climbed down, and swung her knapsack onto her back. They left the vehicle and the motorbikes in a paddock where the fences were in need of repair, and she listened to the conversation as she trudged across the paddock behind them to the base of the hill.

'That's the chimney of the original homestead I was telling you about the other day.'

Emlyn followed the direction of Travis's finger as he pointed to a small thicket of trees at the base of a small hill.

'My father loved the history of the place so much, he never demolished it. It's all that's left. There's not much of the second house left, either. A few posts and chimneys,' he said.

'You need to get onto those fences, Dad,' one of the boys said.

'I know, mate. The fencing's got behind since the winter. As soon as we move the rest of those cattle, I'll get you to give me a hand over here.' Travis glanced back at Emlyn. 'With the amount of traffic that's going to be here for the next three months, we need to make sure these paddocks are fenced off. You don't want the cattle following you.'

'Has Uncle Gavin been helping you since we left?' the taller boy asked.

'Next question,' Travis said wryly as he led the way up the hill.

'Are you supplementing the breeders with lick blocks, Dad?' The other boy caught up to Travis and Emlyn slowed her pace.

'I am.' Travis smiled at his son. 'You're on the ball, Jase.'

'A molasses-based mix?' The young boy frowned.

'It's okay. We've set up a good drainage system. No chance of any water staying in the lick trough.'

The track was obviously well used; a sort of walkway had been defined by rocks and fallen trees edging the scrubby trees. They climbed a hill where a couple of manmade rock steps had been built into the path.

Emlyn bit her lip and frowned. Unless they could get the vehicles closer, it was going to be a long walk up the hill with the equipment each day. They might have to look at leaving some of it in the caves. It should be secure there; it was way off the main road, and not on any tourist track. The photographs she'd seen from the visit of the initial researchers hadn't showed the size of the caves, or the approach that they were now on. She hadn't done her homework well enough.

The savannah woodland was dry, and the grass and the occasional small tree branch crackled beneath her hiking boots. The air was ripe with the smell of eucalypt trees and Emlyn took a deep breath of the fresh breeze.

David would love this. She closed her eyes for a second as a shaft of actual physical pain pierced her chest. Being closeted in an office all day, her husband had taken every opportunity to be outdoors on weekends and on all their holidays. She'd seen more of Australia in ten years than most people saw in a lifetime. She wriggled her fingers to get rid of that awful light feeling that came with overthinking.

Breathing out too much carbon dioxide, the doctor had said. Stress-related.

Focus on your breathing. Forget David. Forget what he liked, or what he thought he wanted. She had to stop this constant thinking and worrying about him.

Move on.

Survive.

She had to focus on the job here. Once the others arrived and they were exploring the caves each day, and recording what they found, it would be easier.

'Did you see this, Emlyn?' She jumped as the taller of the two boys caught up to her and pointed to the side of the path where a ground cover with bright-yellow flowers spilled over onto the walkway.

'What's that?' she asked with her head tilted to the side. 'It is Joel?'

'Yes, I'm Joel.' He smiled for the first time. 'It's the wild Daisy Cress, *Acmella grandiflora.*'

Emlyn glanced up at him as she crouched down at the edge of the path. 'It's pretty. You know the scientific names of the local flora?'

He laughed, and she saw the close resemblance to his father. Similar strong features, minus the tanned and weathered skin.

'No. Only the ones that I've used in my schoolwork. This one is really interesting. Did you know that only a few kilometres west there was a huge gold rush in the late nineteenth century?'

She shook her head. 'No. I can tell you all about insects, but I'm pretty rough on my Australian history. Just about primary school level and that's it.'

'The gold rush wasn't long after the first Carlyles—our forebears—took over the lease for the *Carlyle Downs* land.'

Emlyn smiled. He was his father's son. Joel's voice held the same passion that she'd heard in Travis's as he'd spoken of the history of the station.

'Around the late 1870s, hundreds of Chinese came in and took over the area. As well as gold mining, apparently, they taught the local Aboriginal people about the medicinal value of some of the plants here, like the Daisy Cress. Or so the story goes.'

'You know your history, too.' Emlyn stood, and Joel walked beside her as they continued along the path that was winding around the hill.

'I was born here, and I'm interested, but Dad's the one with all the knowledge. He used to tell us stories about the place when we were growing up. You should get him talking one night. There's a lot of history tied up with the lava tubes, too. It'd be good to get Dad back talking about things again.' He stopped, and his face was flushed as he bent down. 'Look at this, Emlyn, you won't see this one anywhere else in Australia.'

A series of fungi sat beside a flat rock at the side of the path, tucked into the shade of a wide tree trunk. They looked like a pile of pancakes off the grill. Each mushroom—if that's what they were called—was edged with cream and then a light-brown circle surrounded a series of concentric circles in a variety of shades of purple. The perfection of the markings coloured the flat surface as though an artist had painted it.

'Now that's beautiful.'

'Wait till you see inside the tubes. The insects and fungus feed on the roots that penetrate the ceiling and bat droppings.' He waited while she took out her small camera and snapped some shots of the fungi. 'Dad said you haven't actually been in there yet? It's pretty special. We were never allowed to go in there when we were kids, and it was always a special treat when Mum and Dad took us.'

'No. This is my first time. I'm really looking forward to going in.'

And I am, Emlyn thought as she stood and slipped the camera back into her pocket. For the first time in over a year, a spark of interest was firing.

She smiled at Joel. 'Really excited.'

Her counsellor had said that one day she would wake up and life would take on a sense of normalcy again, but she'd rejected that idea outright. She didn't deserve to have a happy life.

What was that old maxim that the doctor had told her? Time heals all wounds. But Emlyn had rejected that; her heart had been irrevocably broken and grief had settled into her soul. Everyone had tried to pull her out of it—David had told her they could work through it together, but she'd closed her mind to any concept of healing.

It might be selfish, but she didn't *want* to. It was her fault and she didn't deserve to.

Joel watched her as she fluttered her fingers again.

'Are you hot?'

'No. No … I'm fine. Thank you.' They'd fallen behind Travis and Jase as they'd talked and looked at the plants.

Travis had stopped at the crest of the hill and called down

to them. 'Come on, you two. It'll be dark before we get there.'

'Oops, we don't want to get your father more offside than he is already.' Emlyn hurried up the hill; Joel was still beside her and he glanced inquisitively at her.

'Don't worry. Dad's bark is worse than his bite. It's just that he loves this place so much, it's his life, and the last few years have been tough. He's looked after the place pretty much all by himself.'

Emlyn strode ahead and didn't answer.

Life was like that. It wasn't particularly kind to anyone. It was a shame that Joel would find that out for himself one day. Everyone did; it was a part of growing up.

'I'm looking forward to seeing how you guys work.' Joel caught up to her and lowered his voice. 'Do you think I could come and watch you some days?'

'I can't see why not.' A smile tugged at her lips and it felt strange. Unfamiliar. Using facial muscles that had forgotten how to function. 'We could probably put you to work.'

'Awesome!' Joel's enthusiasm made her smile again and this time it was easier.

'Looks like I've got a new team member.'

It would be helpful to have some local knowledge on hand as they worked their way through the caves.

'I'll talk to Dad about it.' He kept his voice low. 'But don't tell him why. I'd love to talk to you about going to uni. I can start applying for university halfway through next year. My principal said she can recommend me for early entry as soon as I know where I want to go. You might be able to help me choose the best university.'

This time it was Emlyn's turn to look curious. 'Why not mention it to your father?' Travis and Jase were a couple of hundred metres ahead of them, so she spoke quietly.

'I'm pretty sure Dad wants us both here on the station. He really needs all the help he can get. He's got no idea that I want to study history. I was stoked when he said that people from the university were coming here. For a while, I thought it was to do with the history of the place, but I'd still love to see how you work, and how you write up what you discover. One day I'm going to have to tell Dad that I won't be staying here, and that's going to be hard.'

'I'm sure he'll want what's best for you. Whatever makes you happiest.' She felt like a hypocrite saying the words, but poor Joel looked so unhappy, she needed to say something.

'No.' He shook his head vehemently. 'He'd think I'm as useless as Uncle Gavin, and I don't want that.'

Emlyn was thoughtful as they caught up to Travis and Jase. She was getting to know too much about this family. It wasn't what she'd expected—or wanted—here.

* * *

Travis stood with Jase waiting for Emlyn and Joel to reach the top of the hill. She negotiated the last bit of the track quickly, yet despite the last steep pinch, she was breathing easily. He'd revised his opinion of her slightly. Although very thin, she was obviously fit, and his assumption that she might not be up to the climb was proven wrong. Her pallor had been relieved by the exertion, and for the first time her cheeks held a rosy flush. Huge brown eyes were set in a face with high cheekbones, well-defined lips and a dimple he'd noticed the one time she'd almost smiled yesterday. She was quite pretty—or she would be if she filled out a bit.

'Did Blue get that water pressure sorted for you?' He looked at her thoughtfully. It wasn't so much the gauntness of her face that defined her demeanour; it was the distance that she kept as she observed those around her. Clinical and detached most of the time, she was a strange mix. Obviously a confident woman—to have no hesitation in coming way out here and being by herself in the middle of the bush—her self-sufficiency struck a sympathetic chord in Travis. There was a story behind it; he recognised the barriers that she put up.

'No, he hasn't come yet.'

The wind lifted her hair as they reached the top of the hill and his eyes were drawn again to that fine network of scars on her neck. He shrugged off his curiosity; he had enough problems of his own.

'Sorry, he told me he was going there this morning. I'll chase him up.'

'Thank you.'

'It's much cooler up here. Feel the difference?' he asked as she put her hand on her hair and pulled it down to cover the side of her neck. Her fingers were shaking as she did up the top button of her shirt. He didn't think it was vanity, but more reluctance for anyone to be prompted to ask about the scarring. He knew the boys wouldn't ask even if they did notice. Despite their parents separating as they'd grown up, he was proud of the polite and thoughtful young men they'd grown into.

She nodded.

'Even though we're seven hundred metres above sea level, we experience less humidity with a drier climate during the day and much cooler evenings than down on the coast.'

'Had much rain so far this season, Dad?' Joel asked.

'Use your eyes, son. What do you see?'

'Yep, you've had a bit,' Joel said as he stared out over their land to the western horizon. 'But not enough.'

'Enough to make it look green from up here, but we still need a lot more for the cattle.' Travis nodded as he watched Emlyn take in the view from the top of the hill. At this time of the year, the first rains triggered an explosion of colour as the country transformed from its usual brown and dry environment to one of a rippling green sea of colour.

'You called it the green season yesterday?' she asked.

'Yes, from now on, we should have enough rain to kick off the growing season. The new growth and the water will bring out the wildlife.'

'Are you scared of snakes?' Jase asked with a grin.

'I'm an entomologist. I spend most of my research time in the bush and in places where snakes are looking for food,' she replied. 'So not scared, but always wary.'

'A good way to be. Especially up here.' Travis beckoned Emlyn over. She stood beside him and he leaned down so that her line of sight was level with where he was pointing. 'Have you ever been up to Kalkani Crater?' he asked.

'That's the volcanic crater over at Undara, isn't it?' she replied.

'Yes, the one where they take tourists for a walk up to the top and around the rim.'

'No, I haven't been up this way at all before. I came straight across from Townsville.'

'See the mountains in the distance?' He pointed to the west where the sun hovered over the low Newcastle Ranges.

She stood beside him and a whiff of lemon shampoo wafted across from her hair. Travis moved away slightly.

'If you look halfway out there, you can just see a stand of

bush. In between there and here, if you look carefully you can see a straight line of vegetation dissecting the paddocks.'

She put her hand to her face and frowned as she looked across the plains. 'That way?'

'Yes, the tree line has a silvery hue to it.'

As he stood still and kept pointing, a family of rainbow bee-eaters flitted around in the bushes beside them. The lowering sun caught the reddish gold of their heads above their lime-green chests. A pair of sulphur-crested cockatoos flew ponderously over them, their screeches breaking the quiet of the early evening.

Emlyn stared to where he was pointing and nodded. 'Ah, I see it.'

'That straight line is the main tube that crosses our property. It will have started at Undara.' Travis turned around and then pointed to the curtain of green vines behind them. 'This is an entry point and it goes for over eighty kilometres to the west.'

'Does it come from the original eruption over at Undara?'

He shrugged. 'I'd say so. Until the volcanologists arrived here from Germany a couple of years ago and told us they were a part of the Undara system, we just looked at them as our caves. I'd never even been across to the Undara tubes before then. Now I realise that this is part of the same volcanic eruption. This system has never been explored, not since the Carlyles have owned the land anyway. Even Aboriginal people didn't go far into the caves from what we know.'

'No one else *has* ever explored them, or even mapped them. I've read the papers the Germans published. It was quite an exciting discovery for us. They've examined the geological aspects of one tube, but who knows what new species of insects we'll find in there.'

For the first time since Travis had met her, her voice was filled with enthusiasm and her face came alive.

'It's a whole unknown area, and three months is going to be nowhere near enough,' she said.

Travis shook his head and ignored the frown that Joel directed at him. 'I only agreed to three months.' 'If we find anything of significance, we'll need to extend.' 'I really can't afford to have the running of my station interfered with for more than the three months.'

'Let's leave it open.' She stood and folded her arms and regarded him coolly. 'We'll see when the time comes.' He nodded.

'We'll see what happens.'

* * *

Despite Travis's reluctance to be open to an extension, Emlyn couldn't help the flutters of anticipation jumping in her stomach as he led her over to the curtain of vines hanging over what appeared to be a high rock face.

Unexplored. It was like being an explorer in uncharted territory. The fieldwork and the new discoveries were the best part of her job. Surely with his apparent love of history, Travis could understand how they would have to stay as long as they needed to here. The potential for discovery of new species in this network of caves was extremely high and Emlyn looked forward to being part of it.

And apart from the possibility of new discoveries, the beauty of this landscape soothed her this evening. The colours of the trees, contrasting with the brown dirt, provided a stunning backdrop for the wildlife that was venturing out as the sun set. Mobs of kangaroos grazed in the paddocks below, and myriad bird life darted in and out of the trees.

The only thing missing was David. If he'd been here, he would have the camera out, taking photos of the birds, the trees, the sunset.

She called him the sunset king. They had thousands of photos of sunsets on their computer.

His computer.

Emlyn ignored the ache that kicked into her chest.

'Can we go in now?' she said briskly as she reached into her knapsack and pulled out the headlamp. She'd checked the batteries as she'd unpacked the equipment from the Troop Carrier earlier this afternoon. The small settlement was beginning to take shape as she'd scrubbed and set up an office area and put the equipment she'd brought with her in a secure cupboard. Flying from Brisbane to Townsville had meant that she'd been limited in the amount of gear she could bring with her, and she was looking forward to the arrival of the team at the end of next week. It had seemed unnecessary to be in such a large vehicle by herself, but once the others arrived, they'd need it to get to and from the site.

'Just watch where you're going here,' Joel said. 'The snakes'll be waiting for the bats as soon as the sun sets.'

As they entered the dimly lit space and looked around, Emlyn drew a breath. The light filtered through the lacy foliage above and Travis raised his hand as she went to step forwards.

'Clever buggers, aren't they?'

To their right, a high ceiling of honeycombed grey rock rimmed the edge of the clearing. A pile of tumbled rocks rose in what looked to be a manmade cairn where the grey rock met the ground. High above them at least a dozen snakes hung from the intertwined branches. As she watched, the milky bulbous eyes of a striped green snake looked back at Emlyn and she suppressed a shiver. A soft noise came from in front of them and the boys walked over to the rock cairn and looked up. A large gap in the green canopy revealed a triangle of midnight-blue clear sky. As Emlyn looked up, the noise became louder, and suddenly, with a huge whooshing sound, the space filled with dozens and then hundreds of small black bats as they flapped up to the open space and disappeared into the dusk.

Her eyes were wide as she took in the amazing spectacle, forgetting that she was with anyone else. Soon the space was full of bats and the snakes moved along the branches, their forked tongues flicking in and out as they stretched for the bats in mid-flight.

'Bingo. Got him,' Jase yelled with a fist pump.

A snake as thick as a man's wrist slithered down the tree branch and disappeared into a fissure in the rocks behind. Emlyn shivered; a bat was secured firmly in its jaw.

'Absolutely beautiful.' Her hushed voice was almost reverent as she watched the spectacle of nature unfold in front of her.

Jase and Joel looked at each other and both chuckled.

'By now, our mum would have been a quivering heap outside, heading back for the house,' Joel said. 'It's a toss-up whether she hates the bats or the snakes the most.'

'No need to be worried about them getting tangled in your hair. Their sonar enables them to dodge us,' Emlyn replied.

'We know that, but she'll never believe us,' Joel said.

'She hates them.' Jase shook his head and his voice was respectful. 'But you do this for a job, Emlyn?'

'I do it because of moments like this. It's more than a career. It's hard to explain.' Heat rushed into her cheeks as she noticed Travis staring at her. It was difficult to read his expression in the dim light.

'You right to go in?' he said. 'I think most of the bats have headed out for the night now. With a bit of luck, some of the stragglers will still be feeding inside and you can find your first insects.'

Even though she didn't appreciate his dismissive tone, she nodded and slipped her backpack on. Adjusting the headlamp, she waited for the three of them to lead her into the tube. 'I'm ready.'

Chapter 6

***Carlyle Downs*, July 1879**

Missy Carlyle scrambled up the hill. As nimble as a mountain goat, she searched out rocks and tree roots to pull herself quickly to the top. The stand of deep-green vegetation along the ridge would be the best-ever hiding spot and she knew if she hid in the thicket Tommy and Stanley would never find her. She pulled herself over the crest just as Tommy called out.

'Eighteen … nineteen … twenty. Coming, ready or not!' His voice drifted up the hill from the other side of the fallen eucalyptus tree where he'd been hiding his face in his hands. Stanley had scarpered towards the creek as soon as Tommy had starting counting, but Missy had always had her eye on the thicket at the top of the hill.

As she approached the thick vegetation, Missy was surprised to see that hanging vines fell from the tree branches like a natural curtain. She carefully pushed aside the thick, matted vegetation, keeping an eye out for snakes. It was coming into the dry of winter, and the time of the year when the snakes would be searching out water. Missy shivered; she'd never forget seeing one of their Aboriginal stockmen die right in front of her before Mother had dragged Tommy and her away last summer. The brown snake had struck over and over at Old Billy's bare foot, and his scream had stayed in her head for weeks.

They didn't see many snakes around the house and she knew to be careful out in the bush. Father always said if you made enough noise and didn't try to touch them, they'd get out of your way.

But Missy was still wary, although her immediate problem was not making noise to give away her hiding spot, so she moved very slowly and shuffled her boots on the leaf-littered ground.

Once she was sure the trees and the dirt were clear of creatures, she lifted both hands to separate the greenery and stepped behind the curtain of vines. With a grin, she turned and peered down the hill. They would never find her up here. She could see Stanley as clear as day, his black face peering around the white bark of a tree where the creek split into the two tributaries. Tommy could never find Stanley either when they played; he could be standing right near you, but he was always as quiet as a mouse as he moved from place to place. Tommy always found her first, but this time she knew that he wouldn't. She giggled as her brother walked right past the tree where Stanley was hiding.

If he found Stanley, she knew that the young Aboriginal boy would be able to find her footprints, but it was satisfying besting Tommy for a change. Tommy—Missy's twin—was older by three minutes and he never let her forget it. He thought he was the best at everything, and sadly it was only their lessons where she usually surpassed him. Although he was as smart as a whip, all he wanted to do was get out of the schoolroom and help Father with the cattle. He didn't care about 'stupid book learning' as he called it, but Missy loved every minute of reading her books and learning something new. She just wished she could go to a proper school; she already knew more than their older sister, Eunice, who was supposed to be teaching them.

Tommy—named for their father—had been like a bear

with a sore head since Father had headed off to the gold miners' settlement with a hundred head of cattle early this morning. He'd pleaded and cajoled and finally resorted to tears.

'It's no place for a young boy.' Mother had stood firm even when Father had wavered.

'I'm almost thirteen. Old enough to work with the cattle. Why can't I go?'

Missy hid a smile as she saw him lift his foot and then he obviously thought better of stamping it.

'It's too dangerous over there at the moment. I'm not happy with your father going, either.' Mother had glared at their father as he'd waited while she'd wrapped him some bread and meat in a hessian sack.

'I'll only be gone a couple of days. Young Tom could come with me.'

A grin threatened to split Tom's face, but Missy knew Mother would not budge.

'No, Thomas. You yourself have told me about the troubles in the mining village. The violence! It's no place for a child.' Mother folded her arms and shook her head. 'And it was only last week that the Native Police stopped in on their way to the Lynd River to warn us to be careful.'

Father shook his head. 'They're just a bunch of rabble-rousers, those blokes. Looking for trouble. You know we have no problems with our Aboriginal workers.'

'That may be all well here, but you heard them tell us about the two men that the blacks murdered up at the Lynd.'

'Mother, *please*.' Tommy stood in front of her as Missy watched the battle of wills.

'No. You're not going. Now the pair of you scat to the schoolroom. You have work to do.'

Tommy muttered under his breath as they headed for the small alcove at the back porch that Mother referred to as the schoolroom, but his mood improved when Eunice excused them early. Missy and Tommy then called in at the Aboriginal camp, collected Stanley and went bush. Stanley was the son of one of the Aboriginal stockmen at *Carlyle Downs*, and his father often let him off the work when Tommy and Missy escaped the schoolroom.

Now, Missy stood stock still as Tommy walked past Stanley's hiding place for the second time, paused and then looked up the hill. 'I can see you Missy, so come out.'

She giggled again. There was no way he could see her; she might have fallen for that ruse when she was little but she would not now.

By the time he finally found Stanley with a triumphant whoop, Missy was getting bored. Dropping the vine curtain, she flexed her fingers and turned around. She crossed to a rock in the middle of the space, and after checking around it, she sat down. It was cool in the shade, the lacy canopy of leaves above letting only a small amount of light in. Eventually, the sound of Tommy and Stanley coming up the hill reached her.

The vine curtain was shoved aside and Tommy's voice was full of glee. 'Found you!'

'Only with Stanley's help,' Missy said in a bored voice. 'You never would have found me by yourself.'

'Oh jeepers, Stanley! Look at these vines. It's like a jungle.' Tommy pointed to the vegetation that went for over thirty yards past the rock wall in the centre and then disappeared over the side of the hill into the next gully. 'Let's go and explore.'

Their companion shook his head. 'You don't go down

there.' Stanley's eyes were white and wide in his dark face and his voice was high-pitched as he backed away out of the shady glade.

'Why not?' Tommy persisted with a teasing laugh. 'You scared of bad spirits, Stanley?'

'No. It's just bad land. We no go there.'

'We *don't* go there,' Missy corrected him. Just because Stanley wasn't allowed at their lessons didn't mean she couldn't help him improve his grammar. He was a quick study and they'd been great mates ever since his father had turned up on their lease a couple of years ago.

Stanley hurried back out and Missy followed him out into the sunshine. She put her hand to her eyes; it was dazzling outside after the cool interior of the glade.

Whoever would have guessed there was such a pretty spot close to the house? Spiky brown grass and dusty stockyards surrounded the small house that Father had built when he'd first leased the land. Rooms had been added on higgledy-piggledy over the years, but Missy still shared a room with Eunice; there was never anywhere to sit and be quiet by herself.

The glade was going to be her special place, and she intended coming back up as soon as she could get away from the boys.

Tommy shrugged and gave in to his mate. 'Okay, you go back. Missy and me'll go exploring.'

'Missy and I.'

Tommy glared at her.

Missy patted Stanley on the back as relief relaxed his shoulders. His work shirt was rough beneath her fingers. 'I'm going to go back and get my book to read.'

'Come on, Stanley, we'll go down to the creek and look

for gold,' Tommy said. 'Then if we find some, I won't have to go to school anymore.'

'Father said the Chinese have taken all the gold already.' Missy shook her head.

'There might be some here,' Tommy said scornfully.

'I don't want to. I'm going back to the house,' she said.

'We're a long way from the mining camp. They haven't even looked in our rivers,' her twin said. 'Come on, Stanley. Let's go and get that dish Father had.'

Their father had been enthusiastic when the first gold was discovered west of them just over six months ago, thinking it might make their life on the land easier. For a while, he'd considered joining the constant stream of men trudging west carrying tools and guns across the dry gullies.

'One good find, Lila, and I could build you that fancy homestead I promised you,' he'd said to Mother one night when they'd sat on the porch and watched the pall of dust over the road a couple of miles away from their hut.

'You'd be better off staying here and working the cattle, Thomas.' Mother had looked up from her mending. 'What would suit us best would be if they do discover enough to make it worthwhile for the teamsters and storekeepers to come our way.'

Tommy had been intent on discovering gold on their place since he'd listened to their parents that night.

'Well, when Stanley and I find it, you don't get a share.'

'I don't want one,' Missy replied haughtily.

They headed back down the hill, but Stanley's father was waiting for them at the gate and he jerked his head to Stanley. Wally was a man of few words; his gesture said it all. Stanley looked at them, disappointment pulling his mouth down in a scowl. 'I gotta go work.'

'Okay, I'll help out too,' Tommy said. 'What are you doing, Wally?'

'Moving some cattle. We have to move that herd from the west paddock. It's spooking the horses too much out there.'

'What do you mean spooking?' Missy asked.

Stanley puffed out his chest as he answered, 'It's bad land. Them horses don't like it.'

'What do you mean bad?'

Wally gestured sharply to his son and Stanley put his head down and walked over to the horses.

'What does he mean by bad land, Wally?'

The stockman scratched his head. 'Funny things happen out there. We can be riding along just fine, and then the bloody—sorry, Missy—blasted horses just stop, and won't take another step forward. The one your father was on the other day wouldn't move. Your father almost went head first over the front of him.'

'I wonder why?'

Wally shook his head. 'Dunno, but it's happened too many times now, so we're going to move the cattle. It only happens over there. You want to help too, Missy?'

She shook her head and crossed her fingers behind her back. 'No. I have chores to do.'

Wally nodded and Missy waited until they had disappeared down into the gully where Father kept most of the herd. She looked over her shoulder; it was Monday and Mother was probably still at the scrubbing board in the small shed where the fire heated the water to wash their clothes once a week. Missy ducked behind a tree as Eunice came out of the small lean-to and began to peg out the washing. If she wasn't careful, Missy knew she'd get roped into helping in the hut. It would be full of steam and stinking hot.

Or even worse she'd get called into the cookhouse; she always had to peel potatoes—or even worse, salt the beef.

Missy skirted around to the front of the house. Her book was still on the bench seat on the porch. She picked it up with a grin, stuffed it into the front of her pinafore and then walked backwards, keeping one eye on the house until she was out of sight. Once she was sure she was in the clear, she turned around and then headed back up the hill.

In the distance, she could see Wally, Tommy and Stanley moving the cattle. Brown dust hung in the air as they headed for the perennial spring on the other side of the hill. For a while, she sat in the sun on a rock and watched them. Then the cool of the glade beckoned; she put her book aside and approached the vine curtain.

This time, she went deeper into the shady glade. A rock fall had left a small pile of rocks beneath a rock wall and the sun was shining in through a gap in the canopy high above. As she looked up, she kicked her bare foot on a large stone and stumbled. Putting her hand out, she caught her balance on the rubble before she fell. The rock at the top of the pile rolled and she jumped back as the whole pile shifted and disappeared into a crevice, the sound of them hitting the ground below preceding the cloud of choking dust that came through the fissure in the rock. She screamed and rubbed at her head as a small black creature came through the crevice and flew past her face.

Slowly, the dust cleared and she approached the large hole that had appeared at the base of the rock wall. Walking across slowly in case the ground shifted, or worse still, she fell into the hole, she gripped a tree branch as she leaned forward and looked down.

It was one of the most beautiful things she had ever seen,

and as she became more confident, she moved closer. Beneath her, about twenty yards down the scree of fallen rocks was a huge cavernous opening that went further than she could see. The light from the opening above caught hundreds of cobwebs interlaced through the rocks, each one holding dead leaves woven into a semicircular shape. She shivered and stepped back from the eerie scene as she wondered at the size of the spiders that had spun those webs. The walls were different shades of reds and browns, and for a moment, she wondered how the colours had been painted on before she realised that the colours changed as they followed the shape of the rock walls and ceiling.

Missy stood there for a few minutes and examined the rock in detail, considering climbing down to the cave. As her eyes adjusted to the darkness, she could see further in, and realised that the black spots in the walls and ceilings were hundreds of bats clinging to the rock. Halfway along the cavern, tree roots dangled from the ceiling, forming a forest of greenery.

She jumped as something moved in the red dirt below. A huge snake slithered along the ground, stopping every foot or so at each fallen rock, leaving a trail in the fine dust behind it. It must have been at least twelve feet long, and she backed away, any thought of going down there quickly disappearing.

Maybe with Tommy one day, but certainly armed with a weapon.

Missy backed away from the crevice as the snake began to climb up the rock wall towards her, its tongue flicking in and out as it tasted the air in search of prey.

Chapter 7

***Carlyle Downs**, 3 January 2019.*

Emlyn rose early and pulled on her jeans and work boots. She picked up a jacket before she slipped out of her room. As she went to pull the door shut, she paused and went back inside for her phone. If she was going exploring, she should follow the policy that she insisted on for her team members, although it was a bit hard to tell anyone where she was going, seeing as she was here alone.

She didn't intend to go far. As they'd climbed the hill to the entrance to the tube last night, she'd noticed a higher hill a kilometre or so to the east. It would be a good vantage point to scope out the property and the direction of the tubes from the east to the west. She was going to read more of the German research papers. It might be convenient to enter the tube where they had stood last night, and where the Germans had done their initial research, but their proximity to the accommodation was not really a good enough reason to focus on that section of the tube.

The chances of coming across different species would be higher if she and the team went in deeper. Perhaps to a section where the roof hadn't collapsed and there was no intrusion of vegetation from above. It appeared that the discoveries of the Germans were very similar to the findings of the team that had done extensive research in the Hawaiian lava tubes. Invertebrates had colonised the young lava tubes there and were already evolving as tropical-zone cave-adapted species. The tubes on the Carlyle property were much older than the Hawaiian site, and the possibility of discovering new species was excellent.

A spark of anticipation fired in Emlyn's belly as she shut the door behind her. Seeing the wildlife at sunset last night had awoken feelings that had lain dormant for too long. She switched on her phone and checked the time. Sunrise was about half an hour away. The first rosy streaks of dawn were painting the sky as she ran lightly down the three stairs to the dusty drive. A wallaby stood beside her car as she walked past, not bounding away until she was almost upon it. She crossed the paddocks to where Travis had pointed out the site of the original homestead last night, walking parallel to where they had driven along the track. As she passed the ruins of the old homestead, a movement behind the half-tumbled-down brick chimney caught her attention and she blinked.

Emlyn found a gap in the barbed wire fence, slipped beneath and walked across the paddock. She could have sworn that she'd seen a small girl run from the fence line to the site of the old house. She shook her head and picked up her stride.

'Hello? Is anyone there?' She felt silly as she called out. There was nothing to be seen apart from the hovering mist and ghostly shadows, but still a shiver ran down her back. As she got closer to the chimney, she could see the charred posts that had once supported the original homestead. Greener grass shoots surrounded the posts that were laid out in a rectangular formation; it had obviously been a big house. A rustle in the grass froze her to the spot. She smiled with relief as a wallaby— about the size of a small child—scurried through the gap in the fence.

As Emlyn turned to head back to the east, she noticed a large lump of concrete in front of the fence line and she wandered over. It didn't matter if she missed the sunrise; she had at least another three months to see that.

There was a wooden gate in the fence and she pushed it open, surprised to see that there was a small cemetery laid out behind the ruins of the old homestead. Ground cover with tiny white flowers climbed over some of the graves, and a shaft of grief hit her as she spotted a small jar with some flowers against a fairly new marble headstone.

Her breath caught, and heavy pressure built in her chest. She gripped the gate and closed her eyes and fought the panic attack that threatened, focusing on taking in steady and deep breaths. There was no one here; it was simply a memorial to people who were long gone. It was no one she knew, and it meant nothing to her. Concrete and memories, that's all it was. This feeling of doom that was slowly squeezing her chest wasn't real. She wasn't having a heart attack; it was all in her imagination. Focusing on trying to see three things and identify three different sounds—a strategy the psychologist had given her to stop a panic attack—she dropped to her knees and put her hands over her eyes, pushing back the tears that threatened as her heart beat a fast race in her chest.

The tears that were always there.

Why now? She should have continued up the hill and she'd be sitting up there watching the sun steal over the land, instead of being caught in her own horror.

'You all right there, love?'

Emlyn dropped her hands from her eyes and jumped to her feet as a man appeared from behind the newer headstone.

She put her hand to her chest; the pressure had eased, but

her heart was thundering away. At least the fright of hearing his voice had brought her back to the present.

He was short and stocky, with grey hair, and he wore a stained T-shirt tucked into a pair of khaki trousers held up by a piece of what looked like fencing wire. He held a cigarette in one hand and a toolbox in the other. She looked at him warily as he lifted the cigarette to his mouth and drew in deeply.

'Yes. I'm fine, thank you,' she said.

As he walked over to her, Emlyn put her hand in her pocket and wrapped her fingers around the phone, although that was a waste of time; there was no one to call if she needed help.

'I've been over at the dongas fixing the tap on the tank.' His voice held the gravelly tones of a heavy smoker.

Emlyn swallowed and straightened her back, taking her hand out of her pocket. 'Oh, thank you. You must be Bluey?'

'Yep, that's what they call me. Bluey, Blue, your call.' His face crinkled in a larrikinish smile as he gestured to his head. 'When I was a young fella, I was a ginger nut, and even though I'm old and grey now, I still answer to Blue.'

She nodded.

'Anyway, your water's all good now. There was a dead possum blocking the intake. I hope you haven't been drinking the tank water.'

'No, I brought bottled water.'

'Good move.' He stood and regarded her. 'You're the one Travis told me is going into the caves.'

She nodded and gestured behind her. 'Yes. I was just walking up to watch the sunrise when I noticed the ruins of the old home. You're out working very early. I didn't see you there when I left.'

'Yeah, there's cattle to be moved today. I was parked

around the back of the tank when you walked out. I gave you a hoy, but you didn't hear me.'

'No, I didn't. Anyway, thanks for fixing it. I'll tell the others to be careful with the water when they arrive.'

'I thought you might have come up this way. Be careful up on that hill.' The smell of roll-your-own-tobacco took Emlyn back to her childhood. It was the smell that had always surrounded Poppa, her paternal grandfather. She'd spent much of her childhood at her grandparents' house at Morningside, while her parents had explored the world. The passing of Nana and Poppa within a month of each other had been her first experience of loss and death.

As she followed him back through the gate, he pointed up the hill. 'There's a track up that way. I'll show you. Wait here. I'll just put my tools in the ute.'

Emlyn waited while he walked to the road; she hadn't heard his vehicle as she'd wandered around the headstones, but she could see it parked about a hundred metres away. He hurried back to her, and then set out at a brisk pace, taking a different path up the hill to the one she would have followed. They were on the opposite side of the hill to where she'd been with Travis and his boys last night. They circled right around the hill and walked through a stand of trees where fat and healthy cattle grazed. Beside the grove, a small spring bubbled from the rocky hillside and an expanse of water glistened pink in the soft light of dawn. The incline was gentle, and it was only about five minutes before they reached the crest of the hill that overlooked the property. As Bluey leaned against a tree and pulled out another paper and a packet of tobacco, Emlyn's phone buzzed, but she ignored it.

'That's not good for you, you know,' she said.

'I'm too old to worry about that now. Besides, none of it's true. All that guff about smoking being bad for you. It's a government conspiracy.'

Emlyn waited until he had finished rolling the cigarette and then she walked over to stand beside him. She looked to the east. In the soft light, it was easy to see the alignment of the depressions as they ran from the east, where in the far distance, the rim of the old volcano at Undara was visible. Some of the depressions were oval, some were elongated, but all had dark-green vegetation that was easy to discern in the early-morning light.

She shook her head and spoke half to herself. 'It will take years to explore all of that.'

'Why do you have to go down there? There's been people disappear down there.'

'Die? I haven't read about any accidents here.'

He lifted his free hand and nicotine-stained fingers tapped the side of his nose. 'You need to listen to the locals, love. Snakebite, rock falls and the bad stuff. You wouldn't get me down there in those tubes for quids. And you lot shouldn't be down there, either. Travis didn't want you there, but he kept quiet about the danger. He needs the money.'

Emlyn wondered why he was trying to scare her off. 'What sort of "bad" stuff?'

'Nah, you'll think I'm as balmy as a bandicoot.'

'Try me.'

'The spooks.' Bluey lowered his voice to a husky whisper. 'Those caves are haunted. Back in the 1800s, they reckoned there was gold down there and they say half them prospectors who went looking never came back up.' He put his head close to hers. 'On a still night, if you go close enough to the entrance, you can hear them.'

'I'll keep that in mind,' Emlyn said. 'If that's what "they" say.'

He shrugged. 'Just be careful. When you get scared, just remember old Blue warned you.'

'We will. There's no need to worry, and we're not going to cause Travis any bother.' She kept her tone matter-of-fact. 'We're hoping to find some new species of insects.'

He scratched his head, and his heavily wrinkled face creased even more. 'Why the hell—sorry love—why the heck would you want to go looking for insects? Seems like a funny job for anyone, let alone a young girl like you.'

'It might not change anything, but our entomological studies can help humankind. Agricultural pest control, threats to humans, and animals carrying disease—'

He waved his hand. 'Ya reckon?'

'We'll have to agree to differ,' she said with a smile. 'Do you live around here?'

He nodded. 'I've been here all my life. Born over at Mt Surprise. I've been a stockman here on and off for over sixty years.'

'It's such an amazing place. You know, there aren't many places in the world like this. And this system is one of the biggest.' Emlyn stared towards the volcano, trying to imagine the eruption that had created the tubes here so long ago. When the lava had spewed out, some had found its way into old watercourses. When it channelled along them, the lava hardened on the tops and sides to form the insulated tubes that they were looking down on now. 'They say that the swamps here are created by the drainage being blocked by the lava flows,' she said half to herself.

'And that's why the property here has been able to keep cattle right through the years. Even those years when we've not had much rain. And there's a lot of springs, too.'

Emlyn was impressed with his knowledge of the property. 'Maybe you can help when we get into the tubes.'

'Not if you want me anywhere near them.' His eyes caught hers and held them. 'Depends what you want, hey?' A puff of white smoke surrounded him as he exhaled, and the familiar smell reached her again, filling her with a strange comfort.

Before she could answer, her phone buzzed again, and she turned away as she pulled it from her pocket. 'Excuse me.'

He nodded and leaned against the tree, the cigarette hanging from his lips as he watched her. Emlyn moved away, glanced down at the screen and clicked on her messages.

One from John Kearns; the floodwater had slowed them down more than they had expected, and they hoped to arrive early tomorrow. The other message was from the store where she'd ordered the groceries, wanting to know if the back gate to the property that met the road to the Einasleigh Road was unlocked. She'd have to go across and ask Travis; they were delivering the provisions this afternoon.

Emlyn lifted her head and stared at the sky. The pink of dawn had faded, and the clouds had turned from gold to grey. Shoving the phone back in her pocket, she turned back to the stockman.

'I have to go back and get organised. It was good to meet you, Bluey. Thank you for showing me the quick way up here.'

He nodded as they headed back to the track. 'My pleasure, love. Anything else you need fixed, just give me a hoy. Travis always knows where to find me.'

* * *

Travis sat out on the front steps enjoying the still morning air. The sky had cleared, and there was no sign of any rain. Two and a half Millimetres the night before last had been enough to wet the dirt. When they'd come in last night, the boys had stayed up late watching a DVD, some shoot-'em-up, bang-'em-up action thing, but he hadn't been in the mood. They were still asleep.

He looked up as the old ute roared up the road. Bluey swung it through the gate. Travis stood as the stockman jumped out and ran up the hill. He was puffing by the time he reached the steps.

'Slow down, Blue. You'll give yourself a heart attack. What's the rush?'

'Fuckin' hell, Trav. You haven't been over to the paddock where we put the breeders the other day?'

'Not since the day before yesterday when I checked the lick blocks. Why?'

'What about the Collins idiot?'

'I got him to top up the feed that afternoon.'

Bluey sat on the bottom step. He dropped his head in his hands.

'Blue?' Concern built in Travis's chest, and he dropped to his haunches and squatted in front of him. 'What is it?'

'I told you that young bastard was no good.'

'Who? You're going to have to tell me what's happened.'

'The Collins kid. They're all dead.'

Travis stared at Bluey. 'Mate, I have no idea what you're talking about. Who's dead?'

Bluey lifted his face and his mouth was set in a grim line.

'Your cattle. The breeders. I went over to check the feed and there's not one left alive.'

'What? What the fuck?' The blood ran from Travis's head as he pushed himself to his feet. 'How the hell did that happen?' He dug in his pocket for his keys.

Bluey shook his head. 'Come with me. It'll be quicker.'

* * *

When Bluey dropped him back to the house a couple of hours later, there was still no sign of life. Travis pounded up the front steps and yelled, 'Are you still in bed, Gavin?' He hadn't checked the shed to see if his brother's ute was there. Gavin had spent the last two days in his room or on the computer. There was no sign of the twins, either.

'I'm holding the bloody place together by myself,' Travis thought.

Gavin wandered out of his room, unshaven, with a stubborn look on his face. 'I was asleep until you slammed the door against the wall.' He rubbed a hand over his eyes. 'What's all the noise about?'

'I need your help today,' Travis's words were clipped. He was just keeping it together, trying not to think about the financial consequences of the dead cattle. He strode into the kitchen.

'I can't. I have to go to Townsville.'

'I really need you today. We've got to bury some cattle. You can drive the backhoe.'

Gavin's footsteps were faster than usual as he hurried behind him into the kitchen. 'Bury? Why?'

'Because they're dead.' Travis's jaw clenched as he filled the coffee machine.

'Dead? How?' Gavin looked like he was about to cry, and that helped Travis calm down. He grabbed a chair and flopped into it.

'I don't know, Gav. I must have got the mix wrong. Or I didn't ease them into it slow enough. They had salt blocks for two weeks.'

'Maybe someone hurt them?' Gavin stood and crossed to the coffee machine, poured a cup, and brought it over to Travis.

Travis looked up at his brother as he took the mug. His hair was tousled, and even though he was a stocky man, his blue-striped pyjamas were too big for him. 'Appreciate it.'

'So, did someone hurt them?' Gavin persisted.

'No, it was all my doing. I stuffed up.' No matter what Bluey suspected, Travis knew it was his error. He racked his brain and worked out the calculations again in his head. He'd used a proprietary mix with salt, urea, minerals, and grains because it was convenient to feed out. He knew all the blocks weren't the same weight, and they could vary in nutrient content.

'I can still remember what Dad used to say,' Gavin said. 'An old bushie's thing, remember?'

'No, I don't,' Travis said patiently. 'What did he say?'

'Whenever urea is fed to cattle, deaths can occur.'

Travis nodded. 'He did. I'm surprised you remember that. Dad's been gone a long time.'

'And Mum has too.' Gavin sniffed and wiped his nose with the back of his hand. He went to the fridge and poured himself a glass of chocolate milk. 'I really can't help today. I have to go to Townsville. It's important.'

Travis waved a hand. 'Whatever you have to do.'

Gavin disappeared into the bathroom, and Travis went outside to clear his head. He was used to spending most of his time alone; having the boys home, the rest of the university mob about to turn up down the road, and Alison and Cass coming this morning, he needed some space for himself before they all arrived. And after what had happened, he needed some time to think it through more than ever.

A litany of problems crowded his head as he sipped the coffee. He pushed the financial issues to the back of his mind. He'd think about the bloody gold mine later. He'd move heaven and hell not to accept the offer, but he knew the time was coming when he had no other option. They'd withdrawn their offer after meeting with Gavin, but Travis was sure they'd come to the table and talk again. He'd have to put that Collins boy off; he couldn't afford to keep him on. And maybe it was time for Bluey to retire. Maybe Jase would have to leave school and come home to work with him. And Joel, too.

Or maybe if Carroglen would talk again, everyone would be happy; Alison might come home, too. As far as he knew, she wasn't seeing anyone; the boys would have told him if she was. Maybe it was time to try one more time. Convince her to come home.

Maybe he was kidding himself, but if she had no respect—or feelings—for him, she wouldn't have talked to him for such a long time on the phone the night before last. Okay, she kept her distance, but he was sure there was always a spark in her eyes when they saw each other. Or maybe he was just seeing what he wanted to.

The sound of a car approaching had him lifting his head. He'd been waiting for Alison to text him about when they were going to turn up. She always borrowed aunt's car to get to

Carlyle Downs.

Maureen's old red sedan was coming slowly along the road. Travis smiled; Alison had always driven fast, but after the boys were born, her driving habits had slowed right down.

'We have precious cargo now,' she'd always reminded him when he'd teased her.

His smile faded as the car approached. They'd barely got to share Cass as precious cargo. Alison had left before Cass had graduated from the baby seat to a toddler's car seat. The car turned into the gate and parked close to the steps. He walked over and reached in to undo Cass's belt. He took her out and swung her high as she tried to plant wet kisses all over his cheeks.

'Dadda, Dadda,' she squealed.

'Hello, my chicken. Did you bring me a present?'

The little face was scornful, but she took his face between her small hands. 'I did. Kisses.'

Travis let her kiss him and then she held him tightly around his neck and whispered in his ear, 'I wanna stay.'

Disappointment settled in his gut. Obviously, Alison had said something about a short visit. He put Cassie down as his wife approached. He knew by her stance that something was wrong. God, he knew her so well. He could almost read her mind, but damn it, he was going to push her buttons before she could start on about whatever was bothering her. He reached out his hand before she could move away and took her arm. Pulling her close, he dropped a kiss on her cheek. She'd done something different with her hair colour, but he couldn't pinpoint what it was. And she'd lost weight; her face looked thinner.

'Hi, Al. It's good to see you. You're looking good.'

Her hair had grown since he'd last seen her, and she'd pulled it back from her face. Her skin was unlined, and her blue eyes were bright and clear, although he did notice unfamiliar shadows beneath her eyes as she stepped away from him.

'Hello, Travis.' She glanced up at the house. 'Where are the boys?'

'Out the back in their tents. They had a late night and then they wanted to camp out.'

Her eyes moved down the hill to the shed. 'I thought you said Gavin was going away yesterday?'

Travis shrugged. 'You know what he's like. Apparently, he's leaving this morning.'

Cassie tugged at his sleeve.

'Are you going to stay here?' he asked Alison. 'I'd like to spend some time with Cass.'

'I don't know yet.' Her voice was soft as he stood back and let her walk up the stairs in front of him. 'We'll see.'

'Come in and I'll cook us some brunch.'

If it wasn't for the boys teasing Cassie, the meal would have been a tense affair. Gavin was trying to talk to Alison and the boys about some computer game he'd bought, but she seemed disinterested. Travis couldn't blame her and tried to keep the conversation going, but eventually, he gave up. Finally, Gavin sat back in his chair and rubbed his stomach. 'You did good, Travis. I'm too full to move.'

Travis began to clear the table. 'Do you want another cuppa before you leave?'

Gavin yawned. 'You woke me up too early. I'm too tired to drive. I'll go tomorrow.'

'Good. You can help me with the cattle.' Travis shot a glance at the boys; he hadn't told them what had happened yet.

'No. I'm too tired for that, too.' Gavin stood and headed for the hallway, leaving his plate and cutlery on the table.

Alison pushed her chair back and picked up a couple of plates.

'Leave that. I'll do it,' Travis said.

As he placed the dishes in the sink, he saw a movement at the door. Turning around, he stared at Alison, who was gripping the doorframe, her expression sad. He walked over to her.

'Al. What is it? Is something wrong?'

'No.' She shook her head and blinked, but he could have sworn he saw moisture in her eyes before she did. 'Nothing. I just came to wipe up for you before I leave.'

'Leave? You just got here.' Travis ran both his hands through his hair. 'Why are you leaving? It's crazy to come here for an hour and then drive all the way back to Mt Surprise.'

'I'll leave Cass here and I'll go back to Aunty Maureen's.'

'Why, what's wrong?'

'Cass can sleep in the spare bed in our—your—room.' She gestured up the hall. 'There's not enough room for us here if Gavin's home, so I'll go.'

'No. The boys are in their tents. I'll change the sheets in their room, so you and Cass don't have to sleep in the smell of cows and sweaty socks.'

A glimmer of a smile lifted her lips. 'We should have left our visit until tomorrow.'

'Look, I know my brother is a pain, but he'll go. All I'll have to do is mention work, and he'll be gone like a shot.'

'Yes, I noticed that. Still as slack as ever.'

'He's got worse. And now he can't stay away from the coast. I don't know what the sudden attraction is.'

'Maybe he's got himself a girlfriend?'

Travis looked down at her. 'You know I hadn't even thought of that. We can only hope.'

'Hope?' She moved away from him and picked up a tea towel. 'It'd be good to see him in a relationship. Might settle him a bit.'

'You wash, I'll dry, and then I'll help you change the sheets. For Cass's bed.' As she waited for him to run the water, she stared out the window. 'The cattle are looking thin, Travis.'

'I need to talk to you and the boys later. We've had a major setback.' To his dismay, his voice cracked, and he cleared his throat. 'It's been a hard winter. And last summer was dry, too.'

'What's happened? Whenever I ask the boys how it's going up here they always say, 'everything's fine'. I guess you've schooled them in that.'

'I didn't think you were interested in the place.'

'Well, I am. We mightn't be together anymore, but it's still the boys' home.'

'And Cass?' he said. 'What about Cass? It's her home too.'

He glanced at her and her cheeks were tinged with colour. 'Cass is too little to remember living here.'

Travis bit his lip to stop the angry words. He took a steadying breath. 'It's her home too, Alison.'

She nodded but didn't speak again as she reached for the next plate.

Once the dishes were done and the beds changed, Alison called to Cassie. 'Come on, munchkin. We're going to go for a little drive. We'll go and find Bluey before I leave.'

'Want the cows.' Cass's bottom lip trembled as she ran over to Travis and clung to his leg.

'You can go to the yards, but you've got to stay with Dadda and do what he says. Okay?'

'Mummy, too.'

'Yes.' Travis frowned. 'Come over to the yards with us for a while. I could do with an extra hand on the gate today.'

'All right.' Alison's voice was cold. 'But I'm still going back to Mt Surprise later.'

She hadn't even asked again what the setback was.

* * *

As she started the car, Emlyn patted her pocket to make sure she had the details of the store. If she got to the house early, there was a better chance of catching Travis before he went out to the cattle.

Emlyn pulled up outside the dilapidated old house, surprised to see a couple of one-man tents between the house and the side fence. She climbed out of the car just as Joel stood up beside the one closest to the gate. He smiled as she approached.

'I'm sorry, did I wake you up?' she asked.

'No, we've been up for ages and had breakfast. I was just zipping up the tent to keep the snakes out. Dad needs us to help over at the yards.' His tanned face flushed. 'We must look like little kids having a sleep-out. We used to sleep out here a lot when we were little. But Mum and Cassie are here and they're going to sleep in our room.' He nodded at the small red sedan parked near the house.

Emlyn shook her head. 'Look, if you have guests, I won't bother your dad. I just need to know about a back gate being unlocked.' She pulled out the piece of paper where she'd written down the details. 'The gate that joins the Einasleigh Road.'

'No, they're not guests. It's just Mum and Cass.' Joel

looked at his brother as he came down the steps. 'And I don't know about the gate.' He called out to Jase. 'Do you know if the back gate is open?'

Jase shook his head. 'We haven't been out that way for a while. Not since the holidays before last. There's no feed out that way, and no water for the cattle. Dad kept it locked to stop the mining company coming on our land,' he added.

Joel nodded. 'Sorry, Emlyn, you'll have to ask Dad. Why do you need to know?'

'I've got a delivery coming across from Mt Surprise and they asked if the gate was locked. Apparently, it makes the trip shorter.'

'That'd be right. Old Janet's as tight as they come, anything to save a dollar,' Jase said.

'Although to be fair, Jase, it is about fifty kilometres shorter to come the back way,' Joel said.

The door opened, and Travis stepped out, and a small girl followed him. Emlyn's breath caught, and she tried to focus on what Jase was saying.

'It's a couple of years since Dad was having trouble, so it's probably not locked anymore, but you'd better ask him.'

She swallowed. 'Thank you, I will.' Taking a deep breath, she walked to the bottom of the stairs; there was no sign of the red kelpie today. Keeping her eyes on Travis, Emlyn ignored the child up on the landing and cleared her throat. 'Good morning, Travis. I'm sorry to bother you so early, but I need to know about a back gate being locked for the delivery from Mt Surprise.'

He frowned, and she waited for him to reply for a full minute.

'Yeah, it's still locked,' he finally said. 'When are they coming through?'

'This afternoon.'

'Sorry, we don't have time to go out there now. I'll have to give you the key and get you to unlock it.' His tone held no apology at all and again Emlyn thought what a difficult man he could be.

'I'll tell you how to get out there.'

'I can go and do it, Dad.' Joel flicked her an apologetic look, but Travis shook his head.

'No, I need both of you to help me all day.'

Emlyn put her hands in her pocket. 'I don't mind doing it. If you could get me the key and tell me how to get there, I'll go there now. I won't bother you any longer.'

Travis shrugged and went back inside.

'Just ignore him. Dad can be an old grumpy-bum sometimes.' Joel smiled at Emlyn. 'I'm sorry.'

The little girl came down the steps. 'Dadda's got moo cows.' If her smile was any indication, it was something she was very happy about. She stared at Emlyn and screwed up her face. 'Who you?'

'Emlyn.'

'Come on, Cass. I'll give you a piggyback around to the chook pen, so you can feed them.' Jase squatted down in front of her and she climbed up. As they disappeared around the side of the house, Joel walked over to Emlyn. 'Sorry, the whole family's rude today.'

'Not rude. Just busy.' Emlyn forced a polite smile to her face. 'I'm sorry I'm a bother.'

'Stop apologising.'

Emlyn caught his eye and smiled, and this time her smile stayed. 'I'm just not good with people, either.'

'So, you're not lonely out there? Dad said you're still by

yourself?'

'The others arrive tomorrow.'

As Joel nodded, Travis reappeared and came down the steps and held out a key. 'There's a padlock on the gate. This should open it.'

'Should?'

'Yeah, it should. I think it's the right key.'

'Okay, so how do I get there?' Emlyn was starting to think it would be easier to just tell the delivery driver the gate was locked.

Travis pointed to the road. 'Go back to where the dongas are, go past them and then drive ten kilometres past that and take the left fork where the track splits.'

'A track?'

'Okay, I mean a road. Your Troopie will handle it no problem. You won't even need low range. We haven't had enough rain for the creeks to be up yet.' He turned away and spoke to Joel. 'Get your brother and hurry up and get ready. The cattle truck's meeting us at the yards in a while. We've got a big job to do when the cattle are loaded. Bluey's down there already.'

'What job, Dad?'

'I'll tell you when we get there.'

Again, an apologetic look from Joel. Emlyn dropped her eyes down to the key in her hand. It was rusted and slightly bent. She placed it in her shirt pocket.

'And then you stay on the road for another thirty kilometres and you'll come to the locked gate. You can't go wrong,' Travis finished off. 'Okay? Got that?'

'Yes. I'll head out there straight away.' Emlyn kept her tone even despite feeling cross that a few hours would be taken out of her day.

'Leave the padlock on the gate and just bring the key back. Kev can lock it on his way out.'

'Thank you for the information and the key.' Emlyn turned on her heel and headed back to the truck; by the time she'd put her seatbelt on and started the engine, there was no sign of any of the Carlyles. 'Thanks for all your help,' she muttered under her breath. She had been going to thank him for sending Bluey over to fix the water problem, but Travis Carlyle could go whistle.

Once she'd taken the left fork, she pulled over to the side and texted the store at Mt Surprise. There were just enough bars to send a text.

The gate will be unlocked.

Emlyn pulled back onto the road; it was encouraging that there was some service out here, because the road was rutted and narrow, and there was a good chance of getting a flat. If that happened, she'd have to ring Mr. Cranky Carlyle because there'd be no chance of getting road service out here.

It was more like the track he'd said than a road. An hour later, and another twenty-five kilometres further on, Emlyn's simmering temper deteriorated further. The wheel ruts that she had to negotiate in the road were deep and wide, some of them almost big enough for the Troop Carrier to fall into. When the front wheel teetered over a huge drop as she turned a curve, she wrenched the wheel and turned the vehicle into the long grass at the side of the road. It was safer to risk a flat tyre from grass seeds than risk rolling the vehicle into one of those huge ruts. It looked like a bulldozer had got bogged in the wet season, but she knew that couldn't be right because the ruts continued for the next two kilometres.

Finally, the road smoothed out and she drove back onto it, easing her grip on the steering wheel, and grateful that the four tyres were still intact.

Her hands were sweaty and she was thirsty, but Emlyn realised too late she had no water in the car. She'd taken the eskies out the first night she'd arrived and hadn't thought to go back for water before setting off.

All the more reason to drive carefully and avoid getting stranded out here.

Equally cross with herself, and with Travis Carlyle, she pushed her damp hair back from her forehead and looked out for the gate. She flicked a glance at the odometer; according to that, it should be within the next half-kilometre.

'Bloody hell.' She wrenched the handbrake up and turned off the ignition as she stared at the gate.

The unlocked, open gate.

Chapter 8

Carlyle Downs, **October 1879**

The marriage of Thomas Carlyle and Lila Jane Cragg had taken place at St James' Anglican church in Townsville in 1861. Missy loved hearing the story of how Father had met Mother when he and his brother, George, were travelling up the Burdekin and she'd been helping her own father with their cattle. Mother said that Father had spent three weeks camping at the lagoon where her family had their cattle run, and he'd asked her to marry him before he moved further north with the cattle to the land where he and his brother had taken up a lease. Since then, Father and his brother had taken out occupational licences for four new runs.

It was hard to imagine what Mother would have found here when she arrived as a young bride. An old shanty, very little fresh water and no one within miles and miles. Eunice came along quickly and then five years later she and—

'Missy! Stop daydreaming and hurry up. The next ones are ready for you.' Despite the sharpness of her voice, Mother's smile was indulgent. She stood over the copper stirring the clothes with the washing stick. Her cheeks were flushed as the day was hot and dry.

'Yes, Mother.' Missy looked up from the washboard where she was reluctantly spending her Monday morning. As usual, she had drawn the short straw. Tommy was out helping Father, and she'd been roped into washing day. Of course, being the youngest and female she'd got the hard job. Mother handed over the work clothes, still stained with cattle shit and mud after she lifted them out of the boiling water. Like Mother's hands, Missy's were red raw after two hours at the glass and timber washboard. Being in the small room with the fire burning brightly beneath the old copper tub was where Missy hated being more than anything. She'd much rather be in the schoolroom with her books, but Eunice had gone to Townsville on the coach yesterday. She was catching the train down to Bundaberg and would be away helping Mother's sister with her new baby for a few weeks. And that's where George Fairweather was. Bundaberg. Missy would be surprised if Eunice ever came back.

Missy frowned; she and Tommy had planned a trip back to the cave this afternoon, but it looked like they'd be kept busy all day. Although she'd escaped to the glade a few times, she had not ventured any further in since she'd seen that huge snake there in the winter.

Since gold had been discovered over at Spring Creek on the Einasleigh River almost a year ago, there had been an influx of diggers into the region. A couple of months ago, rumours of a strike in a gully about twenty miles west of their boundary had seen thousands more hopefuls on the road west. The camp was growing bigger every day, according to those who headed back east once they gave up. The storekeepers had set up establishments in the small settlement that was growing there, but Father had seized the opportunity and built a store on the road at the edge of their leased land and stocked it with implements and food that the miners could purchase on their way to the diggings. The small slab hut with a weatherboard front and a glass window now sat on the edge of the road where there had been a constant stream of miners heading west over the past six months. Bags of flour, tea and sugar were stacked against the front wall, and tins of golden syrup and molasses filled the shelves. Mother and the girls baked dozens of dampers to sell to the men as they passed by. When Father had gone to Townsville last month to stock the store, Tommy had been allowed to go with him and Missy had been green with envy. She'd never seen the ocean. She'd been born on the property and the way things were going, she'd never get away from it.

'Not fair,' she muttered under her breath as she scrubbed.

'What have you got a bee in your bonnet about now, young lady?' Mother held the stick high above the tin bucket next to the washboard and steam rose from the clothes piled ready for Missy to scrub.

'Nothing.'

Last night when she and Tommy were in bed, she'd heard the glee in Father's voice as he'd told Mother of the prices they'd got for the cattle he'd taken to the digger's camp. Maybe if things were as good as he'd said, they'd be able to afford for her to go away to school. Missy desperately wanted to learn more than what was on offer with the scant number of books in the schoolroom. She'd begged Eunice to bring back some new books from the coast, but knowing her sister, that wasn't likely to happen.

'I just saw your father and brother ride along the ridge. Go and get that mutton pie out and slice up some of that cold potato, too. Leave those clothes. I'll finish them off and peg them out.'

'Yes, Mother.' Missy ran from the washhouse as though her feet were winged. No more scrubbing; kitchen duty was much more appealing.

By the time Father and Tommy came into the house,

Missy had the table set and the midday meal laid out.

'Father's going down to the station store this afternoon, and we have to catch up on our schoolwork.' Tommy's voice was proper, and Missy rolled her eyes. As soon as Father turned away, Tommy winked and mouthed 'the cave' before he shoved a piece of cold pie into his mouth.

'Yes. I need your mother's help so you might as well get into the schoolroom and keep working while Eunice is away.'

'That will be good, Father.' Tommy's voice was angelic, and Missy kicked him under the table as Mother walked in. If Tommy overdid it, Mother would know that they were up to something.

'What will be good?' Mother asked as she walked across to the stove and checked the fire.

Missy glared at Tommy. He pointed to his mouth and shook his head as he chewed.

'Some decent manners at last,' Mother said. 'Mercy, I never thought we'd see the day.'

'Tommy meant it was good that you were going to help Father in the store,' Missy chimed in.

Their father nodded. 'Yes, business has been excellent these past days. I need your mother over there this afternoon. Is that extra leg of mutton cooked and ready to take over, love?'

'It is.' Mother pulled out a chair and sat beside Missy. 'Have you heard any more about the troubles on the road, Thomas?'

Father nodded. 'Yes, unfortunately. I met a fellow yesterday who told me they're having a lot of trouble west of Spring Creek with the myalls.'

'What's a myall, Father?' Missy asked, only to put her fork down in surprise when Tommy interrupted, his eyes wide.

'They're wild Aborigines and they're spearing the cattle, the bloke said.'

'Tommy,' Mother chastised. 'Don't exaggerate.'

Father put his knife and fork down and sat back. 'Unfortunately, he's not exaggerating, Lila. The children need to know that we all have to be careful. I'm going to show you how to use the revolver. When I go to Charters Towers next week, I want you to keep it loaded.'

Tommy's eyes were like saucers now, and a trickle of fear ran down Missy's back. 'Do we need to be scared?' she asked.

'No. Just careful. We're a long way from the troubles. They say it's where the blacks have been pushed off their land by the gold claims. The claims are moving east and a few cattle have been speared.'

Missy sat up straight. 'It could be the miners after free food. Why blame the Aborigines!'

'You could be right, but I want you all to be careful. No wandering about by yourselves anymore. You pair stay close to the homestead.'

This time Missy and Tommy locked gazes as they nodded. 'Yes, Father,' they said dutifully.

After their parents had loaded up the wagon, they headed towards the front gate where the store was on the main road west, two miles distant from the house.

'Come on, we've got at least three hours before they come back. Let's go.' Tommy waited at the door while Missy put the dishes in the cupboard.

'Where's Stanley?' Missy asked.

'He's busy with Wally, and anyway he's scared of the cave. He reckons something bad happened there.'

'Father will tan our hides if he finds out we went

exploring when he told us to stay close to the house.'

'Wouldn't be the first time.' Tommy's smile was cheeky as he put his hands on his hips. 'Besides, there's probably more chance of trouble at the house, not up the hill in the scrub.'

'I don't believe it's the Aborigines, anyway. It's those damned Chinamen spearing the cattle.' Missy pulled down the hessian on the front of the cupboard and checked the stove was tamped down.

'And anyway, how's Father going to know? I won't tell, and you won't tell. As long as we're back well before sundown, it's all good.' Tommy spoke sense. They would be the only ones who knew they'd been exploring. Neither of them had mentioned their discovery. Missy hadn't because she wanted a place to be alone, and Tommy because he knew they'd be in trouble.

'Come on, sis. You are so slow sometimes.'

Excitement curled in Missy's stomach as she threw off her apron and followed Tommy outside.

* * *

Missy lay on her stomach and held the kerosene lantern high above the rock edge that overlooked the cave. Now that they were here and about to explore the dark depths below them, a shiver raised goosebumps on her skin. What if Stanley was right and it was a bad place? A feeling of dread lodged in her throat and the lantern bobbed as she leaned forward and called to Tommy.

'Maybe this isn't such a good plan, after all.'

'Oh, don't be such a sook!' His voice was hollow as he called up to her. Missy could just see him in the ghoulish shadows as he picked his way carefully down the fallen rocks.

'What if the lantern goes out?'

'It's all right. I can see lots of places where there are

chinks of light coming in through the roof. Take the lantern back from the edge for a minute. Let me see how dark it is without it.'

Missy did as he said and waited until her brother called her back.

'It's amazing. We don't need it and it'll be easier for you to climb down. Leave the lantern at the top and come down. It's safe.'

'No snakes?' She hadn't forgotten that big one that had made her run out the day the rocks caved in.

'No. There's nothing alive down here. It's dead quiet and still.'

'Really?'

'Not much, anyway.' Tommy's chuckle spurred her on. She hated him calling her a sook.

Missy put the lantern carefully on a flat rock near the entrance to the glade and lowered the wick. She waited for the lamp to go out before she walked slowly back to the edge.

'Are you sure it's safe down there? It's awfully dark now.' Her voice quavered.

'It's good. Now hurry up or I'll explore by myself. Go back and do your sewing or something.'

'I'm coming now. Don't go without me.'

Tommy waited at the bottom of the rocks as Missy climbed down carefully. She stepped cautiously from one flat rock to another and gripped tree roots that were intertwined through the rocks. She shuddered and pulled her hand back quickly when her fingers brushed a cobweb. After a few minutes, she reached the bottom and waited for her eyes to get used to the dim light.

'This is so exciting. We might discover something and become famous explorers,' Tommy said.

'What are we going to discover?' Missy still wasn't convinced they should be down here. A hiding from Father was the least of her worries now that she'd climbed down.

Tommy looked at her scornfully. 'If we knew what it was, it wouldn't be a discovery.' He jumped off the rock ledge where he had been waiting for her. A small puff of dust rose into the air and something scurried up into the rocks near Missy.

'There's something down here,' she squealed and jumped down beside him. 'Oh, I knew I shouldn't have left the lantern behind.' Her cry echoed eerily off the high walls.

He ignored her. 'Or even better, the cave might be full of gold. It's not far from the workings as the crow flies. We could be rich. Imagine how pleased Mother and Father would be if we discovered gold.'

Missy grabbed hold of Tommy's arm as he turned to walk across the cavern. She was pleased when he didn't shake her off.

'Keep your eye out for gold nuggets glinting in the light. This is just sort of place we're likely to find one.' Tommy's voice was quiet and Missy wondered if he was a bit scared underneath all his bravado.

As they walked deeper into the cavern, she looked up and saw the small crack along the edge of the roof where chinks of light were shining through from outside. The roof in the centre was high above them, but it was light enough to see the colours on the sloping surface. As her eyes adjusted to the dark, she kept looking back to the opening where they'd climbed down, reassuring herself that it wouldn't take long to get back up into the glade if they stumbled upon anything.

'Don't be scared, sis. If there is anything in here, I'll look after you.'

She squeezed his arm in silent thanks. 'I wonder how far

it goes?' Missy peered ahead as far as the light from above would let her see.

'It looks like it turns up here. Do you want to wait while I go ahead?'

'No way! We're staying together.' She held onto him tightly and looked up. 'Look at the colours up there.'

The ceiling was honeycombed in a regular pattern. Blocks of bright orange sat side by side with cream and dark-brown sections. Small black blobs covered the rock as far as she could see.

'There're thousands and thousands of bats in here.'

'That's probably what Stanley was scared of. He hates bats.'

'Probably.' Missy let go of Tommy's arm as her nerves receded. 'Come on, let's go find this gold.'

His grin was wide before he scarpered ahead of her.

Chapter 9

Carlyle Downs, **3 January, 2019.**

Travis looked up as the Troop Carrier pulled to a halt at the cattle yard. He'd been wondering if Emlyn would return the key on her way back. She'd taken a long time, and Joel had commented that maybe they should go out to see if she was okay.

He suspected that Joel had a bit of a crush on their visitor. The cattle had been loaded, and the truck had left half an hour ago, and he was repairing a broken fence wire at the edge of the yards, but he couldn't stop thinking about the mess over in the breeder's paddock. He'd kept the boys away from there, and he'd asked Bluey not to say anything yet. Bluey had been quiet as they'd worked, and he'd headed back to his place when the truck had left. Travis was sick in the gut thinking about what was over there; he couldn't put the job off any longer.

Gavin had driven past with a wave a while ago. Alison had taken the three kids back to the house to get some lunch going. She'd slipped back into her old job of manning the gate without a problem. Joel and Jase had been a great help, although some of their time had been spent keeping Cass entertained once the novelty of loading the cattle had worn off. Jase had given Cass his whip and a quick lesson in cracking it. A wry grin crossed Travis's face as he walked over to the vehicle.

And damned if the little tyke didn't master it first go.

The door slammed, and Emlyn began striding towards the fence. She held out the key without a word, but her eyes flashed, and her lips were set in a straight line.

'All sorted?' he asked as he pocketed the key.

'I guess you could say that.' She put her hands on her hips and stared up at him. 'The damn gate was unlocked and open, and you didn't tell me about the bloody great wheel ruts at the end of the road.'

'Wheel ruts?' He frowned. 'No one uses that road apart from us. I haven't been that far out for a few months.'

'Well, it looks like a massive truck got bogged and lurched its way out through the mud.' Her voice got louder. 'And then your gate was open. I've had a totally wasted morning, and I doubt if a delivery truck will be able to negotiate that road, anyway.'

'Yeah, Kev's got a four-wheel-drive truck. He'll be able to get through.' He dropped his gaze from the unhappy face in front of him to the key in his hand as her words filtered in. 'You said the gate was unlocked already?'

'Yes, and open.'

'Bloody hell. I wonder who did that.' He stared past her to the ute, at the grass seed and spikes on the tyres. 'Sorry I sent you on a wasted trip.'

'Are you really?' Her voice was cold. 'I don't think you're sorry at all.'

'What?' He narrowed his gaze.

'I said I don't think you care one bit that I've had a wasted day. I know you don't want us here, but it's a bit of a low act when you waste my morning deliberately. I have research papers to read, and I still have to sort out the last accommodation before the team arrives tomorrow.' She took a big breath. 'No wonder you didn't want your sons to—'

'Just wait right there.' Travis was in a foul mood already,

and he hated being unjustly accused. Alison was an expert at it. 'I fully expected the gate to be locked. I'm sorry that you've had a wasted trip.' He took a deep breath. It wasn't Emlyn's fault that his week had gone to shit.

'All right, I'm sorry I snapped too.' She seemed to be happy to meet him halfway. 'I'm hot and I'm tired, and I thought I was going to run out of diesel on the way back.'

'Come to the shed, and I'll top up your tank. It's only fair.'

'I guess I'll have to because I haven't got enough to go to town now.' She lifted her chin. 'Where's the shed? I haven't seen it.'

'It's down the hill behind the house. Follow me.' Before she could protest, he swung himself up onto his horse and headed along the road towards the house.

His anger was swift. Despite not giving the mining company permission to come onto his land, they'd obviously ignored him. He should have gone to Townsville with Gavin when he'd met with them a few months ago to make it quite clear they weren't welcome. It hadn't been necessary to meet with them in the end; Carroglen told Gavin there wasn't enough water on the station to make exploration viable, and they were going to pass anyway. Travis had been relieved; under the legislation, he'd had no choice but to let them on. But he'd made sure he'd locked the back gate after they had approached him eighteen months ago. Whoever had been there had been on his land without his knowledge.

* * *

Emlyn's temper had improved a little by the time Travis

directed her into the shed, and she parked the ute by the pump.

'Jesus Christ!' She jumped when he cursed and strode across to the other side of the shed.

'What's the matter?'

'The backhoe's gone.' He gestured to a large empty space between two posts. 'It was here yesterday.' His brow wrinkled in a frown. 'I need it this afternoon. Bluey must have moved it on his way from the yards.'

Emlyn waited while he filled the tank. He was solicitous, and his voice was pleasant, but she could tell his mind was elsewhere. When he gave her a big smile, she was hard-pressed not to roll her eyes. Talk about an attitude change, but she was still angry after the unproductive morning.

'You still look a bit hot. Would you like to come in and have a cold drink or a cuppa?' He put the nozzle back into the holder.

Emlyn was self-conscious as his gaze settled on her long-sleeved shirt. She was hot and thirsty, and since she'd got out of the ute, feeling a little bit light-headed.

'Thank you. A glass of water would be good. And then I won't take up any more of your time.'

'Leave the Troopie here.' The look he directed at her was sharp. She followed him across the paddock up to the house yard, neither speaking. When they reached the steps, she waited at the bottom, but he shook his head.

'Come on upstairs. It's cooler inside.' He gestured to the air conditioner that was at the base of the wall. 'And the boys have got the air going. Come in and meet Alison and sit down for a few minutes. You look like you're about to fall over.'

Reluctantly, Emlyn climbed the steps, tightly gripping the weathered handrail. Travis held the door open and gestured for her to step through. The sparsely furnished living room was large, and a couple of sliding doors opened out to a narrow verandah on the side. Two single chairs sat either side of a coffee table in the middle of the room, littered with newspapers, catalogues, and an array of used coffee cups. The carpet was frayed, and an old-fashioned, dull-green sofa filled the wall between the sliding doors. She blinked; the wall at the back of the room held a floor-to-ceiling mural painted in garish shades of red.

'Please sit down and excuse the mess. We've been flat out on the property.' He flicked her an apologetic look. 'Cold water, or would you prefer coffee or tea?'

Emlyn sat on one of the single chairs and leaned back. 'Tea would be good.'

Footsteps padded down the hall that led off the living room, and Joel appeared in the doorway, with Cass and Jase not far behind him.

'Emlyn! How did you go? Did you find the gate okay?'

She shared a look with his father. 'Yes. I did.'

'Mum's got a pot of tea made. She's just cutting some of the cake Aunty M sent over. Would you like a cup of tea or coffee, Emlyn?' Joel asked.

'Tea for Emlyn please, Joel,' Travis answered for her.

'Choccy milk,' the small girl butted in.

'Okay.' Travis smiled, and Emlyn was surprised at how much younger he looked when he wasn't stern.

'Did you bring me back some of Aunty Maureen's Christmas shortbread?'

'Silly, Dadda. It's not Christmas anymore.'

'But she might have some left over.'

'Look, I won't stay, after all. I've got a lot to do still, and you've got visitors.' Emlyn went to stand but the room tilted. She grabbed the side of the sofa and sat down again. 'Don't worry about a cup of tea.' She closed her eyes until the room stopped spinning, and when she opened them, Travis was close to her, his expression full of concern. Being in his house with all his family around was ramping up the anxiety she'd managed to keep under control since she'd arrived.

'Stay right there,' he said. 'Alison will love talking to you. She was always fascinated by the tubes and the history of the place when she lived here.'

'Yeah, Mum's not a real visitor,' Jase added. 'This is her other home, too.'

'Dad, Uncle Gavin ended up going to Townsville,' Joel said. 'We passed him on the way while you were still at the yards.'

'I saw him go past.' Travis nodded. 'Good. Joel, did one of you take the backhoe out?'

Joel shook his head.

'What about Bluey?'

'Nope, he went home for a kip.'

Travis frowned as he stared through the window. 'It's not in the shed.'

'I want my dress.' Cass disappeared up the hall while Joel and Jase stayed in the living room, talking to Emlyn. Travis went into the kitchen.

Joel sat near Emlyn on the other single chair. 'Aunty Maureen is actually our great-aunt. She's just turned eighty-eight and lives at Mt Surprise next door to Dad's cousin. She still drives too, and she was always interested in the tubes, too.'

'Sounds like a lot of people are. I'm surprised that there hasn't been much exploration so far.'

Joel lowered his voice and Jase nodded as he spoke. 'I think it was very much a family decision to keep quiet about them. The place has always been a cattle station, and both Dad, and our grandfather before him, hated the thought of people traipsing over the land to get to them.' He shook his head when Emlyn frowned. 'Tourists, I mean, not you. And other companies, too. That's why Dad had the back gate locked, but that's another story.'

She sat up straighter in the chair. 'Don't worry. I already know your dad isn't very happy about us being here.'

'Well, I think it's great.' Joel looked up as a tray rattled. 'Here's Mum now.'

Emlyn was nervous about meeting Alison. From the little Travis had said, she'd assumed there was a fair bit of tension between them. Life had obviously thrown him some curve balls, also. The woman who came into the living room with Travis was not what Emlyn had expected. Alison Carlyle was petite and had a young face with gentle blue eyes. Her smile was shy, and Emlyn noticed the look that Travis sent his wife's way before he bent down to pick up the catalogues from the coffee table.

Alison glanced at Emlyn and Travis cleared his throat. 'Emlyn, this is my—this is Alison. Al, Emlyn is the first of the university group to arrive. She's staying over at the dongas.'

'I was just returning the key to the back gate.' She felt the need to explain her presence in the house, but Alison smiled at her.

'Lovely to meet you, Emlyn. The boys told me you went with them up to the entrance to the main tube the other night. Isn't it fascinating?' She gave a mock shiver. 'Apart from the snakes and the bats, that is. Tell me all about your work. I'd love to hear what you're going to be doing there. I think the tubes are intriguing.'

Emlyn swallowed and was pleased when Travis reached for a cup. Her eyebrows rose when he carefully placed a fine china cup and saucer on the coffee table in front of her.

'I noticed your cup the other day,' he said.

'That's kind of you,' she said.

'Jase, throw the newspapers in the bin at the back door ready to be burned.' He shot an apologetic look at Emlyn. 'Having all males in a household tends to turn it into a pigsty very quickly. And please ignore the painted wall; that's some of Gavin's work. He went through a stage when he tried his hand at being artistic. I'm going to get the boys to paint over it one day.'

Interesting. His rugged face had softened before the shutters came down.

Emlyn picked up her teacup and took a sip. Her head was still a bit wonky, but she welcomed the hot liquid as it slid down her parched throat. She turned to Alison. 'I'm the field entomology coordinator at the university. We've got two research scientists—a professor and an associate—on our team, and both of them are really experienced in the area of tropical insects. One of the scientist's partners is a secretary in our department, and Lucy will be transcribing our notes and uploading the photographs. They're driving up from QU now and Bill, the driver, doubles as our cook, sets up the equipment we need, and he'll be a bit of a jack-of-all-trades. And there's a freelance photographer, too, but I haven't met him yet.'

Alison nodded her thanks to Travis when he passed her a coffee mug. She sat on the sofa between Joel and Jase. 'I'd love to watch you work if that's allowed. Not far in, though.'

Travis's eyes narrowed. 'How long are you staying, Al?'

Alison shrugged. 'I'm not sure. Aunty M appreciates the company, although'—she looked around—'now that Gavin's gone away and there's more room, I'll stay here for a couple of days before Cass and I go home. The boys can't stay all the holidays; there're things to be done at home, too.' She turned back to Emlyn, ignoring Jase's sullen expression. 'Tell me more about the tubes and what you'll do in there.'

'The first week will be mostly looking through as much of the tubes as we can and making a plan. We're really hopeful about the potential of what's in there.' This time she levelled a look at Travis. 'If necessary, we'll be hoping to extend our stay here.'

When he looked away and stared through the window, Alison kept her gaze on him and the sadness in her expression was very familiar to Emlyn.

'Anyway, I won't keep you.' Emlyn drained her cup and put it back on the saucer. 'Thank you for the cuppa, and thanks for the fuel, Travis. Hopefully I'll see you again, Alison. Come over any time you want to. You too, Joel. I haven't forgotten our chat the other day.'

As she stood, their little girl ran into the room. She was wearing a pink dress with a skirt that flared out over plump legs, and pink satin ballet pumps. She twirled and ran across to Travis. 'Dadda, milkshake!'

Emlyn closed her eyes briefly as the dizziness returned. She turned on her heel and headed for the door. 'Don't worry about seeing me out. I'll go down and get the car.' She closed the door behind her, knowing she'd been rude, but sometimes coping with a simple social situation was beyond her these days.

* * *

Travis glanced at Alison as she sat in the chair that Emlyn had vacated.

'She seems nice.'

'Yeah. I haven't had much to do with her. But I'm not happy with the university being here.'

'I saw that. You can be rude, Travis.'

Joel piped up, 'Emlyn's really clever, Mum, and she knows a lot about the different universities.'

Travis shot him a curious look. 'And? What's so good about that?'

Joel shook his head. 'Nothing. I was just saying how smart she was.'

'If you're going to make a go of this place the way things are, you need to be taking every opportunity that comes your way.' Alison's voice was cold, but Travis refused to be drawn.

'I'm not going there again.'

'I'm not talking about the gold mine. Look what they're doing at Undara. They've got a multimillion-dollar business going over there.'

It took a lot for Travis to snap, but talking about money always did it. They'd gone round and round the talk of money and accepting Carroglen's offer in the days before Alison had left, but up until that time, they'd always wanted the same outcome. When she'd taken Gavin's side over that bloody gold mine, they had clashed.

'It's not all about money, Alison. We've got the history of the place to consider.'

She stood, and her coffee sloshed onto the carpet, but she ignored it.

'And that's going to pay the bills and put food on the table and pay for the boys to go to university?'

'Have I ever missed making one payment to you?' His voice was clipped.

'No, you know you haven't, but that's not the point.'

'What is the point?'

'Dead people. You can't protect the history of a lump of land forever.' She shook her head, and her voice was loud. 'I know why you love it. I feel the same about Mum and Dad's place, but it's time to move on. Life changes, Travis. And other things become more important than land. You can protect it so far, but not to the detriment of your family.'

'When have I ever let this family down?' This time his voice came out as a roar, and Cassie whimpered and buried her face in Alison's skirt.

'You don't know the half of it, Travis.'

Travis kneeled in front of Cassie and put his arms around her. His gut clenched when she lifted her small, tear-streaked face to look at him.

'I'm sorry, sweetheart. Mummy and I were having a talk, and I got a bit loud.' He looked to Alison for support.

She brushed back Cassie's curls. 'Daddy's right, Cass. We're just having a grown-up talk.'

'Go into the kitchen and the boys will make you a milkshake.' Travis gestured to the kitchen, and Jase and Joel moved quickly, exchanging an uncomfortable glance.

'With ice-cream?' Cass said with a smile, her tears forgotten.

When their three children went into the kitchen, Travis shut the door. He dragged his hand through his hair with frustration.

Alison raised her eyebrows and nodded towards the

closed door.

'Does that mean more yelling?'

'No. I'm sorry I lost it.' He dropped onto the sofa and put his hand over his eyes. 'What did you mean about university?'

'Joel is desperate to go to uni after next year, and he's terrified of telling you. He thinks we can't afford it.' She stood stiffly beside the coffee table.

'We probably can't afford to pay for a residential hall.' Travis dropped his hands between his knees and leaned forwards.

'It's no more than the private school fees,' Alison said.

'I was counting on that money going back into the property. But if he wants to go, I'll find a way.'

'I've picked up more hours at the club. When the boys are home to mind Cass, I go in at five in the morning and clear the pokies and balance the tills. That will help.'

Disgust curled in Travis's chest that he couldn't provide for his family.

'Sometimes I think maybe I should have let that mine come onto the place.'

'You can't stop them; they will eventually. They took out a mining lease.'

'What? How do you know that?'

Alison wouldn't meet his eye. She crossed to the window as a vehicle revved loudly, and then a door slammed.

'I thought the boys said Gavin went to the coast?'

'Joel did.'

'Well, he's come back.' She shook her head and opened the door to the kitchen.

'Cassie. Come on, we're leaving. Now.'

'I want my drink.' Cass came out of the kitchen holding her

sippy cup with both hands. Joel and Jase followed her. 'I'll make you another one at Aunty Maureen's.' Alison threw a hard look at Travis. 'I'll call you before I go home, and you can come over to see Cass. If it suits you.'

'I thought Cass was staying here for a couple of nights even if you wouldn't?'

'I've changed my mind.

As she spoke, the door opened. Gavin walked in, his bag slung over his shoulder. He glanced over at them and his face flushed.

'I was too tired to keep driving when I got to Greenvale.'

Alison gave a rude huff.

Exasperation filled Travis, and he rubbed the back of his neck as he stood. He knew Gavin was lazy and unreliable, but he had a sweet nature. He'd always been kind to Alison. She had no reason to be rude to his brother, just because they'd had their own marital disagreement.

She walked past the sofa without looking at Gavin. Travis's chest tightened further. He picked up Cassie and held her close.

'Give your dad a big smooch, sweetie.'

Alison got her bag from the boys' room and held the front door open for Travis. He frowned as she hurried down the steps ahead of him, but he carried Cass down.

'Can you put her in the car seat, please?' She threw her bag in the back of the small hatchback, and her face was set as she opened the door.

Travis clenched his jaw as Cass started to cry.

'Dadda.'

He belted her into the toddler's seat, closed the car door, and then leaned towards the driver's window. Alison looked up at him, her eyes wide in a pale face.

'Look, I'm sorry, I didn't mean to pick a fight before,' he said.

She shook her head, put the car into gear, and backed down the drive, narrowly missing Bits as he slunk out from under the house.

Travis stared after the car as it disappeared around the bend, and the usual sense of loss lodged in his chest. He loved his little girl and didn't get to see her often. He'd made the mistake of saying that in front of Gavin one night and his brother had suggested perhaps he should take legal action for more regular access. Maybe it was time to think about it now. Gavin must have said something to Alison; his interpersonal skills were sadly lacking.

He hurried back up the steps and pushed open the door. 'Joel, Jase. I have to talk to you. Gavin, you can come too.'

'But—'

'Gavin, for God's sake, just this once without being like a whiny kid.' Travis's disappointment at Alison leaving fuelled his temper.

'Just pull your weight around here. You know you could go on the books if I didn't have to hire to make up for your slackness. I've already told you that.'

He turned to his sons. 'There's been an accident. We've got some dead beasts to bury.'

'No!' Jase's cry pierced the air. 'What happened?'

'I'll tell you later. Give me half an hour, then I'll meet you at the yards when I find Bluey.'

Travis headed for the shed. 'And the backhoe,' he muttered to himself.

Chapter 10

Travis strode down to the shed, and when he turned around after he checked he'd turned off the pump, he was surprised to see a figure silhouetted in the doorway behind him. For a moment, he wondered who it was—he hadn't heard any vehicles since Alison and Cassie had left—but then he realised it was Joel. It struck Travis how much the boys had grown this year; they were both almost as tall as he was, and they'd left Gavin behind. His temper had blown itself out, and a hard core of sadness and frustration had settled in his chest.

'What's up, mate?' he asked as he opened a new bag of dog food.

Joel walked over and bent down to pick up the bucket and the scoop. 'I wanted to see if you were okay, Dad.'

'Yeah, I'm fine, mate. I'm just angry with myself. We've lost stock because of a stupid mistake I made with the lick blocks.' Travis reached out and took the scoop from his son and half-filled the bucket. 'And I'm sorry your mum and I had words in front of you.'

Joel followed him quietly to the dog enclosure and watched as the dry kibble clanged into the metal feeding bowls. The look on his son's face broke his heart. He looped his arm around Joel's shoulder.

'Come and sit down with me for a while.'

They walked to the hay bales left over from the winter feed, and he sat opposite Joel.

'Mate, I'm sorry you've had to deal with all this. It hasn't been a good time for the three of you growing up, either. That long train trip from Townsville every time you boys come home takes away a lot of your school holiday time.'

'We want to see you, Dad, and we want to be out on the station. This is still home, you know. And besides, now we're almost in our last year of school. It's not long and we'll be home for good.'

'True.' Travis stared past his son and lowered his voice. 'If your uncle would help out more…'

'I hate him for leaving all the work for you.' Joel's voice shook. He jumped off the hay bale and walked across to the opening that looked out over the paddocks. 'He's a leech.'

'That's a bit harsh, son. Your uncle has always been lazy, and he can be selfish, but he's still part of our family. I haven't ever told you this, but you're old enough to know now, and it might help you understand him a bit better. When my mum was having him, she was sick. Gav's always been a bit different and hard to deal with. Our mum made me promise that I'd look out for him after she died, and I've honoured that promise. You'd do the same for Jase if you had to.'

'So why won't he help out more? It's his place, too.' Joel's brow wrinkled in a frown.

'Your grandmother left me in charge of the property in her will, and I think Uncle Gavin resents that in his own way. He was fine until a couple of years ago, and now it's just as though he's lost interest in the place. It seems his life is down in Townsville now.'

'Well, he should move down there and leave us in peace.'

Travis put his arm along Joel's shoulder. 'I know. But I do want you and Jase to know how much I appreciate how hard you work around the place.' He leaned forward and held Joel's eye. 'Now tell me about this university stuff.'

Joel shook his head. 'It doesn't matter. I'm happy to come back here and work with you and Jase. I know Jase wants to stay here.'

'When he finishes school?'

Joel shook his head. 'I'll let him tell you.'

Travis held back a sigh. What else could be thrown at him today? 'But what do you want, mate? If you want to do something else, that's fine by me.'

'Really? You wouldn't be upset?' The hope in his son's voice hit Travis in the gut like a fist. Why hadn't he spent more time talking to his kids? Why had he let work and the property come between them? He barely knew Cassie, and he could see her behaviour needed checking. Everyone spoiled her.

'Dad?'

He looked up again. 'Sorry, mate. I was miles away. Tell me what you want to do after school.'

'One day I'd like to go to university and study history.'

'I guess you're more like me than you know. I was fascinated by the history of this place when I was growing up. I used to read everything I could get my hands on. It's a shame the diaries are gone.'

'What diaries?' Joel asked.

'They were in our old homestead that burned down. In your grandfather's study—diaries, the household accounts, stories about the gold rush in the late 1800s. It was amazing stuff.'

'I could do history at Townsville Uni. I'd love to study some of the local records.' Joel moved to sit beside him. 'That wouldn't cost as much. I could stay with Mum and Cass and I'd get a job at night. I'll get my RSA ticket; there's plenty of bar work going where Mum works. If you could just help me get set up, I could be independent pretty quickly.'

'If that's what you want, we'll make it happen.'

'Let's wait and see how I do this year at school before we go making any plans.' Joel laughed and leaned towards him. 'Maybe I won't get good enough marks and you'll be stuck with me here.'

'Never stuck with you, mate. But we'll do our best to get you to uni.' Travis swallowed when Joel enfolded him in a quick hug.

'Oh, Dad. You don't know what that means to me,' he said, his voice thick. 'Having your support is the best.'

Travis patted his son's back. Now all he had to do was figure out how he was going to support Joel at university. He had a year to get some funds together. If Joel stayed with Alison, and Jase came home to work, maybe it wouldn't be as bad as he'd thought. But he still needed money to keep the property afloat.

Maybe it *was* time to talk to Carroglen Gold again. The idea stuck in his throat like jagged glass.

'Come on. We've got to go and get this job done.'

***

When Emlyn got back to the donga, she turned the air-conditioning on high and stretched out on her bed. The delivery was due soon, and the kitchen was ready. The drive in the heat out to the gate without water had taken its toll, and as well as a bad headache, her shoulder and arm were throbbing. For a moment, she considered taking one of the pills in her medicine bag. The cause was partly emotional, not just the drive and dehydration. Pills might ease it, but they wouldn't help in the long run.

She stared at the fly marks on the ceiling, trying to clear her mind. Being in the house with the Carlyle family—no matter how fractured they were—had been hard. Trying to conduct a conversation had been an effort.

Emlyn knew what the problem was, but she wasn't going to admit it. Even to herself.

She sat up and pulled her laptop towards her. If she focused on work, she would settle and get this emotional stuff out of her head. She calmed as she immersed herself in a recent article about the discoveries in the lava tubes in Hawaii.

The sound of a truck engine revving along the drive interrupted her work after a couple of hours. It would be the provisions delivery from Mt Surprise. She ran her hands through her hair and smoothed down her shirt before she slipped on her boots and opened the door.

'Gawd, that bloody road's a shocker now.' The truck driver was a burly older man in a navy-blue singlet and khaki work shorts. 'Never seen it like that before. I'll have to have a word with Travis if you're going to need more deliveries down here. It needs grading.'

She nodded.

'Blow me down, but I was glad to get here. Now, where do you want this unloaded, love?'

Emlyn pointed out the main donga, and he backed the truck close to the steps.

He climbed out and lifted his cap. 'Sorry, love. Janet's always getting into me for being rude. I'm Kev.'

'Emlyn,' she said quietly as he opened the back doors of the truck.

Emlyn helped unload the items despite Kev's assurance that he could do it. She left the heavy boxes for him.

'So, where are you from, Emlyn? Have you always lived in the big smoke?' Before she could answer, he'd started talking again. She followed him, carrying the smaller bags of fruit and vegetables into the kitchen, and Kev hadn't drawn breath.

'Hard life up here. Since the livestock export stuff's changed out of Karumba and the mines have come in, all our young blokes leave and chase the big money as soon as they're out of nappies.' He chuckled at his own joke. 'Well, maybe when they leave high school. No love for the land anymore.'

He hoisted a box of tinned food onto his shoulder and headed back inside. Emlyn picked up two more of the plastic shopping bags that were near the front of the hold.

'But Travis's two young blokes love the land, so he'll be right. It's his useless brother that makes it so hard for him. Have you met Gavin?'

Emlyn nodded.

'Well, that's another story. He reminds me of that useless old Jimmy from Mt Garnet. Now, he moved here with…'

By the time the truck was unloaded, Emlyn knew the history of most of the families between here and Mt Surprise.

'Mind you,' Kev said as he carried in the last box of meat. 'We were all shocked when Alison upped and left. Broke Maureen's heart, it did. Did I tell you she lives up the road from us?'

Emlyn shook her head, bemused. 'No.' She managed to get one word in.

'This meat'll have to go straight in the freezer, love. But you never know, maybe she's come back to stay this time. I saw her at Maureen's last night. I think Travis would like that. We can always hope.'

Emlyn nodded again as he collected the empty cartons.

'Do you want me to stay and give you a hand to unpack the rest of the stuff? Not too heavy for a little thing like you?' He looked at his watch and frowned. 'I'm a bit short of time. That bloody rutted road held me up. By the time I get back, Janet'll have me dinner on the table and I'll be in the bad books. She told me to get a move on this morning. Hate to say it, but the damn woman's always right. A man should learn to listen. Should be part of the marriage vows. If you ever get married, love, give the poor man a chance.'

Emlyn's head was buzzing. 'No, no, it's fine. I can unpack it. The others will be here soon. But thank you.'

'Well, I'll be off, then. You make sure you ring if you need anything else, won't you? My young bloke's working here for Travis. He can bring down anything you need.' He stood back and looked at her before he patted his paunch. 'You need a good feed of Central Queensland beef.' He chuckled. 'That'll put some meat on those bones of yours. Next time I come out, I'll bring you some good scotch fillets.'

'Um, thank you, I think.' Emlyn couldn't help smiling. She seemed to have been smiling more since she'd arrived here.

Kev climbed into the cab and tooted the horn as he backed down the circular driveway, kicking up red dust as he left. Emlyn leaned on the door and watched as he drove out. Once the truck roared up the hill, peaceful quiet returned.

Pushing away Kev's observations of Travis Carlyle and the state of his marriage—it was none of her business—Emlyn unpacked the boxes and filled the cupboards. When she was done, the fridge and freezers were full of fresh food and meat. Grabbing a snack for dinner and a bottle of water from the fridge, she sat at the desk she'd marked as hers before going back to her reading.

She checked her email, and there was a new one from John Kearns, putting their ETA early tomorrow.

We're sharing the driving, so expect us about nine tomorrow, she read.

It was going to be hard to have others here after being alone at the camp. But one thing Emlyn was looking forward to was getting into the tubes and the fieldwork. She couldn't do it by herself.

The thought of interacting every day on both a work and social level was already making Emlyn nervous, and she wiped her damp hands on her shorts. They were here to work, and the last thing she needed were cosy boy-scout chats around a campfire.

She stared at the puce-coloured wall in front of her, her eyes following the specks of fly dirt that marked it. She was kidding herself. She'd been on many field trips over the years before—before her life had changed—and of course they would relax and talk at night. Just because she'd changed didn't mean that others would fit in with her idea of not wanting to chat over dinner and drinks.

She'd cope. She had to.

Chapter 11

Emlyn slept deeply and dreamlessly. She rose early and showered, screwing up her nose at the thought of the dead possum contaminating the water that was trickling from the shower. As she walked across to the main building, two white vans drove into the compound and parked in the middle of the driveway.

'Emlyn?' A tall, lanky guy with short-cropped dark hair climbed out of the first van. He held out a hand as she walked down the steps. Emlyn forced a welcoming smile to her face.

'Hello, and yes, I'm Emlyn Rees. You must be Larry Robards.' She took his hand; his grip was cool and firm. 'Good to have you here. I've heard great things about your work.'

'And I've heard the same about yours,' he replied as he let go of her hand and shut the door of the van.

Bill Goodwin and the two couples climbed out of the second vehicle and stretched. 'Gawd, that was a long drive. Three and a half days on the road. That bloody Bruce Highway's no better than the last time I drove north,' Bill said as he smiled at Emlyn. 'Good to see you again.'

'It is a long trip from Brisbane. You found the turn-off after Conjuboy okay, obviously,' Emlyn said to fill an awkward silence as they stood there waiting for the others to come across from the van.

'Yeah, we had to detour around Gladstone. They've had a lot of rain down there.' Bill nodded and looked around. 'Looks like a decent enough set-up here.'

Greg and Lucy gave her a friendly wave as they walked across. 'Hi, Emlyn. Good to see you. All settled in?'

She nodded as the professor and his wife joined them. 'Yes, it's not a bad set-up here.'

John Kearns slung a bag over his shoulder and came around from the back of the van. 'Emlyn, this is my wife, Meg.'

Emlyn smiled at the woman standing beside him, aware of dark eyes sizing her up. 'Good to meet you, Meg.' The effort of keeping her voice chirpy and upbeat was tiring, and the humidity was still oppressive. 'Come inside, everyone, and I'll show you around and you can stow your gear. I turned on the air conditioners in each of the dongas last night.' She waited for the others to catch up and then climbed the steps to the main building. 'This is the mess, and the work area.' She pushed open the screen door and gestured to the bench along the front wall where her laptop was set up. 'The wi-fi speed is great. We've hooked into the satellite connection without a problem. I guess this is where we'll spend a lot of our time.'

'Good kitchen set-up.' Bill poked his head into the space. 'Much room left in the fridge? We've got some wine and beer that need chilling.'

'Some. I left a couple of shelves free.' Emlyn focused on relaxing her shoulders. Her breath threatened to hitch as she led them outside again and across to the dongas. She'd gotten used to being here by herself.

'Two double rooms, a single and one shared, plus mine. I'll leave you to sort out where you want to go. I've given them all a bit of a spruce-up, so they should be right. I wasn't sure which rooms you'd want to sleep in.'

Meg Kearns surprised her. 'If everyone's okay with it,

John and I will take the shared room. Two singles?' She quirked an eyebrow at Emlyn and she nodded.

'Yes.'

Meg bumped her husband's shoulder and smiled. 'Even university professors have a snoring problem after a few red wines. We'll take the shared, then.'

'I'll take the single,' Bill said.

'Double for us,' Greg said with a smile at his wife.

'I'll take the second double if no one wants it,' Larry said. He looked down at his lanky frame. 'I hang over a single bed.'

'Good. All sorted.' Emlyn rubbed her hands together nervously. 'So, get unpacked and then we'll meet for a drink and a bit of a talk about our schedule, maybe?'

'Good.' John took control. 'How about we meet at eleven? Does that give everyone enough time to get organised?'

Emlyn stepped away and headed for her laptop. The next few weeks were going to be challenging for her, and she needed to prepare herself for being in company twenty-four-seven.

The day passed quickly, and by five-thirty, the communal area was cluttered and busy. Laptops sat on benches, cables snaked across the floor; a couple of laser printers and a large scanner were set up on the benches on two of the walls. Mobile phones were charging in the spare power points. Bill was on a chair securing a data projector to the frame that was mounted on the ceiling. He'd made a quick stir-fry before he'd come into the workroom, and a delicious aroma of honey and garlic drifted in from the kitchen.

John had put a map of the property on a pin board on the wall. 'Have you been out to the site at all, Emlyn?' he asked.

She nodded. 'Yes, just a quick look. Travis Carlyle and his sons took me over there at sundown a couple of days ago. We went to the entrance of the main tube, but only down into the first cavern.'

'I think we should have a bit of a preliminary walk-through tomorrow. And then we can plan where we'll set up our first grid. There's an awful lot of ground to cover, and we've only got twelve weeks,' Greg commented.

'And to get additional funding to extend the research is going to mean a lot of hard work on your part, guys. There'll have to be some pretty solid findings if we want to get more money. And fast. That's going to mean writing some papers while we're up here, too, as well as the field work. We're all going to be putting in some long days.' John glanced across at Larry. 'Can you set up to take photos on our first trip in?'

The photographer nodded. 'Yep. Everything's charged. It's just a matter of getting my gear into the caves.'

A buzz rippled through the team as they looked at the map on the wall. Emlyn stood and traced the route from the camp to the top of the hill. 'The main tube is here. We can drive some of the way, but there's quite a walk to get the equipment up,' she said to Larry.

'Won't be a problem. My last job was in Nepal. I think I can cope with a hill here. And what's the difference between a tube and a cave?'

Emlyn flushed. For the first time, she detected arrogance in his tone. She sat down and didn't speak again. John flicked a sympathetic glance her way before he turned to the photographer. 'The term 'lava tube' refers to a cave formed as an internal lava conduit within a flow, and we use the more general term 'lava cave' for any cave within a lava flow, no matter how it was formed. Does that make sense?'

' Nope, not one bit, but I'm here to take photos so I don't

have to understand all the scientific stuff.'

'Lucy's going to transcribe our notes each night and put the photos into a database,' Greg said as they all examined the map. 'I've got some quality audio gear for recording, so most of the transcribing will be from that and then I'll edit it.'

Bill picked up the remote. The wall lit up as John's computer desktop was projected onto the large screen. 'Great. All set to start work, then. I think that deserves a drink,' John said.

'Okay, dinner's ready whenever you are,' Bill said.

John stood when everyone was seated and had a drink in front of them. 'To a successful trip.' He raised his glass with a smile. 'And an extra-big thank you to Emlyn for coordinating the trip and getting the place sorted out. You've done well. We really appreciate it.'

Dinner was a noisy affair as plans were made for the following day and a slideshow of aerial photos flashed across the screen.

'Recent analysis of the radar data from a NASA space probe since the Germans were here seems to indicate that as well as the straight channels fanning out from the old crater, there are some aligned depressions,' John said.

'And the thinking is that unmapped lava tubes will connect these depressions that have been photographed from space.' Greg crossed to the workbench and brought his laptop over.

John shook his head. 'Unplug mine, Greg, and hook up yours to the data projector so everyone can see it on the big screen.'

Greg did so, then sat back down and turned on the data projector. The screen was filled with a satellite shot of the area, and Emlyn's eyes widened as he zoomed in. These new images were much more detailed than anything they'd looked at in the days they were preparing at the university.

Greg was beaming. 'Pretty amazing, aren't they?' He traced his mouse pointer over the image and zoomed in on the dongas. 'Look, it's so clear you can even see the taps on the water tanks outside.'

A smile tipped Emlyn's lips. 'That reminds me, don't drink water out of the taps.'

Zooming out again, she concentrated as Greg walked them through the new depressions that had been picked up by the NASA satellite.

She followed the road from the dongas, past the site of the old homestead and the cemetery, and up the hill to the glade where she had entered the tubes with Travis and his sons. Emlyn couldn't hold back.

'Do you mind if I show you something?' She jumped up, grabbed a ruler, and stood beside the screen.

'Can you zoom out a little bit please, Greg?'

She pointed to the glade with the ruler. 'This is where we went in the other night. Once you climb down from the glade, about twenty metres below the scree of fallen rocks, there's a huge cavernous opening that goes for about fifty metres before it turns to the north.' She lifted the ruler and followed the green depression on the screen. 'We didn't go any further in, but the small section that we explored with just LED headlamps was breathtaking.'

John stood beside her. 'May I?' He held out his hand, and she passed him the ruler.

'There're obviously dozens of tubes here if we follow all of the depressions linking the channels. What we thought was one long tube is obviously much more of an interlocking network.' His eyes were bright, and his voice was charged with excitement. 'The only problem is where do we start?'

Greg pointed at the tube that Emlyn had been to. 'Once we establish some clean-air tubes, I think we should start there. Working with oxygen will slow us down, and our time here is limited.'

John grimaced. 'So, we have to find something unique and find it early. I have no doubt that we are going to discover new species, so speed is of the essence.'

'Hang on,' Larry interrupted. 'What do you mean by clean-air tubes? What else are you expecting to find down there?'

'There are two things we've got to watch out for,' John replied. 'Underground water and the composition of the air. In some of the caves, there's a good chance the percentage of carbon dioxide will be high. We'll have oxygen with us, and it means we can go further in.'

'How will we know when the air's not good?' Larry frowned. 'What causes it?'

'Soils have much higher concentrations of carbon dioxide than the atmosphere. Plant roots, bacteria and fungi, and water in the tubes mean the soil absorbs additional carbon dioxide. And it's a by-product of fauna such as bats. We can measure it, so don't worry, we won't have you working anywhere unsafe.'

'Tell me exactly what this 'bad air' does.' Larry shook his head. 'I've just seen six of the last team I was with in Nepal choppered out from Gorakshep with altitude sickness. Is it anything like that? That was bloody scary.'

Greg took over. 'That's one of my roles, Larry. Measuring the air quality. The maximum safe working level recommended for an eight-hour day is zero-point-five per cent.'

'What happens if it goes higher?'

'A concentration of ten per cent or greater can cause respiratory paralysis and death within a few minutes.'

'Jesus Christ, that's great. I didn't know that when I took the job on.'

'No need to worry, mate. We'll be measuring everywhere we go,' Greg hastened to reassure him. 'There's no smell or visual sign, but even without measuring, you'd experience some warning signs like increased pulse and breathing rates. Plus clumsiness, severe headaches and dizziness, and sometimes a dry acidic taste in your mouth can be an early indication of an unsafe concentration.'

'It's more common in the deep caves,' John said, 'but we could still encounter it in shallower caves. So, we'll take extra care in the deep caves and anywhere we come across tree roots or bat guano.'

'One other way we can be sure,' Emlyn chimed in, her voice soft, 'is to work in a tube or a cave where there are entrances at different elevations.'

Greg nodded. 'Thanks, Emlyn. I forgot to mention that.'

'So how do you test it?' Larry asked.

'A simple naked-flame test. Easy: the flame goes out, so do we.'

'That's all you do?' Larry was incredulous. 'I wouldn't trust that. A bit like what they said in Nepal. 'Climb high, sleep low.'

'We do have sophisticated measuring equipment in the van, too.' Greg exchanged a glance with John and Emlyn, and she sensed that he was wondering, like she was, whether Larry had been the wrong choice.

The conversation moved back to a social level, and Emlyn sat quietly and followed the talk as it washed around her, smiling occasionally and nodding when a comment was directed her way. Her limbs were loose, and she relaxed even more when she realised she wasn't required to contribute. After a while, she took her plate into the kitchen and scraped what was left into the bin.

'Not a fan of honey-soy chicken?'

She jumped as Bill's voice startled her.

'Yes, it was good, thank you. I wasn't terribly hungry.'

'You'll have to make sure you have a good breakfast if you're going out early. I'll get a tucker bag ready tonight for you to take tomorrow.'

Emlyn nodded as Bill regarded her. 'You've lost more weight, Emlyn. Do you mind if I ask if you're well?'

She nodded. 'I'm fine. It's just the heat up here. I haven't been very hungry, and being here by myself for the past few days, I haven't bothered much with cooking.'

Bill crossed to the sink and put the plug in before turning on the hot water tap. 'Well, I'm here now, and I'm in charge of the meals. And, young lady, I'll be making sure you eat.' He tempered his words with a smile. 'Especially your meat and veggies.'

Emlyn blinked. 'That's what my mum used to say.'

He turned from the sink. 'Used to?'

'Yes. I lost both my parents last year.'

'I'm sorry to hear that, love.' He stood there looking out the window into the dark. 'I lost my wife last year, too. Bloody breast cancer.'

Emlyn bit her lip. She squeezed Bill's arm before she walked away and unplugged her laptop. Walking back through the dining room that had now morphed into a work area, she put her head down and crossed to the door. The others were still involved in a discussion at the table, and only Meg lifted her head as Emlyn slipped out the door without saying goodnight.

145

Chapter 12

Carlyle Downs, **5 January.**

Emlyn woke with a start when her phone alarm went off at six the next morning. She lay there for a moment after she woke and cleared her mind, breathing deeply as she prepared to face the new day.

She had a quick shower and pulled on her long work pants and long-sleeved shirt. She'd left her boots on the step last night and she tipped them up one at a time and checked them. It was a bad habit to leave them outside, especially this time of the year with snakes on the move. She pulled her boots on when she was sure they were clear, and walked across to the mess. The camp was quiet, although there was a light on in John and Meg's donga. She pushed open the door of the workroom and was surprised to smell something appetising coming from the kitchen.

Bill leaned around the door, a frypan in each hand.

'Morning. Eggs or pancakes?'

Emlyn shook her head as she put her laptop on the table. She stepped back when Larry pushed past her.

'Sorry,' he said. 'Need coffee.'

She nodded and waited until he filled his cup from the coffee machine that Bill had fired up. Larry glanced at her as he walked through the door and headed for his laptop. 'Just ignore me. I'm not nice in the mornings. And it's damn near the middle of the night still.'

Bill shot him a filthy look and took Emlyn's bowl from her. 'Rude bugger. We don't need that when we're living in each other's pockets,' he muttered. 'So, eggs or pancakes, love?'

'Just cereal for me,' Emlyn said.

'Then eggs or pancakes?' Bill's voice was firm.

She looked up with a smile, but he didn't smile back.

'If you can't look after yourself, someone has to do it, love. I'm cooking here, and when I'm cooking, people eat.'

'Okay, then. Pancakes.'

'Ice-cream, too?' Bill asked with a smile, but she shook her head.

He nodded and went back to the stove. Emlyn followed him in and took out a bowl and the packet of muesli that she'd unpacked the day before. She sliced a banana and opened a small tub of yoghurt, took her bowl over to the bench and booted up her laptop. Her hands were shaking.

Ice-cream.

The email that had arrived from David had ice-cream in the subject line, and she knew exactly what he was going to say to her. She'd managed not to open it so far. Her hand gripped the mouse and she hovered over the 'delete' button for a few seconds. With a sigh, she clicked on the message, unable to help herself.

There was no greeting.

It's late Tuesday night, and I'm sitting out in the barbeque area looking at the sky, wondering if the sky is clear where you are. We've had a very warm New Year's Eve down here, and I walked down to South Bank and sat by the river for a while. I thought back to that day when a pretty dark-haired university student gave me an extra scoop of ice-cream on my order.

Butterscotch brickle. When I got to know you, I found out it was your favourite, too. That was obviously the catalyst that sealed the attraction. Just joking.

I waited for you to finish work that night, because I couldn't get your laugh out of my head. Do you remember when you dropped the first cone before I reached for it? I remember your sticky fingers brushing mine, and I knew then I was going to marry you. Yeah, I know it sounds crazy for a systems analyst to have that certainty, but I don't think I've ever told you that I had that thought in that moment.

David had waited at the counter after he'd ordered that day and she'd dropped the ice-cream cone as she'd handed it to him, because she hadn't been able to stop looking at his beautiful eyes. His eyes were blue, a deeper dark blue than she'd ever seen, and they were surrounded by the most beautiful, lush, dark lashes. His hair had been longer in those days and the tumble of dark curls had given him a roguish look as he'd grinned at her.

When she'd finished her shift, sticky and smelling sweet like every variety of ice-cream they sold in the shop, she'd walked along the river, and he'd been waiting for her on the seat near the bridge.

She read on and his email mirrored her thoughts.

I told myself that I'd walk west, and if that was the way you walked home, I'd ask you out. I knew when I saw you coming, wearing that hot-pink apron, that we were meant to be.

Emlyn looked down at the finger where her wedding ring had once circled her finger.

Meant to be.

That was their catchphrase, and they'd danced to the song at their wedding. Maybe *what if* would have been more sensible for them?

What if David hadn't stopped for an ice-cream that day? What if she'd finished her shift early? What if Mum and Dad hadn't talked them into going to Fiona's wedding? What if she'd listened to David?

Emlyn forced away the lump in her throat and kept reading, despite the heavy feeling that was building in her chest.

I'm sorry I swore at you on the phone, but Em, it's taking me a long time to come to terms with not having you in my life. I hope you're reading this and you'll let me keep working through getting used to it by sharing my memories with you. It makes me smile, and I haven't smiled in quite a few months. Anyways, sleep tight and don't let the bed bugs bite. Not that you'd mind, you'd probably have them under a microscope if the little buggers got into bed with you.

Seriously, keep safe and spare me a thought occasionally. Love you.

P.S. Do me a favour. Just hit reply and say you read this. Just so I know you're okay, alone wherever you are. So I don't have to worry about you.

Reluctantly, her fingers clicked on the mouse and she replied.

I'm okay, she typed.

Memories. Damn him, they meant nothing. It was the past. It had gone.

They meant *nothing*. She was going to live in the day and not dwell on the past. Her hands clenched and her face heated. David was living in La La land if he thought he could convince her to go back to him. If he thought reminding her of a couple of stupid things like ice-creams and movies would change her mind, he was kidding himself. Maybe the old Emlyn would have fallen for it, but she would never forgive herself, and she had to hold onto that thought.

David was wrong. There was no chance for them at all.

Wrong, wrong, wrong. The words fluttered around and around in her head.

She stared at the screen. If Mum had still been alive, she would have been horrified at how hard her daughter was now. And Emlyn couldn't bring herself to think of her father's gentle eyes. She was a very different Emlyn to the one who had once been a vital part of a large and loving family.

Damn you, David Barber.

She wasn't going to think about any of his bloody times.

Happy or sad.

Work was her focus now. If David emailed again, it would go straight in the trash with the others.

Unread.

'Bloody hell!'

Her head flew up as a loud cry filled the room. Bill dashed in as Emlyn jumped up, thinking that Larry had burned himself. He was sitting glaring at his laptop screen.

He looked at Emlyn accusingly. 'I thought you said there was a satellite connection. I can't get my email.'

'Mine came through okay,' she said. She looked at his screen as Larry brought up the network icon.

'Hmm. It seems to be down,' she said.

'Well, you'd better get it fixed. My phone doesn't have service here and I didn't bring a dongle because you assured me there was a satellite connection. My work depends on an email connection. I don't want to lose any jobs. If that's how it is, I won't be staying here.'

'All right, Larry. Settle down. Drink your coffee and pull your head in,' Bill said crossly.

'I'll go up to the house and see what the problem is before Travis goes out to work. I should catch him this early.' Emlyn glanced at her watch; it was just after six-thirty.

'Have your pancakes first.' Bill stood there, a tea towel over his shoulder and holding a plate loaded with pancakes. He frowned as Emlyn lifted a shaking hand and took the plate from him.

'I'll have some pancakes, too,' Larry said.

'Well, come in and get them. I'm not your slave.'

'All right.' He picked up his cup and strode into the kitchen and Emlyn smiled as Bill raised his eyebrows.

'Takes all kinds,' he said.

She managed to eat half a pancake, but it was like cardboard in her mouth. She waited until Bill was out of sight and closed her laptop, before she hurried back to her donga to get the keys to the Troop carrier.

As Emlyn drove out, John and Meg were walking back to the mess, and she stopped to tell them where she was going.

'Okay. No rush. We're going to head out about nine. I've got some emails to send first, so if you can get it sorted that would be great.' John smiled at her and she couldn't help comparing his attitude to the arrogant Larry, whom she was fast beginning to dislike.

'I'll see what I can do.'

When she reached the old house on the hill, she kept an eye out for the red kelpie, but there was no sign of the cranky dog. This time she drove through the gate, and she could look down the hill at the shed where Travis had filled up the Troop carrier. There were a couple of utes parked down there, so she assumed they hadn't gone out to work yet. She parked the car near the fence and walked across to the stairs. The front door opened just as she put her foot on the bottom rung.

'Emlyn?' Travis walked down with a cup of coffee in his hand. 'Everything okay?' he asked with a frown.

'Yeah. Not a major problem. Just the internet's not working.'

'So that password was wrong?' He sipped his coffee as he reached the bottom step where she waited.

'No. That's fine. It's been working. It's just dropped out overnight.'

'Ah. It does that sometimes. Seems to be if there's a lot of cloud cover, it resets itself. Or so Joel tells me. He's our resident IT expert.' Travis yawned and glanced back upstairs. 'I'll get him to fix it as soon as he's up. I wouldn't have a clue about it, only what I hear him say. Would you like a cup of tea or coffee? I'm pleased you called in, I wanted to have a bit of a chat.'

She nodded. 'Coffee would be great, thank you.'

'Milk, sugar?' Travis asked. His hair was standing up in tufts and he looked tired.

She shook her head. 'Black with one. Thanks.'

'Wait here,' he said. 'The pot's fresh. I'll be back in a jiffy.'

Emlyn looked around as she waited. The sky was still heavy, and she hoped it didn't break before they got the equipment into the tubes. The green season was not what she'd anticipated; she hadn't realised it could be as wet here as it was over on the coast in the summer.

Travis came back down and passed her a large mug of coffee. She closed her eyes and inhaled the fresh aromatic brew.

'Real coffee?'

He nodded. 'Yes. There's no decent coffee shop within

two hundred miles, and it's one thing I learned to love when I was at university.'

She must have looked surprised.

'Dad insisted that both Gavin and I went to university. I did agriculture at Gatton, and he started an economics degree.'

'Started?'

'Yep. Started.' Travis pushed himself off the post at the bottom of the stairs. 'Come down to the shed. I've got a bit of an office in the back there. Oh, and I asked Joel about the satellite. He's reset it already and it's working here, so it should be fine over at your camp.'

'Thanks.'

'Do you have time to have a bit of a chat?'

'Yes. We're heading out around nine.'

'The rest of the team's settled in?'

'Yes, they got here yesterday morning and we're doing an exploratory walk today.' She looked up at the sky with a frown. 'Do you think it's going to rain?'

Travis shook his head as they walked down the hill to the shed. 'No, there's no rain in that. I think it's going to be a dry run by the look of the long-range forecast and the weather maps.' He laughed. 'You know, that's the only thing I ever use the computer for. The boys call me a dinosaur.'

Emlyn smiled back at him. 'I couldn't cope without being connected.' She wondered what had changed his attitude—or whether he wanted something. Travis was being extremely pleasant and friendly. Coffee and chat about the weather, and not a taciturn expression in sight.

They reached the shed, and he walked across to a door that she hadn't noticed before. As he held it open, a flash of red shot across the dirt floor and she jumped back as the kelpie ran towards her, yipping and teeth bared.

Emlyn screamed and pressed herself against the wall as the dog jumped at her. The coffee mug dropped to the floor as she tried to push it away, and she closed her eyes waiting for the sharp teeth to rip through her jeans and into her leg.

The door closed and all was quiet. Warmth ran up into her neck as gentle hands held her shoulders.

'It's okay. He wasn't going to hurt you. He was just saying hello.'

Her hands shook as she opened her eyes and put her hand up to her mouth. 'It didn't look like that to me. His lips were curled back.'

'He was smiling. Bits is a happy dog.'

She shook her head. 'I can't handle dogs. I was bitten when I was a child and I've never forgotten it.'

Travis held her firmly. 'I'm sorry. You're shaking like a leaf. Next time I'll make sure he's not around.'

Emlyn drew in a shaky breath as he reached up and tucked a loose strand of hair behind her ear. She was so rattled by the kelpie she didn't care if he saw her scarred neck. His eyes held hers and he didn't comment.

'Take a few deep breaths in and out.' His tone was even, and she relaxed a little.

Gradually the shaking eased, but Travis continued to hold her shoulders. The warmth of his hands was soothing. It was a long time since anyone had held her close.

'Thank you. It was kind of you to look after me. I'm sorry for overreacting. I've been a bit—' Emlyn blinked and her voice trembled as tears filled her eyes and threatened to spill over. 'A bit—'

'A bit …?'

'Just a bit fragile lately.' The first tear rolled down her cheek and she lifted her hand to brush it away. As she looked up, Travis lifted his hand and wiped it away with his thumb before he pulled her close.

She leaned her head against his shoulder and closed her eyes again as they stood without speaking. His T-shirt was soft beneath her cheek and it smelled clean and fresh. His hand stroked the back of her hair.

Eventually he pulled away. 'I hope you don't think I was being too forward. I just thought you looked like you could do with a friendly hug.'

Emlyn stepped back and was able to smile. 'A friendly hug was nice, and long overdue. Thank you. I'm okay now and I feel a bit silly.'

Travis shook his head. 'Please don't. We all have our own issues to deal with. It's been a long time since I've held anyone.' His words echoed her thoughts and they both stood there quietly, but the silence wasn't awkward. 'Life can overwhelm us all at times.' He moved across to the desk and gestured to the chair. 'That's why I wanted to pick your brains about an idea I've had. Come and sit down.'

Emlyn crouched down and picked up the coffee mug. Splatters of dark liquid stained the old rug that covered the wooden floor.

'Don't worry about that. It's fine,' he said.

She carried the mug across to the desk and sat down. Travis sat back and observed her.

'I hope you don't mind me asking you to help me out.' He picked up a pen and tapped it against the desk. 'Things have been tough here for a long time. Lots of things you don't need to hear about, but financially we've just been keeping our heads above water. I'll be honest. I didn't want you all here poking around in the tubes, but last night the boys and I had a good heart-to-heart.'

Travis paused and looked past her, and his face was grim. Empathy flooded through Emlyn; it pulled her out of her single focus on herself.

'When Alison left, things really got tough, and we've stumbled through good times and bad. We had an offer from a mining company and I refused point blank to consider it. Gavin was keen, and that ended what little remained of our relationship.'

'How long since Alison and Cassie moved away? And the boys?' she asked softly.

'A year ago.'

'I'm sorry. That would have been extremely hard for you.'

'Hard? Bloody unbearable. I lost my life partner, my twin boys, and my little girl in one hit.'

Emlyn leaned forward, focusing on Travis's words. A ripple of discomfort had shuddered through her, but she pushed it away. 'Tell me to shut up if I'm out of line, but can I ask what happened?' The need to comfort him was strong. From her own experience, maybe she could help him with closure. She was a fine one to try to offer comfort, but seeing something through fresh eyes might help him.

He lifted his face, and his eyes were bleak. 'That's the thing. I didn't see it coming, and I still can't understand why.'

Emlyn took her time answering and then spoke slowly. 'Sometimes, just sometimes, a woman knows that it's better if she goes. Better for everyone. You have to trust Alison to know that she thought she was doing the right thing. You seem to have an amicable relationship now, though?'

'We do, most of the time. For the sake of the kids. I know she was unhappy with how much effort I put into the place, but to provide a decent life for them, I had to spend a lot of time out on the station. You've probably noticed that Gavin doesn't do a lot. He's always been lazy, and he's become even worse over the past couple of years. He barely pulls his weight, but he's still entitled to his financial share.' Travis sat straight in the chair and put the pen on the table. 'Look, I'm sorry. I'm really dumping on you. All I intended was to run a proposal by you.'

'Go ahead.' She waited, but Travis held her gaze, his expression curious.

'First, can I ask you something personal? Tell me to mind my own business, if you want.'

Emlyn steeled herself.

'You said you were fragile, and you seem unhappy. I noticed it the first day I met you. I've dumped my problems on you. I'm always happy to provide an ear if you need one.'

As much as she was tempted, Emlyn shook her head. Her issues were very different from whatever had caused Travis's problems.

'I'm fine, thank you. I've had a bit of a hard time over the past year or two, but I'm working through it. And the opportunity to be here in the tubes is amazing. If I ever do need to talk, I'll remember your offer, though.' She injected as much enthusiasm into her voice as she could summon up. 'So, what did you want to ask me?'

'There are a couple of things.' He paused and looked at the window. 'I don't usually talk to people, or put it this way, I don't have anyone to talk to much these days. I know that sounds a bit needy, but since Alison left, I've become a bit of a loner.

I'm sorry I was so rude and cranky when you arrived. And on New Year's Eve, too! Talk about a great start to the year!' He laughed, but there was little mirth in it. 'My social skills leave quite a bit to be desired. The poor boys cop it, but they're used to me. And Gavin… well, that's a whole other story. He's never really grown up.'

Travis took hold of the pen again and cleared his throat. When he raised his head and their eyes met, his brown ones held the same neediness that formed her core.

She couldn't help herself as she reached out and put her hand on his. 'It's okay, Travis. I get what you're trying to tell me. Now how can I help?' Her hand stayed where it was.

'I think Joel's already told you that he wants to go to university.'

She nodded. 'Yes, he has. He's very interested in the history of your station.'

'No matter what his mother said the other day, I'm grateful for that. It must be a genetic thing. I've always been very interested in the history of our place.'

'So, what's the problem?' She raised her eyebrows, and he held her gaze.

'The bottom line is that the property is struggling financially. And we've had a run of bad luck lately with the cattle dying and some machinery damaged. Remember when we were filling up your Troopie? I noticed the backhoe was missing?'

'Did he own up?'

'No, he denied it, but Gavin saw him take it out of the shed.' Travis moved away and folded his arms. 'So now it's down to Bluey and me and the boys while they're home.'

'Tough times,' Emlyn commented.

'Yep. It's put an even bigger financial burden on the

place. Joel wants to study history, but I'll find the money to support him somehow. The cattle will keep the property going, but there's not a lot left over.'

'I guess you pay support for your kids, too?' she asked.

He ran his hand through his hair. 'Yes, I do, but I don't resent that. I'm sorry, Emlyn. I didn't mean for our conversation to get so intense. You don't need to hear my problems. I know you haven't been in the tubes yet, but do you think there's any chance of the university continuing past the three months we agreed on?'

Emlyn hesitated and thought quickly before she answered. 'I can't promise because it's all dependent on funding, but if we find something…'

Travis dropped his head and moved his hand away from hers. 'I'll have no choice. Alison told me some home truths, and I have to listen. It's time to move on. I guess I was always hoping they'd come home, but that's not going to happen. So I need to do something about Gavin to get him to pull his weight. I need to get some money together to send Joel to university. I'm pretty sure Jase will stay here and work on the place, but I've still got to support Cass. So, if you have any other ideas that you think the university might be interested in, I'm open to them.'

'Leave it with me. I'm sure we can come up with something.' She tipped her head to the side. 'Have you ever considered doing something in the tourist area like Undara? Or maybe some farm stays in the dongas when we finish? Or school camps?'

He shook his head. 'I've looked into camps before; the return isn't worth the effort I'd have to put in. Not to mention insurance and wages and everything that goes with a venture like that. Maybe I need to go over to the tourist thing at Undara and talk to them. See if they want to extend their operation. Maybe I could offer some more accommodation and combine it with farm stays. If I could get some sponsorship, it might be viable. Who knows? It's all too hard, and that's where I've put it over the past few years, but it's time to start thinking outside my boring square.'

He stood and smiled down at her. 'Emlyn, thanks so much for your time. I really appreciate it, and if there's anything else that you can think of, please run it by me. I'd love to talk to you some more.'

Emlyn glanced at her watch. 'I really do hope that I can help you, Travis. It's time I got going. I'll put my thinking cap on today, and I'll talk to John, too. He's been around for a long time. I'll see what we can come up with. I'm sure that we're going to find something in the tubes, and this is going to be the beginning of something big. I'll bet other researchers will be interested in joining us. You have no idea what an exciting precipice we are on in terms of new discoveries.'

'I hope you're right.' He held the door open, but Emlyn looked at him as her nerves kicked in.

'What about the dog?'

'Hang on. Wait here. I'll go and put him in the pen.'

'Thank you. I'm sorry I'm such a coward.'

'It's okay; we can't have you scared.'

As Emlyn walked past the house to her Toyota, the front door opened, and Gavin stood on the top step. He looked down shyly at first, but then he turned a full smile on her.

'Hello. You're out and about early this morning, insect lady.'

Emlyn smiled back. 'I am.'

'You coming out to help me with the cattle today, Gav?'

'If you really need me, I suppose I can.'

'Good. I'll appreciate the help,' Travis replied with a nod. 'But only today, and then I'll go to Townsville tomorrow. I've got a competition at my rifle club.'

Travis raised his eyebrows. 'Nice to have a hobby and time to enjoy it.' He turned back to Emlyn. 'Thanks for the discussion. You've given me some hope.'

Travis smiled at her. The perpetual weariness that was ingrained in his expression lifted. 'I hope you have a good day today. I'll call over and see you in a couple of days, and if you have any more problems with that internet connection, come on over or give us a call. Have a good one, Emlyn, and thanks again.'

Emlyn climbed up into the vehicle and drove off slowly. When she glanced back into the rear-vision mirror, the two brothers were standing there together, watching her drive away. Travis had his hand on Gavin's shoulder, and she realised that his brother was just one more responsibility for the cattleman.

Chapter 13

Emlyn parked the van outside the main workroom and went back to her donga to get ready for the first day in the tubes. Contentment filled her as she focused on the prospect of the research ahead. After a quick wash and collecting a light jacket—it could be cool underground—she closed the door behind her. It was close to nine, so there wasn't enough time to go to the workroom to write the email she'd planned to send. She would email David later to tell him that the team had arrived and there was no need to check on her again.

The ice around her heart was not going to crack, no matter how many times he chipped at it by revisiting memories. If anything, it would harden her more. But strangely, since Travis had held her, the anxiety that was always a part of her had receded slightly, and the anticipation of what they were going find today added to her new calm.

It wasn't what she'd call happiness—that was something she no longer expected—but a sort of acceptance had settled within her. Whatever it was, she was feeling pretty normal for a change.

Larry and Bill had already loaded the photographic gear into the Troop carrier, and except for John, the others were waiting beside the vehicle outside the main building. Even after her cool wash, perspiration trickled down Emlyn's neck; the heat was building as the sun rose higher in a cloudless sky. As she walked across to join them, Lucy's laugh was followed by

Greg's deep rumble.

'Worst punch line I've ever heard, Larry,' Greg said. Coffee—and a restored internet connection—seemed to have had a miraculous effect on Larry's mood.

'Sorry. Are you waiting for me?' Emlyn asked as she stowed her pack and jacket in the back of the vehicle.

'No, we've had a bit of a delay,' Bill explained.

'The Troopie had two flat tyres. We've only just changed them. I'll have to find out where the closest place is to get them fixed. It's left us without a spare.'

'Two flats?' Emlyn frowned. 'I hadn't noticed them. It must have been the ruts on that back road when I went out to open the gate for the truck.'

Bill lowered his voice. 'No, they both had a slow leak. There was a pebble in two of the valves.'

Emlyn screwed up her nose. 'How would a pebble get in two valves? From the dirt road?'

Bill shook his head. 'No. Someone's put them there to cause a slow leak.'

'Who on earth would do that?'

Bill shrugged. 'They could have been there for a few days. School holidays. Kids skylarking around somewhere you might have stopped on the way.'

'I didn't stop anywhere. I picked up the car in Townsville and drove straight to the station. Plus I've been here for a few days. They've been perfectly fine.'

Bill scratched his head. 'Well, it's a bit of a mystery, then.'

'Thanks for the mercy trip to save my sanity, Emlyn.' Larry directed a smile her way as she shut the back of the vehicle. 'Whatever influence you have with the owners worked. The internet is whizzing along like a dream.'

She nodded in acknowledgement.

The screen door banged, and their team leader hurried down the steps, pulling his cap over his fair and freckled forehead. For an almost sixty-year-old, John Kearns was slim and fit. Emlyn knew that he preferred to be out in the field than lecturing at the university. He leaned over and kissed his wife's cheek.

'Have a good day, Meg, and wish us a productive one.'

'We will,' Meg said. 'Lucy's going to keep me company while I take a bit of a drive down to the road at the back of the station.'

'There'll be nothing to do until you guys come back with some data and photos for me tonight. I've already set up the folders ready to load today's work.' Lucy shot a nervous look at John, but he waved a hand.

'That's fine, Lucy. We don't expect you to stay here and twiddle your thumbs while you wait for us to come back.'

She smiled. 'I'd much rather twiddle my thumbs all day than go down into the tubes.' She walked over to Greg and reached up to kiss him. 'You all be careful down there, won't you?'

Emlyn glanced across at the van they'd driven up from the university. 'If you take the road to the west, be careful, Meg. The road is really bad. You won't make it in the van.'

'Thanks. We'll take care.'

As Bill climbed into the driver's seat, Larry and Greg sat in the back of the Troop carrier.

John gestured to the front. 'Emlyn, you sit up front. You can tell Bill which way to go.'

Once she'd given Bill directions to the paddock that led

to the bottom of the hill she'd climbed with Travis and the boys, Emlyn sat back and watched the bush flash past.

'You seem quite chirpy today, love.' Bill grinned at her. 'As noisy as ever. Fair giving me a headache with all that chatter.'

'I'm pleased to be finally getting to work,' she said quietly.

'Once I get you all sorted up here and help you get the gear underground, I'm gonna go back and cook up a nice feed for tonight. You did a good job getting the place ready for us, Emlyn. Is there anything else that needs doing?'

She shook her head. 'No, it's all done, but thanks, Bill. It's nice to have you all here and it'll be good to have our meals cooked.'

'Okay, tell me your favourite.'

Emlyn had a smile for him when she replied. 'Would you believe curried sausages? Mum used to cook it for my birthday dinner when I was growing up. I haven't had them for years.'

'Well, as long as there's some good old curry powder in the stores, I can come up with that for you.'

Again, that feeling of contentment spiked. 'Thank you.'

The glade at the top of the hill was as enticing in the daylight as it had been at dusk. When they stepped into the cool, green space and looked down the rock fall to the first tube, anticipation curled in Emlyn's stomach and Larry whistled.

'I'm pleased I brought the extra lights,' he said as he peered down into the dim cavern. 'We'll certainly need them.'

Once he'd helped them carry the equipment and photographic gear up the hill from the vehicle, Bill turned to John. 'What time do you want me back to pick you up? There doesn't seem to be much phone service up here.'

'And there won't be any down there.' John looked at his watch. 'Say around five? It depends how much gear we have to bring back out. Whether or not we think it's safe to leave anything down there.'

'I'm not leaving any of my equipment down there at night.' Larry shook his head. 'Worth too much.'

'Okay. Maybe around four, then,' John replied.

Bill nodded. 'Have a good day, everyone,' he called as he disappeared through the curtain of greenery.

Emlyn slipped the headband with the LED light over her head and adjusted it so that it wasn't catching her hair at the front. She pulled up her collar and rolled down her sleeves before she slipped the backpack onto her shoulders. She winced as a nerve twitched in the still-tender new skin from her last graft.

'We all set?' John asked, looking at the three of them.

Larry decided to leave the bulk of the cameras and lights in the glade before they went down for a look. Greg was the first to negotiate the rocks as John hammered a metal post into the soft earth at the edge of the glade. He looped a rope around it and threw the other end down to Greg where he would secure a post at the bottom. The plan was to install a rope so that they could climb up and down the rocks more easily.

The posts were secured, the rope stretched tight, and soon the four of them were standing on the fine dust in the cavern at the base of the rocks.

'Oh wow.' Larry's voice was hushed.

Emlyn smiled as his reaction mirrored her response of the other night. 'It's pretty amazing, isn't it,' she said.

John nodded. 'I've been in the tubes in Hawaii, but this is very different. The geology of these is unique. These were formed by the draining of roofed lava channels.' He pointed to the dark end of the cavern. 'For the first hour or so today, I want to get a feel for the caves before we start marking out the grids we'll work in this main tube. From the map, I think this is the main tunnel that heads west. We really don't know what we're going to find today or how far we can go in. Or how deep the lava flows were this far out from the main Undara tubes.'

'It's going to be pretty easy to walk through if it's all like this.' Larry gestured to the flat, silted floor.

'It'll get much harder than this, Larry. Where we are now, we're standing on sediment deposit from years of water flowing through. Once we get deeper I expect we'll see the ropy lava, and there may be distinct marginal channels up to a metre deep.'

'But what about the air? Are you going to test this cave?' Larry looked around.

'This one is fine,' Greg replied. 'You can see another opening across there. Another cave in on the south side, so there's good air flow.'

'Okay.' Larry lifted his camera and took some shots of the ceiling. Reds, ochre and almost black stripes formed a continuous pattern as far as they could see in the dim light.

'John. I'm in two minds about working close to the entrance at all.' Greg directed his torch in the opposite direction. 'I think this first cave has probably been compromised with the number of people in here over the years.'

Emlyn shook her head. 'I don't really think there has been much activity down here to be honest, Greg. Talking to Travis, I think it's pretty much only the family that has been in here and that wouldn't be very often.'

John nodded. 'I can see both points of view, but I think that the focus of our attention is down in this main tube. The Germans took a minor collection of fauna from the beginning of that one'—he pointed west— 'but the main thing I took from reading their work was their observations of the composition of the gas in the deeper cave. They didn't collect any specimens from that far in. Once we get past where the German team collected some specimens here, we're in unexplored territory.'

Emlyn smiled at the eagerness in John's voice, and it added to hers.

'Will any of this impact on me photographing the site or the insects you might find?' Emlyn was surprised to hear impatience in Larry's voice. He'd come highly recommended; surely, he understood the pace they'd be working at? And the care they'd take to make sure this study was valid. She hoped she hadn't made a mistake in recommending him for the contract. His references had been excellent, and he'd interviewed well over a Skype meeting. But you never knew what a person was really like until you worked with them.

'My primary concern is our safety. We'll stay in pairs the whole time. It would be easy to get lost down here,' John said.

'Come on.' Greg took a step forward. 'The only way to decide about where we'll focus on our collecting, is to go and have a look.'

'Yes, let's go. And, Larry to answer your question,' John turned to the photographer, 'as we go in, you'll see the conditions of the tubes. Once we select the best site for looking for specimens, we'll plot some observation points and start our grid. If you could keep the flash as low as possible to start with but get some shots of each section of the tube as we make our way along, that would be great.'

Emlyn moved slowly towards the dark tunnel ahead, the light from her headpiece creating macabre shadows on the variegated walls.

'Are you happy with the plan so far, Emlyn?' John asked as he caught up with her.

'We're in your hands, John, you've done this before. This is pretty new to me, but it's thrilling, and I'm happy to go with what you decide.'

Emlyn blinked as a camera flash went off and bright light blinded her for a few seconds. When her eyes adjusted again, Larry was standing in front of them and grinning. He must have slipped past them in the dark and caught the three of them front on.

'That's a shot I had to get,' he said. 'You should see the enthusiasm on your faces. Reminded me of the blokes when I got to base camp last month.' He laughed. 'Talk about one extreme to the other. From the top of the world to the bottom. I feel like I'm in a Jules Verne movie.'

Emlyn grimaced. Even though she couldn't see John's expression, his displeasure was evident in his body language. The team meeting when they got back tonight was going to be interesting. She put her head down and followed them into the dark tube ahead.

They'd walked less than fifty metres when an unearthly scream came from behind them. Emlyn and John turned swiftly and the light from their LED headlamps lit the space behind them. The red stripes on the walls were broken by the small black dots where the bats clung to the sheer rock face.

'Oh Jesus God, get them away from me.' Larry's expression was almost grotesque in the flickering light. He flailed his arms and backed away from the pile of rocks in front of him.

Greg ran back and stopped when he reached the photographer.

'Jesus fucking Christ. You didn't tell me what this place was like.' Larry's voice echoed around the chamber.

'What is it?' John asked as he and Emlyn hurried back to join them.

'More bloody snakes than I've ever seen in my life.'

They pulled up short of Larry as they stared down at the reptiles.

'Maybe it's a mating ritual,' Emlyn said softly.

Greg shook his head as Larry edged back towards the rock wall behind them. It was hard to estimate how many snakes were in the writhing mass on the fine dirt. Brown and grey twirled in a sinuous dance as the reptiles curled against each other. Every few seconds a head would lift, and the forked tongue would flick out.

'No,' Greg said. 'Someone's trying to scare us away. Look.' He pointed to the wall and dipped his head, so his light shone on the ground. Two hessian sacks were lying on the ground, and as they watched another snake came from each.

'Who on earth would do that?' John exclaimed.

'I don't care who did it,' Larry said. 'But I'm not fussed on spending a few weeks down here.'

'It's all right, Larry. They're harmless pythons and tree snakes.' Emlyn tried to placate him. 'I've got a fair idea who did this, and I'll tell him not to do it again.'

Bluey's word rang in her ears. 'You need to listen to the locals, love.' She'd be having a word to him if this happened again. A bag of snakes wasn't going to scare them off.

* * *

Travis nudged the flank of the horse with his heel and

followed Gavin down the hill. Jase and Joel had gone ahead on the motorbikes, but he'd asked Gavin to come on horseback. It wasn't a bad day out here. The sun was shining, birds were chirping, and the property looked greener than it had last week.

'How much longer, Trav?' Gavin's whine floated up to him. 'I'm getting bored.'

'We'll just move the last paddock, and then we'll break for lunch at the spring.'

'Okay. You got yourself a lady friend now? She was there early. Did she stay the night?' Gavin's eyes were wide.

'No, Gavin, she didn't. Dr. Rees came over because there was an internet problem.' Travis kept his tone patient. He knew Gavin was trying to pick a fight so he could go back to the house in a huff and get out of the work.

Gavin kicked his horse into a gallop and shot ahead of Travis. When they rounded up the last few cattle and got back to the yards, Bluey was shutting the gate.

'What's he doing there?' Gavin said.

Travis gritted his teeth. 'He's helping us get the cattle in.'

'You know I hate the old prick. He gives me the creeps; he always has.'

'He's a good worker, and he takes up your slack.'

'He must be heading for eighty, the sneaky old bastard. I see him in places that he shouldn't be.'

'Like where?'

'Just places. I reckon he set that boy up.'

'What boy?'

'The one you had working for us. The one who took the backhoe out. That was Bluey's fault. And Bluey was out at the huts the other day. Why should he go there? I reckon he still thinks our property should be his. That's why Dad sacked him.

Dad told me about it. Bluey said his grandfather had a fight with ours and lost it. It's in the family diaries. I read it there.'

'The diaries were destroyed in the fire, so you couldn't have.' Travis knew what his brother's problem was. Gavin had a couple of hidey-holes on the property that he considered his own. He'd resent Bluey being out there—if he had been there at all. Lately, Travis couldn't believe a word his brother said.

Gavin had moved into one of the old huts when Alison and Travis had first married, but he'd soon got sick of looking after himself. Alison had put up with him when he'd moved back to the farmhouse, and Travis had appreciated her forbearance.

'Well, Dad must have told me. I still don't trust him. Dad got rid of him when we were off at school, and then you hired him back as soon as you were in charge.'

Travis ignored the resentment in his brother's tone and sighed. 'Gav, despite his age, he's a great worker. If he wasn't here, you'd have to work every day, so just put up with it, okay? And if you were running the property, you'd be the one having to do the worrying, so just can it.'

After they finished at the yards, they went across to the other side of the springs, and Travis pulled out some sandwiches and cold drinks. Joel and Jase sat leaning against the trunk of a huge gum tree.

'So, what do you think of your dad's girlfriend?' Gavin said as he reached for a sandwich.

'Gavin. That's enough.' Travis shook his head in a warning.

'It's okay, Trav. Have you done the sex-education bit yet?'

Joel lifted his head and stopped chewing as he stared at Travis.

'Emlyn's your girlfriend? She's only been here a little while, hasn't she?'

'Yes, she has, and your uncle is being stupid. He's stirring me.'

'I haven't ever had a girlfriend.' Gavin shot a shy look at both boys. 'Your father started young; I can remember back in high school—'

Jase's lip curled in a sneer. 'Ignore him, Joel. He's full of shit. They didn't even go to high school together. I know you went to boarding school and Uncle Gavin stayed here and was homeschooled.'

'Too sooky to leave home, were you, Uncle Gav?' Joel asked.

'Jase and Joel, some respect, please. That's enough ribbing; we've got work—' Travis went to intervene because Gavin had clenched his fists, and he knew the situation was about to get out of control, but Gavin spoke over him.

'Your grandparents could only afford to send one of us, and as usual, your father got all the benefits. I had to stay home and help Dad with the cattle between my lessons.'

Both of the boys rolled their eyes, and Travis was pleased when the conversation stopped as they demolished the last of the sandwiches. When they'd finished eating, the twins headed across to the large expanse of water and walked around the edge, deep in conversation.

Gavin frowned. 'What are they talking about now?'

Travis leaned back, closed his eyes, and ignored him. He listened to the flies buzzing around his head. It was a toss-up what was more annoying: Gavin or the flies.

'Well?'

'I don't know, Gavin. If you're so curious, go and ask

them.'

Travis sat up and reached for his hat, flapping at the small black flies. 'By the way, I've written you a cheque for your share from the cattle sale last month.'

'That'll come in handy in Townsville.'

Travis pushed himself to his feet, carried the pack over to the saddlebag, and slipped it in. He mounted the old horse. 'We've got more cattle to move tomorrow, so I want you to give me a hand before you go.'

'What about Bluey? I suppose he got a cheque, too?' The whine was back, and Travis fought for patience.

'It's a big job. And if you were out with us, you'd know that Bluey hasn't had a day off for a couple of weeks. And you know that he gets a pay cheque, not a cut of the sales. I want to move the small herd right over to the back paddock. And then I want to head out to the back boundary. Apparently, the road needs grading. Did you unlock the back gate and give anyone access to the station?'

'No, I didn't.' Gavin dropped his lip into a pout. 'Just because Mum left you in charge doesn't mean you can accuse me of things.'

Travis put up his hands and kept his voice calm. 'Okay. Okay. Settle down. I'm not accusing you of anything. I was just asking.'

'What do you think I am?' So, the stirring hadn't worked, so now it was time for the hard-done-by front; Gavin had been doing that to get out of work recently. 'You told me to tell the mining company that there's not enough water on the place, and that's what I did.' He shook his head. 'I don't know why you even gave me the responsible job of dealing with that company.'

'Because I didn't have time, and I knew I could trust you

to get our message across.'

Gavin smiled. 'It's good you appreciate me for something.'

'Of course I do. I know you love this place as much as I do.' Travis forced himself to smile back. 'I just wish you could help me more. The property has taken a big hit with the drought over the past few years. I've had to let Jeff Collins go.'

'No loss.' Gavin's mind flitted from one thing to another, as usual. 'So what about the road?'

'I'll check it out when I move the cattle. Can you help me or not?'

'I'm sorry for being mean. If you can leave it a week, Trav, I can give you all the week after next on the property.' Gavin stood and walked to the horse. He put his hand on old Sam's head and gave him a rub as he looked up at Travis. 'Look, I'm sorry. I know I've been a bit slack lately. I've had a lot on my mind.'

'You and me both.' Travis doubted whether the promised week would eventuate. There was always an excuse for a trip to Townsville. 'Well, if you'll give me that week out there, we could get a lot done. I want to have a look at the road myself before I waste money on a grader.'

'Who said it was a mess, anyway?'

'Emlyn did. She went out to unlock the back gate for the delivery truck from Mt Surprise.' He pushed his hat back. 'I might even give Kev a call. He can tell me how bad it is.'

'Trav, don't waste your time or money—our money. She's a city slicker. A bit of a bump would make it a bad road for anyone who's used to driving on tar. If Kev got through in his delivery truck, it's probably just a few channels on the edge from that one storm we had a few weeks back.'

'Yeah. You're probably right. So, I can take your word that you'll give me a week? We'll camp out there to save some time.'

'Scout's honour. The week after next.'

'Okay. It's a deal.'

Chapter 14

Carlyle Downs, **10 January**

Walking across to the mess room for dinner, Emlyn surprised herself as she began to sing quietly. The air was fresh and clean this evening, and a cooler wind, tempering the constant heat, was blowing in from the south. Her shoes clicked on the steps in time with the song in her head. She stopped at the top and took a deep breath. Silence surrounded her; the only sound was the wind high in the trees, and the faint sound of animals. With a smile, she pushed open the screen door.

The idea that could be the answer to Travis's financial problems began to take shape in Emlyn's thoughts last night around the dinner table. The past few days underground had been excellent, and Larry had taken dozens of photographs that Lucy was going to cross-match with the international tropical-insect database after dinner. They had made an unusual discovery today. The conversation was animated as they sat around the table talking well into the night. Emlyn had made their first discovery today after hours brushing the dirt.

'If only we had more manpower,' Greg said. 'Imagine what other troglomorphic species are down there in those kilometres of tubes. Especially where there's been no human intervention.'

'Translation please? Trog what?' Larry asked with a laugh.

'Sorry,' Greg said. 'A troglobite is a species that is bound to underground habitats … like the tubes here or underground caves. So troglomorphic means a species that adapts to living in the constant darkness—the conditions—of caves. You see things like loss of pigment, reduced eyesight, and often with very fine bodies. Not to mention unique appendages.'

'Like that white "thing" you got me to photograph all afternoon.' Larry sat back and picked up his beer.

'That's the one.' Greg nodded. As they ate dinner, Greg's eyes were bright, and he couldn't keep the smile off his face. Emlyn had come across the unfamiliar creature late that afternoon. Encased in a white shell, it was the shape of a leaf and it seemed to be walking backwards as she brushed the dirt away from it, as if the antennae were at the front of its head. The white antler-like sticks were waving around, and when the light from the camera flash had bathed the insect, it had stopped and lifted the front half of its body.

'I reckon it's a genus of the *callipodida*.' Greg hadn't stopped talking about it since they'd sat down, and Emlyn was quietly delighted, too. It was why they were here, and the first indication of new species. The headache she'd been nursing disappeared in an instant as she'd observed the creature on the red sand.

'A similar species has been recently discovered in limestone caves in Southern China with pale colouration, long antennae and long legs,' Emlyn said.

'How do you know all this?' Larry asked. 'You're a bloody walking encyclopaedia.'

'Just as well I made mango ice-cream for dessert,' Bill said with a grin. 'Sounds like a celebration is called for.'

Ice-cream girl. Emlyn put down her fork, her appetite

gone. Even though she'd told David not to email her again, another message had arrived from him last night. She had to force herself to stop thinking about it and focus on her work down in the caves today. She hadn't slept well and had been plagued by a niggling headache all day.

Sitting on the side of the bed last night, she'd opened the email, after a few minutes of trying to ignore it.

So the nerdy IT student thought he had a chance with Ice-cream Girl, did he? Let's show her what a he-man he is, he decided. Let's go camping for our first real weekend away. Let's show her that he's a real man.

Emlyn's chuckle had surprised her.

So, Ice-cream Girl neglected to mention she was a seasoned camper. You grew up in a camping family. How many research camps had you been on by then, Em? Lots, if my memory serves me correctly. How many times had I been camping? Once when I was about four, with my dad, and that had been a disaster.

The trip he had taken her on had been an absolute hoot. They'd gone up to the Scenic Rim on the New South Wales border to the Natural Bridge walk. The car park had been full of Maseratis and Ferraris, and one Lamborghini. Luxury cars—and luxury people—on some afternoon excursion from the Gold Coast.

David had whistled. 'Wow. Feel a bit guilty parking the old Hyundai next to them.' He'd put his hand out and she'd taken it, as he'd helped her down the path. It had been nice being looked after and cared for, and Emlyn had lapped it up. And he was so good-looking, and his voice was deep and sexy like Alan Rickman's. She'd been to every one of his movies because she'd loved his voice; David's had the same timbre, without the posh

British accent.

They'd both smothered giggles as they'd passed the group coming back up to the car park. The perfume had preceded the women wearing heavy makeup and the shortest skirts Emlyn had ever seen.

'I think I'd rather be in the Hyundai,' Emlyn had whispered as she watched the women totter up the path on stiletto heels.

David had shaken his head. 'Why would you bother?'

They'd chuckled together all the way to the campground in the national park.

First disaster: David hadn't brought tent pegs. Emlyn had smiled as she'd continued to read.

So, I had a tent. Who told me you needed to peg it to the ground? I thought I was clever watching it on the YouTube clip. And the food? Did you really have to giggle so much when I'd forgotten the matches? So you can't light a campfire successfully with the cigarette lighter from the car. I know that now. But weren't the hamburgers we bought at Crystal Creek fantastic? Ever since that night, I've measured my hamburgers against them.

I couldn't provide you with shelter, and I stuffed up the food. But you laughed, and told me it didn't matter, and I fell in love with you a little bit more with every second that passed.

The rest of that night is etched into my memory and it will always be there. Remember how I used to tell you about data on a hard drive?

You are etched onto my soul, Em. Even if I never see you again, if I never touch you again, if I never hold you again, I will survive because you are written into my soul.

I love you, babe. Wherever you are today, hold that

thought close to you. David.

She'd closed the laptop and laid down, even though it wasn't dark yet. That had been the first time they'd slept together, and like David's memory, it was imprinted on her mind forever. Tears had welled in her eyes and Emlyn had let them seep from the corners as she lay there until she'd fallen into a restless sleep.

'Emlyn, where would you go?'

She jumped as Meg touched her arm gently. Looking down, she was surprised to see her dinner plate was gone and had been replaced by a bowl of ice-cream and jelly.

'Sorry. I was miles away,' she said quietly.

'Always thinking about work, aren't you, love.' Bill nodded at her as he cleared the plates.

'Yes. Always work,' she agreed.

'We were talking about the best place for holidays,' Meg said.

'It's a shame they can't do something here like that dig we did over at Winton last holidays,' Lucy said.

Meg laughed as she held up her wineglass for a refill. 'You mean to say your scientist husband took you on a dig for a holiday?' She was sitting next to Greg and she leaned over and nudged him. 'If John ever tried that ...'

'I'd be in the doghouse,' John cracked a rare joke. 'Airlie Beach or Hamilton Island, that's Meg's choice for a holiday. But if you'd like to go to the Dinosaur Dig, love—'

Meg held up her still-empty glass. 'Pour me another wine and button it, John.'

Professor John Kearns winked at Emlyn as he did what his wife instructed, but Meg's comment got Emlyn thinking.

'Tell me a bit more about this dig holiday,' she asked quietly. 'I've read a bit about the fossil work over at Winton, but

I didn't know about the holiday program.' Usually the quiet one at dinner, she was content to sit back and let the conversations wash over her. Most nights she'd excuse herself early and head over to the workbench and write up her notes for the day before emailing them to Lucy.

'Yes.' John sat up a bit straighter. 'I can see what you're thinking, Emlyn, and I like it.'

Greg nodded. 'Yes. It could work here, too. Over there, you pay to be a part of the dig for a short period. At the moment it's five to six days. In the beginning, Winton was supported by a national magazine fundraiser and private donations from a heap of volunteers and supporters. Now, it's big business. When we were up there, we had the choice of going out on the dig or working in the prep room cleaning the rock away from the fossils.'

'A tourist facility could be set up here—with sponsorship paying the set-up costs—and the university would benefit with a facility set-up where we had a continuous stream of visitors working on pre-set grids.' Emlyn spoke quickly as her thoughts tumbled around.

Greg and John both nodded. 'But the property owner would have to be receptive to the idea,' Greg said.

Emlyn's interest was growing as she thought about what it would mean for the future of the property, and the research of the university. It was exactly the sort of thing that Travis had been asking about the other day. No, maybe he hadn't considered something on that scale, but the bigger it was the more chance there would be of getting sponsorship and government funding.

'Let me get my computer.' John brought his laptop back to the table.

'What sort of set-up costs would there be?' Emlyn asked.

'Accommodation, and all that goes in the rooms, the cost of staff to cook for the guests, safety equipment … and I suppose here you need vehicles like the Troop Carrier to get up to the entrance,' Greg said. 'Not to mention advertising. Have a look at the dinosaur website and you'll get a feel for what they do out there. The property owner who made the initial discovery back in the late nineties began the build with lots of volunteers and support from the state museum. Since then, the state government has come on board to assist with the cost of building an onsite museum, and the facility where the fossil preparation shed has grown.'

'Emlyn, look at this,' John said as he pulled up the site details. She leaned over and read with him as he clicked through the various pages.

'That's got huge possibilities. I think it's worth taking the idea to Travis. What do you all think?' It was the most Emlyn had spoken at dinner since they'd arrived, and heat ran up her neck as she intercepted a look between the other two women.

She lowered her gaze, feeling self-conscious. It didn't matter what they thought. She was helping Travis, but more, this would also be beneficial to their research. There was so much ground to cover and they would barely scratch the surface—literally—with such a small research team as theirs over a few weeks.

She couldn't help her voice bubbling over. 'Imagine a combination of what's over at Undara, and a research facility here in the unexplored tubes? Imagine how many of the tubes we could get to.'

'There's no volcanic crater here, and no walks apart from the tubes—' Lucy began.

'That wouldn't matter,' Greg interrupted. 'The sort of

clientele that this type of stay would attract is not your usual family-type tourists. It's costly and upmarket.'

Emlyn stood and pushed in her chair. 'I can't wait to tell Travis about this. I'm going to head over there now.'

'Isn't it a bit late?' Bill asked as he took the last plates from the table. 'You know it's heading for nine-thirty.'

Emlyn widened her eyes. 'Really? I had no idea. I'd better leave it till tomorrow, then.'

Before she went to bed, she emailed David. Brief and to the point.

David, the rest of the team has arrived. I am not alone. There's no need to email again.

She ignored the small twinge of discontent that took away from her anticipation about the idea she couldn't wait to run by Travis.

Chapter 15

Emlyn had to wait a few days before she could share her idea with Travis. She went to the house as soon as they came up from the tubes the next afternoon, but there was no sign of anyone there or at the yards as she drove past. Disappointment filled her as she drove around the back of the house and past the shed on the way out. No sign of anyone or any vehicles. For a fleeting second, she thought about leaving Travis a note, but decided to come back after dinner, and she'd make sure it was at a reasonable hour tonight. She also wanted to mention the bags of snakes that had been waiting for them in the tubes. She still suspected it was Bluey's doing.

As each day passed, an easy camaraderie had developed in the team, and Emlyn found herself sitting at the dinner table later each night listening to conversations and enjoying the interaction. Once Larry had realised there was no pecking order to be established, he'd been much easier to take. No more posturing or telling everyone how good he was or who he'd worked with. Since he'd settled in, along with Bill, he'd kept them entertained most nights with funny anecdotes and stories. Even John had thawed a little more each night.

The work had been put back a day yesterday. When they'd entered the first cave, John hadn't been able to find his bag of tools. He stood there scratching his head as the others collected theirs.

'I could have sworn I left it here. I must have taken it back up yesterday without thinking. It'll be in the van.'

Emlyn dug into her small backpack. 'I've got a couple of spares, John, to save you going back up.'

'Thanks, Em.' They were in a daily routine now, and they chatted as they headed for the grid.

'A couple more days here and we'll move deeper,' Greg said as he walked along beside Emlyn. The lights from their headlamps flickered on the loose sandy floor as they made their way to the work area. They always kept their eyes open for snake tracks after that first day.

'Look at that.' Emlyn stopped and pointed to the ground. She pulled the larger flashlight from her bag. The floor was usually smooth, with small mounds along the path they took, but now there were furrows and the usual piles of dirt had been scattered.

Greg crouched down. 'It's not footsteps. Something—or someone—has been in here since yesterday.'

Emlyn shivered as Bluey's words came back to her: Those caves are haunted.

'What do you think it is?' John caught up to them.

Greg shrugged. 'I can't see any animal tracks or footsteps, but something has certainly disturbed the place. No idea what, though.'

'Keep a good eye out.' John moved past them and led the way, Larry taking up the rear. Emlyn smiled. The photographer was staying closer than he usually did.

'Oh no.' John's exclamation reverberated off the walls as he turned into the cavern where the grid was marked out. Or had been. Emlyn stepped into the tube and stared in disbelief at the mess in front of them. Half of the pegs had been pulled out, and their string lines were gone. The dirt floor and the area they had carefully marked out and brushed over the past few days was a mess of scattered dirt.

'My God. What did that?' Larry's voice was hushed. 'It wouldn't be snakes?'

Emlyn folded her arms. 'I think it might be a matter of 'who,' not what.'

As they moved across to the scattered pegs, a loud thumping and a hoarse, ghostly cry came from the dark tunnel ahead. Another shiver ran down Emlyn's back.

'Stay here, Emlyn.' John raised a hand. 'Greg and I will go and see what it is.'

She shook her head. 'No, I'm coming too.'

'And me too,' Larry said. 'Don't leave me by myself.'

Slowly they moved forwards, three flashlights now lighting up the way and disturbing the small bats that usually clung to the roof and walls.

'Jesus,' Larry exclaimed as they swooped low past them.

'It's all right. They won't touch you,' Emlyn reassured him.

John stopped, and Emlyn peered around his shoulder. 'It's all right. Nothing sinister. Macropus dorsalis,' he said.

'A what?' Larry said.

'Just a wallaby,' Emlyn said. 'Oh, the poor thing. We're going to need gloves to get that off.'

A black-striped wallaby lay on the ground in front of them, tangled in the string lines that were missing from the cavern. As it thumped its legs against the dirt, it emitted a harsh grunt.

'How did it get down here?' Larry asked.

'Obviously the same way we did,' Greg said drily.

It took a while to free the creature, and once they'd taken

it up to the top, John made the decision to go further in and mark out some new grids.

Her email icon had been flashing after dinner and she clicked on it. David was at an IT conference in Melbourne. Would he never leave her in peace?

Hi Em, from dreary Melbourne. Who'd believe it was the middle of summer! God it was hot on the way down here, though.

Emlyn put her hand over her eyes. Of course, David would have driven down from Brisbane. He had a height phobia and that had been why he wouldn't fly to Fiona's wedding. But she'd wanted to go so badly, of course he'd agreed.

Eventually.

A shaft of grief pierced Emlyn's chest and it was hard to breathe. She focused on drawing in air, and then focused on the words on the screen.

It's cold and wet, and I've got a head cold.

I hope he took the Vicks with him, she thought. David had ended up in hospital one winter with pneumonia and it had been the longest night of her life, home alone with his side of the bed empty.

Emlyn turned her attention back to the screen and chewed as she kept reading.

The conference is boring and I thought I'd brighten my day by talking to you. You know, if you're ever feeling lonely, just pick up the phone and call, and we can have a chat. No ties, nothing else. Although it would be nice to hear you laugh.

Maybe I could tell you a joke. Remember the one ... nah. You don't want to hear that one again. You never thought it was funny, anyway.

Sleep well, sweets. I'm going to rub my feet with Vicks and put socks on.

What the hell did David think he was going to gain by sending her all that stupid stuff?

Her hands clenched and her face heated.

That Emlyn was gone.

Along with her dreams of love and happiness.

Along with her family.

* * *

Even though she hadn't caught up with Travis, the work in the tubes had been going well, and the results were encouraging. Despite only working into the first two caves beneath the glade, they'd already logged six species formerly believed to be extinct, and the exhilaration of the team was growing more each day. As they entered the glade every morning, the expectation that they would have a good find was creating a cheery and positive atmosphere.

Emlyn was healing. It was hard to believe that it was two weeks since she'd arrived. She welcomed the nights when she was physically exhausted after a long day. The ache in her arm was easing daily, and the tension headaches had stayed away. Physically, she was stronger, and mentally, her focus was on the work.

After she left the deserted house, Emlyn drove slowly back to the camp, keeping an eye out for any sign of horses or the farm utes. She desperately wanted to know what Travis thought about the tourism idea.

As she came to the bottom of the hill near the site of the old homestead, a vine with bright-burgundy flowers spilling down the bank caught her eye. On a whim, she pulled over to the side of the dirt road and climbed out of the vehicle. Walking over to the bank, she touched the cascading blooms. The small delicate flowers were waxy to the touch and the deep-red petals had a star-shaped centre. She reached down and picked a small bouquet and crossed the road, walked past the old ruins and kept going until she reached the old family cemetery.

There were four graves, and she tried to read the engravings on the weathered headstones. The dates were faded, but she could make out three names, all Carlyles: Thomas, Lila and Eunice. The last headstone was a different shape—smaller—but it was chipped and she could only make out an S at the beginning. Maybe it was a child's grave. Sadness tugged at her— melancholy for the past. If it was a child, how did they die? Childhood illness had often been a death knell back in the early days of settlement in the bush. Far from any medical assistance, mothers had coped with the loss of many children to diphtheria and tuberculosis. Even childhood diseases like measles and chicken pox had been fatal to many.

Emlyn crouched down, placing the pretty flowers beneath the stone, and touched the petals. 'Rest easy, whoever you were, little one.'

Sitting at a grave was a new experience for her. Her parents had both requested for their ashes to be spread out on Moreton Bay, where they'd loved sailing. Their plan had been to retire there, but sadly, tragedy had intervened and ensured that had never happened. There were no graves to visit and nowhere for Emlyn to leave flowers.

'That's Stanley.'

Emlyn jumped and turned around as the deep voice interrupted her thoughts. She narrowed her eyes; she was sure he'd been nowhere in sight when she'd walked over from the car, and the paddocks were wide and open; there were few places to hide.

'I saw you tracing over the letters. It's almost impossible to read these days.'

'Oh, hello, Bluey.'

'We've got to stop meeting here.' His face split into a huge grin, exposing missing teeth. 'You'll think I've got some sort of thing about hanging about graveyards. I hate the places. I'll be in one soon enough meself.' His grin faded and he muttered as he stared at the gravestone. 'I'm the last one here.'

Emlyn looked at him curiously, wondering if he was ill. 'I didn't see you there when I walked over.'

'I was up the hill. Flora threw a shoe.' When he gestured up the slope, she could see a horse standing in the shade under the tree.

'Ah, Flora is your horse.'

'Yeah, I'm hoofing it back to the shed to get the ute.'

'Hoofing it?'

He smiled again, revealing nicotine-stained teeth, and pointed to his feet. 'Shanks's pony.'

'I can go back and get the Troop Carrier and give you a lift if you like.' Emlyn's tension eased when he shook his head. He was a funny old fella, but friendly enough.

'Nah. I'll be there in no time.' He took off his hat as he looked at the graves and put it on his chest. 'It was kind of you to bring the flowers to the cemetery.'

'Who was Stanley that you mentioned? A child?' She gestured to the headstone. 'Is that his grave?'

'Yep, he was one of the young stockmen on the place, way back in the early days. Back in the late 1800s. The story is that when he died in his teens, Lila insisted he was buried with the family. She'd lost two of her children and wanted him to be near them.'

Emlyn looked around with a frown. 'Are their graves here, too?'

'Just that memorial stone over there.' Bluey shook his head. 'It's one of the great mysteries of the place. Missy and Tommy were never found.'

'Found? What do you mean?' she asked.

'The story is they disappeared in mysterious circumstances. Some reckon they got kidnapped by the Chinese in the goldfields and put to work, but I won't have a bar of that. Something bad happened. There's been talk about it for over a hundred years.'

Emlyn's throat ached, and she focused on speaking evenly. 'No matter how it happened. it would have been dreadful for their mother.' Her voice hitched, and she fought down the sob that threatened. 'To lose two children at once.'

'Yep, you keep a good eye out, love. Keep safe when you're down in those damn caves. You shouldn't be down there, you know, none of you. It's not right.'

'I know, you've already told me. We're very careful.' She looked intently at him. 'The only thing we've seen is a lot of snakes down there. And one poor wallaby,' she added archly.

'Told you there was critters down there.'

'You wouldn't happen to know how they got down there?'

Bluey frowned. 'Why would I? What exactly are you asking?'

Emlyn hesitated. He looked genuinely puzzled. Had she got it wrong? 'I thought … Nothing.' She shrugged. 'Do you know if Travis is back at the house yet?'

Bluey nodded. 'Yep. Trav and the boys were ahead of me

when Flora stumbled. They'll be back there already.'

'Thanks. See you later, then.' She gave him a wave as he returned to his horse.

* * *

'Okay, what do you need from me?' Travis's voice held suppressed enthusiasm … and hope.

Emlyn was in the living room at the homestead. Joel and Jase had made a cup of tea for everyone and then disappeared into the bedroom. The sounds of a computer game filled the room until Travis shut the door.

'Tell me more about this,' he said. His interest when she'd given him a rough outline was encouraging.

'We need to do a project plan, a feasibility study. Look at the objectives—for you and for continued research for us.'

Travis grinned. 'I suppose it's not enough to say I need the money?'

'No. That might be the bottom line, but we have to define and document the project-management plan to meet the project objectives.'

He shook his head. 'It all sounds like words to me.'

Emlyn nodded. 'It's called jumping through hoops. But we need that to meet your objectives. As well as looking at any permits that might be required and do a costing analysis. And other things.'

'You know what?' Travis scratched his head and Emlyn lifted her eyebrows.

'What?'

'I think I understand why I like working with cattle.'

'I'm with you,' she replied. 'I know why I like working with insects.'

'Okay. If it has to be done, let's do it. How long have we got?'

'The funding applications for the next triennium close at the end of this month, so if you're serious about this, we're going to have to devote the next two weeks to this full-on.' Emlyn looked up as Travis stood and began to pace the room.

'Two weeks?' he said, scratching his head. 'You really think we've got a chance?'

'I think we've got an excellent chance if we take care with the application. The concept is going to be a cross between the Undara tourist facility and the dinosaur work at Winton. As far as I know, there's nothing else like it in the country. If we do our homework, I think we can get it.'

The front door flew open and Gavin walked in. 'Hello,' he said. 'What's going on?'

Travis shot a warning look to Emlyn. 'Just some questions Emlyn had about the tubes.'

'Found any new creepy-crawlies yet?'

Emlyn didn't like Gavin's tone. His initial shyness had disappeared and today he made her feel as though she was intruding. 'We're making progress.'

'Not long till you lot finish up over there?'

Before she could reply, he disappeared into the kitchen.

Travis rolled his eyes. 'Just ignore him. Gavin's feeling left out because he's not the centre of attention.'

'I heard that,' came the reply from the kitchen. The sound of dishes being thrown into the sink reached them.

'If the cap fits,' Travis called back.

'Maybe I'd better go,' Emlyn said. She lowered her voice. 'What night would suit you to talk more about this?'

'I thought you said it would take a while?'

'It will,' she replied. 'But we have to start somewhere. We need to work a few hours each night before the deadline.'

'Jeez, it'll be like being back at ag college.' Travis laughed.

'There'll be big money involved if we get the green light.'

'Don't mention money in front of Gavin. He'll want to put in his ideas,' Travis said quietly. 'He's supposed to be going away again tomorrow. I'm not going to let him stuff this opportunity up. Come over after dinner unless I call and cancel.' His voice was full of impatience as he looked towards the kitchen. 'I don't know what he's doing from one day to the next. He disappears out on the farm, but he's certainly not working.'

* * *

The next day in the tubes was wonderful. Two new species were logged, and the mood was upbeat as the afternoon drew to a close.

'If we keep on with these sorts of results, your project application will be very highly regarded,' John said as they packed up for the day. 'Travis was keen?'

'Very,' Emlyn replied. 'I'm heading over there after dinner to get started on the proposal.'

John stood for a moment looking at her, and she looked around the cave.

'Did I forget something?' she asked.

'No, I was just thinking how good it is to see the spark back in you again. But you've been quiet today. I always worry that you came back to work too soon after—'

Emlyn cut him off. 'No need to worry about me, John. I'm as fit as a fiddle and fully recovered.'

He put his hand on her arm. 'Are you, Emlyn?'

She didn't take offence. John had been a colleague for a long time, and he had been her mentor when she'd studied for her doctorate. They had only ever had a working relationship, but she knew he was a good man. With a brisk nod, she reassured him, 'I am. Now let's get packed up or Bill will be carrying on about dinner getting cold again.'

John took the hint and moved away.

Why did everyone have to worry about her? David wouldn't ease up, either. Another email had been waiting when she'd come home from Travis's place last night. *Please read and don't delete*, the subject line read. Her heart had plummeted as soon as she'd read it. Why the hell couldn't he leave her to get on with her life, and why did she find it so hard not to read his messages?

David's email had touched a nerve and Emlyn had relived the memories all day as she'd worked in the tubes.

Hi Em. It's funny talking to you by email, but it has brought you closer to me, and I find you in my thoughts many times through the day.

Oh, I wish you'd been here today to hear the speaker we had. He was AWFUL. You know how I can usually pay attention, not matter how bad a speaker is? Well, not this time. I cleaned out my email, I organised my files and folders, and it looked as though I was studiously taking notes.

If you could expire of boredom, that would have been me today.

You know, Em, one of the best things for me was how you pulled me out of my comfort zone and right into yours as soon as I met you. I'll never forget that first night. I was so scared of asking you out. I was terrified you'd say no. I mean, why would someone as beautiful as you look at a nerdy IT student? I couldn't stop looking at you when we walked along the river that night. Your gorgeous hair was pulled up into the crazy sideways ponytail on the side of your head. Your lovely lips always in that permanent smile.

Oh, Em, I so miss seeing your smile. That gorgeous laugh of yours. I've even missed that snort you descend into when you really lose the plot. I can close my eyes and hear it now and I'm smiling.

Anyway, you smiled when I asked you out. I waited and then that crazy ponytail bobbed as you nodded. I walked on air for days.

Stay safe, Em. I think of you each night.

For a moment, anger pinged inside her. He *was* checking she was okay. Why the hell did everyone think she was going to hurt herself—or worse? There'd been enough death to do her a lifetime.

A grim smile crossed her face. She'd seen the counsellor's face when she'd filled out the questionnaire at her first appointment. Ever since then, until she'd moved out, David had watched her like a hawk.

If she was honest, it was the content of David's email more than anything else that had unsettled her. Her foot was jigging on the floor and she looked down at her left hand, surprised to see her fist opening and closing. She took a deep breath and focused on being calm.

They'd had some fun times, and their life together had been good. She wondered if he was still living in their house or if he'd moved out like he said he was going to.

'I can't stay here without you, Emlyn.' That was one of the arguments he'd used to get her to stay, but it hadn't swayed her determination. David was playing dirty, but he didn't know that her emotions were dead and he couldn't get to her that way. But reading about the snort he'd always teased her about had lifted the sides of her lips briefly.

Anyway, I digress. I hope you are well and happy, and enjoying your new job.

Wherever you are.

She blinked as a shaft of guilt drilled into her. Being up at *Carlyle Downs* wasn't a secret; she'd tell him where she was when she replied.

As she read on, she changed her mind when David's next words knifed through her. Her breath hitched, and heat rushed through her body. The screen blurred for a second as she squinted and read the sentence again.

How could he? How dare he mention that time of their life? How dare he talk about it as though it was normal and natural?

I'll never forget the day you told me I was going to be a dad. If I close my eyes, I can still feel the happiness that filled my heart that day.

Emlyn also closed her eyes. Of course he'd been happy, so had she. They'd both been filled with joy, and hope, and the future had looked bright.

But happiness was not reality. It could be gone in the blink of an eye. She knew that now. How long would it be before David realised that? Images flashed behind her closed eyelids and the pain twisted in her chest.

Why is he doing this to me? Why is he dwelling on the past?

She leaned back and tried to focus on the sounds around her, but the occasional laugh from the mess room was muted and didn't hide the sounds screaming through her head.

To have and to hold.

The cry of a newborn baby, a sweet little voice, sounds that she had blocked for almost a year.

I do.

The rain pounding on the iron roof of their house. The creaky swing in the back garden. Back and forth, back and forth.

I love you, Em. I'll love you forever. David's voice whispering in her ear, telling her the words she loved to hear.

Emlyn sat there with her hands over her eyes and forced herself to breathe calmly. Gradually the panic receded, and she was empty, her eyes dry, past tears.

She felt nothing. And that was the way it had to be.

It was the only way she could survive.

Opening her eyes, she stared at the screen until she saw weird shapes. She sat up and stabbed at the keyboard button to reduce the brightness. Reading the rest of what David had to say was essential now; it would stop the memories that had flooded in. The little twinges of emotion and the occasional fleeting surge of happiness that past memories had been reviving over the past few days. She'd been weak and let them in. She didn't want that, and she wouldn't let it happen. If reading the rest of this email fed her anger, she would read it all night.

Over and over.

She bit her lip and looked at the screen with determination; it was time to be strong.

Making a child with you completed me. As she grew inside you, my reality shifted, and even though I didn't think it was possible, my love for you grew stronger. Lying beside you at night and watching your tummy ripple as she showed us how fast she was growing, is something I will never forget, Em.

We have both been changed by what happened, but we can survive the loss. We can. Our loss.

Not yours, not mine, but ours. I want us to do this together, and I hope and pray that deep down you agree with me. We both need to forgive ourselves for being imperfect—we did the best we could.

Em, you might think I am cruel writing this, but I had to tell you how I feel. We have to be honest, if we are to have any hope of getting through this. That link between us, that link that you know was there, and was there forever… well, I can feel it shifting. Stretching and getting further away every day.

We can't let it go.

I won't let it go. I won't let us go. I worry so much about you, Em. Every minute, every second of my day is filled with missing you.

I love you, sweetheart. Hold that in your heart.

Emlyn carefully closed the laptop, but her hands were shaking. Her whole body felt detached as though the blood churning through her veins wasn't part of her.

But her thoughts wouldn't stop.

I love you, sweetheart. Hold that in your heart.

She dropped her head, refusing to let the tears come. Although she couldn't control her emotions and thoughts, she could her physical reactions.

And I love you, David. I always will.

But there is no future for us.

Chapter 16

After dinner the next night, Emlyn headed over to the homestead with her laptop and a bundle of folders. She'd printed out pages and pages of details about the initiative over at Winton, to get the terminology for the application correct.

'The timing is perfect. We're just going to make the cut-off date for the funding for the next financial year for the university. They've already got a lot of sponsorship money promised; now it's a matter of matching applications to suitable research projects, and the appropriate sponsorship source. John and I are really hopeful that this is going to get the green light.' She booted up the laptop and brought up the application form. 'There's about seventy zillion attachments on it. I've printed them out and you'll have to sign a few of them, providing proof of ownership of the property etcetera.'

'Seventy zillion?' Travis sat back, and his smile was wide. 'You are amazing, Emlyn. You spend all day in the caves, so when did you put all this together.'

She sat in the chair beside him. 'Trust me. Sleep is highly over-rated.' As she worked with Travis, she'd revised her opinion of him; behind the terse and sometimes gruff cattleman was a sharp brain with a good grasp of the language needed for the formal document they were creating.

After he amended her words for the third time, she looked up at him with an accusing smile. 'You've done this before, haven't you?'

'Not exactly this, but yes, I've done a few feasibility studies in my time.' He stretched his arms above his head and checked his watch. 'You know it's almost eleven. Do you want a coffee?'

When she'd first arrived, the twins had been in the process of moving the television and Xbox onto the back sleep-out.

'For peace and quiet, and concentration,' Travis had explained. The occasional whoop had come over the sound of a game at full volume. Even at this late hour, they were still going. 'And it also gives me some control about them going to bed. If I didn't stop them at midnight, they'd go all night. The rule here now is no devices in the bedroom. I sometimes wonder what they get up to when Alison is at work.'

Emlyn tipped her head to the side, remembering the nights that David would get immersed in a game and play through the night. 'I know,' she said softly. 'My husband was the same.'

Travis was headed towards the kitchen and stopped at the door. 'Was?' he asked.

Emlyn shook her head. 'Oh, he probably still is, but we don't live together anymore.'

'I'm sorry to hear that.' He left, and Emlyn smiled when he returned a few minutes later with the fine china cup and saucer.

'Thank you,' she said. She turned back to the laptop, but Travis put his hand over hers on the keyboard.

'I think you've worked hard enough tonight. Have your cuppa and head off. What time will you start work tomorrow?'

Emlyn couldn't stop the yawn that had been threatening for a while. She put her hand over her mouth. 'Early one tomorrow. About seven, I think John said.'

'Us too. We'll be heading out at dawn.' Travis inclined his head towards the tents. 'If I can get them out of bed.'

'What about Gavin?' Emlyn couldn't help asking.

'He's gone back to Townsville. He spends a lot of time down there.' He looked at her intently. 'He was supposed to be helping us this week, but as usual he's let me down. I've put the work back because we were going to camp out there for a few nights, but this application takes priority.'

'Good,' she said briskly.

Travis held her gaze and warmth touched Emlyn's cheeks. She dropped her eyes as he continued.

'To be honest, I don't mind him taking off. It's a lot easier with him not around here.'

'Have you told him about this?' She gestured to the paperwork.

'No. Gavin would be difficult just for the sake of it. He's got a selfish outlook. If there's no immediate benefit to him personally, he'd find a way to wreck the idea.'

'That must make it hard for you here.'

Travis's laugh was grim. 'Emlyn, you don't know the half of it.'

Before she went to bed, she checked her email and wasn't surprised to see a new message from David.

Just touching base, the subject line read.

Her hand hovered over the mouse and she stared at the screen. With a determined nod, she closed the browser and shut down the laptop.

* * *

Travis began to look forward to Emlyn's visit each night. She was a creature of habit, and he could have set the kitchen clock by her arrival and departure times. She would arrive just as the ABC news began and leave at ten-thirty on the dot. The boys knew that they were working on an application together that had the potential to help the station overcome its financial woes.

Knowing Emlyn would be there at seven made them have dinner and get the cleaning done early; the house seemed to be more organised as they got into a routine. Gavin had stayed away all week.

Travis smiled and crossed to the door as the now familiar Troopie pulled up at the front gate. Joel had pulled out the lawn mower this afternoon, and Travis and Jase had cleaned up some of the junk lying around the house.

Emlyn smiled widely as she ran lightly up the steps. 'Someone's been busy.' She gestured to the freshly cut grass. 'I love that smell. It reminds me of going to my grandparents' every Saturday when I was growing up. Lazy Saturday afternoons when I'd play with my cousins and Poppa would mow the lawn. He used to hunt us down to the chook pen to play so we didn't get in his way.'

Her eyes were glowing, and her cheeks were a healthy pink. She looked much healthier than when she'd arrived on New Year's Eve.

'The kettle's boiled and I've got your cup out.' He stood at the table as she pulled out her chair and set up the laptop.

She looked up at him with a smile. 'Thank you.'

Travis frowned as he crossed to the kitchen. For the first time, he was looking at Emlyn as a woman.

A very attractive woman.

The feeling that had run through him when she'd smiled at him was hard to define. He shook his head and lifted down the Earl Grey teabags. She even had him drinking the damn stuff now.

He carried the two cups to the dining-room table and called out to the boys, 'Tea's made if anyone wants a cup.'

'No thanks, Dad,' Jase said.

'Not for me, either.' Joel's response followed quickly.

The door to the sleep-out shut with a sharp click; it would stay that way until he made them turn off the Xbox at midnight.

Emlyn was reading through the rationale that they had finalised last night. 'This is really good,' she said as he sat beside her. 'I'd give us the sponsorship. I think it's a fabulous idea.'

'So how does it work?' Travis pointed to the screen. He wasn't au fait with the university system. 'Do we lodge it electronically or post a printed copy?'

Emlyn shook her head. 'No, it's a meeting. And I'll be there to present our application and answer any questions.' She stretched her arms above her head and the shirt slipped off her shoulder, revealing the fine network of scars on her skin. She flushed and quickly pulled it up as she saw Travis looking at her skin.

He lowered his voice and reached out to put his hand on hers. Emlyn looked up and held his gaze. 'I don't think I've told you how much I appreciate what you're doing. I was pretty rude to you when you first arrived, but you've gone out of your way to help me with this, when you didn't have to.' He rubbed his thumb over the back of her hand. 'You're a good person, Emlyn.'

To his surprise, her eyes filled with tears. Her voice was low and husky, and she shook her head from side to side. 'Oh, no. Oh, no, I'm far from that, Travis.'

Her bottom lip trembled, and sympathy shot through Travis. He reached out and tucked that always errant strand of hair behind her ear, and then they both sat there without speaking.

'I told you, I'm always here if you need an ear, or someone to dump on, you know. I've got broad shoulders.'

'Thank you.' He was even more surprised when she lifted her hand and settled it on his shoulder. 'And yes, you do.'

Her fingers were warm for the few seconds she left her hand there and then she seemed to come to a decision. She took a deep breath, and he felt the shudder through her fingertips.

'I did something very stupid last year, something that resulted in a … a very sad situation. Something that led to the end of my marriage.'

'I'm sorry to hear that.'

'David won't accept that it's over and he keeps emailing me, trying to resurrect old memories and trying to make me feel something, but I don't want to.' Her eyes were fierce. 'It's over, and he needs to accept that.'

Travis picked up his tea and drank it. It was cold. 'Look, Emlyn, I don't want to tell you what to do. I know nothing about your situation, and it's none of my business.' He reached out and took her hand again. 'But make sure you are very, very certain about what you want to do before you say something you don't mean.'

Emlyn pulled her hand away and Travis sensed he might have overstepped the mark with his words. But it was too late to pull back now.

'I've been there, Emlyn. And I've lived without Alison for almost a year. Let me tell you, if there is any love left in your marriage, don't do it. Fight for it. Because it never gets any easier, no matter how much time passes. I've been fighting all that time, and Al's immovable, but I'll never give up. We have three children together and I'll love her until my last breath.

There's nobody else involved, so I'm going to keep trying.'

Emlyn looked up at him and her eyes were awash with unshed tears. 'I appreciate what you said, but ours is a very different situation. There's no happy ending possible. For reasons that I can't—won't—go into, David and I can't be together. It's the only solution, because like I said, I'm the one at fault, not him. He tells me now there is nothing to forgive, but I know that if I go back there, the past will resurface. It would destroy us eventually.'

'Just think about it, okay?'

She nodded, but he got the impression she was just being polite. 'I will.' She straightened in her chair and he could tell that the laugh that came from her mouth was forced. 'Goodness, how did we get so serious? It's time we got back to work.' She clicked on the mouse and the project application filled the screen.

* * *

Emlyn was exhausted when she got back to the camp. The buildings were in darkness; it looked like everyone had gone to bed, but someone—probably Bill—had thoughtfully left the verandah light of the mess building on for her. The air was heavy and still; there'd been no rain apart from the light showers in the first week she'd arrived. The landscape was getting drier every day, the grass was brown, and the cattle were thin. She really hoped that this sponsorship application got accepted. Travis deserved a break. He was a hard worker, a good man, and it was time something went his way. She'd listened to him tonight, really listened to him, and his words had stayed with her.

She opened the door to her donga and put her laptop next to the bed before she headed for a quick shower. As she stood under the cool water, Travis's words went around and around in her thoughts.

Fight for it, he'd said. Because it never gets any easier, no matter how much time passes. It's worth fighting for.

Emlyn closed her eyes and rested her forehead against the tiles. She didn't know the details of Travis's marriage breakup, but it was different to what had happened to her marriage.

To her life.

Fight for it.

Working closely with her colleagues in the lava tubes and learning how to socialise again in the mess at night, and then working with Travis, plus the easy friendship she'd formed with his boys, had helped her a lot. Emlyn knew she was getting better.

She climbed into bed and pulled the laptop across. Opening the browser, she logged on to her Gmail and scanned the inbox, until she found the unopened email from David.

Hi Em,

I hope things are going well up there for you. I know you said you were okay and the others are up there with you, but I just wanted to say hello.

Don't worry. I can see you rolling your eyes. So I'll be brief.

I thought about what you said, and I've decided you're right.

Maybe we should sell the house.

Emlyn put her hand to her chest as her breath caught. Telling David to sell the house had been easy. Knowing that he was going to do it broke her heart. Not being able to picture him in a familiar environment brought a lump to her throat. And knowing that the home they'd created together and shared, one she still loved, would not be there for them any longer made her feel peculiar.

She stared at the screen, but his words ran into each other as she tried to read them. Blinking, she focused again.

I've got a couple of agents coming to do a valuation. I guess it's time for me to stop being unfair, so you can have your share of the house. I won't email again until I have some news.

Goodbye, Em. And please remember how much I love you.

Emlyn closed the laptop, turned off the light and prayed for sleep to take her away.

Chapter 17

'Sorry.' Travis covered a yawn just after ten o'clock two nights later. 'It's been a bloody long day.' He was still in his work clothes, and Emlyn had ignored the smudge of red dust on his cheek.

She'd come over earlier the last two nights and the boys had cooked dinner as she and Travis put in extra hours to finalise the application. Travis had groaned as he'd gone through his files tonight, looking for the various documents that had to be scanned and sent off with the application. Emlyn had shaken her head; for someone as organised as she was, it was an eye-opener to see the various shoeboxes and crates where Travis stored his station records, with no obvious order or logic.

'I might call it a night and head back,' Emlyn said. 'We've got an early start tomorrow, too. But, Travis, we've broken the back of it tonight. We'll make the deadline. You just look for that boundary document'—she flicked a glance at the boxes on the table and smiled— 'and once we scan that and attach it, you're pretty much done.'

There was an easiness between them now; a comfortable camaraderie that had developed since their talk the other night. At first, Emlyn had been embarrassed that she'd let her guard down in front of him, but Travis's kindness had soon dispelled her discomfort.

She stared up at him now as he stretched. His hair was standing on end where he'd been running his fingers through it as they'd worked, and a puff of red dust filled the air. She'd ignored the smell of cattle that had pervaded the air since she'd arrived.

'How much more have we got to do?' he asked.

'There are only a few things to write up and slot in now, once you find that document. Once we establish for sure that we've discovered some new species in the first three weeks of our research, and I can write that into the application, it will strengthen our case even more. Lucy's checking the international databases, and it's looking good for at least three of the discoveries we've made.'

'You're really making a lot of progress over there, then?' Travis stood at the table with his hands on the back of the chair.

'Oh yes. I don't know what's been the best part of the days lately. When we find a likely specimen in the cave, or when we stand behind Lucy as she cross-matches the photos with the database every afternoon.' Her smile was wide. 'Or the thought of this project that we've put together.'

'There's a lot to smile about, then. It's good to see you smiling.' Travis shook his head. 'I've never seen anyone get so excited over insects before.'

'I love my work,' she said simply. She stood and closed her laptop. 'I'll take this back and finalise the projected costs with John. You could come with me to Brisbane to the meeting if you wanted to.'

'When is it?'

'John's just waiting to hear from the committee. It won't be far off. I'd say in the next week or so.'

Travis frowned. 'As much as I'd love to, I can't afford the time away. And who knows what Gavin would do if I left him in charge.'

'The only thing putting a dampener on the process for me is the time I'll have to take out of the tubes, and that drive down to Townsville.' Emlyn fought the yawn that was threatening. 'I'll have to take one of the vans because they need the Troop Carrier here. Or maybe Bill can drive me down, depending on the flight times.' As she leaned forward to gather the files, Emlyn took a deep breath. 'Travis? I've been thinking about what you said the other night.'

'And?'

'I'm going to see David when I'm down in Brisbane.' She injected determination into her voice. 'I'm pretty sure I'm strong enough to talk to him face to face now. I took on board what you said.'

'So, you're going to fight to save your marriage?' he asked quietly.

She shook her head. 'No. Unfortunately it's past that. But I can be kind to David. He's a good man. Things can be amicable. We can organise the sale of our house while I'm there, and then it'll be easier for us …' Her voice almost broke. 'And we can stay friends.'

* * *

The anguish on Emlyn's face was heartbreaking to see. Travis didn't know what had happened in her marriage, but as much as she tried to kid herself, it was obvious she wasn't dealing with it.

'He'll be pleased about that?' Travis said carefully.

She bit her lip and nodded. In one way, he was pleased that Emlyn had taken that positive step. She'd seemed happier over the past week or so, and that air of fragility that he'd noticed when he'd first met her had almost gone. The dark shadows beneath her eyes had lightened and her face held more colour.

She nodded, and her voice caught. 'It's going to be tough, but it's time for closure. We've survived a lot worse.'

Travis moved closer to her as she unplugged the cords of the laptop. 'Emlyn?'

She turned around and her eyes widened when he held his arms open.

'You look like you could do with a hug.'

She smiled as he put his arms around her, and he rested his chin on the top of her head. They stood there quietly for a moment before he spoke. 'I really hope it works out for you. And that you'll be happy with the outcome.'

'Thank you.'

Travis lifted his head as headlights arced across the driveway. 'Unless one of your colleagues is looking for you, I think Gavin's just arrived home.'

Emlyn stepped back and gathered up her notes and photos before placing them into the small leather satchel she'd brought over. 'I'll head off. As soon as Lucy finishes checking all the databases, I'll add our findings to the application. And you look for that document!'

'Yes, ma'am!'

The door opened, and Gavin strode in.

'Sorry. I hope I'm not interrupting anything.'

'No. Emlyn came over to show me what they've found over there.' Close enough to the truth. Travis didn't want Gavin to know what he was doing. Not yet, anyway.

Gavin shot him a cursory glance as he disappeared into the kitchen. He was out a moment later, pulling the top off a stubby.

'I'll see you later,' Emlyn said to Travis and then nodded at Gavin on her way to the door.

Travis waited at the door until she'd driven off.

'Getting cosier, hey, Trav?'

Travis picked up the two coffee cups and headed to the kitchen as Gavin sprawled out on the sofa. 'I told you, it was work. I've been helping Emlyn with the project.'

'Yeah, sure it is. And how could you help her, anyway? What document of yours did she want?'

Travis cursed that he'd overheard Emlyn, and for a moment he considered telling Gavin about the project.

Gavin put his beer on the floor, disinterested and picked up the television remote.

Travis shook his head and looked at his brother. If the application was approved, and was successful, Gavin would get his share of the proceeds, eventually. There was no point getting him involved now; it was enough that the money might lead to a bit more independence for his brother. Maybe he could move to Townsville permanently

'Just a bit of local knowledge they need. I'm going to bed. Are you back to stay? I could do with a hand tomorrow.'

Gavin shrugged. 'I'll see what I've got on. When does the next lot of steers go to the sales?'

Travis walked to his bedroom and closed the door firmly behind him.

* * *

The first tendrils of dawn were colouring the sky rose-pink, and Emlyn picked up her phone to check the time; it was just after five. There was no point trying to get back to sleep.

After a quick shower, she dressed for the day in the tubes, and headed for the mess.

Bill was there already, and she called out to the kitchen as she pushed open the door. 'Morning, Bill.'

He came from the kitchen, wiping his hands on a towel. 'Hey, Em. We haven't seen much of you this week.'

'You've been eating properly, I hope?'

'Yes, Bill. I have been eating properly.' She shot him a grin. 'Thanks for caring.'

'How's it going over there?'

'Good. It's come together well, and it's almost ready for me to go to Brisbane. I'm just waiting to hear when the meeting is before I book my flight.'

'Well, give me a day's notice if you can, and I'll cook ahead and drive you to Townsville.'

'Thank you. You're a sweetheart. I was going to ask, but I didn't want to interfere with your work.'

Bill's laugh was hearty as he gestured to the kitchen. 'Work? This isn't work! Cooking for the six of you? A couple of years ago, I was on a cattle station down at Innamincka and there were four hundred to feed every night. I call this retirement, love.'

'Thank you, then. That'd be great.'

John and Greg walked in together and she filled them in on the progress of the application as they ate breakfast.

'We're going to go in deep today,' John said. 'I know what a difference it'll make to the likelihood of getting funding if we have something spectacular to include.'

Greg lifted his fork and held it in the air with a smile. 'And you don't know the best of it, Emlyn. John and I have been studying the NASA vision while you've been out each night, and we went exploring. We've found another entry point about ten kilometres to the west. And from walking along the top, it appears that the tube goes for a few kilometres unbroken.'

'That's fabulous.'

John nodded. 'I've got no doubt that there's something down there, so I thought we'd go right into the new one today. I asked Bill last night to load the oxygen into the van in case we need it. The entrance isn't far from the road. It's a bit of a drop into the cave. We'll need our climbing gear.' John's eyes crinkled as he grinned. 'I've got a feeling about this one, Emlyn. I don't think anyone has been down this one before.'

* * *

Three hours later, John, Greg and Emlyn, followed by a reluctant Larry, climbed down into the cave. Bill helped them secure the mounts at the top so that they could easily climb back out. The oxygen tanks and camera gear had been lowered down and a dark void opened up ahead of them.

'I've been reading up on the Undara findings,' Greg said as he secured his LED headband. 'The most significant finds over there of diverse species came from the sections like Bayliss Cave.'

'Where the air was foul?' Emlyn asked as she put the backpack over her shoulders.

Greg nodded. 'There are some specimens in the Australian Museum in Sydney, but it's unclear who collected them. It's thought that it might have been a local explorer's club because there's no documentation. They were found in the early eighties and recorded as coming from Bayliss Cave.'

'We didn't know about any of this at the university, did

we?' Emlyn frowned.

'No, we didn't,' Greg said. 'Lucy stumbled across it while she was searching the databases yesterday. It's never been documented because although museum records note that it was one of the original Hawaiian biology team who discovered them, that was discounted because it was before they first came to Undara.'

'Subsequent to the discovery of those specimens,' John added. 'A couple of members of a caving club from up north collected the first specimens of a blind plant hopper, as well as a juvenile located amongst tree roots in the deep, dark zone of Bayliss Cave. So, I'm very hopeful about what we might find today.'

'Come on, let's get exploring.' Emlyn stepped out towards the dark cave. 'Whatever we find will be documented properly.' She peered ahead at the unusual lava tube structure as Larry flashed his bright light ahead of them. It was very different to the tube and caves they'd spent the last three weeks in. The entrance was confined as the floor sloped down, but it was undulating. Greg followed her as she ducked beneath a wall-like ridge.

Emlyn wrinkled her nose at the same time as Greg spoke. 'I think we need to test the air quality before we go any further.'

Larry took a step back. 'I'll go back and wait at the entrance near the tanks while you do that.'

As Greg opened the case with the testing equipment, Emlyn asked, 'Can you taste the air, too?'

John nodded. 'I can. And the excess intrusion of tree roots and the heavy deposits of bat guano is a giveaway.'

Greg ran his test quickly and their suspicions were confirmed. They made their way back to Larry, and soon, the four of them had donned a small oxygen bottle and masks. Greg went ahead to test the air further into the tube.

'Abnormally high, about fifty metres in,' Greg said as he walked back to where they were waiting. 'I think if we start work here and call a halt where the tube turns, we'll be fine.'

'You only *think*?' Larry shook his head, his eyes wide in the shadowed light.

'Sorry,' Greg said with a smile. 'Poor choice of words. We'll be right.'

Larry followed with the camera as the other three worked quietly and systematically through the fine silt and the overlapping tree roots.

The only sound was the occasional grunt of satisfaction as Larry was called over, or as a specimen was carefully bagged. Emlyn worked near the thick deposits of bat guano and her gloves were soon filthy. Her mood was euphoric as she bagged specimen after specimen, and noted down the grid that she was working in. Long-legged spiders, cockroaches, a white scorpion and several beetles that were unlike anything she'd ever seen before.

Emlyn moved further ahead and focused intently on her collection. She'd gathered more specimens in two hours than in the past three weeks. What a lot of time they'd wasted over in the big cave. She reached for her water bottle. Her lips were dry and there was a foul taste in her mouth.

'Em?'

She looked up and the darkness deepened as David stepped from behind a thick tangle of tree roots.

'I've sold the house, Em.'

Her last thought before she passed out was that she'd gone all morning without thinking about David and now he'd interrupted her work.

Chapter 18

He sat at the corner table and watched the waitress take drinks to punters. He was here to have a good time, but he was short on cash tonight. After a while, he got sick of paying top dollar for his drinks in the front bar, so he wandered to the dark and dingy back bar and sat in the corner and checked out the action. This part of the pub was crammed with backpackers. The smell of stale beer and sweaty bodies filled the air, and he sat back as his gaze settled on a group of female backpackers at a table near the bar. He ordered another beer and took it back to the table as an idea came to him.

Easy money, there for the taking. The group of women had been calling out and yelling, trying to catch the notice of anyone who would pay them some attention.

All bar one.

He caught the eye of the young girl as he walked past to get another beer. She was quiet and obviously not a close part of the group. Redheaded and freckled and a bit on the scraggy side, but she was sure to have money.

They wouldn't even miss her. The next time he went to the bar, he walked close to the table and brushed past her. 'Sorry, love,' he said with a friendly smile. The bitches with her didn't even acknowledge him.

'S'okay.' Her accent was broad northern English, and close up she was even rougher around the edges than he'd first thought.

Didn't matter.

He went back to his stool and smiled to himself when she looked up and caught his eye. When he passed her again, he smiled, and satisfaction filled him when she followed him to the counter.

'Can I buy you a drink, sweets?' he asked.

'That'd be lurvly.' The broad accent grated on him, but by the time he'd sorted her, she wouldn't be saying much.

'What's your poison?' He grinned down at her.

'Aye, just a beer.'

He carried the two beers back to his table.

'I'll just get my pack,' she said.

He took the olive-green pill out of his pocket and slipped it into her beer. It had dissolved completely before she came back.

'Local?' he asked.

'No, I've been down at Bowen picking veggies with that lot.' Her face fell. 'We just got paid, and they're heading to Cairns tomorrow, out to the reef, but I have to go back to work. I can't afford it yet. Got a bit more to save up yet.' Her voice was sharp. 'They're all rich bitches on their uni break. Not a worker like me.'

'You got somewhere to stay tonight?' He'd almost licked his lips as she'd carried a huge backpack across with her. It would be easier than the last few times. He'd slipped up badly last visit; that robbery had even made the papers.

'Not yet. Why? You offerin'?'

'Finish your drink, and I'll show you my place.'

She held his eye as she sculled her drink. 'What's yer name?' Her eyes were already getting cloudy. 'I'm Sarah.'

'Lovely to meet you, Sarah.'

Luckily, when he'd been looking for a car park, he'd got the corner space in one across the paddock from the pub and had reversed his vehicle in. It was the darkest corner, and he'd used it a few times. The girl's head slumped to the side as he leaned her against the bonnet before he took her backpack around to the back of the ute. He rested it against the fence that divided the car park from the creek, and then he went back to put her in the passenger seat. Even though she was slightly built, Sarah had long legs. By the time he had her in the seat, she was out like a light.

He slammed the door and went around behind the vehicle again. He opened her backpack and searched through it until he found her purse in the front pocket. He scowled; she hadn't lied about having to go back to work. Four fifties and a five.

Bloody hell. Bugger all.

He took the money and the one credit card out of the pouch, as well as a handful of gold coins. After glancing at the family photo in the plastic square, he threw the purse into the creek. He dug deeper into the backpack and smiled when his fingers reached another plastic wallet. Headlights swept the paddock, and he picked up the backpack and leaned down on the ute tray so his face was hidden. Once there was darkness again, he unzipped the wallet.

Jackpot. Her passport and a bundle of fifty-dollar notes in a rubber band.

'Thank you, Sarah,' he whispered.

After putting the cash in his pocket, he threw the passport into the creek and carried the backpack to the fence. He walked along it until he reached the skip bin near the road. He looked around, and once he was sure there was no one watching, he lifted the lid and threw her backpack in.

Chapter 19

Emlyn was determined to drive to the homestead to tell Travis about their find. The specimens they'd collected today were like gold and were sure to put the seal of approval on the sponsorship application.

As she sat drinking a cup of tea and eating a muffin Bill insisted on before she left, he hovered around her like a worried parent.

'Bill, for the tenth time, I'm fine.' Emlyn tried to allay his fear that she was about to pass out any minute.

'I'll drive you to the homestead. I don't want you behind a wheel. What if you faint again?'

Bill had been at the entrance to the cave when they'd climbed out, and had taken one look at her pallor and known that something had happened down there.

'I'm fine, and I won't pass out again. There's plenty of oxygen here. And I feel okay. No headache, no after-effects at all. So please, stop worrying.'

John nodded. 'She is, Bill. She was only out of it for a few seconds before I noticed that her oxygen bottle was empty, and she got a big swig of carbon dioxide.' He looked apologetically at Emlyn. 'I'm sorry, Emlyn. We were all so engrossed with what was down there, we lost track of the time.'

'You need to be more careful. Bloody insects.' Bill frowned. 'It could have been nasty. Life-threatening even.' He went back into the kitchen, and a minute later, there was a loud crash, followed by a loud shout of, 'Bloody hell!'

John and Emlyn hurried in after him and were met by the sight of cooked pasta all over the floor, and a broken dish. Bill was running his hand under the cold water tap and his face was screwed up with pain.

'Oh, Bill, what happened?' Emlyn hurried over and checked the burn that covered his fingers and palm. 'John, grab the first-aid kit and I'll sort him out.'

When Emlyn left to go the homestead, Bill was sitting in the mess with a disgusted look on his face, and John and Greg were about to serve up dinner.

* * *

Travis was in the kitchen when he heard the knock on the door. Emlyn was standing there, and her eyes were bright and her smile was wide.

'Hi, Travis. I just wanted to let you know we've had a really good day today.'

Travis frowned at her and glanced across at Gavin as he gestured to the kitchen. He'd come home from the coast today in one of his moods. 'Come into the kitchen, Emlyn. I know Joel wanted to ask you something about coming across to the tubes one day.'

'I'm sorry, I did promise him that he could help, but we've been so busy, it totally slipped my mind.'

Travis held open the kitchen door and turned to Gavin. 'Dinner's almost ready.'

'I won't stay long,' Emlyn said. 'Bill's had a bit of an accident, so I'll go back and help clean up after dinner.'

'Is he okay?' Travis closed the door to the kitchen after

Emlyn stepped through ahead of him.

'Yes, he's okay. He burned his hand on some boiling water. He was a bit preoccupied.'

Travis sensed there was more to it, but he didn't press her as she greeted the boys.

'Hi, Emlyn, Dad told us all about the tourist project stuff.' Joel looked up as he drained a pot in the sink. 'Cool.'

'Ssh,' Travis said, gesturing to the lounge room with a nod.

'It is cool, but be careful. Don't you burn yourself, too.' Emlyn smiled as she watched Joel. Travis was keen to hear what had brought Emlyn over here early. He hadn't been expecting her till later tonight.

'You've found something?' he asked quietly.

She nodded. 'We've had an incredible day. And John got an email from the university. We have an appointment next week.'

'Come outside with me.' Travis held out his hand for hers as he walked to the back door.

Her eyes were wary, but she did as he said. Her fingers were cold, despite the warmth inside the house. He listened for a moment after he shut the back door. An occasional clatter and laughter came from the kitchen, but he couldn't hear the television anymore. He led Emlyn down to the small lean-to beneath the verandah.

'We went in a different way, about ten kilometres further west. It was amazing, although we did encounter some bad air briefly.' Her voice was animated as she outlined the significant finds they'd made in just one day. 'Some are possible adaptations to some troglobitic species we already know, but there were many we haven't seen before. Even John was pumped today. He agrees that this will make the application very appealing.'

Travis looked down as Emlyn put her hand on his arm. 'I'd say that in about eighteen months, the tourist facility and the university research will be in full swing here,' she said.

'That's incredible. I'm going to owe you big time if this comes off.'

She shook her head. 'Oh, no. It's just as good for us. It'll mean that we can spend much longer here, and many research papers will come out of it, too. I'm going to predict that *Carlyle Downs* is going to be as well-known a tourist facility as Undara in a few years. It's also been good for me personally. It will make a huge difference to our work if we get approval, and,' she dropped her gaze, 'it's kept me busy and taken my thoughts away from my personal issues and put a lot of things in perspective for me. I know that your main motivation with this is to do with your family—and your wife—but it's been a two-way street.'

Travis looked up as the front door closed quietly above them. A minute later the smell of cigarette smoke drifted down. He pointed up and put his finger to his lips.

'I'll get going now,' Emlyn said, nodding her understanding. 'I'll just go and tell Joel that he can come out with us one day after I return from Brisbane.'

The kitchen door was open, and Travis was surprised to see Gavin in the lounge room when they went back inside.

'I thought you went outside to have a smoke,' Travis said as Emlyn stayed in the kitchen to talk to Joel.

'You deceitful bastard.' Gavin glared at him. 'You wonder why I'm not interested in the place. Did you ever think it's because you don't include me in any of your plans?'

Travis stared at Gavin, his surprise deepening; it was

unusual for Gavin to lose his temper. 'I do include you. And I know you care about the place.'

'Bullshit. And when were you going to tell me about this big tourist project you've been planning with your girlfriend?' Gavin's voice was petulant. 'I've never heard anything so stupid in my life. You think people are really going to pay you to come out here and look at dead insects?' He laughed and shook his head.

'Keep your voice down, mate.' Concern filled Travis. This was a side of Gavin that he'd never seen before. 'It's not like that. And it's confidential, Gavin, so don't go blabbing to anyone about it.'

'I'd be too embarrassed to. I've never heard such a stupid idea.' His face was red as he kept glaring at Travis. 'You knocked back the offer from the mining company, one that would guarantee big money, and yet you're happy to ask thousands of strangers to come and traipse all over the place.' He dropped his gaze and pointed. 'Are you sure you're not just thinking with your—'

'That's enough. I'll tell you all about the proposal later.' Travis glanced towards the kitchen.

'Don't bother. I'm sure you and your new lady have got it all worked out.' He grabbed the packet of cigarettes from the coffee table and opened the front door again. 'Does Alison know she's on the outer?'

Travis ignored him and walked to the kitchen. 'You about to head, Emlyn?'

'Yes. I've got work to do after I help Bill.'

'Come out the back way. Gavin's smoking out the front, and he's got the sulks about not being included in the project.' He held open the door of the Troopie. 'So when are you off to

Brisbane?'

'Thursday.'

'Next Thursday? So soon?'

'The applications close at the end of the month, so we've got in by the skin of our teeth in this round of funding.' She nodded. 'It's all happening.'

'How long will you be away?'

'The meeting's at five o'clock, so I'll fly down that day. Lucy booked my flight this afternoon.' She smiled. 'Bill was worried about me driving down and wanted to take me to Townsville, the pet. I told him I was fine, and now he's hurt his hand, he can't drive anyway. After the meeting, I'll …' She hesitated.

'You'll see your husband?'

She nodded.

'I'm pleased to hear that.' Travis shut the door after she'd climbed into the cabin, and he waited until she put down the window. 'And, Emlyn, thanks again. I can't wait to hear what they say in Brisbane.'

As Emlyn drove off, Travis stood and looked out over the property. He'd lost his appetite after Gavin's serve, so instead of going back inside, he walked down to the back fence, across the paddocks, and climbed the small hill that overlooked the site of the old homestead.

Next Thursday. He couldn't believe it had been just over a week since Emlyn had come up with the idea, and now she was off to the university with a completed proposal, feasibility study, and all the other hoops you had to jump through these days.

If the application was successful, it would mean big changes for the station. Even though the thought of it might sit uncomfortably with him in some ways, there wouldn't be thousands of strangers on the place like Gavin had said. The numbers would be controlled. He wouldn't have to worry about the organisation of it. He wouldn't have to pay the insurance. If the project attracted sponsorship, it would mean he'd take a share of the proceeds, the university could move much more quickly through the tubes, and it was a win-win situation. It was time he went to see his accountant; he'd been avoiding that for the last few months because he already knew what he would hear. The place was going broke, and something would have to be done. Gregor, his accountant, told him the same thing every year on the phone, but they managed to stumble through.

Well, he was taking the first positive steps in that direction. If the sponsorship didn't come about, he would have to give some consideration to Carroglen. As much as he hated that thought, there weren't many options left open, but it was all positive.

Cigarette smoke prickled Travis's nose, and he sighed.

Shit. He wasn't in the mood for more Gavin tonight; he couldn't understand why he'd gone off like that.

'Hey, boss. You're looking a bit thoughtful there.'

'Gidday, mate.' Relief flooded through him when he turned around.

Bluey leaned against the old chimney, the usual cigarette hanging from his lips. The stockman held out the packet of tobacco, but Travis shook his head.

'I gave it away years ago.'

'So you did. I'm getting more forgetful the older I get.'

'What are you doing over this way?' Travis asked as he leaned against the chimney beside Bluey; it was still warm from the afternoon sun. 'I haven't seen you around for a couple of days.' Bluey lived in a small house about four kilometres back on the Mt Surprise road.

'Just enjoying the night. Last chance to wander around before the rain hits. The place has been busy. The missus still here?' Bluey reached into his pocket for a paper and began to roll another cigarette.

Travis shook his head. 'Alison and Cass went home last week, but the boys are home for a while, and the university people will be here for a few more weeks at least.'

Bluey's face darkened. 'They shouldn't be down there, you know. Not in the caves. It's not right.'

'We have to move with the times, Blue,' Travis said. 'The longer I'm on this place, the more I'm realising that. Time moves on, things change.'

Bluey blew out a ring of smoke, but his eyes were dark as he stared at Travis. 'I don't like it. Interfering with nature, that's what it is.'

'I know.' Travis stared past him. 'The place is important to me, too, you know that. But I have to do the best I can for the land and for my family.'

They stood quietly and watched as the light faded. On the horizon, the towering clouds were shot purple and gold by the setting sun. Travis narrowed his eyes and followed the cloud line as far west as he could see. 'So, you reckon the rain's on the way? We've had very little so far this season.'

'It'll be raining by the weekend. You tell them university people it's time to get out.'

'They're not working in the tubes that flood.'

'You just tell them to be careful.'

Before Travis could reply, Bluey walked away and disappeared into the tree line. Travis shook his head. The old bugger was always right. He'd checked the online weather forecast before Emlyn had arrived, and there was no rain predicted—that was one thing the computer was useful for. He'd looked at the synoptic charts, and they hadn't indicated much would change over the next week or so. If the rain was coming, he was going to have to move the cattle away from the springs.

If that was the case, unless he could hire again, he'd need Jase and Joel to help him all week.

There was no point relying on Gavin being around.

Chapter 20

Emlyn was looking forward to going to Brisbane. The next night she sat in front of her laptop debating whether or not to let David know she was coming. The room was filled with the sound of clicking keys as each of the team members entered their data, and Larry and Lucy manipulated photographs. Bill's singing from the kitchen lightened the working environment.

She hadn't told David she was flying down yet because she had been in two minds. They needed closure and that wasn't going happen if he kept emailing her, but they needed to sort out the house sale, and she wanted to establish an amicable relationship. She was in a good place emotionally since she'd talked to Travis. Even though she hadn't told him everything, his words had stayed with her, and she knew she needed to see David to tell him why they couldn't be together. It was time to be honest with him. This trip to Brisbane was the perfect time to do it.

At the same time, she knew that talking to him, and giving the female perspective, had maybe helped Travis understand a little more about how to cope with the deterioration of his marriage. Before she could change her mind, she typed David's email address into a new message. Even typing his name sent a strange feeling through her fingertips—a shakiness that moved straight to her chest. Learning to live a life without him was going to be hard, but she'd made a lot of progress over the past three weeks. A life that no longer had her parents and a life without—

'Emlyn?' Meg's voice was soft beside her as she typed.

Until she turned her head and looked at Meg through a mist of tears, she hadn't realised she was crying.

'Are you okay, sweetie?'

Emlyn bit her lip and shook her head. Before she knew what was happening, Meg had taken her arm and they were walking out to the verandah. She couldn't help but smile through her tears as the smell of curried sausages followed them.

'I don't know how Bill cooks with one hand out of action,' she said, trying to get a normal tone into her voice, but her words were muffled from a throat thick with unshed tears. Meeting with David was going to be so … so final. 'He's a lovely man.'

'He is. He takes good care of everyone here,' Meg said.

They stood side by side looking out over the driveway as the clouds got heavier.

'I'm very lucky.' Emlyn sniffed and wiped her eyes with the handkerchief she'd found in her pocket. A handkerchief with small sprigs of blue flowers and a lace edge that her mother had crocheted.

'Why do you say that?' Meg's voice was soothing, and Emlyn realised that Meg was rubbing her back gently. That brought a fresh swathe of tears. That was how Mum had helped her get to sleep when she was little.

She sniffed. 'Smell that?'

Meg smiled and nodded. 'I do. I heard you tell Bill it was your favourite meal. You're right. He is a good man.'

'You're all good people. I don't think you realise what a godsend you've all been. I know I've been quiet, but I've appreciated your company, and your kindness. And Travis, too, he's been amazing.' Emlyn pushed the handkerchief into her pocket. 'I need to be grateful and lighten up. I know I've been prickly, and I even snapped at poor Larry the other day for no good reason.'

'From what John tells me, he deserves a serve daily.' Meg gave her a wry look. 'I know you've had some sad times, but I want you to know that I think *you're* amazing. You put your head down and soldier on, and the work you've been doing with Travis is over and beyond what anyone expects. I know John thinks you're marvellous.'

Emlyn chuckled. 'We've got a mutual admiration society going here, haven't we?'

'If you ever want to talk about it, I've got a good ear.'

'Thank you. I didn't even realise I was crying until you spoke to me. I'm about to take a step in my journey of going it alone. I emailed David—he was my husband—to tell him I want to see him when I'm in Brisbane next week.'

'Does that make you happy or sad?'

Meg's tone was just like Mum's had been when she had talked to her. Her throat thickened again and she swallowed. 'Sad, I think. Oh, don't get me wrong. I'll be happy to see him. I miss him so much. He was a part of me for so long. I'm just discovering who I am without him again.'

'How long were you married?'

'Almost ten years.'

'Are you going to try to reconcile?'

Emlyn shook her head. 'No, that can never happen.'

'Did he have an affair?'

She put her hand to her mouth. 'Oh my God, no. David would never do that. He loves me.'

'And you love him?'

Emlyn nodded mutely. 'I do. But we can't be together, no matter how much he wants to. I'd destroy us.'

Meg was quiet for a long time as they stared out at the bush. The light was getting dim and the lights on the timer had come on over on the dongas. 'Emlyn, I don't know your circumstances, but I just want to say one thing. If you love your husband and you trust him, I want you to think about trying. No matter what you are trying to tell yourself, there might be an answer.'

Emlyn dropped her gaze to the floor. Dozens of black ants were making their way along the wooden floorboard that joined the steps.

'We all have sad times and tragedy and grief in our lives, but you know what holds it together?' Meg said softly.

She shook her head as more ants joined the line.

'*Love*. It might be trite, but it is the answer.' Meg's hand rested on Emlyn's on the verandah rail. 'When I was in my teens back in the seventies, long before I fell in love with anyone, and long before I met John, there were these little cartoons. I guess you'd call them memes in these days of social media. Little pencil drawings of a cartoon couple, often hiding behind a heart. Every day there was a different one. I used to look for them every day in my father's newspaper. And you know which one I remember the most?'

Emlyn shook her head again.

'Love is looking ahead, not back.' Meg's voice was sad. 'It's helped me a lot over the years, and it's given me a rock-solid marriage. John and I have had our share of hard times, but I always remembered that phrase, and, sweetie,' Meg took both Emlyn's hands in hers, 'trust me, it's so very true. Live in the day and look forwards. You can't change the past, but you can shape your future. If you love your husband, whatever the issue is, try to work through it.'

Emlyn took a deep breath. Two people had told her the same thing in two days. Confusion ran through her. But they were two people who didn't know what had happened; it was her fault that the future couldn't be fixed.

'Promise me you'll think about it?' Meg squeezed her hand as Bill hit the dinner gong.

Emlyn nodded. 'I will.'

* * *

On Monday morning the following week, Emlyn zipped up her waterproof jacket as she and John came out of the mess. The rain had started in earnest yesterday morning and there'd been some discussion over dinner last night as to whether they'd keep working on the western tube.

'I think we'll go back to the original tube,' John said. 'The new one is a bit low and it's an unknown. As long as we can get up the hill, we'll be fine. There's no sign that the high one has ever been under water.'

A ute came down the drive as they headed for the Troopie. Greg and Larry had gone to change into wet-weather gear, and then they had planned an extra-long day in the tubes. Once they were down there, time meant nothing, and the first afternoon they'd spent in the western tube they'd been surprised it had been almost dark when they'd come up to the surface. With Emlyn away in a couple of days and the weather closing in, they weren't sure what the rest of the week was going to bring. There had barely been a break in the downpour since the wet weather had arrived. The bush around the camp had greened up already, but the driveway was muddy and slippery.

The ute slowed as it approached, and Emlyn smiled when Joel pulled up and climbed out.

'Hi, Emlyn,' he said as he nodded at John. 'Professor.'

'I'll go and say goodbye to Meg,' John said after he shook Joel's hand.

'Come and stand under the awning.' Emlyn led Joel to the small carport at the side of the mess. 'The rain was beating steadily on the tin roof above them.

Once they were out of the rain, she asked, 'Is there a problem?'

'Dad asked me to come over and see you. He's flat out with the cattle, and I've got to get back over there and help him and Jase. He tried to call you, but he couldn't get through.'

'I let my phone go flat,' Emlyn apologised. 'What's up?'

'We're going to be busy out on the far boundaries with the cattle for a few days. We have to move a few hundred head across the station because Bluey reckons it's going to flood. Dad said to wish you luck and to say he'll be sending positive thoughts down there for Thursday. Jase and I do too, we think it's an awesome idea.'

'You all be careful out in this weather.'

'We're used to the wet season. Even Uncle Gavin's out there in the rain with Dad today. They've been out since before light.' Joel grinned. 'Dad also said to tell you to drive carefully.'

'Thanks for passing the message on. Tell him I'll call as soon as I know anything. I'll organise something else.'

'I will. Joel stood there awkwardly for a moment. 'Can I tell you something?'

'Fire away.' She tipped her head to the side and waited. Both of Travis's boys were good young men.

'I just want to say thank you. For how good you've been for Dad. He hasn't been happy for a long time, and you've really spurred him on with this proposal.'

Emlyn put up her hands. 'I can't take the credit. It's not just me. John—Professor Kearns—has had a lot to do with the idea.'

'Well, whoever it was, Dad thinks really highly of you. He told us it was all your doing. It will be so cool if this goes ahead. I'd even think about not going to uni and staying here if it happens.' Joel dropped his head and his boots scuffed at the dirt on the edge of the covered area. The rain hadn't come in here yet, and the dirt was hard and dry.

'We'll talk about that in a couple of weeks. I'm happy to advise you.'

'Thanks, Emlyn, you're way cool.' Before she could react, Joel leaned over and kissed her cheek and then took off towards the ute.

* * *

They put in another long day in the tubes. While Greg and John systematically plotted out another one hundred grids, Emlyn worked on the last of those that they'd set up two weeks ago. Four grids to go, and then when they were finished, they could focus the coming weeks on the western tube.

The work was painstaking; each area was forty centimetres square. Emlyn started clearing the corner of each grid with a small brush and swept the soil aside to see if there were any insect remains in the fine dust. Any rocks in the grid were gently prised out of the dirt and examined carefully before being put aside. Larry sat quietly and patiently with his camera at the ready. Over the past weeks, she'd seen a different side to him, and her respect had grown—along with the certainty that they had chosen the right professional for this job.

Emlyn's thoughts were scattered today, and she had to concentrate on what she was doing. She wondered if David had received her email, and hoped that he hadn't got too excited, thinking that it was going to mean reconciliation.

No, that was the wrong term. He'd broached that with her once about three months ago—just after she'd been discharged from hospital and he'd assumed she would be coming home. When she'd told him she was checking into a bed and breakfast for a few weeks, he'd been bewildered.

Reconciliation was a process of finding a way to make two different viewpoints accepted by each party. The bottom line was David thought their marriage could work again.

Emlyn knew it couldn't.

She shook her head as she focused on the perfectly preserved skeleton beside a small rock. 'More light please, Larry.'

He obliged without speaking; Larry was fitting in well with the team now.

'Photo, please.' She sat back as he set up his light and took a photo of the insect skeleton in situ before she gently picked it up with her tweezers and set it in a jar, labelling it with the date and the grid address. That night it would join the other specimens in the makeshift laboratory they'd set up in the small room off the workroom. Already the shelves were full of small labelled jars filled with hard-bodied immatures. But apart from the one new species they'd discovered here, there had been little of major interest in this cave. These specimens were providing a base line for the study and the reports that would be written up.

They had barely scratched the surface yet. There was a lot more work to be done here; the lure of the bad-air cave was the impetus that spurred them on with the slower work in this cave. After she'd placed the specimen in the jar, she stretched and looked around to see how far Greg and John had progressed. Sometimes the scars on her arm burned if she stayed in the one position for too long.

'Cup of tea, anyone?' she called.

'I thought you'd never ask.' Greg turned around with a grin. 'I'm with you. It seems a bit hotter down here today, don't you think?'

'It's the humidity from the rain,' John replied as he stood. 'I'm keeping an eye out for any water in here.'

'Maybe we should take the equipment that we're not using closer to the entrance?' Larry said. 'Actually, I think I'll take most of it back now.'

Greg nodded. 'Better to be safe than sorry. We should be right here, but if there was a flash flood, we don't want to be scrabbling to pull equipment back at the last minute.'

'I think in the interests of safety, if this rain continues for the rest of today we'll have a couple of days back at camp. There's plenty we can catch up on.' He turned to Emlyn with a cheeky smile. 'And there's no need for you to look so happy, Dr Rees. Were you worried we were going to make some more ground-breaking discoveries while you were down in Brisbane?'

The camaraderie between the group was easy now, and Emlyn had become more talkative over the past weeks. One night over dinner, she'd laughed for a couple of minutes at one of Larry's lame jokes and had seen the satisfied look that Meg and Lucy had exchanged.

But it didn't bother her; the more time that passed, the

better she was feeling. The nights had become easier. She was so tired after a day underground, and often a late dinner, and then working into the night, she simply didn't have time to think about everything she'd lost and for that she was grateful.

Chapter 21

Emlyn was up early the next day. The room was dark, and she had to switch on the light before she headed for the shower. It felt strange not to be pulling on her work clothes and work boots, and she stood looking through her backpack for something suitable to wear. Her denim jeans and a long-sleeved chambray shirt over a white T-shirt would have to do. Not corporate enough for the sponsorship meeting, but that was the best she had with her. At least she'd be comfortable on the flight. It was past time she got the rest of her clothes from the house.

She pulled out the small synthetic backpack that she kept for overnight trips, and slipped in her wallet, a change of underwear and her toothbrush. Her phone fitted neatly into her front jeans pocket. Anything else she needed, she could buy or get from the house. Once there was an email back from David, she'd reply and arrange to meet him there tonight. Closing the door behind her, she walked outside and slipped her good leather boots on before she made her way over to the mess. Even this early, the enticing aroma of bacon and eggs was drifting over the camp, and she smiled as she walked into the kitchen.

'You could have had a sleep-in, Bill. Didn't you hear they're staying in today?'

'I did. But you still need feeding before you head out.'

'I could have grabbed some cereal. Easier for you than cooking with a bandaged hand.'

'Stop fussing.' His grin was wide. 'You've got a long

drive ahead. I could have taken you, you know.'

'One-handed, now that'd be safe,' she joked. 'It's okay. I'm a big girl and quite capable of driving myself to the airport.'

'One-handed, now that'd be safe,' she joked. 'It's okay. I'm a big girl and quite capable of driving myself to the airport.'

'Do you good to get away for a few days, love,' Bill said. 'But it'll be quiet here without you. You're such a noisy bugger.' He grinned at her as he broke an egg into the pan one-handed.

She nudged him as she poured a coffee. 'At least you won't have to cook as much with me gone.'

'You got a point there. So, bacon and eggs or pancakes?' he asked. 'I've cooked both.'

'I'll have both. Thank you for getting up to look after me.'

'Just doing what I get paid for, love.'

Emlyn left the kitchen and headed over to check her email before she packed up her laptop. A niggle of nerves hitched in her tummy, but she tried to tell herself it was merely hunger. She opened the email program and looked at the six unread emails from David. They were still in bold font because she hadn't opened them; she'd read them on the trip down.

Clicking on the most recent one, she was surprised to see the brief reply: I'll be home tonight. You come to the house. Can't wait to see you there.

Even though that had been her intention, the tone of the email made her cross, and she was tempted to disagree. Her fingers hovered over the keyboard for a moment before she realised she was overreacting. It made sense for her to go there. They had the future to talk about, and if she stayed, it would save booking into a hotel for one night.

Maybe she would stay. It would be a good opportunity to grab some of her stuff and show David that they could have an amicable parting of the ways. It all depended on how he was, and how he'd take the finality of her packing up her clothes.

It would be hard, but it had to be done. Emlyn snapped the laptop closed and slipped it into its case with the cables and the spare battery she'd left charging overnight as Bill put a loaded plate on the table.

'Breakfast,' he called over to her.

Emlyn drained her coffee and smiled when she looked at the plateful of food. 'Looks like I won't have to eat again today.'

'I've packed a sandwich and some fruit for you, too.' Bill gestured to the brown paper bag next to her plate.

The move to reach over and hug him was spontaneous. 'Thank you.'

'I hope you have a good trip.' He whistled a happy tune as he went back into the kitchen.

Emlyn did the best she could with the loaded plate, then she pushed it aside and glanced at her watch before she picked up her backpack and laptop bag.

'Don't forget your lunch pack,' Bill said as he came out of the kitchen.

'I've got it.'

He waited while she stowed it in the backpack and reached over and pulled her in for a one-armed hug.

'I hope it all goes well. And drive safe in this rain.'

'I will. Thanks, Bill.'

He looked embarrassed as he went back to the kitchen.

Emlyn pushed open the door and waited on the verandah. The rain was still bucketing down; there was no sign of anyone stirring in the other dongas. Last night at dinner, Greg had suggested spending a night in the caves when she returned.

'Before we start on the new grids. To see how much

activity's in there at night.'

'Shift work, eh?' Larry said. 'Was that in my contract?'

'We can write it in,' John said before Emlyn could respond, but Larry had waved his fork in the air.

'Just joking,' he said.

What they'd found so far had been encouraging, and she liked the idea of spending a night down there. When she got back from Brisbane, things would be sorted with David—hopefully—and she could move on and focus totally on her work.

Maybe start thinking about her future and where she would settle.

Not Brisbane. There were too many memories there. Emlyn stared at the rain splashing into the overflowing puddles in the driveway as she waited for the heavy shower to pass. She'd always lived there and had stayed in her hometown to do her university degree. David was a blow-in; he'd grown up in western Queensland in a small town east of Charleville, where his father was still the local school principal. David had talked about taking her there for a visit, but they'd never got there. With their hectic work schedules, there'd been little time to do the long drive, and every time she'd suggested flying to Charleville for a short visit, David had come up with an excuse.

He'd taken to city life like a duck to water; when they'd bought their house, he'd wanted it to be close to the city.

'It'll give our kids so many opportunities.' His expression had always been animated when he'd talked about the children they'd planned on having one day. They'd both come from families where they'd had no siblings, and both of them had dreamed of a large family. They'd found the perfect house in Bardon not long after David got his promotion. Close to the city for him, and close to the university for Emlyn. Best of all was the huge backyard with six towering mango trees, a tree house in one of them and a swing from the low branch of another.

'The owner thought about taking the trees out to sell the house, but—'

The real estate agent had looked at David, whose eyes had widened in horror.

'God, no. That's the best thing about the whole house, isn't it, Em?' he'd said.

Her heart warmed as she remembered his enthusiasm. They'd lived in that house for five years before the invitation to the wedding had arrived.

After their first disastrous camping trip, and once her dad knew that David was the one for Em, they'd gone camping with her parents every opportunity they could get. In national parks, beside rivers, on top of mountains and on the beach, her father had slowly turned David into a seasoned camper. On the long weekend in October the year before last, they'd packed up the tents and headed down to Northern New South Wales to a fabulous spot that Mum and Dad had been visiting for years. Illaroo campground was on the beach and they could lie in the tent and watch the waves break on the sand only a hundred metres away. It was a wonderful hiatus from their busy lives.

'Hope we don't get a tsunami,' David had said as he'd hammered in the tent pegs on the site closest to the sand.

Emlyn had stood there sipping the coffee that Mum had poured from a thermos and watched children playing on the beach.

'You are such a wet blanket, Davy boy,' she said as she smiled at him over the rim of her cup.

'Speaking of wet blankets,' he looked skywards with a grin. 'Is that a rain cloud I spy?'

'Next time we'll leave you at home,' Emlyn said.

David threw down the hammer, jumped up and grabbed her in a close hug, peppering wet kisses over her cheek and neck. 'Oh, sweetie, you'd miss me too much.'

'Oh, you are so romantic.' Emlyn went straight for his ticklish spot, spilling warm coffee over both of them in the process.

'Speaking of romance, you two,' her mother said with an indulgent smile—she was well used to the way that Emlyn and David teased each other. 'Fiona's getting married. The invitations go out next week. A Valentine's Day wedding.'

David picked up the hammer and got back to work. 'Who's Fiona?' he asked.

'One of my cousins from the country,' Emlyn said, turning to her mother. 'Is she getting married in Warwick, Mum?'

'No. They're flying all the guests to North Stradbroke and putting us up in luxury tents for the night after the wedding.'

'Sounds wonderful,' Emlyn said.

'Am I invited?' David asked with a frown.

'Of course you are, David,' Mum said.

He shook his head. 'This little black duck doesn't fly anywhere.'

Emlyn closed down the memory as the rain eased. She unlocked the van and put her laptop and backpack on the passenger seat. With a smile, she put the brown paper bag that Bill had handed her within easy reach. Hurrying around to the driver's side, she ducked her head as the rain began to fall heavily again. It was going to be a wet trip to Townsville. She glanced at her watch, hoping she'd left enough time to get there with the road conditions slowing her down.

'Fingers crossed,' she said quietly as she turned on the car and reversed down the circular drive. As she went to turn onto the dirt road, she remembered her phone charge was low and pulled over to plug it into the car charger.

The road was slippery, and Emlyn eased back on the accelerator. The house was deserted as she drove past and she thought how difficult it would be for them working with the cattle out in the rain and mud. At least Gavin was out there helping.

The road widened as she approached the thicket of black tea trees, but the ruts on the edge were overflowing. As she slowed, the engine coughed and the car almost stalled.

Emlyn frowned. John had asked Bill to check the water and the oil in the van, and she knew he'd had a close look at the tyres after the incident with the Troop Carrier. He'd assured her all was good, but she bit her lip as she considered whether to turn around and swap vehicles.

Another glance at her watch decided her to keep going; she'd just have to risk it. The engine seemed to recover—maybe it had been a bad batch of fuel and had cleared itself. She'd fill up at Greenvale and get the mechanic there to have a quick look at the engine if she had time. She was almost to the Kennedy Development Road when the motor stopped dead. She eased the car over to the side of the muddy road and tried to start it, but the engine didn't even turn over. Reaching for her phone, Emlyn groaned. She hadn't pushed the charger all the way in and the phone was almost flat.

'Bugger, bugger, bugger,' she cursed as the screen flickered and then went black. There was nothing she could do apart from walk back to the dongas. By the time she swapped cars, she wouldn't have enough time to drive to get to the airport to catch her two o'clock flight.

Why hadn't she left earlier? It was too late now to do anything; she wouldn't make it.

She narrowed her eyes. Unless she walked to the main road and could flag someone down who might have a phone. She could call John and one of them could bring out the other van for her.

Coming to a quick decision, she dug in her backpack for her waterproof jacket and slipped it on before climbing out of the van. Leaving everything in the van, she set off for the road as best she could in the slippery red mud.

It was only a minute or so later when the sound of a car reached her. She stopped and turned, waving her arms at the ute appearing out of the mist.

'Is that your van back there?' Gavin peered at her through a half-wound-down window.

'It is. It died on me. I'm so pleased you came along, Gavin. I'm in a tearing hurry, can I use your phone?'

He shook his head. 'Sorry. I don't have one.'

She bit her lip. 'I'm on the way to the airport and I'm running out of time. Could you give me a lift back to the donga so I can swap cars?'

'I can do better than that. I can give you a lift to Townsville. I guess that's the airport you're going to.'

She nodded slowly. 'I thought you were helping move the cattle.'

'I've been out there since dawn, but I have to be in Townsville by lunchtime for a meeting at my rifle club.' He gestured to the other side of the ute. 'You're getting soaked. Jump in.'

Emlyn hurried around to the door, but Gavin had reached

over and opened before she got there.

'Thanks,' she said.

'Have you got stuff in the van?'

'Yes, my bag and computer.' Emlyn looked at her watch as Gavin did a three-point turn. It was almost seven-thirty. 'Are you sure you can take me to the airport and get me there by one?'

'I can. My club isn't far from there.'

'Okay then, thanks. I'll take you up on your offer, I appreciate it.'

Gavin pulled the ute up close to the van and she quickly grabbed her things. The rain had eased slightly, but the clouds loomed dark overhead.

'Thank you,' she said as she stowed the two bags at her feet. Wiping a hand over her wet face, she glanced across at him. 'And thanks again for the offer of a lift. I do appreciate it.'

'My pleasure.' He put the car into gear and the back fishtailed as the wheels churned in the mud. 'We all appreciate the plan you've thought up to save the farm. Least I can do.'

Emlyn looked out the window for a moment before she replied. 'How do you think the road will be?'

'Fine. But I'm going to take another way out to the main road, because I reckon the creek in the first gully on the main road might be up. You probably wouldn't have got through, anyway. There's another road that comes out the other side of Conjuboy. It was good that I found you. I've got something to show you, too. You might be able to mention it at your meeting.'

Emlyn frowned. If Gavin had thought the creek was up why had he been going that way? 'Okay, as long as we're not late getting to the airport.' She nodded and reached for her bag. 'I hope you don't mind, but I'll take the opportunity to go over my notes while you drive.'

'No problem, love. Besides, we haven't got that much to talk about, anyway. I'm not that interested in what you're doing over there, but Travis seems to think it's worth pushing on with, apparently.'

She looked across at Gavin; he was different today. He had an air of confidence that she hadn't seen before, but then she realised it was the first time she'd been alone with him. Maybe he was overshadowed by the other males in the family. 'You don't think it's a good idea?'

'Shit, no! Insects?' A snort followed his laughter. 'It's almost as bad as Travis and his bloody son's obsession with the history of the place. It's all a waste of time, but if it floats your boat, who am I to criticise?'

Emlyn shrugged and tried to be a bit sociable. 'What do you like to do?'

The smile that crossed his face and the silence that followed made her uncomfortable. They weren't even off the station and there was five hours to go—at least. Emlyn bit her lip; she'd dealt with much harder things in her life than being stuck in a car with a jerk for a few hours.

'I've got my rifle club and other things I do. Just a bit of this and a bit of that. Have my fingers in a few different things.' He reached over to open the glove box and Emlyn shrank back as his hand brushed her leg. 'How about some music?'

'That'd be good.' It would mean no more conversation. 'Oh, and I've got some food in my bag, too, so yell out if you get hungry.'

'I will.'

She frowned at him as he rested his elbow on her knee while he fiddled in the glove box. 'Do you want me to get a CD out for you?'

'Yeah. There's a Bloodhound Gang one in there. Do you like them?'

'I don't know. I haven't heard of them.'

Gavin inserted the CD and turned the volume up loud. Emlyn reached forwards and pulled out her laptop as the cabin was filled with a heavy guitar riff.

'Can you work with the music up high? There're a couple of songs you'll like here.' His loud laugh filled the cabin. 'A bit of biology in them.'

Emlyn turned on her laptop, aware that Gavin was glancing at her frequently. Her discomfort increased as the lewd lyrics got louder.

Charming. She set her lips and logged on.

'You got one of those dongles?' he asked over the music as he nodded at the computer. 'Mobile internet for watching movies?'

'No. I'm just working on some data files and then some more work on the sponsorship application.' She put her head back down and focused on opening the program. 'I've got plenty to keep me busy.'

'Shame,' he said. 'I could have suggested some good movies.'

Emlyn lifted her head and regarded him coldly. 'I'm in the mood for work. I appreciate the lift, but I'd be grateful if you'd let me get on with it.'

'Oh, la de da. Too good for some cow cockies from the bush, hey, Doc?' Gavin changed back a gear and Emlyn looked through the windscreen. The terrain was familiar and she realised they were on the road that led to the back gate. They were heading west not east.

A little ripple of anxiety added to the discomfort that had

settled in her chest. 'Where are we going?'

'I told you I've got something to show you. Might make all the difference to your application.'

'There's not time. I have to be at the airport by one.'

'Yeah, I know, you already said.'

'I can't afford to be late. I have to check into my flight.'

'Don't stress. We've got plenty of time. This is a shortcut to the main road.' He reached over and turned off the music. 'You'll be really interested in this. How far do you think you'll get along the tubes?'

'Why do you ask?'

'I was just wondering whether you think you'll get this far.'

'Why? Do you think there's something there that will interest us?'

'Don't stress,' he muttered as the car slowed. 'There's no need to stress.'

Emlyn took a breath as uneasiness trickled down her spine. She knew that she'd been oversensitive with people over the past few months, but there was something about Gavin's behaviour that unnerved her.

She stretched back in the seat and reached into her pocket, wrapping her fingers around her phone. Gavin glanced across at her; his mouth was set, and as he started to slow the car down and turn onto another track where the trees encroached on the narrow dirt road, Emlyn pulled out her phone, hoping there might still be a smidgeon of charge in it.

'What are you doing?' he said.

'I'm just seeing what time it is.' She kept her voice brisk.

'You just looked at your watch.'

'I'm checking my flight times,' she said, relieved when

the screen came on. Opening up a new text message, she started to type.

I'm in a car with Gavin and we are heading west.

Bloody hell. Who could she send it to?

'No point trying to send a text, Doc. Way out of service here.'

'I was just confirming my flight.'

'Were you?' He raised his eyebrows.

The ute travelled along a narrow track. To the right was a high hill covered in the telltale green vegetation that covered the tubes they were working in at the glade.

Maybe I'm worrying for nothing.

But all Emlyn's senses were on high alert. Mum had called it her 'spidey sense,' and right now it was screaming at her to get out of the car.

And how was she going to do that? They must have travelled twenty kilometres already. She'd been out on this track the first week she was here, and she knew there was nothing out here. No farmhouses, no people. Not even any cattle.

'Gavin, I'll ask you one more time. Please turn around and head for the main road. If I don't get to the meeting, it means that the sponsorship won't go ahead. The deadline for the current round of funding applications is today. And it's the only appointment that was left. That's why Travis and I had to rush the application and we worked so hard last week. You can show me when I get back. Okay?'

'Five minutes. That's all it will take.'

She folded her arms, frustrated. He wasn't listening to a word she said. 'All right. Show me whatever it is you want to show me, and then we have to hit the highway.' She glanced down at her phone again. 'Five minutes. Five minutes max.'

The ute slowed, and Gavin nosed the vehicle into a thicket dripping with rainwater.

Chapter 22

***Carlyle Downs*, 1879**

Every opportunity that came their way, the twins headed for the caves. With the road busy with the gold miners heading to the diggings and Father going to Charters Towers to get stores, they were left to their own devices as the weeks went by. Each time they went to the glade they'd followed the long circular caves in a different direction but had seen nothing apart from bats and one large snake.

They still hadn't told anyone about their explorations, although Stanley had quizzed them one morning when he'd overheard them talking. Mother had sent them up to the yards with some fresh baked damper to where Stanley and Wally were working, and then they were supposed to go out to the paddocks and pull out those weeds with the long cottony-looking flowers.

'You didn't ever go back in that place, did you?' Stanley asked as they sat and watched Wally rope the last of the steers.

'What place?' Tommy said innocently.

'Under the ground.' Stanley's eyes were wide.

Tommy caught Missy's eye and shook his head. 'No, Eunice is back from Townsville and we've been at lessons every day.'

Missy crossed her fingers behind her back. 'And we've all been busy with the miners going through.'

'Yeah, them buggers is causing trouble.' Stanley spat out

the gob of tobacco he was chewing and Missy frowned.

'You need to learn some manners.'

'Sorry.' Stanley looked sheepish, but Tommy laughed.

'This is men's work out here. You take the basket back to the house if you want to be a girl.' He leaned away when Missy thumped his arm.

'You can come back now, too. We've got things to do,' she said.

'Wanna go for a swim this afternoon in the springs?' Stanley passed the enamel mug back to Missy and she put it in the basket.

Tommy nudged Missy. 'We have to go and pull out weeds all day.'

Stanley's eyes widened again when Tommy knocked back the offer of a swim, and he shook his head. 'I'll be there if you come at sunset.'

'Okay. Race you back, Missy.' Tommy took off and Missy walked slowly behind him.

They weren't going back to the house, or to the paddocks to pull out weeds. Mother and Eunice had gone to help Father in the station store and the twins had been given the task of taking the morning tea to the yards before they went to the paddocks. Missy had packed extra damper for them and now they were heading off on an adventure. Tommy had stumbled upon another entrance to the caves further from the house when he and Father had been coming back from the far paddocks last week. As soon as he'd seen the rock fall, he knew what it was; he'd told Missy about it that same night.

'I called Father away, because I didn't want him to know it was there. Cripes, Missy, he was almost on top of it, and I ran in the other direction and pretended I'd rolled me ankle.'

'My ankle,' she'd said automatically.

'All bloody right, then. *My* ankle.'

'Is it like the other cave?' she asked.

'No, this one looks easier. I only took a quick look before Father got off his horse and it is sort of like a hole in the roof, but it looked really easy to get into. There's a whole lot of rocks pushed up to the top.'

'And it's closer to where the goldfields are,' Missy said slowly. After they'd seen the big snake, it had taken Tommy a full two weeks to talk Missy into going up to the glade with him again.

'There's sure to be gold in this one. I know there will be. For sure and certain!' Tommy was so happy his words ran together.

'Father did say the miners were moving close to our fence. It's exciting, isn't it? I was going to write about the other cave in my diary, but I was scared Eunice would find it. Imagine what they'll say when we find the gold.' Tommy's eyes gleamed. 'We'll be rich.'

'And I can go to a real school and have all the books I want.'

'Come on, then! Let's go.'

They had the rest of the day to explore before they would be missed.

It was a long walk to the cave entrance that Tommy had stumbled upon. Occasionally, guilt got the better of each of them as they walked, and they stopped to pull weeds along the way.

'We've already walked about five miles.' Missy lagged behind after an hour. 'How much further?'

'There it is!'

She looked across the paddock to where Tommy was

pointing. 'Are you sure? I can't see anything.'

'See that funny-shaped rock over there? That's where the hole was. I'm sure it is.'

Missy walked over and put her hand on the rock. It was warm from the winter sunshine. She leaned forward and peered down. 'It is better than the other one at the glade.'

Once they'd cleared the bush from the edge of the hole, they saw it was easier to enter than the other cave. The roof had caved in and provided a walkway of large rocks straight to the floor.

'Do you think it's safe?' she asked.

'Don't you dare squib out on me now.' Tommy put his hands on his hips and scowled at her.

Missy hitched up her skirt, threw him a glare and climbed over into the hole. 'You can bring the basket with you.'

Half an hour later, they'd walked through two long circular caverns, very different to the ones under the glade. The third cavern was huge with a high roof that had lots of places that let the light in. Tree roots hung from the roof and the occasional bird flitted through the holes before disappearing. As they walked they came to large patches of sunshine where there were more holes above them. Beneath each hole was a small pile of rocks, but it was light and airy; Missy had got over her fear of the dark, and they hadn't seen any more snakes.

Apart from the bats on the ceiling, the flitting birds and the occasional scurrying insects—different to any they'd seen before—there was little life in the caves.

Tommy was determined to find gold, and they'd both whooped as they'd come across some glistening streaks on the rock wall beside them. Today he'd packed a pick in the morning-tea basket.

'Yuk. Look at that.' Tommy stopped in front of her and Missy had to halt suddenly so she didn't bump into him. Even though she was more comfortable in this cave, she still hadn't ventured far from her brother.

'What?'

A strange creature about two inches long edged its way along the ground in front of them.

Tommy leaned down, and Missy pulled him back. 'Don't touch it. It might sting you.'

He shook his head. 'It's only a cockroach, but a big white one. They don't bite.'

'I've never seen a white cockroach before,' she said.

'Our first discovery. We'll have to start a journal and write it all up.'

Missy nodded. 'That's a good plan.'

They were quiet as they trudged further into the cave. As they went deeper, it got darker and Tommy lit the small lantern he'd packed in the basket.

'Maybe this is far enough for today,' Missy said. The flat floor had ended and they had to pick their way up and down through ridges and hollows that went from one side of the cave to the other. She reached for Tommy's arm and held him back. 'Do you think this might flood in the rain?'

Tommy lifted the lantern and looked down at the uneven ground beneath their boots. 'Sure looks like that, don't it.'

'Doesn't it,' Missy corrected him absently as she wrinkled her nose. 'It smells different here, too.' She followed as Tommy moved deeper into the cave and the light behind them faded. Ahead was the entrance to another cave, and they walked until they reached it.

'We have to be getting close to where the gold is,'

Tommy said hopefully. He stumbled and the lantern swayed.

'You be careful with that lantern. If it goes out, we'll never find our way back.'

'Will I turn it off to see how dark it is?'

'No! We need to turn around now. I don't like it in this cave. It smells funny.' Fear began to prick at Missy's neck. There could be monster snakes down here and they'd never see them. She bit her lip as it began to tremble, but there was no way she would let Tommy see she was scared.

Tommy held the lantern higher and the shadows danced across the rock ceiling.

'Look, the ceiling's getting much lower and the passage ahead is narrower.'

'Come on, we've seen enough today. I don't like it here. It's hard to breathe,' Missy said as a strange, shaky feeling ran down her arms and legs.

'Maybe an animal came in here and died. That's what it smells like. A dead beast.' He held the lantern up to his chin and pulled a face. 'Or a dead snake.'

The shadows beneath his eyes and mouth made him look ghostly and Missy squealed. 'Stop it.'

Tommy lowered his voice and pretended to moan. 'Or maybe a person came down here and got lost and it's them we can smell. A body! Maybe the Chinks have beaten us to the gold.'

'Stop it! Right now! You're being stupid.' Missy's voice hitched on a sob. 'And you're really scaring me.'

'I'm sorry.' Tommy moved the lantern to his left hand and held out the other one to her. 'Come on, we'll just go to the end of this passageway and then we'll go back up into the first cave where the sun is and have some dinner. And then we'll have a swim with Stanley later. How's that sound?'

She nodded slowly. 'Just a little bit further, then.'

They shuffled along together, and Missy fought her fear as the passage narrowed and they went deeper into the small cave.

'Oh, gosh. Look at that!' Tommy's voice was full of wonder and Missy stepped to the side and peered around him. The cave came to an end, but there was a circular hole surrounded by fallen rocks ahead of them. The rocks glittered in the light of the lantern.

'Do you think it's gold?' Tommy's voice was hushed.

'Maybe.' Missy followed him over. 'I'll hold the lantern while you get some to take home. Where's your pick?'

'In the basket. We can show Father if we get some.'

'We're not going to tell him we came down here, though.'

'We'll have to if it is gold.'

'He'll skin us alive if he knew we came down here, even if we have gold,' Tommy said.

Missy pondered their dilemma. 'Just see if you can get out a chunk. Look.' She held the lantern up high after he passed it to her. 'There's some over near that hole that's even got more golden bits in it.'

Tommy bent over near the small hole that led into the next cave. He picked one up and held it up to the lantern light, and his eyes widened.

'I think this is a gold nugget. Bring the light closer.'

Missy moved reluctantly to the rock pile as Tommy began to climb up the rocks to look into the next cave. He turned around when he got to the top and gestured for her to climb up.

'Golly, come and see this. It's like a treasure cave. It doesn't go any further. I think we've reached the end.'

'Good, we won't have to come down here again. I really don't like this.' She picked her way to the top of the rocks, holding the lantern in one hand as she used her other to keep her balance. The small cave was about ten feet below them.

'Come on. We'll go down there.'

'I'm not being a sook.' She shook her head as tears threatened again. 'I don't want to.'

'Aw, come on, sis. We'll fill the basket and our pockets and then we'll leave. I'll look after you.'

She shook her head stubbornly.

'Okay. You give me the lantern and you wait here.'

'I'm not staying by myself in the dark.'

'Well, you'll have to come with me. Five minutes, tops. Come on.'

With an exasperated sigh, she took his hand and they climbed down the rock pile.

'Five minutes. I'll be counting. I've had enough of this exploring.' Missy's mouth was dry, and they'd finished the water they'd brought in with them half an hour ago.

The rock pile sloped down steeply to the floor of the smaller cave. As she climbed behind Tommy, a large rock tilted precariously beneath Missy's feet and she grabbed for Tommy, one arm flailing to keep her balance.

'Oh, I thought I was going to fall.' He held onto her until they finally stood on the floor of the cave.

'Look at this, the ground's different here.' Tommy put down the lantern and picked up a clod of dirt. In the other caves, the dust had been fine and silty, but this was sticky like wet mud.

'Yuk, it smells awful,' he said, looking around.

'It smells really wet, just like it does over at the springs. That mouldy smell when the swamp dries up.' Missy wrinkled up her nose.

For the first time, Tommy sounded scared. 'There's no gold in here. It's all dark and dank. Look at the wall, there's water running down it.'

Missy's eyes widened as she stared at the wall. As her eyes became accustomed to the darkness, she could see rivulets of water trickling down where they'd climbed down the rocks. 'I wonder if we're near the river at the gold diggings?' she said quietly.

'We could be. We've walked about the right distance.'

'I've had enough.' She turned away from Tommy. 'Come on.'

'Yes, let's get out.' Tommy shook his head. 'I don't like it in here, either.' A low rumble began above them, and Missy screamed as the rocks they'd climbed down began to roll towards them. Tommy jumped on top of her and pushed her to the ground, shielding her body with his.

It took a few minutes for the loud noise to subside and the choking dust to settle.

'You okay, Missy?' Tommy's voice was croaky.

'I will be when you get off me. The ground's all wet and sticky.'

He stood and held his hand out to her. 'Look, it's light now.'

High above them, a patch of bright sky was visible where some of the roof had fallen in.

'Come on,' he said and then turned around and swore. 'Bollocks.'

'What?' Missy turned to face him and gasped.

The opening they'd climbed through was now a solid wall of fallen rocks.

Chapter 23

Carlyle Downs, **31January**

Gavin opened the door and came around to her side. Emlyn shoved her phone back into her pocket as he walked around the back of the ute. He opened her door and held out his hand to her.

'I'm fine, thank you.'

'You think?'

Irritation and impatience filled her as she climbed out of the car.

'Oh, come on.' He threw her an impatient look. 'I just wanna show you something. Can't you take a bit of teasing?'

Gavin reached for her arm and his fingers bit into the tender skin on her biceps. She tried to pull from his grip, but he started to lead her up the steep incline.

'Gavin, please let me go. I'm quite capable of walking up the hill myself.'

'Come on, Doc.'

Emlyn frowned. 'How far up is the cave?' She looked around as he kept hold of her arm and pulled her up the slope.

'Not far. It won't take long.' His eyes were hard and glittering, and she dragged in a shaky breath. 'Come on, Em.'

'Don't call me that.' Irritation pushed out her sharp response, but he got the message and let her go.

'We're almost there.'

Emlyn looked at him and clenched her hands behind her back, so Gavin couldn't see how much she was shaking. Her arm was burning where his fingers had pressed into the scar tissue. Her mind spun as she tried to think of a way to get him to go back to the car. She didn't know how to react, but one thing she was picking up loud and clear. Gavin's behaviour wasn't normal. Her heart thudded, and her hands were clammy.

How she could get away from him?

'Come up here. I guarantee you're really going to like what I'm going to show you. It's a special place.'

'Is this another entry to the tubes?' She caught up with him; the quicker he showed her, the sooner they'd get back on the road.

Gavin nodded. 'Yes. And the stupid part is, my brother has forgotten all about it. Even though it's raining, it's still bloody hot, isn't it?' His tone was conversational as he rolled up his sleeves and looked up at the clouds. Emlyn had noticed before when the rain had eased patches of blue dotted the western sky. But now her eyes were fixed on his arm. The skin on his right forearm was white and shiny; puckered and wrinkled, the same as the top of her arm had been before her skin graft.

'What happened to your arm?' she asked.

'What happened to your neck?' he threw back at her.

'I was in an accident.' She lifted her head to meet his eyes steadily as they walked towards the top of the hill. She wasn't going to show him how ill at ease she was. 'What about you? What happened?'

'I was trying to do the right thing,' he said, but his smile was ugly. 'But the sad thing was I could never take any credit for my efforts.'

She slipped her hand into her pocket, reassured that her phone was still in there. 'What couldn't you take credit for?'

'I tried to save the house.'

'What house?'

'The house we used to live in when we were kids. The big house where we had our own rooms, and lots of nooks and crannies to hide things. Not like that shit pile Travis calls the family home now.'

'The one that burned down?'

He stared past her and his words were quiet. 'But I couldn't tell them I tried to save it for one very good reason. I wasn't supposed to be there.'

Emlyn's blood ran cold. 'So how did you tell them you burned your arm?' she said slowly.

'I was supposed to be out with Bluey, working with the cattle. Travis was at boarding school. I was always lucky back in those days. Not like now. Blue went back to his ute to get his smokes. I said I'd wait in the paddock, but I got bored when he didn't come back quickly. So, I went home. And I took what I wanted out of Travis's room and out of our father's study.'

He rubbed at his scarred arm. They had almost reached the top of the hill.

'I didn't expect the fire to spread so much. I was only trying to get back at Travis and take the stuff that was important to him.'

'Why?' she asked quietly.

'For bloody always getting everything he wanted. It was only supposed to be a bit of a scare. How was I to know the whole bloody house would burn down? I tried so hard to stop it, but because I wasn't supposed to be there I couldn't tell them I tried to put the fire out.'

'So, what did you say?'

'I told Dad I fell in the campfire while Bluey was shirking

off. And boy, did Bluey cop the blame over it. He moved away to another property for a while after that. Thought the bastard had gone for good, but he fucking came back, of course.'

Emlyn shook her head. 'It sounds like you really tried to do the right thing.'

'And you know, I didn't mind one bit when he went. I hated the way that smug bastard used to look at me. He reckoned he knew everything. I was always scared he'd tell, but he never did.'

'But he came back?'

'As soon as Mum died, Travis got him back to help. Bloody useless old bugger, he is too. If he pulled his weight I wouldn't have to work on the place.'

Gavin turned quickly and grabbed her arm again. His eyes were wide as he shook his head from side to side. 'But poor Travis knew nothing. He thought he'd lost all his wonderful books. And he's lost a lot that's been important to him since then.'

Emlyn stiffened in his grasp and didn't speak. Her eyes dropped to the car keys that he held loosely in his other hand.

Gavin straightened, and his voice changed back to normal as he let go. 'The track's a bit easier now. So, I need to know, do you think your research will bring you this far into the caves?'

Keep him talking. It was her only chance. As he turned to walk between two thick-trunked trees, he held her arm, but she took the opportunity to have a quick look around. About fifty metres to the right there was a thicket of tangled bush.

'I don't think so,' she said. 'We're a long way east of here. It would take years to get this far. We don't have the funding.'

'Good.' His eyes were dark and intense. 'What about if this tourist shit gets going?'

She shrugged, and his grip loosened. 'I doubt it. Or if it does it won't be for a long time.'

'Now come and see what I've got.' He let go of her arm and gestured for her to follow him.

Emlyn held up her arm and pointed to her watch. 'We don't have time. This is taking longer than five minutes.'

He shook his head slowly. 'You're not catching any plane today, Em.'

She ignored the abbreviation of her name this time as the hair lifted on the nape of her neck. 'What are you talking about?'

'I thought you were supposed to be smart.'

Emlyn didn't like the way he was looking at her. She stepped back away from him, her leg muscles tightening, but his eyes narrowed.

'There's no point. There's nowhere to go.'

'Yes, there is. I'm going back to the car. I'll wait for you there.' She went to turn, but he was beside her again.

He held up the car keys and jiggled them in front of her face. 'Forget about the car. And give me your phone.'

Her fingers went to her pocket, her fingers closing around the iPhone. 'Why?' Fear dried her mouth, but she managed to get the word out.

He smiled and held out his hand. 'Give me the phone.'

As she looked over her shoulder, Gavin stepped forwards and shoved his hand into her pocket and squeezed her fingers hard. 'Give me the fucking phone.' He wrenched the phone from her pocket and held it up. 'Well, look here, no service at all! What a shame.' He put it into the back pocket of his jeans. 'But you know what? There is service at the top, so that's why you can't have it, just in case.'

Emlyn stepped back again, but Gavin moved swiftly.

Although she resisted, he pulled her up the last three metres until they reached the crest.

A thick stand of matted vines blocked their view, until he reached in and held up enough of the vine so there was a small space to walk through. He nodded for her to step inside. 'Look what's down here.'

'No. I'm going back to the car, and you can take me back to the camp. I'll get to the airport another way.' Panic was making it difficult to breathe; her lips were trembling, and her words were choppy. Emlyn didn't care about the flight or the meeting anymore; she just wanted to get away from Gavin.

He let the vine drop and grabbed her shoulders, then firmly pushed her towards the curtain of greenery.

'Look inside.' His tone was normal again.

The entry was very different to the glade that had become so familiar to her over the past weeks. The tube in front of her was like a mineshaft with a narrow opening only a couple of steps in front of her feet. She leaned forwards; a rope hung between some rough steps hewn into the dirt at the side of the opening.

'Okay, that's great,' she said. 'Thanks for showing me this. I'll be able to tell the guys how to get here now in case you're not around. Now let's go back to the car.'

'Go down there, Doc.'

'We don't have time. Gavin, I don't know what you're trying to prove, but the joke's over.'

'Get down the fucking hole.' His eyes were dark, and his mouth twisted into a sneer.

'Why?' Emlyn backed away, but he grasped her hand tightly and shoved her towards the hole. She reached desperately for the vines above her head as she teetered on the edge, but the dirt beneath her feet gave way and she pitched forwards. With a scream, she twisted to the side and fell, rolling down the dirt steps and landing with a thud on the hard floor below. Pain shot through her back and hip. It wasn't as far up as she'd first thought. Gavin leaned in and grinned down at her as he began to climb down into the cave, one hand holding the rope.

Emlyn rolled over onto her back and half pushed herself up, using her hands to crab away from the bottom of the rough steps. She pressed herself against the damp dirt wall and a sob broke from her throat as Gavin came closer. He jumped down the last steps and walked over to where she was hard against the wall. Reaching down, he pulled her foot so that she slid back into the area where the light was coming from above. 'Em, it doesn't have to be like this. You play along with me, and it'll be fine. I'll let you go.'

Her breath was coming in short pants as she stared at him.

'Wait till you see what I'm gonna show you.'

The dusty floor was similar to the one in the cave they'd been working in for the last few weeks. Gavin watched as she sat up, and Emlyn grimaced when the sharp pain gripped her back again.

The space was much smaller than any of the caves they'd been in at the glade, and only dim light was coming in from the hole above the centre of the space. Emlyn put one hand on her side as she looked around. The surroundings slowly became clear as her eyes adjusted. She reached behind her with the other hand and her fingers closed around the rock that she'd felt beneath her back as he'd dragged her away from the wall. It was small, but it had a sharp, narrow edge.

'Unfortunately, you won't find any of your special insects in here. I keep the place sprayed,' he said in a soft voice.

A small table with two chairs and a stretcher bed were against the wall next to the steps. The remains of a fire were against the other wall. He watched her look around and up at the perfect, natural chimney. 'I don't light the fire much. It's only to keep the bats out. I don't want the smoke to be seen.' His voice was normal again and he held out one hand to help her to her feet. 'I'm sorry you fell in. I hope you're not too sore.'

Emlyn shook her head. 'I'm fine. Just my back's a bit tender.' She kept the hand holding the rock behind her, as though she was rubbing her back. 'Do you camp out here?'

'You could call it that,' he said.

He pulled her to her feet and Emlyn froze as Gavin's hands settled on her shoulders. Her fingers gripped the rock as she tried to take a step back.

'Come on, Gavin. Let's stop mucking around. You said you had something to show me in here?'

He gestured over to two large metal toolboxes that she hadn't noticed behind the stretcher. 'Before I leave, I wanted you to see how clever I am. No one knows what I've managed to do over the years; they just see me as the hanger-on brother. "Poor Gavin, he's not real smart." Well, I fucking showed them up, didn't I? But you know Travis, and you'll understand what this means.' She sagged as he released her and walked over to the chest. 'One thing you don't know is that I took Alison away from him. He doesn't know why, either. It was fun to see him suffer. God, that hurt him when she left. And now he'll lose you, too.'

'Gavin, there's nothing for Travis to lose. I'm married, and I have a business relationship with him.'

His laugh echoed around the small cave as he opened the toolbox. 'Sure you do. Do I look stupid?'

'No. You don't. I can see how clever you are. Show me what you've got there.' Emlyn's legs shook as fear kicked in.

'Come over here.' He reached into the box and pulled out a plastic zip-lock bag. 'I did a lot of research on document preservation, and I think I've done it pretty well.' He held up a bag and there was a book with a faded cover inside. 'What do you think?'

'It looks like you knew what you were doing. Is it an old book?'

'It is.'

'Can we go back to the car now, please?'

He lifted a book out of the chest. 'You still don't get it, do you?'

He lifted another book out of the chest. 'I took these from the study before I lit the fire. It's the diaries and the stuff that Dad and Travis used to drool over. I tried to get involved, but they wouldn't ever let me be with them. Ironic really. According to them, it was the gold mining that had made the fortune for the first settlers on *Carlyle Downs*. They didn't find the gold. They ripped off the miners and sold them food and cattle and took their gold and any money they had when they arrived.' He held up the old book and laughed. 'And it's all in here. Maybe I inherited the entrepreneurial gene from the first Carlyles.'

'Maybe you did. Now it's time we left.' Emlyn kept her voice strong and matter-of-fact.

'You still don't get it, do you?'

'Tell me what I'm supposed to get.'

'I tried my best to scare you lot off, but it didn't work. It would've been all right if you hadn't hatched this plan for the tourist stuff. I can't let you go down there and chase sponsorship. And once you're off the scene, Travis won't have the get-up and go to do anything about it. With you gone, he won't agree to any more research on the station.'

Emlyn swallowed. He obviously didn't know that the rest of the team had been involved in the discussions. Or that the preliminary information had already been emailed to the university. 'What if I didn't go? What if I said it wouldn't work? Would that make a difference?'

'Of course it wouldn't. Why would I believe you?' He walked over to her and Emlyn held the rock tightly.

'Why don't you want it to go ahead? Surely you can see it will contribute to the saving of the station?' she asked, her voice becoming more desperate as she realised that he wasn't going to listen to anything she said.

'No,' he said slowly. 'What I see is an interfering bitch who's going to ruin all of my plans. You know when you disappear it'll cause enough havoc for them to stop their research.'

'Disappear?' She tried to step away from him, but he grabbed her wrist.

'We're about to sign off on a multimillion-dollar deal with a gold-mining company. A company that wouldn't be interested if there was this sort of crap going on at the station and tying it up in national-park legislation, and God knows what heritage conditions.'

'We?' She widened her eyes. 'Why didn't Travis mention it?'

'Because he's not a part of the deal.' His grin stretched wide over his lips. 'He doesn't even know. Jesus, you should hear him. Blather, blather, blather … gold mines generate about twenty tonnes of toxic waste for every third of an ounce of gold. And that's not to mention the sludge laced with deadly cyanide and toxic heavy metals.' He stared at her, his eyes cold and flat, and a shiver ran down Emlyn's spine. 'And you know what, I don't give a shit. Give me the money, and they can do whatever they want with his precious land.' His laugh chilled her blood. 'And his lovely wife. He never could understand why she took my side. That'll teach him for leaving me to look after her and those three kids while he was out on the boundary.'

'But, how—'

He let go of her hand, turned back to the toolbox, and leaned into it. He pulled out a glossy photograph, and her breath caught as he waved it in front of her.

'This was enough to get sweet Alison to do whatever I wanted her to. She thought we were good mates and she trusted me.'

Emlyn stared at the photo, and her skin prickled.

'Travis went away for a few nights, and Alison and I had a few drinks. She really did like me once. It was easy to slip a little extra something into her glass. So when she was out to it, I was a good brother-in-law and I carried her into bed. It took no time to get her gear off and climb in and take that selfie of us.'

He waved the photo in her face. Alison was naked, and her eyes were closed. She had her head on Gavin's shoulder as he smiled for the camera.

'It looked just like we'd slept together after a few drinks.'

'What did she say when you showed her?'

Again … that awful laugh. 'Oh, she was beside herself. She calmed down when I told her we didn't have sex. I wouldn't go that far. She's my brother's wife.'

He was crazy. Emlyn looked back at the steps, judging the distance.

'Why did you do it?'

'Don't you get it?' His brow wrinkled in a frown. 'I told her I'd show Travis the photo unless she told him to take the offer from Carroglen. But the stupid bastard wouldn't even listen to his own wife.'

'So did you show him?'

Emlyn backed away a couple of steps as he looked at the photograph.

'No. It wouldn't have been fair. Poor Alison did her best, so I did the right thing and brought the photo out here. But they fought about it, and she was so upset, she didn't want to stay on the farm. Her guilt and her worry got too much for her.'

'Poor Alison,' she said softly, taking another step back.

'Yeah, it didn't work out, but the photo was another addition to my collection out here. And now she doesn't like me anymore.'

Gavin lifted out another plastic sleeve, and Emlyn saw her chance.

'Travis isn't going to be happy,' he muttered.

As he flicked through the contents, his back was to her, and she took four silent steps towards the rope hanging from the top of the hole. Her mouth was dry, and her heart was thudding. She gripped the rope with one hand and stepped onto the first rough-cut step.

'Hey! Where do you think you're going?'

The lid of the toolbox slammed down, and Gavin lunged across the small distance between them. Emlyn held the rope and managed to scurry up three more steps before he stretched out one hand, reaching for her leg. Looking down, she flung the rock at his face as hard as she could.

With a harsh yell, he dropped the photos and put his hand over his face. 'You little bitch. You're going to pay for that.'

Her breath ragged in her throat, Emlyn dragged herself up the remaining steps without turning around to see if Gavin was close. Ignoring the pain in her back that was getting worse with each breath, she pulled herself over the edge of the hole onto her stomach, let go of the rope, and rolled.

Dragging herself to her feet, a whimper broke from her lips as Gavin's head appeared through the opening before she pushed the vines aside and took off down the hill.

On each side, dense walls of bush were broken only by a sheer rock cliff on the northern end, and she ran towards the thicket on her left. The rain was misting now, and the ground was slippery with small rocks skittering beneath her boots as she crossed the open scrub. A flash of colour impacted her peripheral vision before she heard Gavin's panting close behind her.

'You might as well stop,' he called out. 'There's nowhere to go that way.'

Anywhere was better than being with him. Emlyn would prefer to trust her survival skills out here in the wilderness than spend another minute with Gavin Carlyle. Flicking her glance from left to right, her heart sank. The bush was thicker ahead, and it would slow her down. If Gavin caught up to her there, she'd have no chance. Cold fear crawled through her stomach— she had to get away from him.

She pushed through the dense undergrowth, ignoring the pain that sliced through her back with each step. Desperately looking around, she noticed a small thicket slightly to her left and ran towards it. Her wet boots slipped in the mud, and she stumbled for a second, grabbing a narrow tree trunk to regain her balance.

Her breath hitched as she ran, perspiration mingling with the raindrops as trailing branches scratched her face. Taking the final step towards the tangle of vines, Emlyn gasped in despair.

She wasn't going to get away from him.

As every second passed, the stream of curses grew louder.

'Stop, you fucking bitch! You are going to be so sorry.'

She risked a glance behind her, but Gavin was still a good thirty meters away. Blood was running down his cheek, and Emlyn pushed on as fast as she could. She spurred herself to run faster, despite the excruciating pain in her back. The ground had evened out, so she ignored the thicket of bush; he'd see her go in there. She ran and ran until the shouts behind her faded.

As the incline began to descend again, her boot caught on a tree root, and she fell, landing hard on her front. The breath rushed out of her lungs, and the pain in her back was unbearable, but she forced herself to go on. Half rolling and half sliding, sharp rocks and tree roots bruised her until her right leg jarred against the rough edge of a fallen tree.

Emlyn leaned against it and listened, but there was no noise coming from behind. The pattering of raindrops on the broad leaves in the trees was the only sound. Lying there, she closed her eyes, trying to ignore the incessant pain burning in her back. She swallowed and fought the wave of nausea.

There was no time to stop. Rolling over onto her front, she strained her head back and looked behind her—Gavin was picking his way slowly down the muddy hillside. Desperately looking around for somewhere to hide, she hitched a sob as a branch snapped under his feet. Emlyn lurched up and willed herself to run.

Suddenly, the ground disappeared beneath her feet, and she was in midair. Her arms flailed as she fell, and darkness surrounded her. Excruciating pain exploded in her neck and head as she hit the ground.

All was still. Dark and quiet.

She lay on her back as waves of pain washed through her. Jagged points of rocks pressed into her back, and she curled her fingers into the wet, sticky ground. Her right leg was at an uncomfortable angle, and she straightened it, but the movement increased the pain in her back. Her head pounded, and the metallic taste of blood filled her mouth as she drew a deep breath, but a strange smell surrounded her.

Emlyn whimpered as prickles of icy cold moved from her chest to her head. As her vision faded to black, Gavin's mocking laugh surrounded her.

Chapter 24

Carlyle Downs, 1879

Tommy had spent the afternoon trying to climb the rocks to reach the opening above them. When he'd realised that there were no handholds within ten feet of the gap above them, he'd starting building a pile of rocks. The small patch of blue sky taunted them with freedom, and Missy helped him carry rocks and stack them into the middle of the cave.

Insects scurried away as she lifted the small rocks away from the edge of the rock fall that had trapped them. She shivered and watched out for snakes each time she lifted a rock.

By the time the light faded, and the first stars pricked the small patch of now indigo sky, they were both puffing from the exertion.

'Tommy.' Missy tugged at his arm as he picked up another rock. 'Stop. We have to have a plan. We can't go on like this. I feel like my heart is going to burst out of my chest it's beating so fast.'

'Mine too.' His voice was trembling as he put the rock he was carrying on the pile in front of them. The pile wasn't even up to waist height yet. 'I have a plan. I'm going to build an escape so we can climb to the top.'

Missy grabbed her brother's hands; they were wet. 'Did you spill our water?'

He shook his head and she peered closer in the quickly fading light. His hands were scraped and bleeding, and blood was running down his arms.

'Oh, Tommy. Look at your poor hands.' The worst Missy had done was scrape her fingernails raw. 'I'll light the lantern for a little while. Come and sit down. We have to make a better plan.' Her voice broke as she looked up at the hole high above them. 'We're never going to reach up there.' The thought of sitting here in the dark was terrifying her. That was when snakes came out; she wasn't going to go to sleep, she would sit up all night. She felt in the front of her pinafore and was relieved to feel her book still in her pocket. And then she realised they couldn't waste the lantern fuel just so she could read through the night.

'Every time I sit down I get dizzy. I don't want to go to sleep. What if they come out to rescue us and we don't hear them?' Tommy sat on the dirt and pulled his legs up. He put his arms across his knees and his back shook. She knew he hated her seeing him cry, so Missy pretended she didn't know he was fighting back tears.

'I'm scared if we go to sleep, we won't wake up.' Her voice quivered, and she swallowed. 'I've got a funny taste in my mouth, and my head is hurting.'

'I know, Missy, me too. What are we going to do?'

Missy sat beside him and pulled her skirt beneath her, so she couldn't feel the cold dirt on her legs. 'It's okay. Father will be out looking by now and he'll have Wally out with him as well.'

'And Stanley.'

'They'll find us. We have to keep our energy so that we can call out. They'll hear us from up there.'

'Do you really think so?' Tommy yawned.

'Of course I do. Wally will track where we walked today.

And they'll see where we pulled weeds out, and the rock fall in the cave. Maybe Father's even digging the other side of it already. We'll have to listen really carefully.'

'He won't be there yet.' Tommy's voice was scornful. 'They would have only just missed us at dinnertime.'

'Mother will be really cross. And then she'll get worried when we don't come home.' Missy screwed up her eyes and pretended they were sitting at the dinner table and this was all a horrible dream. 'She'll probably cry.'

The light from the skylight above gradually faded as scurrying clouds covered the stars. It was pitch dark down in the cave; they hadn't lit the lantern yet.

'You go to sleep and I'll listen,' she said after a while. Tommy sat close beside her as the temperature dropped and the cold seeped up from the floor. Gradually, his head drooped and she moved around so he was leaning on her.

Missy jumped as a slithering noise reached her. 'What was that?' She held herself stiff, waiting for the cold scales of a snake to creep across her bare legs. She tucked her feet up beneath her skirt and folded her arms.

'It's only the leaves brushing on the rocks up there.' Tommy yawned again and Missy fought the yawn that was building in her chest. 'We haven't seen any snakes and there's no mice down here so they won't come looking.'

'They might.' Her voice wavered, and she took a deep breath to fight the tears that threatened again.

'Lean on my shoulder and go to sleep.' Tommy held out his arm. 'It's too early for them to come here. We'll listen in the morning.'

Missy snuggled into his side and closed her eyes.

'Don't worry, sis. I'll look after you.' His voice seemed

to be coming from a long way away and she struggled to hear what he was saying. 'It'll be easier for them to find us in the morning when it's light.'

* * *

Missy woke with a start at the noise of running water. Somehow during the night she'd sat up and now she was leaning on a rock behind her. Her eyes opened, and confusion filled her for a minute, before she realised where she was. Her head was pounding, and she could feel her heart racing. Cold mud was seeping into her pinafore onto the backs of her legs. She rubbed her eyes and looked at the patch of sunlight dappling the rock wall beside her. Tommy was over by the rock wall. He turned around as he tied up his pants.

'I'm sorry, Missy. I had to go. I couldn't hang on anymore.'

'It's okay. Neither can I.' She stretched and looked at the rock wall behind her. 'How did I get here? I don't remember moving over here.'

'When I laid down, I felt funny,' Tommy said. 'I got real tired, and I kept yawning. I couldn't wake you. So, I pulled you up so we were both sitting against the wall. That way I could breathe better.'

'Thank you.' Missy stood and walked over to the corner, and Tommy turned his back while she squatted in the dirt. When she'd finished, she straightened her skirts and walked across to stand in the small patch of sunshine. Tommy had climbed to the top of the rocks he'd piled up yesterday and was craning his neck looking at the high wall. 'I dreamed there was a way to climb up last night, but it's gone.'

'It wasn't real. It was just what you were wishing for.'

'Do you think Father will be here soon?' He pointed up to the opening. 'Maybe we should start calling out now.'

'That's a good idea. We'll take it in turns.' Missy put her hand on her stomach as it gurgled.

'I'm hungry too. I wish we'd brought the basket down in here with us,' Tommy said. He walked over to the rock fall that had blocked the way they had come in. 'Maybe I should climb to the top and try clearing a hole there?'

'No. It's too dangerous, and your hands are too bad.' Missy pointed up to the hole where freedom beckoned. 'That's the way out. We'll each call twice and then count to one hundred under our breath before the other one calls. That will help pass the time till they come.'

'Who goes first?'

'You do,' she said.

'Father! We're here!' Tommy's yell echoed around the cavern and Missy closed her eyes as she began to count.

* * *

When it began to get dark again, and there'd been no one calling out from above them, Missy put her arms around Tommy.

'I'm hungry, Missy.' He stumbled as he walked over to her, and she caught him before he fell. His voice rasped as his tears soaked her shoulder. 'I've got a pain in me belly.'

Hours of calling out had made Missy's voice hoarse, too and she swallowed before she answered. They'd run out of the water in Tommy's canteen just before the sunlight disappeared, and her lips were already dry and sore, but she tried not to think about it. 'It's okay. They'll be here soon. Father will find us.'

'Do you really think so?' Tommy lifted his head.

'Of course he will. Father won't give up.'

'Maybe he thinks we've run away to the goldfields. Maybe that's where he's looking.'

Worse thoughts than that had gone through Missy's head as she'd called out through the day. *Carlyle Downs* was so vast, and there were so many places to look. 'I just hope that Stanley tells Father about the glade and the other cave.'

'But then he'll look there, and they go forever. They won't reach us.'

'Wally will track us. He can do that.' She nodded as she walked across to the middle of the cave and sat down. Tommy followed her over and he put his hand on his belly.

'Come and lie down with me,' Missy said with a yawn.

'Do you think we should lie down?'

'Yes, we need to get our sleep. If we sleep a little bit, we won't get as tired or thirsty.'

Tommy sat beside her and Missy took off her apron. She wrapped it around her book and put it carefully behind them. She lay back and put her head on one side of the padded shape, leaving enough room for Tommy to lie beside her. After a moment he rested his head next to hers.

'Missy?' He sniffed and wiped his nose with the back of his hand.

'Yes?'

'Will you hold my hand, please?'

She reached out, held his hand in hers, and squeezed her eyes shut.

Chapter 25

Carlyle Downs, **31 January 2019**

It was late afternoon when Travis took the call. He pinched the top of his nose and closed his eyes as he listened to Alison. 'Are you sure she's okay?' he asked.

In the year since Alison had left him, he'd only been to Townsville once to visit them. He'd gone down three months after she'd left, foolishly hoping that maybe Alison would be more amenable to reconciliation by then. Over the months, he'd missed out on school functions and milestones in his children's lives, but there'd never been enough time to justify driving down there to go to some minor function and then turn around and come straight back to a station that needed his constant attention. At first, he'd been angry at Alison for taking the kids away from him, but every time he'd tried to talk about it, she'd get upset. In the end, he'd stopped fighting. He couldn't afford legal action for shared custody, and he hadn't wanted to destroy the amicable relationship they had maintained most of the time.

Her call from the hospital this afternoon had jarred him; Alison had been lucky to catch him in the house. He'd only come in to get drench out of the fridge on his way back to the yards. They'd moved most of the cattle in and Jase and Joel had gone out on horseback to collect a few stragglers in the bush.

'No, she's fine. It's some sort of infection. She's on an antibiotic drip and her temperature's come down already.

There's no need to come down. But, Travis, I—' Alison's voice shook. He waited while she paused and cleared her throat; he knew she was crying as the background noise of the hospital faded.

'Yes, what's wrong?'

'I hate to ask you, but I need some money. I've got medical insurance, but I need to pay the three-hundred-dollar excess. I'm a bit short this week, and I'll have to miss some shifts to look after Cass when she comes home.'

'Don't worry. I'll transfer it over now.' Travis opened his eyes and the first thing he saw was the picture of Cassie with the boys that he kept on the fridge. Three beautiful children. All three were blue-eyed and fair like Al, but Cassie had his curls and the same dimple in her chin as he did.

How the hell had he stuffed up so badly?

If he had his way, Alison and Cass would still be home here; he'd take her back in a heartbeat. Talking to Emlyn as they'd worked together over the past few nights had hit him hard. Travis usually managed to keep his feelings contained, but he'd never got over losing Alison. Stupidly, he'd coped with it by working even harder on the station. Ironically, the main catalyst that had caused their marriage to implode had turned out to be the way he dealt with the loss.

'Thank you.'

'Are you okay, Al?' He lowered his voice and imagined her standing alone in the hospital ward. Disgust curled in his stomach; how had it come to this? Their children shared from *Carlyle Downs* to Townsville—almost five hundred kilometres apart. At least the boys were home for a while, but that would only make it harder for Alison, alone in a unit with a sick child. 'Do you want me to send the boys home?'

'No, it's fine. I'll cope.' Her voice was soft, and he closed his eyes again. God, he still loved her so much it hurt.

He'd fallen in love with Alison the first time he'd laid eyes on her in the bar at the agricultural college. Her fine blonde hair, wide blue eyes and quiet manner had drawn him over to the corner where she'd been sitting alone. A friendship had formed that day—a friendship that had eventually turned to love on her side, too, but the friendship had endured through a marriage breakup.

'All right, love. I'll call you tonight. Okay?'

'Yes. I'll talk to you then. And, Travis, tell the boys not to stress. She's fine and they've got it under control. It's nothing sinister.'

'Take care.'

The call disconnected at Alison's end and Travis put the phone back in the cradle. Maybe with all the cattle in, he could get the Collins boy to help Bluey for a couple of days and he and the boys could fly south to surprise Alison and Cass.

He opened the fridge and took out the box of drench. If only he had the time to drive to the hospital, that would be supportive for Alison, but the way things were at the moment it was out of his reach. There was no way he could leave the place with the possibility of a flood looming. Maybe he could send Joel down.

Again, he realised how much he needed Emlyn to get this sponsorship deal. If it was approved, their lives would change. He'd make sure they would, and not just on a financial level. He went to the pantry and took out a box of muesli bars; the boys had already eaten all the food he'd packed this morning. Another hour or so, and they could come in and have some downtime. The boys could have a day off tomorrow; they'd worked hard.

Gavin had left them out there after an hour. He'd complained incessantly about the rain, and Travis was pleased when he'd finally taken off muttering about getting something from a hut. There was no sign of him or his ute in the shed. If only he could trust his brother to look after the place, things would be different.

As Travis pulled the front door shut behind him and turned to go down the steps, the noise of a vehicle coming along the road from the north caught his attention. He went down to the ute and threw the two boxes onto the seat and waited. It was unusual to have passing traffic on this road, and especially in wet conditions after the few inches of rain they'd had.

A white Pajero, the sides splattered with mud, slowed and then turned into the driveway and parked beside his ute. His eyes widened as two men in suits got out and closed the doors, before walking across to him.

'Travis Carlyle?' the taller of the two men asked.

'Yes.' He nodded. 'What can I do for you?'

'I'm Detective Inspector Jim Blake, and this is Detective Brett Baker. We'd like to have a few words with you.' Both their expressions were closed, and the introduction was terse.

'What's wrong? There hasn't been an accident, has there?'

'No. Can we do this inside?' Blake gestured to the house.

'Certainly.' Travis frowned. A few months ago, a couple of police officers from Stock and Rural Crime Investigation Squad had called in to ask him about some cattle thefts on a neighbouring station, but he'd heard no more.

'Can I get you a cold drink or a cuppa?' he asked once they'd sat down. 'It's a long drive from Mt Surprise.'

'No, thank you,' the detective inspector replied. 'And

we've come from Townsville.'

'Townsville?' Travis sat on the chair opposite the sofa. 'Okay, how can I help you?'

'First of all, we need to confirm you are Travis Thomas Carlyle.' The detective inspector was doing the talking and the other guy had pulled out a notepad and a couple of sheets of paper.

He nodded. 'That's correct.'

'And you are the owner of an apartment in Stuart Street in North Ward in Townsville?'

Relief coursed through Travis; he hadn't liked their attitude. 'Sorry, it looks like you've had a wasted trip. That's not me.'

'I need you to be truthful, Mr Carlyle. This is a serious matter, and if necessary, we'll take you back to the station in Townsville for further questioning.'

Travis shook his head, bemused. 'Look, you've obviously got me mixed up with another Travis Carlyle here. I don't own any property anywhere apart from here—*Carlyle Downs*. Surely there are records you can check.'

The detective nodded, his expression grim as he stared at Travis. 'You're correct. As you say, there are, and we have. What's your date of birth?'

'The tenth of the third, seventy-five.'

The other detective picked up one of the pieces of paper and passed it to the inspector with a brief nod. He glanced at it and passed it to Travis.

'This is a copy of the strata invoice for the apartment.'

Travis looked down at it. The invoice was made out to someone with his name and was addressed to a post-office box in Townsville. Again, he shook his head. 'Look, there's a mistake. I don't have an apartment or a post-office box in Townsville.'

'Were you in Townsville on the fifth of January?'

Frustration coursed through Travis. 'Mate, I haven't been to Townsville in the past six months or so. I'm not sure what you're on about, but I'll say it again. You're talking to the wrong person.'

The inspector glanced across at his colleague and he handed another piece of paper to Travis. 'You have an account with the City Bank in Townsville? And can you confirm this is you identified on this bank record?'

Travis skimmed the document, and anger gripped his chest at the breach of privacy. The details on this document were correct: his name, address at *Carlyle Downs*, and his date of birth. 'Yes, this is my *private* bank information, but I'd like to have it noted down that I'm angry that my private details have been accessed. That's one of the reasons I don't do online banking. But it seems my details can be pulled up at a whim? Where's the privacy in that?'

'We're investigating a very serious matter, Mr Carlyle. If you'd look at this, you can see that we know that the apartment is yours. This is a record of the strata fees coming out of your account. The account you've just confirmed as yours.'

Travis took the bank statement that was handed to him. His name was at the top, but when he scanned the document, he laughed. The account number was unfamiliar, and the deposits and withdrawals were larger than any he'd made since the last cattle were sold for live export about seven years ago. 'Mate, you've got the wrong end of the stick. This isn't my account.' His eyes flicked to the bottom of the page. 'About the only thing like my account is the current low balance.'

'Perhaps you can explain to us how that's occurred. It's in your name, it uses your identification, and it pays the fees on your unit. It's also been used to purchase significant amounts of cryptocurrency.'

'What?' Travis's breath caught as he stared at the detective. 'What did you say?'

The inspector repeated the words. 'It's been used to purchase significant amounts of cryptocurrency.'

A cold feeling settled in his chest as the words hit Travis. 'Cryptocurrency?'

'Enough of this prevarication. Mr Carlyle, would you please roll up your sleeves?'

'What?'

'Roll up your sleeves.'

Travis unbuttoned both cuffs of his work shirt and rolled them up to his elbows. Both men stared at his forearms and then exchanged a glance.

'Can you confirm your whereabouts on the fifteenth of January?'

'Yes, I was here. I haven't been off the place since I went to Mt Surprise for a cattlemen's meeting about three months ago.'

'Is there anyone who can confirm that?'

'Yes, my boys have been home since just after Christmas, and I see the group over at the university camp a few times every week.' When the inspector frowned, Travis went on to explain about the research that was currently underway in the tubes. He picked up one of the newspapers from the coffee table and glanced at the date. 'The fifteenth, you said? That would have been a couple of weeks ago?'

'Tuesday, two weeks ago.'

'Okay, as well as my sons, my stockman, Dr Rees and most of the university workers will be able to confirm that I was here.'

'Thank you. We'll talk to your sons and to Dr Rees. It does sound like there has been some confusion.' The detective leaned back in the chair and his set expression lightened slightly. 'Is that offer of a cuppa still on?'

Travis went to the kitchen and put the jug on. As he reached for the teabags and the sugar, his mind was working furiously. Until he knew what was going on, he didn't want to mention Gavin, but the mention of cryptocurrency had sent a hollow feeling in his stomach, but the unit and the bank account were a mystery.

As he carried the mugs of tea into the lounge, the boys rode past, heading towards the yards, a couple of beasts ahead of them. 'There're my boys now. They'll be here soon.'

'And Dr Rees? Where would we find her?'

'Normally over at the camp. It's about three kilometres further along this road, but I know she's away. She left early this morning to head for the airport at Townsville. She's going to Brisbane this afternoon for a couple of days.' Travis lifted his mug and took a sip as he gathered his thoughts. Finally, he set his cup down and held the detective's eye.

'There must be something serious going on if you've taken the trip from Townsville to talk to me. May I ask what the investigation is about?'

Detective Inspector Blake held his gaze steadily. 'Over the past few months, there have been several assaults and robberies involving female backpackers around pubs in Townsville.'

'Yes? Go on. I'm interested to hear how the hell you think

I could be involved in that. How that led you up here to me?'

'Last week, an English girl was robbed and taken to a location in a car. When her assailant left her in the car, she woke and took note of her surroundings. She pretended to be asleep when he came back. We have good reason to believe she was drugged with a date-rape drug.'

'Are you saying she was sexually assaulted?' Travis's gut churned as he thought back; Gavin had been in Townsville on the fifteenth.

'No. At this stage we don't believe any of the assaults are sexually motivated. It appears that robbery is the main motive.'

'Can I ask one more thing?'

The detective nodded.

'Why did you want to look at my arms?'

'The man who assaulted the English girl had a severely scarred right forearm. A burn injury. And the address was the unit that you say isn't yours.'

Travis leaned forward and covered his face with his hands.

* * *

'Gavin.' Travis nodded at the detective when Gavin picked up the call. 'Where are you?'

Once he'd told them that it was Gavin whose right arm had been scarred from a childhood burn, they'd swung into action. At their request, he'd called Gavin. The revelations about the unit and the bank account that had somehow been started in his name, and the amounts that had gone in and out of the account had left him reeling. He knew his brother had issues, but the thought that he'd been involved in the sort of thing the detective had described made him sick to the stomach.

'Travis? What's wrong?' Gavin sounded impatient.

'I've got a problem up here. I need you.'

'What problem?'

Travis thought quickly. 'Cassie's in hospital and the boys have to go down to Alison's to help her out. I need you back here as quick as you can get here. Have you dropped Emlyn off yet?'

'Yeah. But I already told you I had an appointment down here. I'm not going to turn around and drive straight back up there.'

'So where will you be tonight?'

'Why?'

As Travis waited he thought he heard a flight called in the background. 'Are you at the airport?'

No,' Gavin snapped. 'I'm at the shops. Is that all right with you?'

Travis looked up as Blake gestured to him to let it go. 'Okay, okay, don't get shitty with me. Just get back here as soon as you can. I've still got cattle to move and the water's coming up fast.' He ended the call without saying goodbye, as he would if he had the shits with Gavin. He turned thoughtfully to the detective.

'He said he's at a shopping centre but I'd swear I heard a flight called when I was waiting for him to answer.'

'What do you think he was doing? Would he be flying somewhere?'

Travis shrugged. 'I doubt it. But from what you've told me, I'm beginning to wonder if I know my brother at all.'

Chapter 26

Travis was too wired to sleep. He sat at the kitchen table in the dark, long after the boys had gone to bed. Alison had called earlier to tell him that they were home from the hospital and that Cassie was much better. Relieved to know that she was on the road to recovery, he'd let his thoughts go to Gavin. Disgust warred with disappointment and anger that he'd had no idea what his brother was up to. He cupped his hands around the now cold mug of coffee and wallowed in self-disgust.

If everything that the police had said was true—and he had no doubt that most, if not all, was right—Gavin would be up on fraud charges, and even worse, assault and robbery. In a way, he blamed himself for letting Gavin get away with so much, but he'd always felt a strange sort of responsibility for him, even as adults, particularly since their mother had begged Travis to look out for his brother.

His mum's eyes had been full of sadness as she'd gripped Travis's hand, her own hand thin and her rings rolling loosely around claw-like fingers.

'Please promise me you'll take care of your brother, please. He's not like you, Travis. He's different and he needs a lot of guidance. That's why we couldn't send him away to school like we sent you. We tried once. I never told your father …'

'Told him what, Mum?'

'Gavin hurt me a few times—physically—but I didn't want to make things worse for him. I blamed myself. I was the only one he was cruel to. I went to a doctor and he gave me some anger management things to try, and it seemed to work for a while. So you have to promise me you'll take care of him …'

He'd promised, and he could remember the day as though it was yesterday, but it was over fifteen years ago. Alison had been out in the waiting room on the verandah with the twins—he could still hear the toys clattering on the wooden floor of the cottage hospital at Mt Surprise. Gavin hadn't even bothered to come to the hospital. It was at times like that Travis knew there was something different about him. Most people took him as being shy, but he used that perception to cover a calculating nature where getting his own way was the only thing that mattered. He was whip-smart, and his mathematical ability and computer skills were extraordinary, but his lack of a work ethic—and the fact that he let a lot of people down—never seemed to bother him. Having to pull his weight on the station had caused so many disagreements over the last two years Travis had almost given up.

It was always about Gavin, and Travis knew he'd been guilty of letting him get away with it, too. Maybe if he'd been harder, it wouldn't have come to this. He stood and crossed to the sink and rinsed his cup.

Fraud and assault. And that bloody bank account. The amounts that had gone in and out of the account were staggering. Anger began to simmer. Not only had he somehow started an account in Travis's name, Gavin had had the hide to keep taking money from the property, when he'd been making so much on the side. He closed his eyes and wondered what the hell he was going to do. One of the first things would be a trip to Townsville to the bank.

As Travis turned towards the door, headlights arced

across the wall before a vehicle turned into the driveway. He hurried to the window, wondering what he would do if it was Gavin. Blake had said if his brother turned up to call the police, no matter what time of day it was. The headlights went out, and as the door opened, Travis realised it wasn't Gavin's red ute but the Troop Carrier that Emlyn usually drove.

In all the drama of the afternoon, he'd only given a fleeting thought to her meeting at the university. He'd half expected her to call when it was over, but he knew she'd been going to see her husband tonight. She'd call with news when she was able to—if there was any news. Now he had a hell of a lot more to worry about than the sponsorship deal.

Travis opened the front door and walked down the steps, surprised to see both Greg and John get out of the Troopie.

'Is everything okay?' he asked.

John stood beside the car. 'We hope so. Have you heard from Emlyn?'

The hair rose on the back of Travis's neck. 'Why, what's wrong?'

'She didn't go to the meeting, and she hasn't turned up at her husband's place. David called a little while ago, trying to find out which flight she was on and where she could be.'

'Has he tried calling her?' Travis frowned. 'Come inside, it's too wet to stand out here.' He opened the front door and ushered them in. 'I've been dealing with the cattle most of the day, but there weren't any messages on the phone when I came in.' Travis sat down and stared at John as he sat opposite him.

'Yes, we've all tried to call, but her phone goes straight to voicemail.' John leaned forward and lowered his voice. 'David is very concerned for her wellbeing. She's had some pretty rough times over the past year, and he'd been worried about her being up here alone for the few days before the rest of us arrived. He said he called her once and then she turned off her phone, so he was emailing her every night, and she was replying.'

A muscle jumped in Travis's cheek, and he bit down as a surge of concern shot through him. He held the professor's gaze steadily and focused on keeping his voice level.

'Can you talk to the airline? Maybe the flight was delayed.'

John shook his head. 'The meeting was scheduled for five. I've been on tenterhooks waiting for her to call as she promised, and then David rang.'

'Lucy said she booked her onto the early-afternoon Jetstar flight,' Greg said. 'She should have landed in Brisbane about three and Lucy said she had a cab charge to go straight to the uni.

'Lucy's already tried the airline,' John interjected, 'but it's almost impossible to talk to a real person. The lines are busy, and with school going back this week, it's worse than usual. Besides, there're privacy issues, and they probably wouldn't be prepared to say if she was on the flight or not.'

Travis sat back down. 'Has anyone called the police yet?'

'I don't think so. It's only been a few hours, and David wondered if he was overreacting, but I do know he's worried. And so am I.' He held Travis's gaze. 'Do you know much of Emlyn's story, Travis?'

He shook his head. 'I know she's separated from her husband, and I assumed she'd been in an accident. She did tell me she'd been in hospital when she felt faint one afternoon, and I've noticed the burn scars on her forehead and arms. And she didn't look well when she arrived.' Travis ran his hand through his hair.

'It's not common knowledge at the university. Emlyn is a very private person. But in terms of mental health, she's struggled significantly over the past year. All I know is that she was in a light plane crash last year, and she lost several family members, including her parents.'

'Jesus, that'd mess with anyone's mental health. But surely you don't think …?'

'Emlyn's mental health wasn't good for many months, but David said she was recovering well. I know that she's over the moon about our research here, and she's been particularly focused on the initiative that you've been working on with her.'

'But there's still some concern that she's decided to disappear?' Travis shook his head. 'Mate, I know I don't know Emlyn's history, but she hasn't given me the impression of someone who was considering disappearing.'

John's voice was controlled, but it was clear how concerned he was. 'David would know her better than anyone, and he's worried that she has decided to disappear—or worse.'

Travis stood and walked across the room; it was too hard to stay sitting down. 'No. I can't accept that. Emlyn and I have had some heart-to-heart chats as we've worked together. As you say, she was excited about this project, and she was looking forward to seeing her husband. When she left here last night, she was almost bubbling over with anticipation of talking to the university about the project.' Travis didn't want to breach Emlyn's privacy and share with John the intimate discussions they'd had about her marriage, even though he knew how determined she'd been to talk to her husband about the future. Maybe he'd misread her, but he didn't think so.

John nodded. 'I know, that's why we've come over at this late hour. Maybe something's happened. Maybe she took ill and is in a hospital somewhere. Maybe there was an accident.' He shook his head. 'Emlyn was very keen to get back here quickly; she didn't want to miss out on something while she was away. She was only staying away two nights because she didn't want to miss any time in the tubes.'

Travis sat back down. 'I need to be frank with you.' He lifted his hand to his chin and the stubble rasped beneath his fingers. 'The police have already been here this afternoon. My brother is involved in something—something I had absolutely no idea about—but that's another story. I think David's right, though. We need to be worried.' He pulled his phone out. 'I'm going to call the detectives who were here today. I'm sure they'll get onto the airline and see if Emlyn was on the flight.'

He pulled his mobile out of his shirt pocket and checked the bars. He'd put Blake's number into his phone. Despite the late hour, the call was picked up straight away.

'Detective Blake, it's Travis Carlyle. We have a problem.'

Chapter 27

Brisbane CBD, I February, 9 am

Eric de Vere, CEO of Carroglen Gold, welcomed Gavin and his mate, Rod, into the conference room of the Park Regis Hotel in Brisbane. Having to fly to Brisbane for the final meeting with the gold-mining company—along with the new suit he'd bought—had almost taken the whole cheque that Travis had given him the other day. But if the deal was to go ahead, Gavin knew he had to look and act like a player. Everything—his finances and his future—hinged on this final meeting today. He'd sorted out that sponsorship issue, but having to leave the bitch in the bush had worried him.

With a bit of luck, she'd bloody die out there. If she was ever found in that cave—and the chances of that were very slim—he'd be long gone. He'd only just made the airport with a few minutes to spare, after he'd taken a quick detour to dump her phone at the top of Castle Hill lookout. He hoped she had location services turned on, because he'd held it with the bottom of his T-shirt and made sure it was switched on before he'd thrown it out of the window. Once it was found, they'd think she'd been up there.

Then Travis had called full of bloody questions while he was waiting for his flight, and for a while he'd thought that the bitch had already got out and made her way back to their house. On the plane, he'd calmed himself; there was no way she could have got out of that cave. And she was miles from anywhere; no one ever went out that way.

A huge sense of relief rushed through Gavin as they entered the conference room, and he glanced at Rod. The beauty of the meeting being in Brisbane was that Rod lived there—and worked as an actor—and he'd agreed to come along with him and take on the persona of Travis Carlyle. He'd stayed at Rod's place in West End last night and taken him through the whole scene. It had cost him the last of the cash he'd taken from the English girl's wallet, but it was worth it.

But after today ...

De Vere shook his hand and looked at his face. 'Nasty cut you've got there, Gavin.'

'Yeah, I took a tumble off a horse yesterday. I was lucky.'

De Vere held his hand out to Rod. 'I'm very pleased you could come this time, Travis. It's good to finally meet you.'

'I'm pleased I was able to come. The station and my kids keep me busy, but I had every faith in Gavin's ability to negotiate us to this point. We're a solid family alliance now that there're only the two of us left.'

Don't overdo it, Rod, Gavin thought.

'It's time for all of us,' de Vere began once they were all seated at the conference table. 'Gold is certainly living up to its reputation as a haven for investors to park their currency. Brexit, Trump and volatile global interest rates have been good for our industry. The contracts have been drawn up, and once we clear up a couple more questions, we can sign off on the deal this afternoon.'

Once the social chit-chat was over, de Vere turned to Rod. 'We've taken your brother through the process in detail over the past couple of months, and I need to confirm that you are also behind us one hundred percent. There'll be significant disruption to the back end of your property, and if the initial seam that we've found continues east, we'll be following it all the way over the next few years. The lease we've taken up extends twenty kilometres into your property.'

Rod raised his hand. 'Gavin has kept me in the loop after every meeting and I'm happy to sign the agreement. Our solicitor has looked it over, and there's nothing to amend.'

Good, Rod was sticking to the script now.

'Excellent.' De Vere's words echoed Gavin's thoughts. 'There've been some interesting finds. The drillers came across some of the historical diggings from the nineteenth century. The pioneer miners were on your property. There's no doubt there's gold in "them thar hills."' He put on a fake cowboy accent on top of his American accent and Gavin laughed politely. He could have told de Vere that. He had more in his cave stash, and he'd planned to sell them one day, but now he didn't need the money and he had no intention of going back to *Carlyle Downs* after he got the funds. He only had one regret: he would have loved to see the look on Travis's face.

Despite the air-conditioning pumping into the room, perspiration was soaking Gavin's shirt. He just wanted to get this over and done with, take the deposit cheque and run. De Vere sat back and folded his hands.

'My PA is just running off copies of the documents down in the business centre. So a couple more points to clarify, and then I think we're right to sign.'

Gavin slipped a finger inside his collar and loosened it; it was getting hard to breathe in this monkey suit.

Rod leaned forward. 'Yes?'

'Heritage listings.' De Vere stared at Rod. 'We've

checked the state heritage register, of course and there's nothing on there, otherwise we wouldn't be here today. There are no buildings, homesteads or anything else of significance that could impact us in the future that you're aware of?'

Gavin bit back a smile and frowned. 'What year was it the old homestead burned down, Rod?' He hadn't primed Rod about the fire. 'That would have been the only building. But sadly, it's gone now.'

'Ah, let me think? How old was I?' Rod came back quickly, holding Gavin's eye.

'I was fourteen, so that would have been 1987.'

'Good. I'll get you to sign that addendum on the contract when Peter comes back. Now, to the best of your knowledge, is there anything of archaeological significance or Aboriginal cultural heritage on the property?'

Gavin schooled his face into a serious expression and looked at Rod.

Rod shook his head. 'Nothing.'

Gavin chipped in. 'Just acres of flat grasslands that are good for nothing except cattle.' He shook his head. 'As much as we didn't want the mine to go ahead, financially we have no other option.'

'And finally,' de Vere looked up as the door opened and a man walked in holding couple of folders. 'Excellent. Thank you, Peter,' he said as he took the folders before sitting at the end of the table. De Vere quickly introduced them to his PA and Gavin fought the urge to tap his fingers on the table.

Just get to the bloody money.

'So back to where we were.' De Vere looked steadily at them both. 'Finally, to the best of your knowledge, there is nothing on the property that may be environmentally sensitive and impact on the future of mining on the land?'

Gavin tried not to let his relief show. He put his hand to his mouth and muffled the sigh with a cough. The final handicap was overcome. It looked like they hadn't seen either the early interest of National Parks a few years back or knew about the university stuff that was happening. None of it mattered because they'd be gone in a few weeks. Travis's sponsorship deal was dead in the water, anyway.

He and Rod looked at each other and both denied any knowledge. 'No, just a working cattle station.'

De Vere nodded to the fridge in the corner. 'Peter, if you would?'

As Rod and Gavin signed the contracts that were on the table—Rod had practised Travis's signature last night until he had it down pat—the PA put three glasses on the table and opened a bottle of champagne.

'Thank you, gentlemen. Carroglen looks forward to a long and happy, and of course mutually beneficial, relationship with *Carlyle Downs*.' He took the glass that the PA handed him and held it up, waiting for Peter to pass one to Gavin and Rod. With his other hand, he slid an envelope out of the folder and held it up.

'Which one of you is the finance person of the station?'

Rod took the glass and gestured to Gavin with a nod. 'Oh definitely Gav, here. He's the brains. I'm a simple farmer, out with my dairy cows and horses.'

Fuck. Gavin's breath stilled as he took the cheque and slipped it into his coat pocket. *We're a beef cattle station, not a bloody dairy.* He sat there and gripped the glass, wondering whether to let the comment go or say something.

But de Vere was obviously as dim as Rod when it came

to cattle. He slid the envelope across the table, lifted his glass and proposed a toast to the venture. 'The record of deposit that has just gone into your account. To a long and prosperous association.'

'To a long and prosperous association.' Gavin raised his glass and drained it.

He didn't have to wait for the cheque to clear. The money was already in there. He could barely stop himself from laughing out loud.

* * *

Rod drove Gavin to the airport. He pulled his car into the area for dropping off passengers, and Gavin opened the door.

'Can I ask you a favour, mate? I've got no cash on me and my card's been playing up,' he asked. 'Can you lend me a twenty, and I'll add it to the money I put in your account when I get to the bank at Townsville.'

Rod pulled out his wallet and passed Gavin a twenty. 'No problem, thanks for the job. Every little bit of work helps these days.'

'You did well, *Travis*. I'm happy to give you a bonus.'

'I did. You've still got my account details. Two grand, you said?'

Rod asked as Gavin went to get out of the front seat.

'Yep, and it's now two grand and twenty dollars.' A car hooted from behind, and Gavin patted his pocket. 'Thanks for what you did. You convinced me, although when you started going on about dairy cows, I thought you'd blown it.'

Rod laughed. 'Sorry. I don't know one end of a cow from another.

I'll have to come and visit you one day on your cattle

station.'

'You must,' Gavin said, but his smile was cold. Rod had served his purpose, and there'd be no need to ever see him again. Bumping into him on the Strand in Townsville a few months back had been handy. The one year he'd gone away to boarding school at the end of primary school, he and Rod had forged a sort of friendship. Two misfits together, Travis had taunted him. Gavin had never forgotten that.

Everything that was coming to Travis, he deserved.

'I'd love to see the look on your brother's face when you tell him the good news,' Rod said as Gavin slammed the door. He ignored Rod's last words and walked towards the terminal. Two hours in the air, a visit to the bank, transfer the money across to his account and his new life was about to begin.

Anticipation vied with anxiety until he had the money in his hands. It was a shame their parents were dead; they could have seen that he was the son who deserved the admiration, and more respect. Oh, the satisfaction of besting his bastard of a brother, and having a quarter of a million in the bank.

Life didn't get much better.

CHAPTER 28

***Carlyle Downs**, 1 February*

Bluey called in on his way to the yards.

'You okay, boss?' He looked at Travis long and hard, but Travis shook his head and gestured to the boys. He'd been quiet since they'd got out of bed, but there was no point worrying them until they knew for sure that Emlyn was missing.

'You pair head over to the yards,' Travis said. 'I'm just waiting on a couple of calls. We'll be over directly.'

'Is everything all right, Dad?' Joel asked. 'I heard you talking to someone late last night.'

'A couple of problems, mate. I'll tell you about it later.'

'Mum and Cass are okay, aren't they?' Jase's brow wrinkled.

'They're fine.'

Happy with that, the boys climbed onto their bikes. Travis stood on the last step and waited until they'd disappeared around the bend.

'You look like you've got the weight of the world on your shoulders.' Bluey crossed the yard and stood at the bottom of the steps.

'Feels a bit like that.'

'You need me later, you just ask. Okay?'

Travis frowned. 'What makes you say that? Later?'

'It's that brother of yours who's in trouble, ain't he?'

Bluey pulled a cigarette from his pocket and put it in the corner of his mouth. 'It's been building for a long time. Just remember, it's not your fault,' he said before he cupped his hand around his lighter. 'Gavin brings it all on himself. Always has.'

'He is getting harder to deal with. It's like having another child in the house, lately. His moods and his bloody unreliability are hard to take.' It wasn't necessary to tell Bluey his suspicions about Gavin. Travis looked at the cigarette in the corner of Bluey's mouth. For the first time since he'd given up smoking ten years ago, he craved a nicotine hit. Last night, after John and Greg had left, he'd opened the bottle of Glenfiddich whisky that the boys had given him for Christmas, but he'd limited himself to one small nip in case he had to drive anywhere. Worry had pressed heavily on his shoulders, and the whisky hadn't helped him sleep. He'd lain there until the early hours, worrying about Cass, wondering where the hell Emlyn was, and the financial problems that were imminent if they didn't get top dollar for the cattle. He couldn't bring himself to think of the accusations against his brother.

'It's not going to be a good season, boss.' He looked up at the house. 'Where's Gavin gone?'

'Who knows?' he said with a shrug. 'I can't trust him anymore.'

'Never should have,' Bluey said. 'I knew he was up to something when I saw him speeding down a track yesterday.' He blew a smoke ring away from Travis. 'Actually,' he said half to himself, 'he's been up to no good since he was a young'un.'

Travis leaned forward. 'What track? Where was he?'

'Gavin was heading down the track from the Conjuboy turn-off in that red ute of his. He must have been doing a hundred k. I was expecting the ute to roll after he flew past me, but he slowed it down before he got to that bad corner. You know the one, just before the track veers off to the west gate.'

'He was supposed to be on his way to Townsville, but I don't know why he'd go out there first,' Travis muttered before he looked at Bluey. 'What time was that?'

'Wasn't far off eight. I had a morning cuppa with Billy Bates over on the main road, and then we had a bit of a yarn.'

Travis knew his eyes were wide. 'Bluey, I need you to think carefully. Was there anyone in the ute with him?'

The old stockman nodded. 'I thought it was strange, but yeah, I think Dr Rees was in the front.'

'Jesus Christ.' Travis turned and took the stairs two at a time. 'Wait there. I'm going to need you. I have to make a call.'

Last night, Detective Inspector Blake had taken his call and promised that he would look into Emlyn's flight details as soon as he got a chance, but Travis had sensed that he hadn't seemed worried about it. It was Gavin that he was interested in.

Travis's stomach roiled when Baker replied. Before he could pass on what Bluey had told him, the detective kept talking.

'What I can tell you is that Dr Rees didn't travel to Brisbane on any flights yesterday. And her ticket wasn't cancelled. She was simply a no-show. The vehicle that Dr Rees was driving has been found abandoned on your road not far from the main road.'

'Jesus.' Travis kept his voice calm as he relayed to Baker what Bluey had said.

'We're on our way,' the detective said. 'We also have a witness who says that she wasn't in your brother's car when he stopped for fuel at Greenvale. He was there about one, about the time her flight was due to leave. He had a chat to the guy behind the desk and bragged about going to Brisbane to make his fortune.'

'Brisbane?' Travis shook his head in disgust. 'And a fortune? He can't help himself,' he mumbled.

'And we've confirmed he was on the late-afternoon flight. A ute registered to your company is at the airport in the short-term car park. Do you know why he'd be going to Brisbane?'

'No. I have no idea.' Travis put his hand on the door jamb and braced himself as a shudder went through him. 'I'll head out to where Bluey saw him driving and see if we can find her. Maybe her phone's gone flat and she can't call?'

'We've located Dr Rees' phone,' the detective said. 'Strangely, it was in the car park at the top of Castle Hill.'

'Castle Hill?' Travis frowned and lifted his arm to wipe the perspiration from his face. 'In Townsville?'

'Yes, not far from the airport.' The detective's voice was firm. 'We're concerned for Dr Rees' wellbeing and we're just about to board the search-and-rescue helicopter. Are you sure you have no idea why he'd be going to Brisbane?'

'No.' Travis's voice was flat.

'And, Travis, I want you to stay where you are. Don't start a search until we get there. We'll organise a search grid when we arrive. We've also got ground-search crews coming from Mt Garnet and Mt Surprise.'

'Do you have any idea how big *Carlyle Downs* is?' Travis's stomach was churning. He couldn't bring himself to think of where Emlyn might be. *Or what Gavin might have done.*

'I'll go see the university team before you get here. It's probably a better base to plan a search from.'

'Okay. If you see or hear anything, I'll give you a number

to ring, and they can contact us while we're in the air. Is there a clearing near there to land?'

'Yes, it's clear all around the dongas.' Travis hurried to the desk in the corner of the lounge and wrote the number that Baker gave him on a slip of paper. When the call ended, he looked at the computer sitting silently on the desk. The one that Gavin was always on. It reminded him to call the main branch of his bank in Townville and sort out this mystery account. Once the boys were back in the house, he'd get them to help him log on and have a ferret through Gavin's files. Joel was a computer whiz. Maybe there was something there that would explain what his brother was up to.

He glanced outside as he dialled the number. It had rained until almost midnight, but now the sun was out and glinting on the narrow channel of water trickling down the drive from where the water tank had overflowed.

'Townsville City Bank, may I help you?'

'Good morning, it's Travis Carlyle from *Carlyle Downs* calling. I need to speak to Graham Edmonds as a matter of urgency.'

'Just one moment, Mr Carlyle. I'll see if the manager is free.'

Travis held back a groan as the blasted music chimed in. Finally, the phone picked up.

'Travis. It's been a while. Haven't seen you down here for a long time.'

'Graham. I need to be brief. We have an emergency up here. The police are involved, and I have to go out and search for someone who's gone missing.'

'Sure, Travis, but what can I do to help?'

'A new account has been started in my name, and I know

nothing about it. How do I put a stop to anyone accessing that account until I can get down there and sort it out?'

'You say it's in your name?'

'Yes. Apparently. This is the account number.' He read off the number that Baker had given him.

'Just a moment.' A keyboard clicked as he waited.

'Okay. It's in your name, and your identification is on file against it. It was opened at a branch in Brisbane about three weeks ago.'

'The bastard,' Travis muttered.

'Sorry?' Graham asked.

'Nothing.' Travis tried to relax his clenched jaw. 'Can you put a stop on any access to that account until I get down there next week?'

'I can. Just some security questions for you,' Graham said. 'I know it's you, but I have to follow security protocol.'

Travis provided his date of birth, his mother's maiden name and the name of his first pet, the third security question, and it was done quickly.

'Okay, Travis. All good.' Graham's voice was brisk. 'Are you aware a sizable deposit went into that account overnight?'

'No, I don't know anything about the account. That's the issue. But what do you mean by sizable?'

'A quarter of a million dollars.'

'What? Are you frigging serious?' Travis sagged against the wall and held the phone tightly against his ear. 'Are you able to tell me where the deposit came from?'

'I can. Give me a moment.'

Travis waited, tapping his foot on the floor as he stared at the wall, not seeing anything.

'A company called Carroglen.'

'The fucking bastard. He's sold out.' White-hot fury filled Travis. 'Just make sure you put a stop on it, and Graham, if my brother comes into the bank, delay him somehow and call the police. I'll give you a direct number to call. Whatever you do, don't let him withdraw any of that money.'

'Okay, it's guaranteed. No one can access those funds until you personally come and sort this out.'

'Thanks, Graham. I really appreciate you doing this over the phone for me. I'll get down there on Monday … if I can. If the situation here is resolved.'

'Okay, Travis. I'll see you when you get here. Ring first to make sure I'm free. And I hope everything works out up there.'

CHAPTER 29

Townsville City, 1 February, 2.30 pm

It wasn't long before the gloss rubbed off Gavin's mood. His flight had been delayed by two hours, and once he'd bought some lunch and a coffee and a newspaper at the airport, he'd run out of cash. At first, he'd scowled when he read the headline, '*Cryptocurrency crash as bitcoin and other prices tumble*,' but then he'd realised that if it was going to crash, it couldn't have happened on a better day. The day he was *buying* again.

All he had to decide was how much to spend and how much to leave in cash reserves. Prices had dropped before and he knew it wouldn't last. Now that China was clamping down on digital currencies, the western world was taking it up more and more. But the little niggle of concern unsettled him, and as the plane got closer to Townsville, he thought about the unit. He had to decide whether to sell it or rent it out.

Selling would be a problem, because they'd want addresses and other details, and Gavin intended to disappear. And if he rented it out, that would be a steady little bit of pocket money going into his account. That could be kept anonymous, too, once he set up an agent to manage it.

'Should have thought of that before,' he muttered, and stopped when the woman sitting beside him looked at him. 'I could have made some cash out of that when I was short.' He stared back at the woman until she looked away.

The problem of what to do with the unit was still on his mind as he walked through the car park to the ute, but he figured renting it was the way to go. As soon as he finished at the bank, he'd go to the real estate agent who managed the block and put it up for rental.

And then the only problem was deciding where he would book a flight to. Vanuatu looked good; he'd met a guy at the bar one night who'd told him about all the Americans who were hiding on some of the smaller islands there.

Not that I need to hide. I've done nothing wrong, just taken what is mine by rights.

He'd like to see someone try to take it off him.

He drove around for ten minutes before he could find a park, and in the end, he had to park two blocks away from the bank. The smile on his face was wide as the automatic doors opened in front of him. He'd brought the folder he'd left in the car with his identification in it in case there were any problems transferring that amount of money into his account.

As he walked into the bank, he frowned. It had been refurbished and there were no counters where the tellers used to be. Looking up at the huge red-and-gold sign above, emblazoned with the bank's logo, he read, *Technology, Leading City Bank Forward.* Underneath the sign was a line of individual booths with a computer in each.

As he stood hesitating, a customer service officer approached him.

'Welcome to our new technology branch, sir. What service would you like to use today?' She was tall and blonde and her shirt moulded a nice pair of breasts.

Gavin slowly lifted his gaze from her chest. 'I want to transfer some money from account to account, and I want to withdraw some cash, too,' he said.

'This way, sir. All of the instructions are straightforward, but if you have any issues just press the button beside the terminal, and I'll come out and help you.' Her perfume wafted around him as she left him at the terminal.

Gavin could barely contain his excitement as he pulled out his wallet and took out the cards for each account. He inserted the card for the new account and the balance came up on the screen.

Two hundred and twenty-five thousand fucking dollars.

He wanted to turn around and call everyone over to see how clever he'd been. He glanced up and bit back a smile. Apart from the old pensioner on a walker, the cool, air-conditioned space was empty. Gavin stood there for a moment, wondering if it would let him empty the account. Another grin lifted his lips.

Nah, he'd leave Travis ten bucks in it, and then it wouldn't bring up any account closure flags. Although if it did, the pretty blonde would see how much money he had. When he'd opened this account, he'd linked it directly to his account so there were no daily transaction limits. He'd picked his time carefully and made sure that the manager who knew Travis had gone to lunch. Watching the bank and checking out his routine had filled in a few days for Gavin a couple of months back.

He pushed the 'transfer funds' button on the side of the screen, and when requested he entered his pin number for a second time, and then chose his linked account. Pride filled his chest as he typed in the transfer amount on the keyboard. Two hundred and twenty-four thousand dollars, nine hundred and ninety dollars.

Enjoy your ten bucks, Trav. Who needed to go to some fancy boarding school and university? He'd done neither and had more brains than anyone he knew.

The timer on the screen whirred in a circle, and when the circle closed a message appeared: '*This amount exceeds your daily limit. If you wish to continue, please press for assistance.*'

Good. Blondie would get to see how wealthy he was, after all. Gavin pressed the button for assistance, and after a moment, the blonde girl came out of the office.

'Yes, sir?'

'I need to increase my transfer limit, so I can transfer funds to my other account.'

'Certainly. All I need is some identification, Mr—?'

'Carlyle. Travis Carlyle.' Perspiration beaded on Gavin's brow as he pulled out the fake driving licence he'd bought in Travis's name. The girl glanced at it and nodded before she looked at the screen.

Her eyes widened. 'I'm sorry, Mr Carlyle. I'm only a customer service officer. This exceeds the amount I have authority to clear for transfer. I'll have to wait till the manager comes back from lunch to authorise a transfer of that size.'

Jesus. What now? Panic began to churn in Gavin's gut, and he thought quickly. Glancing at his watch, he shook his head. 'Look, I don't have time now. I have an appointment, I'll come back later and do it. I'll just withdraw some cash now, and I'll come back and see Graham later. What time does he finish lunch?'

'He'll be back in about fifteen minutes.'

'Right, I'll be back in an hour or two.'

'Okay. If you're happy to do that, I'll leave you to it.'

Gavin nodded and pulled his handkerchief from the pocket of his trousers. He wiped his neck and turned back to the screen.

How much? How much could he withdraw before he got another stupid message like that? He settled for two thousand to start with and pressed the 'withdrawal' button. The circle whirred as he stared at the screen. This time, when the error message came up, anger began a slow burn in his stomach.

'*Funds not available.*'

Jesus, he'd give them fucking funds not available. Gavin pressed the 'cancel' button and lowered the withdrawal to just under two thousand dollars. He'd have to go back to the unit and go online and change all of the account limits on his laptop. It was strange that there were limits; when he'd set up the account, he'd tested it a few times with some of his bitcoin profits and he'd never had an issue before.

'*Not so clever, after all, Gav.*' Travis's voice filled his thoughts so clearly, Gavin turned around half expecting to see his brother standing beside him, but no one was there apart from the old bloke stabbing at the screen.

'Shut up,' he said.

The other man glanced at him and Gavin glared back as he put the new withdrawal amount in. This time as the circle whirred, he knew it wasn't going to work before the error message appeared.

Fucking hell. What was he going to do now? He didn't have more than five bucks in his wallet. Biting his lip, he stared at the screen. From memory, there was about thirty bucks in his account. He inserted the card and asked for the balance to be displayed on the screen. Thirty-eight dollars. He pressed 'withdraw' and this time the transaction went through. As he opened his wallet to put the money in, a shadow fell across him.

'Hello, Gavin. Deandra said you were having some issues with your account?'

Gavin looked up at Graham Edmonds, the manager. The blonde girl—Deandra—was hovering in the doorway, the phone pressed to her ear, her eyes fixed on him.

'Oh, hello, Graham. No. Not at all. No problems.' He held up his wallet. 'Have to run. I have an appointment.'

Graham shot a glance at his assistant, and Gavin saw her nod as she walked back into the office. Suspicion flared as he looked at Graham. If the blonde bimbo had told Graham he was Travis, Graham would be wondering what was going on.

What to do? What to do?

'Come into my office for a moment, Gavin. We can get it sorted for you now. It'll be quick, and there'll be no need for you to come back later.'

For a moment Gavin hesitated, wondering if he could wing it, and then common sense came into play. Of course, they wouldn't let him transfer money from an account that purportedly belonged to his brother.

'No. I'll come back later.' He turned for the exit, but Graham grabbed his arm.

'I think you need to do it now.' His grip was firm, and Gavin stared at him. There was something in Graham's eyes that told Gavin he knew something was going on. 'We'll sort it out now.'

Gavin wrenched his arm from his grip. 'No.'

He raced for the exit as Graham yelled to the blonde, 'Tell them he's taking off!'

Tell bloody who? What the hell had happened?

As he stepped out onto the footpath, two cars came flying around the corner into Sturt Street and pulled up on the footpath outside the bank.

Gavin put his head down and ducked into the doorway of

the next office block. Four men hurried from the cars into the bank; he knew by just looking at them they were plain-clothes cops.

Muttering under his breath, he made his way through the building. He'd been in here before and knew there was a shortcut to Walker Street at the back of the foyer. Trying not to run and draw attention to himself, Gavin hurried across the tiled floor. He pushed open the back door and ran for his car.

They must have found that stupid insect woman. How had they found her so quickly? He'd depended on her dying on the floor of that cave. There was no way she could have got out, and with a bit of luck, the air would be bad down there and she should have carked it quickly.

'Fucking hell, what's happened?' Gavin muttered under his breath as he unlocked the car door.

There was no way on God's earth that Travis would have got wind of the bank accounts, so how the hell did they know to look for him at the bank? He clenched the steering wheel with one hand as he tried to put the key in the ignition; his hand was shaking so much he dropped the keys on the floor.

'Jesus bloody Christ!' His scream echoed around the car and he sat there for a moment trying to calm himself.

What to do, what to do?

He started the ute and pulled out into the traffic on Walker Street. He couldn't go back to the branch now. They were looking for him.

But why? How?

Gavin fought for control.

Calm down.

He was clever. He had more brains than the lot of them; he just had to think calmly and work out what to do. If he knew what was going on, he could plan. He was tempted to ring Travis and suss out what had happened up there.

No. Stupid. Don't show any weakness.

The light ahead turned red and he slowed, glancing nervously in the rear-vision mirror. Would they be looking for his ute? But there was no one behind him.

Think, think.

Taking deep breaths, he counted to twenty. His mother had taught him that when he'd been in one of his rages. It had been a few days after the fire, and he'd realised that he'd lost his Nintendo. He knew his mother was scared of him, and that he enjoyed hurting her. Only little things, pinches and scratches, and sometimes he'd bite her, but the stupid bitch had never told his father. Only that stupid doctor who'd told her about the counting. Maybe he hadn't been that stupid, because it worked.

As he drove along the Strand towards his apartment, he counted again to twenty—twice—and his thoughts began to form a coherent order again.

Even when he hadn't been thinking straight, his subconscious hadn't let him down.

Of course. He could change all of the bank limits at his unit, and then go to another branch, transfer the money and withdraw the cash.

Cairns. He'd go to Cairns. Gavin smiled. And there was an international airport there.

He turned into his street and he drew a sharp breath. Anger settled deep as he saw one of the cars that had been at the bank pull up outside his building.

CHAPTER 30

By three o'clock that afternoon, the search for Emlyn was in full swing. The police helicopter had arrived, as well as two ground crews. The research team's dongas were being used as a base, and a meeting was about to start. Joel and Jase had been horrified to hear that Emlyn was missing somewhere out on *Carlyle Downs* and both had been eager to help in the search.

'The helicopter is doing a sweep to the west until it gets too dark,' Detective Baker told the assembled group. 'Because Dr Rees has already been out there for over twenty-four hours as far we know, we need to start the ground search this afternoon and continue it through the night.'

Sergeant Brennan from Mt Surprise was organising the search grid, and after Baker had thanked them all for being there, he called Travis over to the table where they had spread out large maps of the locality. 'Are you and your boys confident to go out on horseback in the dark?'

'Of course.'

The sergeant nodded and traced his finger over the map. 'We have to assume that they were on the road or a fire trail, so we'll map the search grid two kilometres either side of the roads that a car could have been on.'

'Travis. Are there any buildings in the scrub? Any reason why your brother would have taken Dr Rees out there? An old hut, or any place that he would need to go before they went to Townsville?'

Travis shook his head. 'There's nothing out there at all. We rarely go out that way, and there's no cattle out there, either.'

'The land is too barren? So it's open and dry?'

'No, quite the opposite. There are some lush areas out there, and many bush thickets, that we now know,' he nodded to John, 'that indicate there're more caves out there.' Travis looked at Bluey, who was sitting quietly in the room. 'There's no point for us to ever go to the western paddocks. We can't muster the cattle on motorbikes because of the terrain, and over the years, my forebears have recounted the stories of how the horses won't baulk in the far paddocks.' He shrugged and Bluey nodded.

'We've tried it, and it's true,' the old stockman said. 'You can be galloping along, and the horse will just come to a dead stop. You have to turn around, because they simply won't cross some of the land.'

'It's only since the university has shown us the NASA maps that we've realised that the area is crisscrossed with more caves and tubes,' Travis said.

Bluey stood and walked across to the map. His nicotine-stained finger traced a line from the western boundary to the property, to the road. 'This is bad land. Everyone knows that. Nobody goes there.'

Brennan frowned. 'Why do you call it bad land?'

'I think it's as simple as the horses sensing the openings in the ground,' Travis said, but Bluey shook his head.

'No. It's more than that. There's been people go missing over the years. Those two little kids were never found back in the 1800s, and local legend has it that a lot of prospectors disappeared out there, too.'

The silence that followed was long as the group looked at the elderly man.

Joel broke it and his voice shook. 'Uncle Gavin goes out there.'

Travis turned to his son in surprise. 'What? How do you know that?'

'I heard him bragging to Mum one night. 'One night you were away … before we left. He cooked dinner and opened a bottle of wine, and he was talking to her about those caves and about the gold mine.'

'We listened after we went to bed.' Jase sounded upset, too.

'Yeah, he sent us off to bed the same time Cass went to sleep.' Joel's lips curled.

Travis placed a hand on each of his son's shoulders. 'It's okay. Just tell me what you heard, Joel.'

'He said he had a place where he kept his special things. I remember he laughed when he told Mum. He said if you knew about it, you'd think all your Christmases had come at once.'

Travis frowned. 'I wonder what he meant by that, and where he was talking about.'

'No ideas?' Baker asked.

'No, but I'll go looking. Maybe that's where he's taken her.' Travis stood. 'We'll go home and get saddled up. It'll take us a few hours to ride out there. I don't know how the phone service will be so far out, so I'll get Bluey to take the ute out with the CB radio. What channel do you want us on?'

Sergeant Brennan stood and addressed the group. 'How many of you have CB radios in your vehicles?'

John nodded. 'Yes, in the Troop Carrier and the van we came up in. Larry?' He turned to the photographer.

'Yes, there's one in mine, too.'

'Okay,' Brennan replied. 'Channel nine if you have a

forty-channel set, and channel five on an eighteen channel. That's the emergency channel as most of you probably know.'

Bill called from the back of the room. 'I've got enough food, so make sure you come and stock up before you leave.'

John walked over to Travis as they were about to leave. 'I thought you'd like to know. Emlyn's husband is on his way up. He's flying into Townsville in a couple of hours and hiring a car.'

'I'm pleased to hear that.' Travis nodded. 'Come on, boys. Go and get some food from Bill, and we'll get out there.'

'I'll radio you when David arrives, and we'll come out that way,' John said. 'Even though it's a dreadful situation, he was relieved to know that—'

'That my bloody brother is somehow responsible.' Travis couldn't keep the disgust from his voice. 'When he comes home, it's going to be very hard to stay civilised. I just hope that he hasn't hurt her.' The things that Detective Baker had told him, the violence that Gavin had shown the backpacker didn't fill him with confidence.

If Emlyn Rees was on his station, he would not give up until she was found. The thought of her being hurt—or worse—at the hand of his brother brought bile to his throat.

'Do you think he'll come home, Dad?' Jase asked as they saddled up the horses a short time later.

'Who knows?' Travis tried to keep the anger from his voice. Anger with Gavin, and anger that his brother had duped him for so long. 'It appears he's arrogant enough to come home and carry on as though nothing's happened.

CHAPTER 31

Emlyn lay on her back and opened her eyes. Since she'd fallen into this cave, she'd drifted in and out of sleep—or consciousness. The pain in her back was bearable when she lay still. The first time she'd woken up, she'd worried about the air quality, and had tried to sit up so that she wasn't low on the ground, but pain had sliced through her and she'd fallen back onto the hard floor. The next time she'd come to, she'd forced herself to move because she needed to relieve herself.

The effort of that movement had sent excruciating pain through her back again, and she'd only just managed to return to the centre of the cave under the skylight before she'd passed out again. Being able to see the gap above calmed her. Mercifully, she'd slept most of the night. The couple of times she'd woken, Emlyn had calmed herself with deep breathing.

She dreamed of David and Sophie. He would have been disappointed when she didn't arrive last night. Over and over, she dreamed the same thing. She was standing at the pretty leadlight door of their home. Sophie was crying in the background, but she couldn't get inside to soothe her. Sometimes Emlyn knocked; other times she pulled out the key, but each time the door stayed firmly shut. She could hear David's beautiful voice on the other side, and that helped her through the night. As the dream repeated itself, she began to hate that door.

'When I come home, David, we'll get a new one,' she muttered in her sleep.

I love you, Em. It's going to be all right. I'll come out there and I'll find you.

Suddenly he was there. His breath warmed her skin, and Emlyn reached out, trying to get him to stay with her. His arms held her close until she began to wake.

Blinking, she looked around in confusion as the darkness lightened, fighting to keep her eyes open.

For the first time in many long months, Emlyn ached to feel David's arms around her. To hold her. To comfort her. He would keep her safe.

'David,' she called out as her eyes closed. 'I'm at the bottom of the trees. Come and find me.'

* * *

A few hours later, Emlyn opened her eyes and put her fingers to her lips. She had to get out of here; she needed to find water. Already her lips and tongue were dry, but she was relieved there was no telltale metallic taste of bad air in her mouth. Apart from the wrenched back muscle—and a slight concussion, she suspected—she wasn't feeling too bad. The skylight was now filled with a bright patch of blue, and the lacy branches above were waving in a soft breeze. Her strength had returned along with her determination, and she was going to try to find a way out of here. She knew how these caves worked. Somewhere behind her, there would be another fall, and she would be able to get out eventually. As she lay there, she could feel a slight rush of air on her face and it wasn't coming from above, so her thoughts about the air quality were right. There was a flow-through of air, so unless she was in a low pocket of carbon dioxide, she didn't need to worry about that.

The fragment of a pleasant dream floated at the edge of her thoughts, but as she tried to grab it, it floated away, and she felt sad to lose it. Lifting her arm carefully, Emlyn peered at her watch. The fuzziness that had clouded her vision when she had woken up the first time was gone, and she could see clearly now. She couldn't believe how much time had passed. It was after three—obviously in the afternoon by the sun shining in from above. The pain had eased but it was worse on her right side, so Emlyn rolled slightly to the left, and pressed her right hand against her back where it hurt the most. Breathing in deeply, she knew it wasn't her ribs, perhaps just a torn muscle when she'd fallen at such an awkward angle. It eased as she moved slowly to the left, as long as she kept the pressure on her back. As she rolled, she encountered something hard beneath her side, so she moved onto her back again and slid it out from under her. Lifting the object, a piece of what felt like fabric dissolved into dust in her fingers. She held up the rectangular object; it was a book of some sort, or what remained of a book. Reassured, knowing that someone had been here before her, she placed it carefully on the ground to her right and felt around with her hand to see if there was anything else there. Her fingers touched something hard and round, and as she smoothed her fingers over the shape and they felt a gap, cold dread lodged in her throat. Emlyn pulled her hand away and forced herself to sit up. Once she was upright, she looked down to her left. The sunlight played over two identical shapes, side by side. She drew in a quick breath and looked down at the sad remnants of two young lives.

Two small skeletons were lying in the depths of this cave.

Immediately, she knew who they belonged to.

The two children who had gone missing over a century ago.

Travis's—and Gavin's—forbears. She wondered if Gavin had known they were down here. After he had shown her what was in the cave that he'd taken as his own, she wouldn't be surprised if he had known all along.

She wondered what he'd tell Travis when he went home. Would he say that he'd taken her to the airport? David would have been beside himself with worry when she hadn't turned up.

And she'd missed the sponsorship meeting at UQ, and probably missed the deadline for the funding for the next triennium. A wry grin crossed her face; unless attempted murder and kidnapping counted as extenuating circumstances. Despite what she'd been through, Emlyn was feeling calm.

And strong.

Because she would get out, and no matter what it took— she knew how far away from the house and the dongas she was— she would go back, and she would be able to tell Travis about the diaries and the missing children.

Worse still, she would have to tell him about his brother.

Seeing the two skeletons had renewed her determination to survive. She had to tell David she loved him.

She pressed her hand against the torn muscle and pushed herself up to her feet. Her breath hitched as she straightened, but stretching seemed to help. She could move without that intense pain now. Standing in the warm sunshine, she stared down at the skeletons of the two children and thought of their poor mother. Never knowing what had happened; never having closure.

At least she'd had closure. It was time to take her life back in hand and move forward. And she could tell Bluey that she'd found Missy and Thomas. They deserved a proper burial in the little cemetery by the house.

Tears pricked at her eyes and she said a silent prayer for

the children and their parents. 'We'll take you home,' she whispered.

Emlyn turned and began to make her way to the back of the cave where a glimmer of light peeked through the top of the rock fall.

* * *

They rode down the back roads and they were only an hour away from the dongas when they picked up the tracks of Gavin's ute. They followed them on horseback for another few kilometres and Travis called Bluey to let him know where they were. It wasn't long before they heard Bluey's ute following behind them. The tracks turned into a break in the trees and they had to duck to miss the low branches. About a hundred metres in, they could see where Gavin had been parking in the bush. The wheel ruts were deep; deep enough to show that the car had been there many times. A well-worn footpath headed up the hill.

Jase dismounted, crouched down and looked closely at the tracks. 'Yep, it's the same tread as the tyres we've got on both of the farm utes.'

'I want you to stay here with Bluey please, boys.' If there was anything—anything bad—up ahead, he didn't want his sons there. 'Or better still, get on the radio and tell them I've found where he's been. Tell them we'll call back if we need help.'

Joel nodded and got into Bluey's ute, while Bluey and Jase tethered the horses. Travis walked quickly up the hill. At the top of the ridge was a curtain of vines like the ones at the glade near the old graveyard. He stepped over to them quietly and lifted them. There was a narrow opening and a rope hung between some rough steps dug into the dirt at the side.

Travis pulled out his phone and turned the flashlight app on. Holding it up high, he shone it down into the cave. Finally, he called out softly, 'Emlyn? Are you there?'

All was quiet and there was no movement below. He grabbed the rope and made his way down to the opening, his eyes widening when he reached the base.

'Very cosy, Gavin.' Now he knew where his brother had disappeared to over the past couple of years. A table and chairs—why two? he wondered—a bed and two large metal toolboxes filled the small space, but there was no sign of Emlyn. A plastic sleeve and some coloured papers lay on the floor and he bent to pick them up.

Travis's breath caught and he almost gagged as he stared at what was in his hand. It wasn't paper, it was a photo. A photo of Alison in bed with Gavin. Gavin was beaming at the camera, but Alison's eyes were closed and her head lolled at an awkward angle on his brother's shoulder.

'You filthy bastard.' The growl from Travis's throat reverberated around the small space. The detective's words came back to him in waves.

Date-rape drug.

Robberies.

Assaults

Rage like he'd never experienced before consumed Travis. His blood thrummed in his ears and his vision blurred as he stared at the photograph of the woman he loved. He knew Alison well enough to figure out what had happened. It explained why she'd suddenly sided with Gavin, why she'd fled their home. His brother had taken away more than a year of his family from him.

'I'll kill you for this, Gavin.' His jaw ached where he'd

clenched his teeth.

At the same time, beneath the disgust and the hatred, a tiny burst of joy flared. Surely once he told Alison that he knew what had happened, what it seemed Gavin had done, she would come home. His only fear was that she wouldn't return to the station because of his brother.

If it came to that, no matter how hard he had to work, he'd build a new house for them. A home where they could be happy, a home where there was no Gavin. A home that was full of love instead of bad memories.

Even if it meant selling the station. They didn't have to stay here.

He knew Alison had always loved him, but Gavin had tried to destroy it, and he'd almost succeeded. If he ever came home, the police would have to queue up to deal with him, because Travis was going to have the first go. When he thought of what Alison had endured alone over the past twelve months, he had to fight back the sharp nausea that burned in his gut. He knew he was guilty, too; his hurt at being left had caused him to lash out at her many times. There was a lot of forgiveness to come and many harsh words to be taken back. Travis felt sick to his stomach when he thought of what Alison had suffered at his brother's hands.

Gavin would pay. That was the one thing he had no doubt about.

Travis stumbled as he headed for the steps carved into the dirt. His mother's words kept coming back to him.

Please promise me you'll take care of your brother.

That promise was about to be broken. His own family would come first; that was who he had to take care of now.

'Dad! Where are you? Are you okay?' Travis hurried out

and was in the open before his sons reached the top of the hill.

'She's not here.'

'We'll saddle up and head further west,' Jase said.

'Thanks, guys. Jase, you go in the ute with Blue. I'll ride Sam. Head to the fence line and work your way back along the road. I'm going to stay on this ridge and look from up here. I'll meet you at the back gate. Okay?'

The boys nodded and headed back down the hill. Once they were far enough away, he checked his phone for service.

Nothing

Travis climbed to the next high point of the ridge and was pleased to see he had two bars of service. He dialled Alison's number, but it went straight to voicemail.

He stared out over the land beneath him, keeping his sight fixed on Joel as he and the horse blended into the undulating granite landscape surrounding them. The thick vegetation at the top of the ridge thinned out into grassy woodland country. The only colour was the occasional yellow splotch of the flowers of the spindly kapok trees scattered among the ironbark eucalyptus.

Travis pressed 'redial' and waited as the phone rang this time. His hands were slick with sweat, and he gripped the phone tightly.

'Travis? Is everything okay? Are the boys okay? Are you okay?' Until Alison asked about his well-being, Travis had been holding it together.

He swallowed, taking in deep gulps of air before he could speak. In the background, he could hear music and children's voices. It was Friday; Cassie had dance lessons at the local scout hall on Friday afternoons. He mightn't be there with them, but he knew their lives.

'Al.' His voice broke, and he brushed his knuckles against

his eyes. 'I'm so sorry.' He couldn't hold it back, no matter what his intention had been.

Her voice was sharp with fear. 'Who is it? Who's hurt?'

'No one. We're all okay. The boys are fine. I can see them from where I am.' Travis took another deep breath. 'I don't want you to ask any questions. I want you to come home. I need you and Cassie here. Now.' This time his voice shook. 'I know what Gavin did to you. Al, I am so, so sorry. I want you to come home. It doesn't matter.'

When he heard her gasp at the other end, Travis fought to stay calm. 'Listen to me, sweetheart. Listen to me carefully. Gavin is in trouble. Big trouble. He's taken one of the university women—you met Emlyn—and we're all out on the station looking for her. And I know he threatened you.'

'Where is he?' Her voice was thick, and he knew she was crying.

'I don't know.' In a flash, he wondered if his brother would try to go to Alison. He would probably see her house as somewhere safe.

Her voice hitched, and she cleared her throat. 'He was your brother, Trav. And I was so afraid of him. What he might do to Cass or the boys if I didn't do what he said. But I was most afraid that you'd believe him. It's all right, sweetheart. I want you here. At *Carlyle Downs* where you belong, and where I know you and Cass are safe.'

'Really? Even after what happened, you can say that? I trusted him.' Travis closed his eyes as she started to cry. 'And he had those photographs.'

'And he betrayed our trust. What sort of man do you take me for? Al, I will spend the rest of my life making it up to you for what my brother did. I want you to come home. I love you.

I've never stopped loving you.'

Travis gripped the phone as he waited. His heart beat slow and heavy as the silence lengthened.

Finally, Alison's soft voice broke it. 'We need to talk before you make any promises. There's a lot to consider. I don't even know what happened that night.'

'There's a lot to overcome, but I know we can do it. I just need to know one thing, and we can work together from there. I need to know you love me. That somehow you've continued loving me through all this shit my brother caused.'

'Yes. Of course I do, Trav.' Another sob, and then Alison's voice steadied again. 'I'll come home, and then we'll see what happens.'

'Is Cass well enough for the drive up?'

'Yes, she's bounced back to normal.'

'Will you come as soon as you can?' Travis held his breath.

'We're on our way.'

* * *

Joel had ridden the fence line to the edge of the property, and it was almost dark. Travis had followed the road to meet him, his torch playing on the path ahead. Just before he'd reached him, he'd spotted fresh tyre tracks in a gully where the road was soft from yesterday's rain. He followed the tracks up the hill until they came to a stop. He climbed out of the saddle and pulled the larger flashlight out of his saddlebag. A vehicle had been this far and then turned around. He followed the tracks in an arc, and then back the way it had come. This was obviously as far as Gavin had driven. No one else would have been out this way since the truck had come in with the first grocery delivery for Emlyn a few weeks ago. Kev had refused to come back that way due to the state of the road, and he'd brought in the subsequent deliveries via the Kennedy Highway.

'Emlyn!' Travis cupped his hand to his mouth and called as loudly as he could. He waited and listened before he called again. 'Emlyn!'

The sound of horses' hooves was the only response, and Joel appeared over the ridge.

'What did you find, Dad?'

'Some more tyre tracks.'

'Where're Blue and Jase?' Joel looked around.

'They're following the road and exploring all the side tracks off it. They should catch up with us soon,' Travis replied.

Joel shook his head as he looked into the dark bush surrounding them. 'It's like looking for a needle in a haystack, Dad. She could be anywhere. If we knew why he came out here, it would give us a clue. What would he have been looking for?'

'We'll find out. You take a break. I'm just going to ride through here and call for a while.'

Travis rode slowly through the bush and called until he was hoarse, while Joel rode back along the road to meet Bluey and Jase. The fear within him grew the more he rode. He had no doubt now what Gavin was capable of, and it horrified him.

They had to find Emlyn.

He spurred his horse along and cantered back across the flat downs at the base of the ridge. Suddenly, he was hurled forwards as the horse came to a dead stop. He gripped the mane and held the reins tightly to stop himself from pitching over its head.

'What's wrong, boy?' He stroked the horse's head until it

had calmed. Swinging himself off carefully, he looped the reins around an ironbark tree and held his flashlight in front of him as he walked forwards. Taking care where he stepped, he came to a thick covering of vegetation on the ground and leaned forwards. There was a gap, and as he pushed at the scrub, the hole yawned deep in front of him. Travis played the flashlight into the deep hole, but there was nothing to be seen below. No movement, and to his great relief, no body lying prostrate below. Just some fallen rocks and tree roots dangling into the gaping space.

The property was dotted with entrances to the tubes; he'd forgotten how he and Gavin had come out here when they were boys and explored. He'd never realised that it was a system of caves linked to the volcano over at Undara. Once he'd started boarding school, he'd rarely come to this side of the property unless they were searching for missing beasts, but it appeared that Gavin had had reason to be out here.

Travis led the horse back to the road, calling Emlyn until the lights of the ute lit up the bush around him, and dispiritedly, he walked back to join Bluey and his boys.

* * *

Emlyn would have given anything to have her phone with her, and to have a drink to ease her dry lips. She was in a quandary; she could wait for help to arrive, and risk dying of dehydration, or she could expend her energy trying to find a way out and locate some water. How long that would take was an unknown, but she decided that was the risk she had to take. Rocks skittered beneath her feet as she made her way carefully to the top of the rock fall at the back of the cave where a shaft of light shone through a gap.

Her breath caught each time she turned the wrong way and the sharp pain spiked in her back. She was almost to the top, and as she stretched to move a small rock that was impeding her progress, the pain gripped her again. Stars filled her vision and she fought for breath. She sat for a moment with her head in her hands. As she sat there, the rocks beside her began to roll, and she lifted her hands to cover her head.

Finally, the rumbling stopped, and a cloud of dust rose to meet her. She wiped her eyes, and relief filled her when she turned around. A huge gap had cleared between the rocks and the roof of the cave. With renewed energy, Emlyn scurried to the top, using her hands to drag herself up. She lay on the rocks and looked over into a cave full of light. It was so long, she couldn't see the other end, but skylights dotted the roof every few metres. She leaned further over the gap; a rock fall like the one on the side she'd come in from, gave her access to the large tube. She turned around and swung her legs over, finding solid purchase with her feet, before she crabbed backwards down the rock fall.

She stared around her as she reached the bottom. There was still enough light coming in to see that she was in an intact lava tube much larger than any they had explored on the other side of the property. Despite her situation, awe filled her as she stood in the massive tube. The floor was covered with silt, and she knew that meant there was an opening somewhere as the silt had washed in and covered the original basalt. Stepping out, she followed the cave as it progressed in a straight line. Apart from the bats dotting the ceiling, there was no sign of any life. After a while, she stopped and tilted her head to the side, hope rushing through her. Moving as fast as her back would let her, she followed the sound. The cave narrowed, and ropes of tree roots filled the space in front of her, but the sound was getting louder the further she went. As she moved forward the long cave split into three tubes, but she followed the middle one where the sound was pulling her.

The light dimmed, but it was still bright enough to see the shining surface on the cave wall ahead. She stepped carefully over the wet mud to where spring water emerged from a crack in the cave wall. Reaching out tentatively, she held her fingers beneath the water until they were wet. She brought her hand to her face and sniffed her fingers, before putting her index finger on her tongue and tasting the liquid.

Sweet, fresh water, with no taste of dirt or metal in it. Talking care not to overdo it, she cupped her hand beneath the flow and took small sips until her dry mouth and lips were eased. Relief flowed through her, and as she relaxed, the constant ache in her back eased.

Now all she had to do was find a way out. Wherever she searched, she knew she could come back to the spring and stay hydrated. Deciding to explore ahead before the light faded for the night, she moved forward. The skylights ended, and the cave roof lowered the further she walked; there was no sign of any light ahead. As she entered the last small chamber, she yawned, and her neck prickled a warning as her heart rate began to speed up. Aware of pockets of bad air, Emlyn held her breath for as long as she could before she turned and hurried back the way she had come. Taking a couple of shallow breaths as she made her way back, she finally reached the spring.

Disappointment came to the fore, and her hope plummeted. There was no path out that way. She sat beside the spring and glanced at her watch as she considered her options.

Six-thirty. It was the middle of summer, but it would still

be pitch dark down here by seven. Even if there was an opening out to the bush, apart from the skylights in the roof, she'd never see it in the dark. It mightn't be five-star accommodation, but there was water, the air was clean and it seemed to be a safe spot. As she considered her options, there was a rush of noise above and a flurry of wings as the bats headed out for their nightly hunt for food. There was a flow-through of air, and she looked around for somewhere to lie before it was too dark. There was a wide, flat lump of basalt over near the cave wall, surrounded by deep, fine silt. She used her hands to scrape a deeper mound of soil, and then went back and washed them under the water. Sitting on the rock with her legs stretched out, her back was supported against the wall and hurt less.

Emlyn closed her eyes, wondering how she was going to endure the long hours until it was light again. As she sat there dozing, her eyes flew open; she could have sworn she heard her name echoing around the vast chamber. She lifted her head and listened, but all there was to be heard was the dripping of the spring, and the rustling of the leaves in the bush above. Her eyes closed again, and she let sleep take her.

* * *

As midnight approached, Travis insisted that they all return to the base camp. They'd searched and called along the fence line and road, with no sign of anyone.

'There's no point searching in the dark,' he told the twins when they wanted to keep going. They had taken a break and eaten the last of the food Bill had packed for them.

'It's not safe with the entrances to the tubes around here, and besides, if Emlyn is unconscious, we could walk within a metre of her and not see her,' he said.

Bluey nodded. 'She's out here somewhere. I have no doubt about that.'

'We'll leave the horses here and go back with you in the ute.' Travis turned to Bluey. 'Then have something to eat and let them know about the tracks. I'm sure they'll focus the search in this direction. We'll have a bit of a rest until daylight.'

Jase stared at him. 'What about you, Dad? Are you going to take a break?'

Travis shook his head.

'So, we won't either,' Joel said. 'We won't stop until we find her.'

They drove into a brightly-lit base camp an hour later. There were more vehicles parked there and Travis noted that a long table had been set up on the verandah of the donga where the mess was. A couple of groups of people stood where the vehicles were parked, and he could see more people inside the building. He'd radioed the base as they'd travelled in and told them they'd found car tracks. The police had coordinated two searches: one out on the Conjuboy Road, and another on a road that led to the south-western corner of the property. There had been no result at either location.

Detective Baker came out of the building followed by another tall man with dark hair. Travis swallowed; he had to share what he'd found with the detective.

'Travis.' Baker nodded to the man beside him. 'This is David Barber, Emlyn's husband.'

Travis held out his hand and it was taken in a firm grip. 'I'm sorry we had to meet this way,' he said. 'I want you to know that whatever my brother has done, he'll pay for it.'

'Thank you.' David nodded. 'You found tyre tracks, Brett

said?'

'Yes.' Travis turned to Baker. 'I think it would be a good move to intensify the search out that way, Brett.'

'Let's go, then.' David turned, but Travis put a hand on his arm.

'In the morning. It's not safe out at night. There're too many places where it's dangerous to walk in the dark.'

'I can't stand around here doing nothing.' David's eyes were shadowed. 'Em could be out there, hurt … or worse … we need to be looking.'

Brett held Travis's gaze as David ran his hands over his face.

'We'll set out from here half an hour or so before first light,' the detective said. 'That's how long it takes to get out there, is that right, Travis?'

'Yes. We can be there in about twenty-five minutes in the dry. You'd never find your way to the tracks without us. There's a rabbit warren of old fire trails and tracks out there, but we know the main trail to the back gate. That's where the ute tracks are. I know he's been out there.'

'Good. I'll get Sergeant Brennan to work out some new search teams. Come inside both of you. There's been a couple of developments I need to talk to you about.'

Travis came to a decision. 'And I need to talk to you, too. In private.'

Bill had toasted a huge pile of sandwiches, and a large pot of coffee sat on the table outside the door, but Baker led them inside. There was no sign of the university team except for Bill, and Larry, who was helping in the kitchen.

After they sat down, and Bill had put a plate of fresh toasted sandwiches in front of them, Brett Baker filled them in on the incident at the bank the previous afternoon. 'The manager said Gavin was quite agitated when he couldn't access the account.'

'I'm not surprised,' Travis said drily. 'A quarter of a million snatched from his reach. I still can't believe he got that far with Carroglen.'

'Your brother appears to be a very clever man, Travis.'

David stood. 'I'm getting a coffee.'

Travis watched as he walked outside to the verandah before he spoke. 'Brett, I need to fill you in on something. It might be relevant to what's happened today. You've already said that Gavin has robbed at least one girl in Townsville. Without going into details, I need you to know something.' He cleared his throat and stared past the detective's head. 'My broth— Gavin—drugged my wife in our house twelve months ago when I was out working the boundaries.'

'What? Why are you only telling me this now? Why didn't you have him charged? It would have saved—'

'I've only found that out this afternoon. From a photo. I found his lair. I didn't touch anything but there're two large metal boxes there. Who knows what else you'll find in them.' Travis switched his gaze back to the detective's face. 'I didn't want David to hear that. My brother is capable of anything.'

'And you never had an inkling of what happened?'

Travis stared at him. 'If I had, I would have killed the bastard with my own hands.' He managed to keep his voice steady. 'My wife is on her way home now. We'll know more when I talk to her.'

CHAPTER 32

The Strand, Townsville, 2 February, 6am

The rage that had filled Gavin when he left the bank stayed with him and escalated to white-hot anger when he saw the police car at his unit. He was in desperate trouble. 'Bloody cops,' he muttered to himself as he turned the ute around. He'd slept in the back seat of the ute in a large car park at the harbour.

The grand total of thirty-five dollars was in his wallet, not even enough to fill up with fuel to go back to *Carlyle Downs*. Driving to the Strand, Gavin parked near the restaurant strip. He might as well get something to eat while he thought up a plan. Sleep had put him in a slightly better mood and he was thinking a bit straighter.

He was going to have it out with Travis, and he could give him access to the station account. He had no doubt that Travis had got wind of the new account and stopped him. There was no way he would know about the insect woman. Travis could pay him half the money that Carroglen had deposited and he'd disappear.

Mr High and Mighty Travis who thought he deserved everything.

Gavin knew he could run rings around his brother with anything he tried to do. He had all the brains in the family, and he'd made sure that Travis's family life had gone to shit. At least it had given him somewhere to live while he waited for his cryptocurrency to make him a wealthy man.

He considered his options.

He could threaten Travis with something unless he gave him the money.

Or he could tell Travis to come to Townsville, and show him the photo of Alison.

Damn. He gripped the steering wheel tightly when he remembered the photo was at the cave, along with the photos of the backpackers he'd robbed over the last two years. It would be worth going back there to get it. He'd love to see the look on his brother's face when he saw the photo. Maybe he'd even tell him that they'd been having an affair and that the little bitch of a girl was his daughter, not Travis's. That would make his bloody holier-than-thou brother very unhappy.

What sweet revenge.

Gavin started to feel better and he chuckled as he sat in the ute watching the tide go out. The mud flats were brown, and the white foam of the small waves picked up the mud as they broke on the seaweed-strewn shore. He hated this city; there was nothing here for him. He was going to find somewhere else to live; somewhere with a good climate, blue seas and plenty of bars.

And a good internet connection.

He got out of the ute and walked down to a coffee shop and ordered a big breakfast and a strong coffee. As he ate, he kept an eye on the customers as they parked their cars and came into the coffee shop. A middle-aged woman parked a Toyota Corolla in front of his ute and then sat at the table beside his. When the woman got up and disappeared into the toilet, leaving her keys on the table, he wiped the egg yolk from the plate with his toast and shoved it in his mouth. The keys to a plain white sedan that wouldn't get anyone's attention.

Gavin stood casually and scooped them into his pocket on the way to the counter. The waitress was yakking to the cook in the kitchen.

Serve her right. She missed out on a sale. He might as well keep his money. He sauntered out, hit the unlock button on the key remote and slid into the driver's seat. He laughed as he drove off; by the time the woman got back to her seat, he'd be heading for the highway.

And in a car that had a full tank of fuel.

His day was finally looking up.

Carlyle Downs, here I come. Satisfaction coursed through him. It had been a long time coming, but this brother was about to get everything he deserved.

* * *

Carlyle Downs 6 am

As soon as it was light enough to see, Emlyn took a long drink from the spring and set off along the tube that led off to the right. Her inbuilt sense of direction told her she was heading to the north. Her back pain was tolerable and the slight headache had gone completely. Her sleep had been fitful, and she'd kept starting to wakefulness thinking she heard someone calling her name, but each time she'd listened there'd been nothing more.

A wishful dream.

The tube had many openings in the roof to the ground high above, and the further she walked the lighter it became. Some of the openings were at the side of the roof, and her hope increased that there would be a low one with a rock fall that she could climb to escape.

As she walked, her mind buzzed with thoughts, and she wondered what had happened at the research base. Did they know yet she hadn't arrived in Brisbane? That she'd missed the meeting? What had David done when she hadn't turned up?

And where was Gavin? That was her only fear about getting out of the caves. That he'd be waiting up there for her to come out. That she'd encounter him, and it would happen all over again. He had serious mental health issues; some of the things he'd said to her had been bizarre.

When she got out, she'd take extra care.

She nodded. Yes, *when*, not *if.*

An hour later, her confidence had slipped again as the roof began to lower and the gaps above became less frequent. There were no tree roots hanging down here, and the space ahead was narrow and confined. She stood there debating whether to turn around, or whether to keep going, but she decided to press on and explore this way fully. It would be stupid to go the other way and find nothing and then have to retrace her steps. There could be something ahead; there was still room to stand up although it was very dark.

Taking a tentative step, she noticed a narrow strip of light appear a few metres in front of her. She stepped forward and gasped as icy water filled her shoes and rose up past her ankles.

An underground lake.

She stepped back with a sigh, and very wet shoes. There was no escape that way.

* * *

Carlyle Downs western gate 6 am

Sergeant Brennan had briefed the searchers before they left the base camp, and everyone was familiar with the search area they'd been allocated. Eight groups of three—more police had arrived from Croydon overnight—as well as Travis and his boys. David had chosen to search with them and he rode in the front of the ute with Travis, while the boys sat in the seat behind the cabin with Bluey.

Alison and Cassie were on their way with Alison's. cousin who lived in Townsville. Travis wanted more than anything to go down to Townsville to get them, but he was needed here.

'We've just left. I called Bette, she's bringing us up in my car.' Her voice shook. 'I didn't think I could drive safely.'

'Good idea. Just keep an eye out for Gavin,' he'd warned her.

'Oh, don't worry, I will be.' Alison's voice had been easier than he'd heard it for a long time.

David was quiet as they travelled along the back road to the far boundary of the property. He stared through the window as though he was searching every second.

'Have you been up this way before?' Travis asked to make conversation.

David shook his head. 'No. I haven't been north of Hervey Bay before. It's a very inhospitable landscape.'

Travis stared ahead, seeing the station from a different perspective. He was used to the brown and ochre around them. The only colour breaking the monotony was the occasional flash of yellow from the kapok flowers on the flat plains.

'It looks boring, but you'll find some of the most ancient

geology in the state out here.'

'Like the lava tubes?' David turned from the window, and Travis figured while he could keep him talking he wouldn't be dwelling on Emlyn and where she was.

'Yeah, that's a big part of it, but there're also other volcanic formations to the north-west, past these sand plains. There was a gold rush back here in the nineteenth century.'

'Interesting. I didn't think there'd be enough water out here to support gold mining.'

'The Einasleigh River is just west of our boundary, and it flows into the Gulf. It greens up a bit when we get closer to the back boundary. There's a swamp out there where drainage has been blocked by the lava flows, but you're right. We've been fighting the advances of a gold-mining company for about five years now. What little water we have out here would be compromised by that sort of mining.'

'Fair enough.' David turned back to the window and Travis left him in peace as they drove the last fifteen kilometres to where they'd left the three horses.

He parked the ute beneath one of the few shade trees near the gate, and Joel and Jase went to attend to the horses.

'Blue, you go on horseback with the boys and I'll walk in with David.' Travis pointed to the north. 'We'll head along that ridge where I was last night, and then work our way east. You three ride to the top of the ridge and then ride west.' He walked around to the back of the ute and passed one of the guns he'd brought to Bluey. 'Three shots if you find anything, and then we'll radio in.'

David glanced at the second gun as Travis slung it over his shoulder and put some ammunition in the front pocket of his shirt. 'Is that necessary?'

'We're a long way from any communication signals here, mate. It's the only way we'll hear a signal when we find Emlyn.'

David lifted his gaze and his eyes were bleak. 'You really think we've got a chance of finding her out here?'

Travis held his gaze steadily. 'I do. She's a strong woman, and she won't give up.'

David took a deep, shuddering breath. 'When she didn't arrive the other night, I thought that was it. It was my last chance of trying to talk her into coming home. And then when I heard she was missing, I thought she'd finally given up.'

'Emlyn and I have been working closely together over the past couple of weeks. I'd like to think we've become good friends.'

David looked at him curiously. 'What are you trying to tell me?'

'It's not really my place to tell you, but I know it will make you feel better. We had a good talk the night before she left. She was looking forward to seeing you.'

'Really? You're not just saying that? When I first heard from John that she was missing, I thought the worst. I didn't know how stable she'd been. I knew she'd stopped taking the anti-depressants and—'

'David,' Travis interrupted. 'She's been happy. I've seen a massive shift in her attitude since she first arrived. And it's not just because of the work and the project we've initiated. She seems to have come to terms with life. She told me how much she was looking forward to going home. She told me all about your house, and what you've done there. I've seen her come alive. I've listened to her, and I've watched some of the sadness leave her.' Travis cleared his throat; he felt as though he was saying too much, and David would think he was intruding on their personal territory, but David stopped walking and put his hand on Travis's forearm.

'So … she told you about … about Sophie?'

'Was that her mother's name? John told me she'd lost her parents recently.'

'Sophie was our daughter. She died in the same plane crash as Em's parents.'

Travis looked away as David lifted his hand and brushed at his eyes.

* * *

Carlyle Downs caves, noon

Emlyn made her way back to the spring, her footsteps slow as frustration filled her. She'd walked as far as she could in the long tube that led to what she was sure was the west. The compass on her watch wasn't working and the battery was almost flat. Even though the roof on the tube was at least ten metres above her, there were very few gaps where the light came in. Numerous rock falls blocked her way, and a couple of times she'd considered turning back, but she'd clambered over them, always hoping for that glimmer of light ahead. She stood at the spring and drank thirstily. Her stomach was rumbling with hunger, but at least she had water.

Emlyn was not going to give up. She'd seen the maps of these tubes many times as they'd decided where to start their research, and again with Travis over the past few nights as they'd looked at the feasibility of locations for the proposed development; and there was always an entry where you could come in from ground level. She just had to find where it was.

If she let doubt set in, she might as well give up. There

was no way she was going to give in and die down here like those poor children. There was a life out there to be lived, and one that she was determined to take up again.

David was waiting for her, and she knew he loved her. When they were old they'd sit back and talk about the event that had brought them back together after the tragedy that had broken her for a while. The lava tubes would always be significant to her; it was where she had discovered that life did go on.

Emlyn rubbed her arms, aching again for the feel of David's arms holding her close, and refusing to consider that she would never feel them around her again. With a deep breath, she turned and headed back the way she had come; there were two side passages that she hadn't explored yet.

A little tendril of fear rippled in her stomach as she headed that way; the passages she'd passed were both dark and narrow, and she'd only given them a cursory glance a couple of hours ago. She'd been so sure that the high cave would have a rock fall where she could climb up to the surface.

She shook away the fear; at the first sign of any bad air, she'd turn around.

More than three hundred metres along the wide tube, she stopped at the first narrow opening. Stepping in, she let her eyes adjust to the dim light, and sniffed the air.

Stupid really, because you couldn't smell carbon dioxide. Her eyes widened as they adjusted to the dark. The sides of the opening were not vertical as they had been in all of the other caves; this wall was multi-layered and at a sixty-degree angle. At the top of the wall, about two metres above, were vertical spaces where shards of light shone through. She mustn't be far underground; the fall had been going up at a slight angle over the past couple of hundred metres, but she hadn't realised how far she'd climbed. If she squinted, she could see glimmers of blue sky through the rock wall above. The floor of the passage was at a steep angle, in alignment with the crenulations on the wall, but to her dismay, the passage narrowed as she stepped forwards. The light became brighter, but she barely had space to move forward. Breathing in, she turned sideways and forced herself to push into the passage where the walls were pressing on her front and back. Fear came in waves, and light pricked at her vision, but she forced herself to breathe evenly until her heart beat slowed and the panic receded.

I won't get stuck between the rock walls, she told herself. If she could get in there, she could turn around and get out.

With a determined lunge, Emlyn forced her body through the narrow space.

Chapter 33

'Your daughter?' Travis waited for David to compose himself.

'Yes, Sophie was two. We were on our way to a wedding.'

'I'm sorry. I didn't know. Emlyn didn't talk about her at all.'

David stood still and stared past Travis. 'That was a lot of the problem. She wouldn't listen to the counsellor, and she wouldn't talk to me about her, either. I wasn't even allowed to say Sophie's name. It was as though she didn't want her to have ever existed. The doctor said it was her way of dealing with her grief.'

'I can't imagine losing a child.'

'As soon as Emlyn came home from the hospital—even though she was still in bandages after the skin grafts—she took everything away. She stripped Sophie's room, the furniture, the toys, all her little clothes. I got home after work and it was empty. Four bare walls. Pink walls. I think if she could have taken them out, she would have too. Emlyn was sitting on the floor. She looked at me without speaking and got up and walked out.'

David began walking again; it was as though he'd forgotten they were searching, so Travis scanned the bush around them as he listened. 'I can't lose her as well. I have to convince her that it wasn't her fault.' David's words hit Travis in the chest as he walked along beside him. 'I'll never forget that phone call. I was on a boat because I wouldn't fly over to the island. It was a family wedding. I told Emlyn to take Sophie in the plane so she could see the water. She loved the sea. From the day she could speak, it was all about water, and swim, and fish. We used to laugh and say she'd be a marine biologist when she grew up.'

'I think when we find her you're going to see a much stronger woman than the one you've described. It's not important in the scheme of things, or what you've been through, but Emlyn talked me through a problem I was struggling with. She knows what matters.'

The vegetation had thickened as they'd climbed towards the top of the ridge.

'Thanks, mate. No matter what happens, I'll hold that close.'

'What's going to happen is that we're going to find her.' Travis stopped and looked towards the top of the ridge as David kept walking. He hadn't been this far along for a few years and was surprised to see how many trees had come down in the last cyclone that had come across from the coast. A lot of trees were down.

'She's been missing almost two days, do you—'

'David! Stop!'

The hill had levelled out on a false plateau before the top of the ridge. A thicket of vines had tangled around a fallen tree, and Travis had spotted the telltale gap as David had been about to step into it.

He grabbed for a tree, leaned forwards and looked down into the depths. 'What is it?'

'There's been a rock fall, and it's an entry point to one of the tubes.'

David's throat worked, and his eyes were wide. 'And

you're thinking that Emlyn could have fallen down one of those?'

'She wouldn't fall. She knows the terrain too well, but she could have gone in one to hide.' The unspoken meaning behind Travis's words made the anger rise in him, and his tone was brusque. 'Come on, just watch where you're walking.'

* * *

Gavin had to take the Hervey Range Road because the small sedan wasn't capable of taking any of the bush tracks. He watched the fuel gauge get lower and lower as the vehicle struggled up the mountain road. It must have a bloody small fuel tank.

'Fuck it,' he muttered as he changed back a gear. At this rate, he'd be lucky to get to Greenvale before he ran out of fuel.

It was almost mid-afternoon by the time he drove into the small village. He pulled his cap down low over his face and parked by the browser close to the road. He smiled as a large four-wheel drive towing a massive caravan drove in, blocking the shop from his view. He was hungry; it had been a long time since breakfast on the Strand, and he'd been in too much of a hurry to get back to the station to think about bringing anything to eat. The owner of the vehicle had kindly left a couple of bottles of water on the floor of the back seat, and he'd had to make do with them.

If things went to plan and he could make Travis see sense, then he could leave this car at the house and come back down in one of the farm utes. And then he'd be on his way.

Gavin filled the car, ignoring the caravan owner as the man tried to strike up a conversation. He put the fuel pump back in the cradle and drove out. As he drove off, he glanced in the rear-vision mirror. Reg and the other customer were standing there watching him drive away.

Gavin laughed. Let them chase that number plate and send the lady the bill. Old Reg at the garage couldn't call the cops to chase him because there were none between here and Mt Surprise. Besides, he'd spent so much money there over the past few months the old bastard owed him a tank of fuel.

The road to Conjuboy was busier than usual and Gavin was surprised to see a couple of police Pajeros parked in the bush on the side of the road. He tapped his hand on the steering wheel as he drove past, wondering what to do now.

Jesus, all he needed to do was find Travis and make him share the money. He had no doubt he could talk sense to his brother, but if there were police sniffing around looking for that woman, he couldn't risk driving to the house in daylight.

Impatience flooded through Gavin, and he swore again. Why couldn't anything go right for him? He deserved better than this.

* * *

Parrots rose squawking, breaking the stillness of the late afternoon as three shots rang out below them. Travis and David looked at each other and took off at a run down the hill, back to where the ute was parked. By the time they reached the two boys and Bluey, they were both out of breath.

Travis looked around, but there was no sign of Emlyn.

David ran across to the ute and looked inside. 'What's happened? Has she been found?'

Bluey shook his head. 'I came back here for a bit of a

breather, and the detective radioed in. Travis, they've spotted Gavin. He drove through Greenvale about one o'clock.'

Travis looked at his watch. It was just before five and would be dark soon. 'Shit, he's had enough time to get out here already. I wonder if the police have an eye on the house. 'All he could think of was Alison and Cass on the same road.

'The policeman said not to worry. They've got everything covered,' Bluey said.

'Did he say anything else? Have they found anything?'

'No, they haven't.' The old stockman shook his head. 'We need to keep looking.'

'We'll take a bit of a break and then go out for another couple of hours. Until it's dark.' Travis took the gun off his shoulder and put it in the back of the ute. 'As much as I hate to say it, I'm pleased he's come back.' The anger he'd put on hold began to boil inside again.

'Because he can tell us where he left Emlyn?' David asked.

'Yes, that and I have a long conversation to hold with my brother.' Travis glanced at the gun and decided that it wouldn't be anywhere within reach when he came face to face with Gavin.

Because he knew he couldn't trust himself not to use it.

He pulled open the door of the ute and picked up the microphone. 'Travis Carlyle. Detective Baker, come in please.'

'Baker here. Have you got something for us?'

'Negative. I just wanted a word about Gavin. My stockman said he's been spotted up here.'

'We think so. But not one hundred percent sure.'

'Okay. I just need to let you know my wife and daughter are on their way home from Townsville. Can someone look out for them, please? They'll be in a white Isuzu SUV.'

'No problem. I'm on it. I'll send a vehicle to meet them at the main road.'

'Thanks, mate. We're going out for one more sweep and then we'll head back in. Over and out.' He hung the mike on the hook at the side of the CB radio and climbed out of the ute. Jase and Joel were standing shoulder to shoulder watching him.

'Dad?'

'Yes, Joel?'

'You just said Mum and Cass are coming home.' The look on both his sons' faces made his throat close.

Travis nodded, unable to trust his voice.

'Did you mean coming home, as in staying here?' Jase asked tentatively.

Travis took a deep breath. 'I wasn't going to say anything until I talked to your mother, but I'm pretty sure that'll be happening.'

'That is so cool.' Joel looked embarrassed as he blinked away tears.

'We'll talk about it all later. Now go and have a drink and something to eat, and we'll head out again.'

Chapter 34

The passage Emlyn was in was different to any that they'd encountered over on the eastern side of the station where they'd been working for the past few weeks. If she hadn't been so determined to find her way out, she would have spent longer looking at the composition of the walls, and the strange markings in the silt on the floor of the passage. As she'd made her way further along—she judged she'd forced herself through fifty metres of the confined space where the walls had pressed in on her at times—she'd seen some peculiar cocoons and shells that she hadn't been able to identify. The light was too dim to get a good look, so she could have been wrong. Tears clogged her throat as desperation took hold. She was hurting, and her head was beginning to ache again. Her legs and arms were burning, and her stomach was sore.

Emlyn fought the fear that was trying to take hold of her and pushed herself to keep going. There was a curve in the wall ahead and she prayed it wasn't a dead end. She doubted if she had the energy to go back to the spring. As she got closer, the ceiling rose higher and the light brightened. When she saw the first tree root hanging past the bend in the passage, hope flooded through her. The walls were further apart and the space got wider with every step she took.

As she hurried past the curved wall, Emlyn looked up and blinked as she stepped below a massive cavern bathed with light. Sunshine poured down a rock fall that led up to a huge gap at the side of the cave.

She could see the trees above, the sunlight dappling their leaves, and as she watched a couple of brightly coloured parrots rose into the air, their squawks like music to her ears. The sunlight played on cobwebs caught between the rocks, but she gave no thought to spiders or snakes. All she could think of was the freedom at the top of the scree.

Taking a deep breath, she put her head down and climbed, making sure each rock was firm before she put her weight on it. It took less than five minutes to climb to the top, and she braced herself on her hands and pulled herself onto the ground. She rolled over onto her back, taking deep breaths of fresh, sweet air and smiled at the bright, blue sky above.

She lay there for a moment, trying to regain some energy. She still wasn't out of trouble. Even though it had been over two days since he'd left her in the cave, Emlyn wasn't going to risk bumping into Gavin out here. She sat up and looked around. She was on a plateau, halfway up from a gully and the top of a ridge. There was no point wandering around aimlessly; she needed a plan.

As well as water and trying to find something she could eat. Hunger gnawed at her stomach as she thought of food.

She pushed herself to her feet and looked around. It was nothing like where she'd run from Gavin, but she knew she'd have to be careful. If she fell into another cave, she'd have no hope of making it out again; her energy reserves were almost exhausted. Her head spun a little as she straightened, and she leaned against the trunk of a large tree. Emlyn put her cheek against it. The bark was rough, but to touch something apart from cold rock, something that was living, was the most incredible feeling.

She'd got this far; she could make it from here, as long as Gavin wasn't waiting for her.

As she closed her eyes and took a breath waiting for her head to steady, a twig snapped close by and Emlyn tensed. She pressed her back against the tree and the skin on her neck crawled as she waited. Low voices reached her, and cautious hope began to unfurl in her chest.

Emlyn listened, incredulous as the voices got louder, now accompanied by the sound of more twigs snapping and grass rustling beneath the feet of those approaching. She moved forwards a little bit and her hands grasped the tree as she peered around down the hill.

Her head spun, and her legs shook, and she grabbed the tree to stop herself falling.

Travis and David—her David, her husband, the man she knew she loved more than life itself—were twenty metres away, and walking up towards where she was hiding. She stepped out slowly, unable to get her voice to work as she waited for them to see her.

David was the first to look up.

'Emlyn!' The emotion in his cry filled her with joy and hope as he ran towards her. The look on his face was something Emlyn would remember for the rest of her life.

Her hands were shaking as she held them out to him. 'David.'

'Oh, Em!' He took her in his arms and Emlyn buried her face against his chest as he held her close. He cupped the back of her head with one hand as his other held her firmly against him. 'Oh, sweetheart.'

They stood together, not speaking, until Travis reached them.

Emlyn lifted her head and stared up at David. She reached up and touched his face, still not believing that he was here. Standing on the side of a hill close by to where she had come out of the caves.

'David? How did you get here?' Her voice was husky and shaking.

'I flew.'

'You got in a plane?'

His eyes were full of love as he nodded. 'Of course I did.'

'But you don't fly.' Emlyn couldn't hold her tears back any longer. 'You hate flying.'

'Not as much as I love you.'

* * *

David and Travis made a chair with their hands, and despite the difficult nature of the terrain, they wouldn't let Emlyn walk. When they reached the bottom of the hill, the going was easier. Every time she tried to speak, Travis shook his head.

'There's plenty of time, Emlyn. Save your energy. Everything's okay. Just know you're safe now.'

She leaned her head against David's chest as they walked, but even though she was exhausted she didn't let herself drift off. Excitement and joy were bursting inside her as the beat of his heart comforted her.

Finally, they stopped beside a ute, and they lowered her feet gently to the ground.

David took her weight and held her close, his eyes holding hers, his hand stroking her hair. 'It's okay, Em. It's going to be fine. You're safe. I've got you.' His voice was fierce. 'And I'm never going to let you go.'

She whispered a reply as she leaned into his embrace. 'That's good.'

'Put your hands over your ears,' Travis said. He walked to the gate a short distance away from the front of the vehicle and fired three shots into the air. Soon after, three answering shots sounded from a distance. As David held her, murmuring to her and dropping light kisses onto her forehead, Travis came back and slid into the vehicle.

Emlyn listened as he picked up the radio and told someone that she'd been found.

'Yes, not in bad condition, but yes, we'll need a medico to check her over.' He paused and listened. 'Yes, that would be good. Yes, she's able to stand and speak. It'll take us about half an hour or so to drive back in. The boys and Bluey will come on horseback.' He looked out at Emlyn and the grin that crossed his face was wide. 'Tell Bill to put on a good feed. I think I know someone who might appreciate it.'

Emlyn looked at Travis as he got out of the car. 'Thank you,' she whispered as she squeezed his fingers

Fifteen minutes later, they'd left the fire trail and were back on the main track heading to the base.

* * *

Gavin was getting more desperate with every kilometre. He'd driven along the Conjuboy Road into *Carlyle Downs*, and all he could see were police cars and vans. And as he drove closer to the house, a police helicopter flew low, but he had time to park the sedan in thick bush before it spotted him. Anger choked him as it circled around and then landed over in the direction of the dongas.

What the hell was going on?

And then he remembered. They must be looking for *her*. The insect woman.

Stuff it. The stupid bitch was going to interfere with his plan. His hands gripped the steering wheel of the pissy little car that had taken him so long to get here. It looked like he was going to have to lie low for a few days.

The unfairness of it all fed the rage that was building inside him. He had no money, half a tank of fuel, and if he went to his cave, he'd have no internet access on his phone. At least he had some tinned food and bottled water there.

Once things settled down, he'd go and see Travis. They'd find her phone down in Townsville and move the search down there. If things went his way—for a bloody change—she'd still be lying on the floor of that cave, and they'd never find her.

Things would die down soon.

He'd be patient. He'd let a day or so pass, and then go out and have a look. Gavin kept a careful eye out as he drove down the track to his cave, but he didn't see anyone. He drove the car into a thicket twenty metres from the track and covered the back of it with some small branches. With each bit of energy he expended, his rage grew.

I deserve better than this.

Chapter 35

Once the relieved welcomes from the university team had been made, and Emlyn had been hugged at least ten times, even by Larry, she sat quietly on the side of her bed as the doctor examined her. David sat in the chair next to her; he'd refused to let her out of his sight, even for the medical examination. The doctor had raised his eyebrows in question as he'd followed them in to her donga, but Emlyn had nodded. Her legs were weaker now, and the cuts on her hands from climbing up the rock scree were stinging. Once the doctor had dressed them, and finished his examination, he stood back and regarded her.

'I don't think there's any need to take you to the hospital. Make sure you stay hydrated and eat well. With a couple of good nights' sleep, your physical recovery will be fast.' He pulled off the medical gloves and put them into the bin beside the door before he turned back to her. 'How are you feeling? Emotionally, I mean.'

'A little shaken. Very grateful, and extremely happy that I got out safely.'

'I'll leave some sleeping pills. You might find you'll suffer from nightmares when the reaction sets in.'

She shook her head and looked across at David. He held her gaze. 'I'll be fine. I've been through and survived much worse than being lost in a cave for a couple of days.'

David reached out and took her hand and she held it tightly as the doctor closed his bag. Warmth settled in her chest as he smoothed his thumb over her skin.

'If you have any problems, even if you want to call and ask about anything, or if you would like a referral to someone to talk to, give me a call.' The doctor passed his card to her, and Emlyn put it on the table next to the bed.

'Thank you.' She waited until the door closed behind him and lifted her head.

She held David's eyes with hers as he let go of her hand and stood. 'I did a lot of thinking when I was down in the tubes.'

He moved onto the bed and sat close beside her. 'I want you to be honest with me, Em. If you don't want me here, tell me now, and I'll go.'

Her bottom lip quivered and the uncertainty in his voice almost broke her heart. She moved across the bed and put her head on his shoulder, her hands twisting together in her lap. 'Oh, David. I want you to stay. I want to have the chance to say I'm sorry. For shutting you out when you were suffering as much as I was. It's not the way to remember Sophie. I know it's going to be hard, but I want to focus on the happy times.' Emlyn drew in a deep, shuddering breath. 'She's gone, and she's not coming back. Neither are Mum and Dad. I tried to bury myself back in my work and pretend that it never happened. That *we* never happened, and that Sophie hadn't existed, but that was stupid. I was wrong. So very wrong.'

She leaned back and lifted her face to rest her cheek against his and David put his arms around her. As she leaned against him, his face was wet, and his chest shook with silent sobs.

'We've lost a beautiful little girl who was a part of our future, but when I was down there in the dark, I made a promise. As hard as it might seem, I promised myself that if I got out alive,

I would make a commitment to life. A life with you, and a life where maybe we might one day have more children.'

David lifted his head and looked down at her. Although his eyes were awash with tears, he was smiling. Emlyn lifted her hand and wiped his cheeks.

'Can I come home?' she asked.

'Of course you can, Mrs Barber.'

As his lips gently brushed hers, Emlyn tasted his salty tears. She closed her eyes and cried with her husband.

* * *

The main donga was filled with the aroma of curry. Bill had a variety of pots bubbling on the stove and insisted that Travis ate before he left, although he was anxious to get back to the house and wait for Alison. She'd called when they landed in Townsville, and he was expecting them to arrive about nine. He glanced at his watch; it was just past seven-thirty.

Baker sat beside Travis as Bill walked over and put two loaded plates in front of them. 'Where are your boys?' the detective asked.

'They're going to camp out tonight and ride back in tomorrow. It's safer than riding in through the night.'

'You think so? With your brother unaccounted for?' Baker raised his eyebrows.

'How sure are you that he's come up this way?'

The detective picked up a bread roll and broke it in half. 'I spoke to the guy at the service station at Greenvale myself. There's a bit of doubt. He said he didn't get a good look, but he's only about fifty percent sure that it was Gavin. The man he saw was in a white Toyota sedan, but he didn't get the plates.'

'So, what's next?' Travis picked up his fork.

'I need to interview Dr Rees and see exactly what happened. And then we go from there.'

'The bank account and the assault? I imagine he'll be up on charges there.'

'The assault for sure. If we can prove it was him. The bank account? That depends on the bank, I guess, and what can be proven. But what Dr Rees has to say is critical at this point.' He held Travis's gaze. 'I'll also need to interview your wife when she gets here about what you told me earlier.'

'I just want it all to be over. So I know everyone's safe.' Travis rubbed the back of his neck. 'It's hard to accept that my brother is responsible for this.'

'I imagine it is. But at least there's a good outcome, Travis,' Baker said. 'Everyone is safe.'

'Yes. The best we could have hoped for. I'll feel better when Alison is here safely. I just wish we knew where he is.'

'Did Dr Rees say anything about what happened out there?'

'No. I didn't want to press too hard. After what I've discovered about my brother in the past few days, I didn't want to upset her.'

They were quiet as they finished the meal, and as Travis stood to leave, Emlyn and David walked into the donga together. She had a lot more colour in her face, but her eyes were red-rimmed. His heart sank; he'd hoped that things would work out for them.

Baker stood and nodded as they came to the table. 'Dr Rees, how are you feeling?'

Emlyn glanced up at David. 'It's Mrs Barber. And I'm feeling fine, thank you.' She sniffed at the air and smiled at Bill as he came over and enfolded her in a gentle hug. 'Is that curried sausages I can smell?' she asked.

Bill nodded and smiled back at her. 'I made a fresh batch today, ready for you. I knew you'd come back.' He blinked, and Travis was surprised to see the older man choke up.

'Serve it up, then,' Emlyn said. 'I'm starving. And I think David is too.'

David put his arm around his wife.

'Are you up to talking to me about what happened tonight?' the detective asked.

Emlyn nodded, but she glanced at Travis. 'Would it be okay if Travis was there? He needs to hear some of the things I have to say.'

'Travis?' Baker asked.

'Yes. I want to be there.' Travis frowned. 'Would it be too much to ask if we did it over at the house? After you've eaten. Alison and Cass are on their way home. I can't settle until I know they're safe. It would be a bit more private there, also. If you're up to it, Emlyn? It's your call.'

* * *

Emlyn was happy to be interviewed at Travis's house. David drove the Troop carrier, and she sat close to him in the middle of the front seat. The search teams had eaten and headed back to the towns they'd come from, and the university team had settled in with a couple of bottles of red wine.

'Well deserved.' John lifted his glass as David and Emlyn headed out. Meg and Lucy hugged Emlyn again and she smiled.

'I'm feeling very popular all of a sudden,' she said quietly.

'It's good to have you back safe and sound,' John said.

'Back to work tomorrow?' she asked.

There were calls of dissent from the team, and David shook his head. 'Not for you.'

'Perhaps we can have a meeting, and I can tell you what I saw down there.' Emlyn threw out a teasing comment as they walked out. 'I have so much to tell you.'

The old house was ablaze with lights and it looked like Travis had raced around and had a tidy-up. The coffee table was clear, and there was a clean cloth on the dining-room table. The piles of newspapers that had been there on her last visit were gone. Detective Baker had come over before them, and he was sitting at the table with a laptop open in front of him.

They sat down, but Travis stood behind his chair.

'David. Tea? Coffee?' he asked. He seemed nervous, and as Emlyn observed he kept looking at his watch and crossing to the window.

'Just water, thanks,' David replied.

After going to the kitchen, Travis returned with a jug of water and put some glasses on the table before sitting across from Emlyn.

The detective looked up from the laptop. 'Any time that you feel stressed by what I ask you, you can call a stop to this, and we'll do it later.'

Emlyn shook her head, surprised by how strong she was feeling. David was sitting close and held one of her hands tightly between his. She still couldn't get her head around him being there. 'I'm fine now. And there was only a short time over the past few days that I felt scared. Once I got away from Gavin and I knew I wasn't injured too badly—' she shot an apologetic look at Travis, but he shook his head— 'I was fairly calm.'

She took them through the events of the day when the van had broken down, and Gavin's behaviour had been bizarre.

'We've had a look at the van. It had been tampered with,' Baker said.

'I agreed to his offer of a lift, but I started to worry when I knew we were heading in the wrong direction. I knew because I'd gone out that way to unlock the gate when I first arrived here.' She looked at the detective and explained, 'For the first delivery of provisions for the camp. Gavin stopped the ute and made me get out.' Emlyn watched Travis closely as she explained about Gavin's cave and what he had bragged about.

'He told me he lit a fire that destroyed your family's homestead.' She reached out to touch Travis's hands clenched on the top of the table. 'Your family diaries are out there, too. He showed me.' Her voice shook. 'Even though he intended killing me, he had to brag and show me what he had down there.'

'He articulated that to you exactly?' the detective clarified.

Emlyn nodded. 'Yes.' She closed her eyes as she thought back to those terrifying moments she was in the cave with Gavin. 'He said, "I was an interfering bitch who was going to ruin all his plans. And that when I disappeared it would stop the research." Poor Bluey; I thought he was interfering with our work. It must have been Gavin all along.'

Travis dropped his head into his hands. 'I'm having trouble processing his. How could Gavin hide all this for so many years?'

'Your brother is a very clever man, Travis,' Baker said. 'The things he's done with the bank, and from what you say, cryptocurrency, as well as the forged documents, shows a very calculating persona.' He turned to Emlyn. 'What happened then?

How did you get away from him? Take it slowly.'

In a calm, clinical voice, she told them of throwing the rock at Gavin and getting away. When David squeezed her hand beneath the table, emotion clogged her throat and she picked up the glass and took a sip.

'I fell down a tube and landed heavily, and the last thing I remembered for a while was Gavin looking down at me.'

* * *

The bastard.

Disbelief slammed through Travis. The house fire that had taken the old homestead, the diaries that he had thought were lost. The dead cattle? The backhoe? And interfering with the university team? What else had he done?'

How much more grief was his brother responsible for?

Lights swept across the front window and he jumped to his feet.

'I'm sorry; you'll have to excuse me for a few minutes.' By the time he reached the door, nerve endings were firing all over Travis's body. His legs were like jelly and his hands were shaking. A car door slammed, and as he turned the front light on, it lit up a white SUV.

Alison was running towards the house, holding Cass to her chest, her hair flying loose behind her. But it was the happiness on her face that brought him to a stop. Her smile was wide, and her eyes were full of love. Travis held his arms open, and for the first time in over a year, he held his wife close against him. There were no words spoken as he buried his face in her soft hair, and she slid her arms around his back and held him tightly.

'Dadda, we home!' Cass wriggled between them.

Travis dropped a kiss on her curls. 'You are.' His voice cracked as he looked down at Alison. 'Both my girls are home.'

Cass wriggled some more and Alison put her down and she ran to the stairs.

His wife lifted her face, and her familiar sweet smile made him catch his breath as she stared up at him. Her face was damp with tears and he wasn't ashamed when his own tears began falling.

Alison reached up and gently wiped it away with her fingers. 'Now that you know. Now that you know and still love me—' Her voice broke as he held her close. 'But you have to be sure, Trav.'

'I'm sure.' Travis put his finger against her lips. 'Later. We'll get a removalist to pack up your things down there,' Travis said. 'I'm not letting you out of my sight.'

'We still have a lot of talking to do before then, Trav.' Alison smiled up at him tentatively.

'We do.' Travis ran a hand over his unshaven chin. 'But unfortunately, we'll have to wait. The police are here interviewing Emlyn. It's been a few days of revelations.' He looked down at Alison and hesitated as he flicked a glance at Cass. 'Al, he wants to talk to you, too. About what happened. But you and me? We'll talk later, even if we have to talk all night.'

'Yes. I'll talk to him. I just need you to know something first.' Alison's voice was full of pain.

He took his wife's hand as she stood on the bottom step, her eyes level with his. 'It's okay, love. We'll be right.' He brushed his lips over her fingers.

'You have to know why I was so awful to you.' Alison's voice was full of pain.

Travis put his forehead against Alison's. 'I know, sweetheart. I understand.''

The joy that spread across Alison's face reached deep into his heart. Travis couldn't wait any longer. He lowered his head and Alison lifted her face to meet him halfway. His wife's lips clung to his for a few seconds before he pulled back as Cassie called out to them.

'Hurry up, Dadda.'

'We're coming, Cass.'

'You go up to Cassie,' Alison said. 'I'll just say goodbye to Bette; she's going to go over to Aunty Maureen's for the night.'

'Tell her thank you,' Travis said as he waved towards the car. 'We owe her for getting you here so quickly.'

As the SUV backed out, Travis put his arm around Alison and held her close as they walked up the stairs to their daughter. 'I've missed you so much, sweetheart. We have a whole year to catch up on.'

'Where are the boys,' Alison asked.

'They're with Blue. They'll be back in the morning.' He kissed her once more. 'And then we'll be a family again.'

Emlyn turned as they came in through the front door, and her smile was wide when she saw hi arm around Alison.

Travis held her gaze and smiled back. He introduced Alison to Brett and David as Cassie disappeared into the kitchen.

'I'll put a cuppa on before I put Cass to bed.' Alison hovered in the doorway. 'If anyone wants one, just say and I'll bring it out.'

'Thank you.' Travis found it hard to bring his attention back to the group at the table as Alison went into the kitchen. He sat and filled his glass with water from the jug. 'Where were we?'

'There's only one more thing I need to tell you.' Emlyn spoke softly. 'And I think it's one of the most important. Apart from the diaries, of course.'

Travis focused on her face as she smiled. 'Knowing that the diaries are still there has been enough,' he said. 'What could be better than that?'

'The children.' Her voice shook as she held his gaze. 'I found the children. The missing children. Missy and Thomas are in the cave I fell into when I ran away from Gavin. In a way, I think it makes it all worthwhile, don't you?'

Travis looked up at the ceiling and blinked as her words sank in. He turned to David. 'I hope you know what an amazing woman your wife is.'

'Oh, I do. Don't you worry about that,' David said.

Colour stained Emlyn's cheeks as she lowered her eyes. 'But there's only one thing that I'm worried about. Finding the two caves again. I walked a long way in the tubes underground, and I don't know if I can remember exactly where we went in.'

'How far is it out to that back end of the property?' the detective asked.

'Just under twenty kilometres as the crow flies,' Travis replied. 'I know exactly where Gavin parked the ute on that back road, so I'm sure we can find it.' Travis stood, anxious to get back to Alison. 'Let's leave it for a few days to give you a chance to recover. The children and the diaries have been there for a long time. A few more days won't hurt.'

''We won't need you out there, Emlyn, if Travis knows where to look.' The detective stood. 'I'll speak to your wife now, Travis, if that's okay. I'll organise for a forensic team to come in by chopper. I think we'll need one to investigate what's in that cave. It might take a couple of days to organise, but in the meantime, I'll leave a couple of men up here to keep an eye out there. I won't be confident until we have your brother in custody.'

Travis nodded. 'Me either.'

Baker walked around the table and held out his hand to Emlyn. 'I'm pleased to see you looking so well. You go back and get some sleep.'

'Thank you,' she said. 'For everything.'

David took her arm to help her stand, but she shook her head. 'There's no need, I'm fine, really.' Letting go of David's hand, Emlyn walked over to Travis and reached up and kissed his cheek. 'I'm very happy for you,' she said quietly. 'It's been a big week for all of us. Now we'll leave you and your wife in peace.'

Travis walked to the door and waited until David had helped Emlyn into the Troop carrier. He turned to Brett. 'Is it okay if I stay while you talk to Alison?'

Until Gavin was found, he intended keeping his family close.

Travis took a deep breath as they returned to the table and waited for Alison to join them.

He feared the rage that consumed him as he thought of what Gavin had done to his wife.

And their life.

Chapter 36

Three days had passed at the station, and although things were slowly getting back to normal, Travis was still being careful and keeping the boys, Cass and Alison close by.

There'd been no sign of Gavin, or any communication from him, and Travis was beginning to think that the sighting of him at Greenvale had been mistaken identity. The police were patrolling out around where Emlyn had been found, and there'd been no sighting of Gavin or a vehicle.

At dawn on the third day that he had his wife and family home, he lay in bed holding Alison close as she slept. Normally he'd be up and heading out onto the station, but he was putting off all the cattle work that was waiting until he knew it was safe to leave the house. Detective Baker was coming back today with the forensics team and he'd take them out to the cave. The thought of seeing the family diaries again lifted Travis's mood even higher, and he was looking forward to sharing them with his sons.

He stared at the ceiling as the room lightened and the first rays of the sun hit the wall opposite the door. Alison's breathing was slow and even, and he let her sleep. They'd talked until well after midnight each night. They were still being careful around each other, and he knew it was going to take a while before things were back to what they'd been.

As he lay there, anger began to rise in Travis's chest and he fought it back. How ridiculous was it to be worried about your own flesh and blood hurting your family? How hard was it to accept what Gavin had done to Alison, and the emotional trauma she had endured over the past year? The money and the deal Gavin had made with Carroglen was unimportant. That could all be sorted.

What he couldn't deal with was the betrayal of his family by his own brother.

He eased his arm out gently and Alison murmured in her sleep, but she didn't stir. As Travis headed back from the bathroom, he debated between getting back into bed and heading out to the cattle yards.

Normal life had to resume soon, but Travis couldn't shake the uneasiness that stayed with him when he'd realised what his brother was capable of. And that he still hadn't been found.

He pulled on his work trousers and a T-shirt. He'd go down to the shed and feed the dogs before the police arrived. As he walked across the living room, he could hear the sound of a computer game coming from the boys' bedroom and he tapped on the door. He shook his head. The games-on-the-back-verandah rule hadn't lasted long.

'I hope you pair have had some sleep,' he said as he looked around. Jase was still asleep, but Joel was glued to the screen.

'Yeah, Dad. I woke up at first light.'

'I'm just going down to the shed. Mum's still asleep. Just keep a bit of an ear out, will you?'

'I will.' Joel's eyes were shadowed, and Travis walked across and sat next to him on the bed.

'You okay, mate?'

'Yeah.' His son shrugged, but his tone didn't convince him.

'What's bothering you?'

Joel's eyes were hollow as he stared back at him. 'What Uncle Gavin did.'

Travis gut tightened. 'He's got a sickness, mate. He's always been like it, ever since he was a kid. We're going to move on with our lives. Mum and I have done a lot of talking, and there're going to be a lot of changes. But all for the better, okay?'

Finally, a small smile crossed Joel's face. 'Okay.' He turned back to the screen and Travis touched his shoulder lightly as he stood. 'I won't be long.'

He closed the front door quietly and stood on the top step looking out over the station. The grass had greened up from the rain they'd had last week, but he couldn't get enthusiastic about it. Once he'd sorted out the mess with Carroglen, he was thinking about selling up.

This place held too many memories. It wouldn't be fair on Alison living in a house that held such memories.

Bits started barking down in the pen as Travis stood on the step and he frowned. As he looked around, dust rose on the road down near the river, and he waited for the vehicle to reach the corner. He held his breath when he heard the gear change as it approached the corner, but let it out slowly as a white Pajero appeared.

It was one of the police vehicles.

He hurried down the stairs and waited while the policeman opened the driver's window. 'Sorry to swing by so early, but Brett asked us to call in and let you know the chopper is on its way. They'll be here a bit after eight.'

'No problem,' Travis said. 'I'll be here.'

'There's been no sign of a vehicle, so we're heading out today.'

'Okay. So, you don't think he's on the property?'

'Doesn't seem to be.'

'Thanks for hanging around.'

The two policemen waved, and Travis waited until the vehicle reversed out of the driveway and headed out towards the main road before he walked down to the shed.

Bits was barking and stirring the other dogs up, and he didn't settle even after Travis had filled his bowl with kibble.

Travis put the scoop back into the bin and frowned. He looked back to the house and froze. The back door was open, and there was no one on the steps or in the yard. He took off up the hill at a run, keeping the house in his sight the whole way. There was no sign of a car, but Bits was still barking. Travis went around to the front and walked quietly up the front steps. He pushed open the door and stopped as he heard voices.

His fists clenched at his side as he stepped into the lounge room. Gavin was sitting there with Cass on his knee. Alison was standing in the doorway of the bedroom, clutching her nightie across her chest, her face drained of colour and her eyes wide. She put one hand out to Travis and he could see her shaking.

Gavin looked up and a strange smile crossed his face. 'Hello, Travis. I was hoping I'd catch you before you went out to the cattle.'

'Cass, go to Mummy.' He tensed as Gavin snaked one arm around his daughter's shoulders.

'Why? Do you think I'd hurt my pretty little niece?'

'Let her go, Gavin. Or God help me—'

'Jesus, Trav. Settle down.' Gavin gave Cass a shove and she jumped off his lap and ran across to Alison. 'It's all good. I only came here to sort out the money. Nothing more.'

'What money?' Travis didn't know how much Gavin

thought he knew.

'Don't play dumb. The money that I can't draw out of my account.' He laughed, and it sent the blood chilling in Travis's veins. 'You've blocked me. Putting the account in your name backfired on me.'

'I don't know what you're talking about.'

'All I want you to do is get on the phone to the bank and tell him to transfer it to my account. And, Travis, it's only a down payment, there's a lot more to come. You have to appreciate that. When the money starts flowing in, I'll give you some for the property.'

Travis glanced at Alison. 'Al, take Cass into the boys' room and lock the door. I'm not transferring any money, Gavin. I can't afford it. There haven't been any cattle sales, and the account is low.'

Gavin stood and shook his head. 'No, *Al*. You stay right there. Travis, stop talking shit, and get on the phone.' He looked across at Alison and smiled. 'You were a stupid bitch to come back here. Don't you know you've been replaced? How's your little girlfriend going, Trav?' Gavin's eyes were cold and hard.

'My girlfriend?' Travis said.

'The insect woman. Did the university come good with the funding?' He stared at Travis and frowned.

Travis narrowed his eyes as he realised that Gavin was fishing for information.

He doesn't know she's been found.

He caught Alison's eye and shook his head slightly. 'Dr Rees is missing. The police thought that you kidnapped her, but I told them you had no reason to.' He tried to inject a level tone into his voice. 'Her husband came up here, and he thinks she took her own life. They found her phone down at Townsville.'

Reel him in. Get him confident.

'If I tell you where to find her, will you transfer my money?'

'Do you know where she is?' Travis stood straight, his hands clenched tightly beside him. 'The bank won't be open yet.'

'They'll answer the phone from eight-thirty.'

'It's only eight.' Travis pointed to the time displayed on the digital clock next to the television. As Gavin looked over at it, Travis held Alison's gaze and mimed putting a phone to his face. 'How do you know where Emlyn is?'

'Because I'm smarter than you, that's why. Now get on that phone, and I'll tell you where to find her.'

'You tell me first, and then I'll call the bank in half an hour.'

'How does it feel, Travis?' Gavin said.

'How does what feel?'

'The world's about to find out that you're not the best in this family, and you never have been.'

Travis clenched his jaw, fighting to stay calm. He wanted Cass and Alison out of the room, and then he was going to beat the living shit out of his brother.

'It wasn't my fault. Silly bitch fell down into a tube, a hundred and fifty metres west of where the fire trail joins the road. I tried to stop her, but she wouldn't listen.'

'Was she hurt? Why didn't you get her out?'

'She was out to it, and I couldn't reach her if I'd wanted to. Besides, I had a flight to catch.' Gavin's voice was devoid of emotion, and Travis realised the depth of his brother's mental-health issues. He had to protect his family; Gavin had no feeling for anybody apart from himself.

Play for time. Stay calm.

Gavin looked at his watch. 'Go and make us some breakfast while we wait, Alison. I'm bloody hungry.'

Travis gestured to Alison with his head. She grabbed Cass and went into the kitchen. Travis walked slowly to the sofa and sat down. He kept his tone casual.

'When does the next payment come from Carroglen?'

'Three months, and then another one after twelve months.' Gavin sat beside him and put his feet on the coffee table. A half-full cup of coffee fell to the floor, and the stain spread onto the carpet.

'And you're going to give some to the property? Do I have your word on that?' Travis ignored the spilt coffee.

Keep him talking. Keep him calm.

'You can hunker down on this piece of dirt and do whatever you want.'

Travis tried to keep the disgust from his expression as Gavin leaned back on the sofa.

'What? What are you looking at?'

He shook his head. 'I'm wondering how our parents could have produced such—'

'A piece of shit?'

'If the cap fits.'

'Just be careful, little brother, or I might change my mind about giving you any money from Carroglen.' Gavin chuckled. 'I did a great job of passing myself off as you. I wish you could have seen it.'

'All right. I'll make the call.'

'I knew you'd come around. I want the first payment, and then I'll share.'

'Fair enough.' Travis knew he had no intention of sharing anything, but he wanted to keep him calm. A bit after eight, the chopper would be here, the policeman had said. But it would land at the dongas, and Gavin would hear it if it came over this way. The door opened, and Alison slipped out of the kitchen and pressed her back to it, staying out of reach. She gave an almost imperceptible nod to Travis.

He had to mark time and keep his brother focused. Keep him talking until the police came back.

'How did you do it, Gavin? How the hell did you manage to swing the whole gold deal without me having a clue you were doing it?'

'Because you're so wrapped up in the bloody cattle you wouldn't have a clue what was going on.' He pointed to the phone on the table beside Travis. 'Try the bank now. They might be there early. The sooner I get off this fucking place for good, the better.' The look on his face was sly as he turned and stared at Travis.

'It's too early.'

'Make the fucking call.' He leaned across Travis and grabbed for his hand and forced it to the phone.

Travis snapped. He closed the fingers of one hand around Gavin's forearm, and grabbed the back of his collar with the other. Dragging him off the sofa, he pulled his brother to his feet and slammed his back against the wall.

'This is for the pain you've caused my family.' He let go of Gavin's arm and slammed his fist into his stomach with all the rage of the past year behind it. Gavin grunted and leaned forwards, but Travis was ready for him as his brother brought his head up fast and tried to headbutt him.

'Oh no, you soft bastard,' Travis snarled. 'Maybe if you'd come out and helped me on the station, you might have been strong enough to take me on, but you were too fucking lazy and self-absorbed.'

As Gavin lurched forward and went for Travis's eyes, Travis pulled his fist back and hit his brother on the side of the jaw. But Gavin kept coming, so Travis punched him again.

'That's for Emlyn, who you left for dead. And this is for Mum. You hurt her and you broke her heart.' He held both his shoulders and shook him. 'I'm not a lowlife like you, but if I was, I'd kill you for what you did to Alison. It would be satisfying to hurt you, but I'm not like you. But it will give me great satisfaction to see you rot in jail for the rest of your life.'

'What's that noise?' Gavin's eyes widened as a helicopter flew low over the house and the sound of sirens filled the air.

'You can't prove anything. Let me go, you bastard.' He struggled, but Travis held him tightly.

'I forgot to tell you, Emlyn's been found and has talked to the police. They know about your cave and all the backpackers. You're going down for a long time, Gavin.'

Travis turned to Alison. Tears were rolling down her face. 'Al, when I get him out the front door, get the boys to take Cass down to the shed. I don't want them to see any of this.'

He put his face close to Gavin's. 'From this minute on, you have no family. I want nothing to do with you ever again.'

He turned Gavin around and held him in a tight arm lock and pushed him over to the door as footsteps pounded up the stairs.

* * *

Apart from an occasional twinge in her back, Emlyn made a swift recovery over the next week. Physically, she grew stronger every day, but her emotional recovery was helped by having David by her side.

At night, lying beside her, talking quietly, smoothing her hair with his gentle fingers, he made her talk about what had happened.

'Get it all out, sweetheart. Don't bottle it up.'

'Not like I usually do,' she said with a sad smile. A slight breeze ruffled the curtains and the intense heat of the day was eased by the gentle wind puffing through the window as the night closed in. She talked, and he listened, and Emlyn's determination to get over the last few days was strengthened. For a few minutes there was a comfortable silence, and she reached up and tangled her fingers in David's hair. 'I still can't believe you're here, David.'

'Of course I am. And I'm not leaving you ever again.'

'Ever?' she asked with a smile as she pulled his head down to hers.

His lips roamed over her face before he laid his head beside hers. 'Enough, you need your rest.'

His voice sent a shiver though her.

'I need you more,' she whispered as she rolled over and put her body as close to his as she could.

'I love you, Em.' David's whisper soothed her to sleep in those first dark nights, and his smile was the first thing she woke to each morning.

She knew that his presence stopped her from slipping into that dark place where she'd thought she wanted to be alone. For the first time in many months, she had managed to get past that barrier that had prevented her feeling a part of the real world. She'd tried to explain it to David, but he'd stopped her words with a lingering kiss last night.

'Put your scientific mind away, sweetheart. There's no need to analyse how you've felt, or document your recovery.'

David rolled over onto his side and his breath puffed warm on her lips. 'Just tell me. Are you happy?'

She nodded.

'Do you love me?' His words were tentative, as though he couldn't believe that she needed him.

She nodded again and moved her lips closer to his.

'Are you sure you want to come home with me?'

This time her nod was slower. 'I am. But I'm going to have to spend a lot of time up here in the tubes.'

'I can deal with that. I've got a proposition for you.'

When she giggled at his words, his eyes darkened. 'Oh, Em, it's so good to hear you laugh. We're going to be okay, aren't we?'

Emlyn lay close beside him, the hard planes of her husband's chest pressed against her breasts. She closed her eyes and smiled, taking comfort from his closeness, from the warmth of the body she knew so well. He moved closer and Emlyn lifted her head to lose herself in David's hazel eyes.

He looked back at her steadily, his gaze intent.

'So, what's this proposition?' she asked, letting the tip of her tongue run across his lower lip. Love and certainty of their future ran through her even as she teased him.

His voice was husky. 'Would you believe it's got nothing to do with what you're thinking?'

Emlyn sighed as his hand reached down and cupped her breast.

'Although I can come up with another proposition along those lines as soon as I tell you what I organised today.'

Emlyn leaned back and watched the smile play over his mouth.

'I've been asked to write a new software package for a

supermarket chain the company has just signed up,' he said. 'And the good news is, I don't have to be in the office to do it. I can work remotely. The boss has already agreed to it. As long as I go to Brisbane once a month or so to liaise with the company, I can work from anywhere I choose.'

'And where would you choose?'

'That depends where you're going to be. If it's the lava tubes, the company will pay a share of the rental for a bit of office space for me and my access to the internet.'

Emlyn lifted her head and brushed her lips against David's. 'That's where I'm going to be. And it would be wonderful if you were here, too.' She could feel the slow, heavy beat of his heart against her skin as his mouth opened against her lips.

Epilogue

Winter, two years later

Travis looked at his watch as they turned onto the Conjuboy Road. They hadn't been up to the station for over a year, and he was surprised to see how green it was looking, even as winter approached. There were no cattle in the paddocks anymore to keep the feed low, and the road edges were mown and tidy. As they reached the turn-off to *Carlyle Downs*, Cass leaned forward.

'Are we nearly there, Daddy?'

Alison pointed to the new large sign at the gate. 'I think we are, Cass. Look at that, it says, FIND-AN-INSECT. BE A SCIENTIST FOR A WEEK.'

'Oh wow. Can I be a scientist too?' Cassie jumped up and down on the car seat.

'I'm sure Emlyn will have a spot for you,' Travis said with a smile.

'Jase and Joel too? Ethan's bit little.' Cassie's words were almost a high-pitched squeal.

Since he'd bought the property down at Giru, and they'd moved into the new house that Travis had had built on the small property sixty kilometres south of Townsville, Emlyn and David often visited for weekends. Cass was in love with Ethan, their fifteen-month-old, and Alison and Emlyn had forged a strong friendship.

'Yes, I think Ethan might be a bit young. But guess

what?' Alison smiled at Travis as he replied to Cassie. 'Jase and Joel are meeting us up here.'

Cassie sighed and put her hands to her mouth. 'Oh, I don't think it gets any better than this, does it.' Cassie had settled in at a small country kindy on the coast only ten kilometres from their new house. For the first few months, Jase had helped Travis get set up and build new fences and cattle yards, before he'd decided—to everyone's surprise—to go to agricultural college. Joel was at university in Townsville and living in a unit at the beach.

They'd retrieved the family diaries from the metal boxes that Gavin had stored them in, and Joel was transcribing them onto the computer with the plan to publish a family history.

'The first of many historical books,' he'd promised.

Travis had decided to grow sugar cane, as well as run a few cattle, and Jase was now full of advice about soils and fertilisers. They drove along the river, and as they turned the last bend, Travis slowed the car. The old house had been rebuilt and converted into the administration block for the new tourist facility. A lump settled in his throat and Alison reached across and squeezed his hand.

'This is still home in your heart, isn't it, darling?'

Travis shook his head. 'No. My home is wherever you are, Al. And we couldn't stay here, not after the memories the place holds. It was time for a new start.'

He parked the car and then walked around and opened the door for Alison. Cass shot out of the car and squealed. 'There's Ethan!'

Emlyn was standing at the top of the steps holding her little boy. Travis smiled up at her as Alison followed Cass up the steps; she'd put on weight and her cheeks were glowing.

Alison hugged her before taking Ethan, and Emlyn hurried down the steps. Travis leaned over and kissed her cheek.

'Well, Travis, what do you think?'

He laughed. 'If it's anywhere near as flash as the new sign at the gate, I think you've done pretty well.'

Emlyn and David had returned to Brisbane the week after Gavin had been arrested, and she had presented their sponsorship application to the university. It had been met with an enthusiastic response, and today, just over two years later, the official opening was about to take place.

Emlyn looked up at him. 'Alison told me you've been in Brisbane for the trial.'

'Yes. He's being sentenced next week.'

'I read about it in the paper.' Emlyn put her arm through Travis's as they walked up the steps together. 'It's very sad.'

'Yes, but at least there's a diagnosis and he's getting treatment.' Despite his harsh words the day that Gavin had been arrested, Travis had supported him through the trial and his medical tests. The evidence in the metal boxes in the caves— there were photos of each backpacker after he'd drugged them— and Emlyn's testimony had been enough for a multitude of charges to be laid.

'Narcissistic personality disorder. Speaking to his doctor has helped me understand his behaviour.'

'You're a good man, Travis.'

'That may be, but I'll never forgive him or condone what he did. The doctor explained that even as young children narcissists learn to mimic the emotions they need to present to the world.' He shrugged and shook his head. 'He's family, but even when I go to see him, I don't know if his remorse is genuine or just what he thinks he needs to put across to get a light sentence. But we have to trust in the judicial system, don't we? Speaking of which, we've got more good news, too. The other court case is almost done, and it looks pretty certain that Carroglen have decided to pull out of their proposed gold mine.'

'That's great news. For you, and for the facility.'

* * *

Two hours later, Emlyn stood in the doorway of the new administration office and smiled. She'd taken the Carlyle family on a tour of the facility, and after having a private lunch in the conference room of the administration centre, they were about to go to the main cave for the official opening by the head of the Queensland Museum.

'I don't know how you've managed all this in such a short time,' Alison said as they headed back to the cars. 'It's only just over twelve months since we moved out of the house. Not that you'd ever recognise the building as the old house.'

'It's been a hard slog, but I couldn't have done it without David staying here and being a house dad for Ethan.' Emlyn smiled at her husband; she was proud of what had been achieved here in just over two years. Not only a new facility that was already booked out for the first six months, but the continuing scientific discoveries made by the team that had now grown to eight scientists.

And she and David had created a new family. She put her hand on her still flat stomach. A family that was about to grow some more.

Sophie, and Mum and Dad, would never leave her, but she'd learned to cope with the raw grief that still overtook her at times. But those times were becoming less frequent as the months passed. Her emotions had healed along with her physical scars.

Emlyn put her hand on Alison's arm. 'Is it okay if I take Travis across in my car? I want to show him something on the way over. We've got a few minutes spare.'

'You go with Travis, and we'll go with David in your car. I can help with your little man.' Alison held her arms out for Ethan, and Emlyn smiled as he laughed at her.

Travis was quiet as he drove them towards the cave. Emlyn glanced across at him. He stared ahead at the paddocks as they flashed past. She didn't speak until they reached the site of the old homestead, letting him enjoy the land that he had leased to the university and the museum.

'Pull over here for a minute,' she said.

The grass was still long and wild, and the old chimney of the original homestead stood as a sentinel guarding the old graveyard. Travis climbed out and closed the car door quietly. Emlyn walked behind him as he crossed to the graves. There were two new headstones.

One white marble, and one dark grey.

Travis crouched in front of the grey headstone and looked up at Emlyn as she caught up. He put his hand on top of the most recent addition.

'It was very thoughtful of you to order a headstone for Bluey,' he said. 'He took a liking to you.'

The old stockman had passed last winter.

Travis leaned across to the white marble headstone and traced his fingers across the words.

Thomas John Carlyle and Missy Lila Carlyle. Born September 23, 1866, departed this life together, 1879.

Laid to eternal rest, June 2019.

'Joel is transcribing their mother's diary entries from the time they went missing,' he said. 'It's heartbreaking to read her anguish.'

'It's so sad,' Emlyn said.

'It is, but they were found.'

She was pleased to see a wide smile cross Travis's face.

He stood and held out his arm out to her. 'Now, come and show me what you've done to *Carlyle Downs*, clever lady.' His grin grew wider. 'A lot's happened since a skinny, feisty woman turned up on my place on New Year's Eve a couple of years back.'

Emlyn bumped him with her shoulder as they walked back to his car.

'Not to mention the cranky bloke who didn't want a bunch of scientists poking around on *his* farm.'

They stood at the car and looked back down over the flat plains. The sky was a brilliant blue and the stillness of the landscape and the bright light over the brown paddocks filled Emlyn with serenity. She was learning to love this land.

Travis looped his arm around her shoulder.

'Thank you, Emlyn.'

'Thank you, Travis. We've done well together.'

They turned away from the landscape that was the same as the one that two small children had looked over before they'd climbed down into the cave many years ago.

'Come and show me what you've created.'

As they drove off, a puff of wind blew across the graves, dispersing the red dust that hung over the brown grass.

THE END

Acknowledgements

Undara is probably my favourite story out of the many books I have written over the past fourteen years. As I edited the manuscript for this, the second edition, I realised once again how much I love this story. Having the rights reverted to me by the publisher meant that I could give the new edition the cover that I had always wanted, and I could also add a few minor things that I preferred to be in this edition, including the beautiful lines from *Silver*, the poem by Walter de la Mare.

It would be impossible to write without support in your personal life. To Ian, the love of my life and my partner in research, as we travel this magnificent country seeking stories each winter. My sounding board, my research assistant, my chef, my driver on outback trips, and my rock—I could not do this without you.

A special thank you to Susanne Bellamy for providing moral support on a daily basis, being a true friend and answering grammatical questions; to Roby Aiken—your proofreading skills are extraordinary; and to Colin Noy for the inspiration that made my heroine an entomologist.

A special mention to Elly Gooch, who took time from her Higher School Certificate studies to create the map of *Carlyle Downs* and Undara at the front of the book.

And to you, the reader: thank you for choosing this book to read. I hope when you read *Undara* that you love it, talk about it, and that maybe you will want to visit this unique part of Australia for yourself.

Awards

2023: Winner - Long contemporary novel category, RUBY award for *Larapinta*.

2023: Finalist - Australian Romance Readers Awards for *Kakadu Dawn,* the sixth and final book in the Porter Sisters series.

2018 and 2020: Finalist - for the NZ KORU Award.

2017: Winner - Best Established Author of the Year 2017 AUSROM

2017: Winner - Author of the Year 2014 AUSROM Best Established Author, Ausrom Readers' Choice.

2016, 2017, 2018, 2019: Longlisted - Sisters in Crime Davitt Awards

2016: Finalist - Book of the Year, Long Romance, RWA Ruby Awards for *Kakadu Sunset*

2015: Winner - Best Established Author of the Year AUSROM

I would love to hear from you.
Drop me a line at annie@annieseaton.net
Reviews on Goodreads are always welcome and much
appreciated!
All Annie's books are available in print at Annie's store
eBook links:
https://www.annieseaton.net/books.html

Print Store:
All books are available in print at Annie's store and on
Amazon in paperback
https://annieseatonstore.ecwid.com/